Praise for  ces

"A star of the genr[...]"
— *RT Book Reviews*

"Coffman's writing is deft, capable, and evocative."
— *Publishers Weekly*

"Brimming with adventure, humor, likable characters, and suspense. Coffman shows us why she is a *New York Times* bestselling author with this gem of historical fiction."
— Romance Reviews Today

"A rare and poignant glimpse into the shadowed realms of the human heart. With an eloquent pen, Ms. Coffman weaves words into a tapestry of beauty beyond measure. With the lyrical prose of a bard, you are drawn into the midst of her tale, captivated with the realism of her creation until you are completely consumed."
— *RT Book Reviews*, 4½ stars

"Simply the best book I've read in a year. Elaine Coffman touches the heart while making her readers laugh and cry."
— *The Atlanta Journal*

"This lusty, tension-filled romance perfectly fits the strong-willed characters' personalities. Coffman writes a purely romantic tale that captures the essence of the genre... the fast pace and heated story are compelling."
— *RT Book Reviews*, 4 stars

"An intensely moving tale of emotional growth and discovery. Once again, Ms. Coffman spins a complex tapestry of the human heart, a vivid portrayal of life, and the grace and redemption of love."

—*RT Book Reviews*, 4½ stars

The Return of
BLACK
DOUGLAS

The Return of
BLACK
DOUGLAS

ELAINE
COFFMAN

sourcebooks
casablanca

Published by Sourcebooks Casablanca, an imprint of Sourcebooks, Inc.
P.O. Box 4410, Naperville, Illinois 60567-4410
(630) 961-3900
FAX: (630) 961-2168
www.sourcebooks.com

Printed and bound in Canada
WC 10 9 8 7 6 5 4 3 2 1

*Don't turn someone away who knocks
at your door one day and claims to be
your future great-great-great grandchild.
They may be right…*

Michio Kaku, American theoretical physicist (1947–)

Chapter 1

I can call spirits from the vasty deep.
Why, so can I, or so can any man;
But will they come when you do call for them?

—*Henry IV, Part 1*: Act III, Scene 1
   William Shakespeare (1564–1616)
   English poet and playwright

St. Bride's Church
Douglas, Lanarkshire, Scotland
In the year 1515

THE LANARKSHIRE HILLS OF SCOTLAND LACK THE SHARP AND ridgy majesty of the rugged Highland mountains, for they resemble rounded loaves of bread fresh from the oven, all huddled together. The lonely hills are somehow irresistibly attractive, with their pasture-covered slopes and fairy-like meadows, where clear streams murmur through rolling undulations of thick woodlands, and the wood mouse and roe deer reside. Here, the sterner features of the north give way to a grace of forest and tenderness of landscape, where the gentle Douglas Water flows.

Alysandir Mackinnon thought it a good day as he rode across the rolling hills, accompanied by the rhythmic clang of his sword tapping against his spur, while larks, hidden among the leathery leaves of trees, broke into song as he passed beneath the heavy branches. A glance skyward told him the sun had passed its zenith, as it dipped behind a cloud to begin its slow descent into afternoon. Just ahead, spangles on the river danced and sparkled their way downstream.

Alysandir pushed back his mail coif. Sunlight brought out the rich darkness of his black hair and the vivid blue of his eyes. He turned toward his brother Drust. "We will follow the river until we find a place to ford."

Drust followed Alysandir's lead and pushed back his own coif, the shiny links of mail almost matching his silvery, blue-grey eyes. He wiped the sweat from his face and gave a silent nod. They continued and drew rein at a point where the terrain sloped gently downward toward the river, before it narrowed to make a meandering turn.

"This looks like as good a place as we have seen," Alysandir said, and he spurred his mount forward and plunged into the water. His horse staggered with the first splash and the water washed over his hocks, but Gallagher was a hobbler, a sturdy Highland pony known for its stamina and ability to cover great distances over boggy and hilly land at high speed. Alysandir only had to spur the horse lightly as he urged him slowly forward until Gallagher gained his footing as the water rose over the stirrups.

When they reached a point where the water became deeper than they expected, Alysandir was about to turn back, but Gallagher leaped ahead with a mighty splash, and they began the climb upward toward the opposite bank.

Wet and dripping, they rode into town and attracted a great many curious stares from villagers who gawked as if they rode into town to slay a dragon or two. Although a small town, Douglas was large enough to have a two-story tavern with a stable out back and streets that were fairly busy at this time of day. They rode between uneven rows of buildings stacked on each side of curving streets that had been laid out more than three hundred years before.

They passed a steep cobbled path that ran through an archway to a small, walled garden next to a house in ruins, and as they threaded their way among carts, wagons, barking dogs, clucking chickens, and the occasional darting child, they observed the slow progress of a lone rider coming toward them. He was leading a prisoner riding a hobbler, the unfortunate wretch bruised and blindfolded, with his hands bound behind his back. Alysandir wondered what the Highlander's crime had been—probably no more than trying to eke out a living in a harsh and unforgiving land.

Just ahead, near the center of town, stood St. Bride's Kirk, where mail-clad heroes of yesteryear lay entombed within, most of them with the surname Douglas. But Alysandir's fiery thoughts centered not upon the long-dead knights but upon his own desire to be away from the Lowlands, Douglas, and Lanarkshire, and back in the Highlands and his home on the Isle of Mull.

Drust, meanwhile, was giving his attention to a young lassie with copper-colored hair who was standing in the kirkyard and holding a bonnet full of eggs. Alysandir caught a glimpse of her standing beneath the graceful branches of an old tree and felt a strange yearning tug at him, but he hardened his heart and dismissed her. Aye, she was a beauty and his body stirred at the sight of her, but he still wasn't interested. The sound of Drust's voice cut into his thoughts.

"That lassie with the russet ringlets is a beauty, and she has taken a fancy to ye, Alysandir, for already she has wrapped ye in her tender gaze."

"I am leery of any lass standing under a wych elm," Alysandir replied.

"I know ye have no desire ever to have a woman in yer life again, but just suppose ye did find yerself in a position where ye were forced to take another wife. What virtues would ye seek?"

"Ye ken I have no desire to marry again. Not ever."

"So make up a list just to keep me happy. We've naught else to do right now."

Alysandir did not know why his brother insisted on having high discourse with him. Of late, Drust had been making too many inquiries as to Alysandir's unmarried state. "Ye are becoming a great deal of trouble, Drust. Next time, I will let Ronan or Colin ride with me."

"Fair enough," Drust replied as a wide smile settled across his face. "I will start the list. Loyalty would be one, am I right?"

Loyalty. The word evoked pain. "Aye."

"Ye canna stop there," Drust said with a teasing tone. "Give me the rest."

"I will give ye the virtues that any man should want in a woman, but only if ye promise to keep quiet the rest of our journey."

"Aye, I agree. Now, give me the virtues."

"Chastity, loyalty, honesty, wisdom, strength, courage, honor, intelligence, confidence, and a strong mind. A woman who knows when to yield as readily as she knows when to take a stand. A woman equal to the man in question, not in might but in nature, virtue, and soul. She would possess a true and steadfast love for him, and in return, she would have his undying love, respect, and honor."

"What aboot silence and obedience?"

"If a man had a woman's love in the truest sense of the word—which I have yet to see any proof of—then he would have all the others for they are but parts that make up the whole."

"I hand it to ye, brother. I didna think ye could give me one virtue, yet ye named many. Surely ye miss having such a woman."

Alysandir pinned him with a cold stare. "I never had such a woman, so how could I miss her?"

"Ye changed once. Perhaps ye can change again."

"Changed? In what way?"

"I remember when ye would as soon tryst in the kirkyard as in a hayloft. How is it that knowing what ye or any man would want in a woman, ye refuse to find her?"

"'Tis easy enough to answer, for such a woman does not exist."

The words were barely uttered when the faintest echo of a man's laughter reached their ears. The sound of it seemed to break into a thousand pieces and fall like tinkling glass. Alysandir and Drust exchanged glances as the laughter faded and a slight wind stirred the heavy branches of the old wych elm.

As they rode on past St. Bride's Kirk, a tossing and rustling of the leaves sent a chill wafting down upon them. Across the way, a startled flock of sheep bolted, running across the meadow and up the hill to the pasture on the other side. The hair on Alysandir's neck stood, and his scalp felt as if it were shrinking. "Did ye hear the laughter?"

"Aye, I heard it and felt the cold wind that blew through the trees. Unless my senses deceive me, there is an oddity aboot."

"What oddity is that?" Alysandir asked.

"We are riding by the crypts of the ancients. Perhaps they wish us to pass by quickly and not linger."

Alysandir laughed. "Perhaps ye are letting yer imagination take the lead. The Mackinnons never had a quarrel with any Douglas, living or dead."

"What aboot the laughter? Ye heard it as well as me," said Drust.

Alysandir's face looked drawn as he replied, "Mayhap it was the bleating of a winded sheep."

"Aye, and mayhap it was not." Drust gazed at the river.

Alysandir knew his brother was thinking about the Douglas Water that flowed through the village of Douglas, past the ruins of Douglas Castle. The name Douglas Water came from the Gaelic *dubh-glas*, which meant black water. The Norman Douglases took their surname from the river in the twelfth century. Superstitious Drust was probably searching for some connection between the laughter they heard and the Douglases. Let Drust think what he would, especially if that would keep him quiet for a while.

The brothers rode on in silence, taking no notice of a dark shadow that came out of nowhere to pass overhead, mysterious and foreboding as the cry of a raven as it darkened the sky. Thunder rumbled in the distance, yet there was no scent of rain in the air. Engrossed as they were with their own thoughts, they did not turn back for one last look at St. Bride's Kirk. If they had, they would have seen a pale mist, of a greenish tint, that bubbled up from beneath the old kirk door.

Chapter 2

Better be courted and jilted
than never be courted at all.

—"The Jilted Nymph," 1843
  Thomas Campbell, British poet (1777–1844)

St. Bride's Church
Douglas, Lanarkshire, Scotland
Present Time

IF THINGS HAD GONE DIFFERENTLY, SHE WOULD BE ON HER honeymoon in Argentina right now, instead of tromping around Scotland with her twin sister, Elisabeth. That morning, Isobella had written in her journal the exciting header: *Visiting tombs of Douglas ancestors,* which reminded her of her engagement, in that both were dead. However, it was the sisters' first day in Scotland, and she was driving to the village of Douglas to visit St. Bride's Church, where Sir James, the Black Douglas, was buried.

Isobella drove slowly down Main Street, passing buildings that looked much as they had when they were built during the Middle Ages. She turned into the parking lot and imagined the quaint, slate-gabled church bustling with medieval life—armored knights and fair ladies with tall headdresses hurrying to attend their weekly worship. Only now those noble warriors lay buried beneath mail-clad, cross-legged effigies, entombed in abbeys and small parish churches.

When they entered the kirk, she and Elisabeth crossed a large marble slab at the entrance to the Douglas mausoleum. It contained three canopied, medieval burial tombs with damaged effigies recessed in walls. Isobella stopped to give her eyes time to adjust to the diffused light, her gaze resting upon the exquisite stained-glass windows. A sense of a supernatural presence enveloped her as they paused to look at a glass box that held a silver case containing the heart of the Black Douglas.

"Since his death, the Douglases have carried on their shields a bloody heart and crown," Isobella said, so overcome with emotion that she could almost hear the ancient heart beating. She glanced around the dilapidated choir to the north wall and saw the effigy of Sir James, the Black Douglas that lay below a finely cut, fifteenth-century pointed and arched canopy.

The effigy, carved from sandstone shortly after his death, had been a splendid example of medieval artistry and as grand as any found in Westminster Abbey. Sadly, the once gracefully carved effigy was now badly worn and its facial features chipped and impossible to make out. Neither sister spoke as they read the plaque on the wall.

THE GOOD SIR JAMES OF DOUGLAS
KILLED IN BATTLE WITH THE MOORS
IN SPAIN, WHILE ON HIS WAY TO THE
HOLY LAND WITH THE HEART
OF KING ROBERT THE BRUCE,
25TH AUGUST 1330

Isobella was touched to see that someone had left a bouquet of Scottish heather on Douglas's tomb. "After almost eight hundred years, he is so beloved he gets flowers."

Elisabeth, who was busy inspecting the foot of the effigy, said, "I find it sad that half of one of his legs has broken away."

Isobella studied it for a moment. "Thankfully, enough remains that you can still see his legs were crossed."

Puzzled, Elisabeth asked, "Is that supposed to be something special? The crossed legs, I mean."

"Crossed legs denote a Crusader. They cross above the ankle for one Crusade and below the knee for two," she replied, knowledgeable because of her recent degrees in Celtic studies and archaeology.

"So he went twice." Elisabeth stared at the effigy and sighed. "My, he must have been quite a man."

She had no more than finished speaking when Isobella was overcome with emotion once again, as if strings in her heart that had never been touched began to vibrate. Without realizing it, she placed her hand on the cold stone of the effigy. How deeply, inexplicably sad she felt for this powerful man whose life had changed history and whose death at the age of forty-four had been both noble and tragic. *I'm so sorry*. Without being conscious that she did so, she moved her hand to the place where the beating heart of Douglas would have been, had the stone effigy been a mortal being. She found the place numinously warm. A waft of spine-chilling air passed over her, and she knew the spirit of Douglas resided here.

"Oh, my God!" She let out a frightened squeak and jerked her hand away. For a moment, she was frozen in place, gasping for breath and feeling as if something had traveled straight to her heart, completely bypassing her sense of reasoning. The next instant, she was overcome with acute distress touching her heart so powerfully that she began to cry—not soft, gentle weeping, but anguished sobs and great gushing tears.

And she was unable to stop, in spite of the curious look Elisabeth gave her. "Good Lord, Izzy, why are you crying?"

"I can't help it," Isobella barely managed to say before more tears drowned the words in her throat.

Elisabeth put her hand on Isobella's arm. "What's wrong? Please tell me you aren't thinking about that jilting jerk Jackson."

Isobella shook her head. "No, it isn't that."

"Good," Elisabeth said and handed her a Kleenex, while patting her on the back. "Then, why are you crying?"

"I don't know. There's just something about his story that's so tragic and sad. The way he died in Spain… how they embalmed his heart… his body boiled in a cauldron of vinegar until the flesh fell away so they could bring the bones back to Scotland for burial here in the kirk.

"It's so moving. Oh, I don't know what is wrong with me. I feel compelled to tell him I'm so sorry for the way everything turned out. I wish he could have lived longer and happier."

Elisabeth nudged her. "Maybe we should go. You're acting weird. Now I'm starting to feel a bit creepy. Stop sniffling, or you'll get dehydrated." She rubbed her arms. "It's getting cold in here, and I want to get back to Edinburgh in time for dinner. A good bottle of wine will do us both good."

Only Elisabeth would worry about dehydration at a

time like this, Isobella thought, but she fell in step beside her twin, who would soon start her last year of residency at Johns Hopkins. Elisabeth always walked faster, because she was accustomed to walking down long hospital corridors. She had a long stride, while Isobella, with her anthropologic mind and tendency to take in everything around her, took her time ambling along.

Elisabeth reached the car first. "Gracious, Izzy! You're as pale as a ghost. Are you okay?"

Isobella was light-headed, but she didn't say anything. Elisabeth would want to talk about it and take her pulse and temperature and maybe pull out her stethoscope right in the middle of the parking lot, so Isobella shook her head and said, "Maybe I'm hungry. I didn't eat much at lunch."

Elisabeth mulled that over and held out her hand. "Okay, give me the keys. I'll drive. You look like you've had all the blood drained out of you."

That was a good description of the way she felt, Isobella thought. She walked around to the passenger side and opened the door. When she sat down, the hair on the back of her neck stood out. A cold shiver traveled across her body. She had the disquieting feeling that the two of them were not alone.

Elisabeth put the key in the ignition. The sky began to darken. Thunder boomed, and the trees began to sway and bend. Leaves flew every which way as jagged flashes of lightning ripped across the sky. An earsplitting clap of thunder was followed by pounding rain that pelted the earth with great fury.

Isobella held her breath as an odd greenish glow lit up the shadowy darkness of the trees with a pale, ghostly radiance. Another flash, and she saw a vision of herself standing beneath the trees with a basket of eggs in her hand. The sound of a man's laughter rode on the wind.

Then, as suddenly as it came, the storm stopped. The sun was shining, and all was quiet. She wondered if Elisabeth had heard the laughter. Judging by the expression of stunned bewilderment on her sister's face, she had. Elisabeth's hands flew up to her face, and she let out a long-held breath. "Did you see what I saw?"

"I saw a thunderstorm."

"And a greenish light," Elisabeth added, "and the sound of…"

"A man's laughter," Isobella finished. "Did you see the girl with the bonnet of eggs?"

Elisabeth spoke with an unsteady voice, "It was you, Izzy. She looked exactly like you."

"I thought so, too, except that she was dressed in a gown from the Renaissance period."

Elisabeth's face was pale, her voice barely above a whisper. "Izzy, what have we gotten ourselves into? Things like that don't just happen."

"And yet it did. We both saw it," Isobella said, surprised at the calm acceptance that washed over her. Something was going on here, and it had to do with Scotland, this kirk, and the Black Douglas.

"You don't think it was something supernatural, do you?"

"That's exactly what I think," she said, and quoted Samuel Coleridge, "'Beware! His flashing eyes, his floating hair! Weave a circle round him thrice and close your eyes with holy dread, for he on honey-dew hath fed, and drunk the milk of Paradise.'"

"Thanks. That was so comforting," Elisabeth said. "I don't believe in the supernatural. There are no such things as ghosts. When people die, they stay dead. What we heard was the wind blowing, not laughter."

Isobella turned her head to gaze out the window. "You will notice that, in spite of the thunderstorm, our car is bone dry and there isn't a drop of water anywhere on this entire parking lot."

Elisabeth paled. "Oh, Izzy, I'm scared. We don't belong here. I wish we hadn't come. Whatever spirits are lurking are not happy with our coming. They want us to leave, and they are going out of their way to make it known."

"If they wanted to get our attention, they would do something we couldn't explain."

The words were barely spoken when the car started. Elisabeth gasped. "Oh, my God!"

"Now what?"

"The car is running."

"That means you are supposed to put it in gear so we can drive back to Edinburgh."

"You don't understand." She opened her hand. The key was lying in her palm. "What do we do now?"

"Put the key in the ignition, I guess. You will need the key to turn the car off."

Elisabeth was about to insert the key when the motor stopped. "I need a drink. A big, stiff one." She started the car with the key this time and burned a little rubber leaving the parking lot.

Chapter 3

I arise from dreams of thee
In the first sweet sleep of night.
When the winds are breathing low,
And the stars are shining bright.

—"I Arise from Dreams of Thee"
  Percy Bysshe Shelley (1792–1822)
  British poet

"WHAT ARE YOU THINKING?"

Without taking her gaze off the road, Elisabeth said, "I am wondering why I allowed you to drag me to Scotland on a wild-goose chase to trace long-dead ancestors. You've just completed six years of college. You have your bachelor's in anthropology and Classical studies, and a master's in Celtic studies. Shouldn't you be concentrating on what you are going to do, as in going to work?

"I don't want to find myself on an archaeology dig, buried up to my armpits in piles of Celtic crockery bits. Do I have to remind you that I have to be back at Johns Hopkins in three weeks?"

"You've plenty of time," Isobella replied.

"Do you think traipsing through musty old castles and creepy kirks is going to ease the pain of being jilted?" She gasped. "Oh, Izzy, I'm so sorry."

Isobella barely heard her sister because she was wondering why it was so difficult for her to meet a man she could fall deeply in love with. She decided that Jackson had truly done her a favor, because she didn't love him any more than he loved her. She had gone along with the idea of marriage because she wanted to be loved and married, but she'd gone about it all wrong. Perhaps it was time to give up believing in happily ever after.

Was the problem the men, or was it her? How would she ever know the answer? However, there was something about being in Scotland, and hearing the stories of the Black Douglas, that called out to her. She longed for such a man in her life and sighed woefully. "I think I was born a few hundred years too late," she said, which sounded pathetic even to her own ears.

Elisabeth almost ran off the road. "A few hundred years too late? Good grief, Izzy! How do you come up with these things?

Isobella sighed, caught in a churning muddle of sadness, regret, and confusion. "It's the men. I feel like a fish out of water. I long to find Mr. Darcy, and he doesn't exist in the world I live in."

"Good Lord above, where is all this coming from? You just make bad choices, Izzy. That doesn't mean there aren't wonderful men out there."

Isobella gazed out the window, apparently not listening. "I wonder what I'd do if a man said, 'I love you.' like Mr. Darcy did. A man who could speak so…" Her voice drifted, borne away by another woeful sigh.

"Who is Mr. Darcy?" Elisabeth asked. "He sounds like a librarian."

"He's the hero in *Pride and Prejudice*. Don't tell me you never read the book or saw the movie."

"You mean Colin Firth? What on earth does Mr. Darcy have to do with you finding Mr. Right? And what did he say that has you so enamored?"

As if right on cue, Isobella began to recite, "'In vain have I struggled. My feelings will not be repressed. You must allow me to tell you how ardently I admire and love you.' Imagine a man of today saying that. He would rather throw you on the bed to press his case."

Elisabeth exploded with laughter.

Isobella wondered what Elisabeth would do if she told her that she owned copies of *Dating Mr. Darcy: The Smart Girl's Guide to Sensible Romance*, or *Jane Austen's Guide to Dating*, not to mention *Jane Austen for Dummies*, and, God help her, *The Jane Austen Cookbook*.

"Is 'press his case' a euphemism for penile penetration?"

"Do you have to make fun of everything? I may be too idealistic, but you are too clinical. What a pity that we can't all be as practical as you."

Elisabeth looked contrite. "Dearest Izzy, I don't know where you got such a romantic soul. You're a dreamer and a believer in the myth, the fantasy that doesn't exist. Why would you pine for a man who spent most of his time sighing and looking bored, or gazing forlornly out the windows of his country house?" She paused, and then added, "If I didn't have a medical degree, I wouldn't believe it possible that we have identical genes."

Isobella had already turned her head away and tuned Elisabeth out. Staring out the window lost in her own thoughts, she asked herself, *just what do you want?*

My very own Mr. Darcy.

Wishing for Mr. Darcy. She could write a book about it. She had been looking, wishing, and waiting for a man who lived between the pages of a book. Was it too much to ask for a darkly handsome man—heroic, upstanding and moral, with a heart filled to overflowing with love—to come to her rescue and sweep her off her feet and into his arms?

Where was he, this man of deep feeling, inner struggle, and fiery pride? How beautiful it would be to have a man who did not want to win her love by mastering or overpowering her, but by becoming her ideal; the man of her dreams, a man reformed by love and desire.

How she yearned for a man of strength and quiet reserve, a man of brooding countenance, who would play the hero. If she could only be the woman who unlocked that tortured soul and released the hidden passions that smoldered within! She knew it was hopeless. To find Mr. Darcy, she would have to go back in time.

She dozed off, but she did not sleep long. Awakened, she said, "You won't believe the dream I had."

"With all the strange stuff that's been happening to us, I'm almost afraid to ask."

"Eggs," Isobella said. "I dreamed about eggs. I was standing under a big tree holding a bonnet full of eggs when two men on horseback rode by, dressed in the garb of knights."

"Well, if you're going to dream about eggs..." Elisabeth started laughing. "I hope they were hard boiled."

Back at the hotel, Isobella did a computer search for interpreting dreams about eggs. "Listen to this.

Dreaming about eggs is symbolic of fertility and that something new and fragile is about to happen. It can also mean entrapment."

From her bed, Elisabeth said sleepily, "It was just a dream. Good night, Izzy."

Isobella slept fitfully, tossing and turning until the bedding was twisted and tangled and her gown around her waist. She turned on the bed light, removed two Benadryl from a bottle and downed them with a gulp of bottled water. The Benadryl would ease the stuffiness in her head and make her sleepy—both welcome.

She dreamed of floating weightlessly through the mist and over the roar of the ocean, while strange shapes and colors produced weirdly distorted visions, a bizarre mixture of real and imaginary characters, places, and events. She heard waves crash, breathed the tang of salty air, and felt herself floating low over a vast body of water and into the darkness of a place she feared she would never leave.

Her soul was caught in the sweep of powerful forces, and she existed in a vague way above the earth, weightlessly adrift in an imaginary sphere of being. Her mind filled with pleasant thoughts, and fantasies crowded into her memory—beguiling shapes, beckoning shadows, whispered words, and hands that knew just how and where to caress. She breathed deeply, puzzled by the scent of wax candles that filled her nostrils, and when she stretched, she touched warm skin.

She wasn't alone.

He was there, warm and alive, for she felt the honed smoothness of his flesh. Her eyes popped open. She was in a medieval castle. The trappings of a warrior lay scattered about the room. A candle burned down on a table by the bed and further over, in an enormous fireplace, a fire smoldered from its bed of glowing coals.

She thought him a mythological being with a face and body created by the gods, lying there, with his head propped up with one hand, watching her. The confident, drowsy, hungry look from his dangerous, mesmerizing eyes of vivid blue held her trapped.

He was dark, frighteningly and desirably bare to the waist, and, more than likely, bare beneath the bedding that covered him. His skin looked hard and smooth, beautifully sculpted with muscle. She tugged the bed-covering upward, for he gazed at her like he was starving and she was the only thing on the menu. Even in her darkest, deepest desires, she couldn't imagine conjuring up a man this perfect. And he looked so real!

She poked him. He was real. Her body trembled. She felt a craving thirst for him that she couldn't explain or understand. She wanted to feel the strength of his arm around her and to be warmed by the heat of his body against hers. Her gaze dropped lower, lingering upon his torso, so wickedly bare and beautifully toned, and then lower still, where the bedding rode dangerously low on his hips. Suddenly, his mouth was on hers, and a rippling of sensation cascaded through her, like a series of waterfalls tumbling over rocks.

And she was as naked as he. Another shiver rippled over her, and she opened her mouth, undecided if she should scream or invite him to keep up the good work. She had no time to think further, for he moved so swiftly that she was not aware he had moved at all, until she felt the delicious weight of him. She had a fleeting thought that they had yet to be introduced, but that did not seem terribly important at the moment.

He stared directly into her eyes, watching, inviting, and igniting a fire within her. Oh, my! She could feel the flex of powerful muscles, the kiss of his breath against her skin. This was unlike any dream ever. The room, her lover, it was all tangible. She must have had too much wine. Or had he cast a spell over her?

"Are you Merlin?"

Firelight danced in his eyes. "Nae, lass. I am no' a magician."

His voice was low, throbbing, soothing, and as seductive as the rest of him. It set her heart to pounding, and she began to think: medieval castle… candlelight, not electricity… a perceptibly irresistible Gaelic burr… animal skins, a tunic, and a mail shirt lying across a trunk.

"You are King Arthur."

The faintest shadow of a smile tantalized her. "Nae, I am not an imaginary being but a mortal man in every sense of the word. Would ye like me to show ye?"

"Who are you?"

A hungry look settled upon his beautifully sculpted face. He spoke with a low, throbbing voice. "I am the man who will, in a moment hence, make love to ye. Abide wi' me." He kissed her intimately. "Abide wi' me, my mysterious lass." One talented finger drew an imaginary line from her lips, across her throat, and between her breasts.

Stupidly, she asked, "What are you going to do?" as if he had to draw her picture. Her brain didn't seem to be functioning properly. Everything, each thought was distorted and her perception was all off. Way off.

"It is not so much what I will do but rather what we will do together." His finger began to draw lazy circles around her navel.

She sucked in a breath, and when her eyes widened, he said, "Dinna worrit. No harm will come to ye."

His hands traveled over her with unflappable skill, learning the texture of her skin, the curves, the indentions, the places that made her moan. Something low in her belly tightened, and she felt consumed by a wild heat unknown to her. She didn't care who he was, what he was, or where he was from.

He wanted her, and she needed so desperately to be wanted, to be loved by a man who desired her and let her know it. He didn't simply kiss her; he made love to her mouth, his tongue plunging and stroking her in a way that made her groan and ache for him to teach her the rest. Heat shot throughout her body.

He kissed her breasts, while strange, unfamiliar feelings fluttered inside. He whispered to her in Gaelic with a hot breath that made her want to mate with him, this stranger, this dream lover her mind created. She gave in to the aching need, the incredible pleasure.

Paralyzed with wanting, she relaxed and opened to him. Surrounded by his warmth, his nearness, his nakedness, and bewildered by her unrestrained desire for him, she lay passive, knowing that whatever consumed her was stronger than she was. He seduced her with hands that coaxed and persuaded with the promises of the erotic, the unknown.

I'm dreaming, and I don't want to wake up. Please don't disappear. I don't think I could handle being rejected again. Not by my own dream.

Alysandir had no idea who she was, why she was there, or how she managed to get into his bed. But, she was naked and lying beside him, with the face of Helen of Troy and the body of Aphrodite. He wasn't about to let her get away, this divinity among mortals, this giver of pleasure. He was adrift in a realm of desire where sea nymphs sweetened the salty sea air with their delights. She was both goddess and courtesan who offered him the joy of ecstasy and a long night of lovemaking; be it imaginary, idealized, or false in nature. She was here, and she was his.

In spite of her appearing quite suddenly and naked in his bed, she had a stormy look of uncertainty laced with fear that made him think she was a maiden. That was absurd. No maiden would be in his bed, inviting him to have his way with her. Where was she from? How did she get into his bedchamber without one of the guards stopping her? Or was this all a dream?

The sight and scent of her aroused him, and he had been too long without a woman. He chuckled as she drew the coverlet up beneath her chin. As if that would stop him. Firelight worshipped her face as he gazed into golden-green eyes full of puzzlement and something darker and arousing. This was not the wooing of a simple maid, nor would it be rape. Something about this night and their coming together transcended that. They were Adam and Eve in the Garden before sin entered the picture.

Consumed by mounting desire, he drank in the pure lines of her lithe limbs, the perfect silence of her nudity. He took delight in her lack of shyness as he uncovered her. Her body came alive in the glow of the fire, rendering it translucent and as priceless as a rare vielle waiting for its strings to be strummed.

He saw the look of uncertainty in her eyes. He wondered if he might have misjudged her, that she wasn't in his bed of her own free will. Unless, of course, she had been sent to seduce him or to inflict bodily harm. But how could she do so? The only weapons she possessed were a body and face created to seduce and rob a man of his wit and wisdom.

He kissed her throat. He kissed the hard crowns of her breasts. He threaded his hands into her hair and leaned forward to kiss her soft, full lips, gently nipping, tracing their shape with his tongue, and then plunging into the sweet, warm depth of her mouth. When she groaned, his body hardened with desire.

He kissed his way across her throat and down to her breasts, moving possessively over them, kneading and learning their shape and softness. His thumbs teased her nipples to hard peaks that he warmed with his breath, before he tasted them, while his hand skimmed the flat planes of her belly and dropped lower. He held her close, for she was too perfect and too precious to let go. He wanted her to desire him, to put her arms around him, giving of herself as completely as he would himself to her.

Lying there, listening to her soft breathing, his thoughts consumed with images of what they could do together, he did not feel the ghostly touch of a hand to his brow, for it was as soft as the breath of a sleeping babe and gone swiftly. He was ready to make love to her one moment, and the next he was suddenly groggy, as if he consumed too much ale. The overpowering need for sleep began to creep slowly over his consciousness, and he fought against it. He held the woman fast, as if by doing so their entwined bodies would become one.

Alysandir slept on, not knowing that although he was the chief of the powerful Clan Mackinnon and protected that which was his, he had no power over the shimmering, sifting grains of time slipping beyond his grasp. Nor could he keep the delicate beauty beside him in his bed.

Chapter 4

O, then, I see Queen Mab
hath been with you.
She is the fairies' midwife…
And in this state she gallops
night by night
Through lovers' brains,
and then they dream of love.

—*Romeo and Juliet*, Act I, Scene 4
  William Shakespeare (1564–1616)
  English poet and playwright

"WAKE UP," ELISABETH SHOOK ISOBELLA AGAIN. "YOU'RE sleeping like you've been drugged." She placed her hand over Isobella's forehead and saw the bottle of Benadryl. "How many of those pills did you take?"

Isobella groaned and opened her eyes. "Two, I think." She put her hand to her forehead. "My head is splitting. I had the strangest dream."

"You look like you've been ravaged and washed up by the tide. I hope the dream was worth it."

"It was wonderful." She remembered strange, vague images of lying in bed. She sat straight up and gasped. "Oh, Lord!"

"Don't stop there."

"I dreamed I was in a castle, in bed."

"Were you alone?"

Isobella put her hand to her head. "I was in bed with a great looking guy, and he wanted to make love to me." She sighed dreamily. "And I wanted him to." She shook her head. "I don't know. I can't recall what he looked like, but I remember thinking he was gorgeous."

Elisabeth laughed. "Aren't they all? If only we could swap the duds of reality with the gods of our fantasies."

"I never realized the mind could be such an erogenous zone."

"Heavens, Izzy, you've got sex on the brain this morning."

"Yes," she said, woefully, "and what an unfortunate place to have it." She grinned impishly.

Elisabeth looked at her watch. "Okay, enough daydreaming. It's time to bid Romeo good-bye. I'll go down and order breakfast, and you can join me when you're dressed."

"Order me a doppio macchiato in about half an hour."

"Sex always works up an appetite," Elisabeth said, laughing as she dodged the flying pillow and slipped through the door.

Half an hour later, Isobella was eating and thinking she was happy Elisabeth was with her. She hoped the trip would draw them closer, for they had never been as close as most twins. Their interests and personalities were quite different. They couldn't agree on books, movies, clothes, cars, or what constituted a handsome man. Elisabeth was outspoken and impatient. She got to the heart of the matter quickly. Isobella tended to take her time and smell the roses along the way, wandering down unknown paths and sometimes getting lost. About the only thing they had in common was that they were identical twins.

While Isobella daydreamed, Elisabeth paid the tab. Soon they were on their way to the ancient Douglas strongholds of Threave, Castle Douglas, and Beloyn Castle, located in Dumfries and Galloway.

Elisabeth was driving. Isobella wanted to remember the night before, but a vague, greyness prevented her from recalling anything concrete. She wasn't sure if her experience had been a dream, reality, or both, although she did have bruises and love-bites, which made her think it had been both dream and reality. And that could land her in a mental institution if she dared tell anyone.

She didn't have a clear image of him. Other than that he was devilishly handsome, no distinct features came to mind. Weren't his eyes blue? She feared a gloomy state of sadness and hopelessness as her future. Why was he a dream lover instead of the real thing?

"If you're thinking about Jackson, stop!" Elisabeth said.

Isobella sighed. "There are 8,395,963 men in the state of Texas, and I can't hold on to even one."

"Stop thinking about him. Who would take tango lessons to be able to dance with his fiancée on their honeymoon and then run off to Argentina with the dance instructor instead?"

"A jerk!"

Elisabeth nodded. "Exactly. The best thing he ever did for you was to give you the check for five thousand that we used to pay for this trip. Who knows? You might meet someone here."

Isobella was already drifting off to sleep.

An hour later, she was jarred awake and heard Elisabeth say, "Sorry, I didn't see that pothole."

"I needed to wake up." Isobella looked around. "Are we almost there?"

"Yes. I'm getting excited to see Douglas's portrait, but I have my doubts about his being a ghost. You've always believed."

"I believed in ghosts when we were kids. Later, I knew it was impossible. Now, I don't know. A lot of references in those old family documents attest to the fact that he appeared a time or two other than to our four—or was it five—times great-grandmother, Meleri Douglas."

"What century was that?"

"Eighteenth. Back to your question, I think I *want* him to be a ghost. I had very strange feelings at St. Bride's yesterday."

"Those documents might be based upon myth, rather than fact. In real life, there aren't many happy endings. Prince Charming's line died out a long time ago, if it ever existed. I wish I could be more like you, Izzy. You got all the dreamer genes. As for me, I'm a boring reality check. I think Scotland's getting to me."

Isobella laughed. "Perhaps that's why I was so moved when we visited St. Bride's Kirk. The Black Douglas could be considered the romantic ideal, could he not?"

"Tell me you aren't going to fall for someone who has been dead for almost eight hundred years!"

"I can't. We might be related."

Later that afternoon, after visiting the first two castles on their list, they turned down a narrow, winding road in picturesque countryside and Isobella caught a glimpse of Beloyn Castle. It sat upon rock, as if it rose straight out of the ground. Part of the structure lay in ruins, for over the centuries the owners had never wanted to repair the damage, preferring to leave it as a reminder that the castle had been destroyed by King James. Now, it was a stalwart fortress, with its crow-stepped gable, baronial turrets, and unusual combination of aloofness and warmth.

Isobella studied the massive walls of yellowing stone, with creeping ivy growing in a roofless tower and dangling from arrow slits. Her imagination ran rampant as she envisioned the walls covered with fine tapestries and silken arras and set with fine glass windows. Beneath those rudely cut stones, scattered among the gaunt ribs and splintered timbers of once-vaulted ceilings, lay the stories of great love, lavish feasts, and births and death, of betrayal, torture, mayhem, and murder. She was irresistibly drawn to this tangible link to the past, both romantic and tragic, for it was the home of her Douglas ancestors.

She stretched lazily, for it was a warm, sunny day and the world around her was as splendid as any rendered by an artist's brush. The sun shone down with an almost liquid brilliance that turned the trees in the distance into a shimmering of great shadows and light, just as it had for centuries. She was awed at the secrets and whisperings the trees could tell of great warriors and battle-weary knights who once rode beneath their noble branches or hid from the English in the shielding embrace of dense foliage.

The road curved and she saw the white fence of a cottage, the tawny gold of a thatched roof, the glazed green of a chestnut tree, and the sparkling blue of the river against the rich brown tones of the road that curled before them. She caught the haunting sound of a bagpipe, the dull humming faint and melancholy. "I wonder who is playing."

Elisabeth slowed and turned onto the graveled parking area. "Playing what?"

"The bagpipes."

"I don't hear anything."

Isobella rolled down the window. "Hear them now?"

"No."

Isobella shivered. "It's freezing in here. Turn down the air."

"We didn't rent a car with air conditioning."

Suddenly, Isobella felt very cold and very frightened.

Chapter 5

Sometimes I think we're alone in the universe,
And sometimes I think we're not.
In either case the idea is quite staggering.

—Attributed to Sir Arthur C. Clarke (1917–2008)
  English science fiction writer

Beloyn Castle
Scottish Lowlands
Present Time

THE DOOR WAS HUGE, HEAVILY CARVED, AND STUDDED WITH brass. The marks of hundreds of years did nothing to mar its beauty. Isobella rapped the lion's head knocker. A group of birds flapped out of a nearby tree as the door opened.

A stout, middle-aged woman said, "You must be the Douglas twins. I am Mrs. Kinsey, the housekeeper you spoke with earlier. You may call me Claire." She opened the door wider. "Do come in."

The entry was dark until Claire drew back the heavy, velvet drapes and sunlight spilled into the room. "As I explained earlier, the castle is closed while the earl and countess are in Italy. If you will follow me."

They passed a true medieval hall, huge, with thick walls covered with tapestries and deep-set windows.

The fireplace was enormous, and the stone floors, although bare, were highly polished. A lovely rood screen stood along one wall. "I bet these walls know a lot of secrets," Elisabeth said.

"Yes, and some are quite blood-curdling," Claire replied.

The sisters exchanged glances and followed her through a long gallery, which contained a great curved stairway, massive and wide. "Who plays the bagpipes?" Isobella asked.

"No one, not since the earl's grandfather died."

Isobella's attention was suddenly captured by a painting, and her heart pounded excitedly. At least five feet wide and eight feet tall, the portrait was ornately framed in gilt and worth a fortune. She wondered why it captivated her. Beloyn Castle was in the background. The two dogs were Scottish deerhounds. She shivered and felt a chill to her neck, for what disturbed her was the man in the painting. He was quite magnificent and so lifelike he seemed a living, breathing entity.

He stood with his legs planted far apart and his arms crossed in front of him, with a great black cape swirling out behind him, a glimmer in his deep blue eyes, and a smile upon his lips. His hair was as black as sin, and she felt she had seen that face before, which was impossible, considering that the brass plaque beneath the portrait declared it to be of Sir James Douglas.

A chill passed over her. "The Black Douglas," she whispered.

"Yes, it is." The phone rang. "If you will excuse me," Claire said, and hurried away.

"So, that is what he looked like," Elisabeth said.

Without realizing she did so, Isobella put out her hand and touched the bottom of his boot, where the cape curled around it. "It's really you, isn't it?"

And everything went black…

———~~~———

When Claire returned to the gallery, the twins were gone. She went upstairs. She searched the eight bedrooms and then the rest of the castle. When she saw their car still parked outside, she called the earl.

"Yes, my lord, I searched every bedroom in the entire wing and then the rest of the castle, top to bottom." She glanced toward the great staircase and gasped. "Dear Mary and Joseph! The Black Douglas is gone from the painting.

"No, my lord, I haven't been in your Scotch. Yes, I am standing two feet from the portrait. I see the place where he was, faintly outlined, but his image is no longer there. It is as if he stepped right out of the painting and took those girls with him."

Chapter 6

But he was not so fair that we
Should speak greatly of his beauty.
In visage was he somewhat grey,
And had black hair as I heard say;
But of limbs he was well made,
With bones long and shoulders broad.
When he was merry he was lovable,
And meek and sweet in company;
But who in battle might him see,
Another countenance had he.

—Description of Sir James, the Black Douglas
   from the epic poem *The Brus*, 1375
   John Barbour (1325?–1395), Scottish poet

A BITTERLY COLD DRAFT SWIRLED AROUND ISOBELLA, a windy and destructive force that grew in strength. A glowing light surrounded by a shimmering green mist stood on one of the steps of the staircase a few feet away. There was something terribly exciting and horribly frightening about the swirling green mist, for in its center a solid shape had begun to take human form. If she'd had a lick of sense, she would have bolted. Paralyzed with awe, she murmured, "Oh, my God!"

From out of the mist a baritone voice boomed like

thunder, "Mistress, I am not God. Ye hae only yerself to blame for my being so hastily summoned forthwith."

Right before her eyes, a real, live former human being was assembling his ghostly self. It was one of the few times in her life that Isobella was completely speechless. She wanted to scream, but her vocal chords were frozen. Her feet felt like concrete blocks. She relaxed, completely mesmerized by the pleasing masculine face looking at her with an almost tender expression.

She blinked, yet he was still there, a man well built, strong and slim, with black hair, a stern countenance, and eyes that were darkly, deeply, beautifully blue. But, it was his suit of armor that identified him. While her heart pounded fearfully, she whispered, "I know who you are."

His eyes twinkled merrily. "Do ye now?"

"You are Sir James, the Black Douglas. You returned as a ghost in 1759, when Robert Douglas owned this castle."

His eyes shined brighter than before, "Ahhh, Meleri. Now, there was a lass!"

"That's what I've always been told. She was my many times great-grandmother." Isobella saw the amused way he was looking at her. She felt like such a dolt. Like he didn't know that.

"I know you were Scotland's bravest knight and greatest warrior. You fought beside Robert the Bruce, were feared by the English, were sung about in ballads... and I don't have the faintest idea why you are standing here, or why I'm babbling like the village idiot when I should be fainting from fright."

"Ye do have a way o' talking overmuch," he said.

"Yes, I know. Am I dreaming?"

"'Tis no dream, but reality, lass."

Ye gods! I'm talking to the ghost of the Black Douglas. She felt as if a bolt of lightning had flashed through her skull. Her mouth was dry, and Elisabeth was squeezing her hand so tightly that Isobella was certain all her blood had given up trying to get through and rushed back to the sanctuary of her heart. Even her eyeballs ached. And her brain! It ached like someone had used it for first base.

"You're a real person, yet you're a ghost."

His brows rose in question. "I am not always an invisible nonentity. Why do ye look so stunned? Ye did summon me forthwith, did ye not?"

"Summon? Oh no, I would never. I don't know how."

"Aye, lass, ye did, for it was ye who touched my ancient heart with the warmth of yer tears shed over my effigy at St. Bride's. No one has ever done that, ye ken—not once in the eight hundred years since my puir boiled bones were placed there. 'Twas yer words that awakened me and summoned me forth."

"My words?" she said, sounding like a hoarse crow. "But I didn't say anything." Then suddenly, she remembered. *I'm so sorry.* "Oh, you mean you read my thoughts?"

Were his eyes twinkling? "Aye, ghosting doth have its privileges, ye ken."

Isobella's brows rose and she said, "What kind of privileges?"

"Mayhap I will show ye."

She studied him with close scrutiny. "You didn't happen to whip up a little surreptitious interlude for me last night, did you?"

With eyes as full of mischief as a four-year-old, he asked, "What do ye think?"

She gasped. Was her dream lover real? She was about to ask for a repeat performance, but Elisabeth was gouging her ribs. She turned toward Elisabeth and everything began to darken and spin, wobbling noisily with a great whirring sound. Isobella's breath caught in her throat, and she felt as if the air was being sucked from her lungs. She heard a loud roaring—louder than a freight train flying by at great speed. She put her hands over her ears to stifle the sound but to no avail.

The earth beneath her feet vibrated wildly, and she feared she was being sucked upward into a tornado. Elisabeth's face was bloodless, and her wild hair rivaled Medusa's snakes, as she held Isobella's hand in a death grip. Debris swirled, and trees were stripped of their leaves, laid almost flat from the force.

Isobella's long hair whipped about her face, tangled as seaweed. She feared her clothes were being ripped asunder as she was drawn into a whirling, swirling mass of debris. Even the light of the sun dimmed and, for a time, went out like a snuffed candle.

Surrounded by an inky blackness, Isobella knew the world they loved was lost to them. Then, in the blink of an eye, everything changed.

Light returned. Grey and smoky at first, but then infused with pale, soft color. The world grew still and eerily quiet. For a shimmering moment, Isobella saw the Black Douglas's majestic figure as it had been in life, and then it began to fade. Somewhere, in the maze of her mind, his voice spoke to her and she felt comforted by the words, clear and sharp, with their lilting burr.

Fear na ye…

Chapter 7

From ghoulies and ghosties
And long-leggedy beasties
And things that go bump in the night,
Good Lord deliver us!

—Scottish prayer

Isle of Mull
Scotland, 1515

IT WAS DARK WHEN ALYSANDIR AND DRUST STEPPED INTO their small boat and rowed the short distance across the Sound of Iona to Mull, where their brother Colin waited with their horses. The night was inky and black. A furtive moon slid between slow-moving clouds to illuminate everything below, including the boat that navigated a labyrinth of craggy rocks, dim in the moonlight. With a yank of the reins, Colin led the horses closer, anxious to hear if their sister Barbara was safely tucked away in the nunnery.

The boat rocked as Drust stood and steadied himself. The current lapped against the hull as he searched the rocky shore for a sign of his brother and spotted Colin's fiery hair. "Troth, brother! 'Tis good to see ye."

"Did ye have trouble finding me?" Colin called back.

"Aye, 'tis as difficult to see ye as the flame of a stick of resinous wood."

Colin grumbled, and Drust chuckled loudly enough for Colin to hear. It always set Colin's temper on edge to be teased about his red hair, and teasing his brother was something Drust rarely resisted.

Tonight, Colin ignored his brother's taunt and quietly stood guard while Alysandir heaved himself over the side of the boat and landed with a gentle splash. The hull scraped against rocks as Drust pulled the boat ashore. Eager horses pawed at the sand, tossing their heads with impatience. Colin extended his hand, and with a toss, threw the reins toward his oldest brother.

Alysandir caught them in one hand and spoke a few soothing words. Gently stroking Gallagher's neck, he mounted. The moment he was in the saddle, the sturdy hobbler broke into a canter along a sandy stretch of sand, splashing through the shallow water and throwing up clumps of wet sand. As Alysandir turned his mount toward higher ground and broke into a gallop, he fleetingly thought of the Macleans and how old Angus must be raising their clannish ire. That did not bother Alysandir, for he preferred Angus's anger to his cunning, for an angry man was ever a stupid one.

However, it did rankle to be spending so much time on a gnat like Angus Maclean when more important matters needed to be dealt with. Besides his troubles with the clan elders who wanted to see him married, Alysandir had to deal with Scotland being trapped in the middle of a power struggle between England and France. It was like crossing a vast chasm on a rope bridge burning behind them, while all manner of poisonous vipers waited at the bottom.

Behind him, his brothers quickly mounted and rode after him, accompanied by the muffled sound of horses' hooves against the boggy soil. "Did all go well with ye?" Colin asked when he slowed his horse to ride next to Drust.

Drust gazed at the leather bag tied to Colin's saddle and asked, rather good-naturedly, "What have ye there in those bags, Colin?"

Colin shrugged. "I like to be prepared. Did all go well?"

"Aye, Barbara is comfortably settled in with the nuns, cozy as can be, and our uncle said to give ye his blessing."

Colin nodded. "Our uncle... did ye warn him that there could be trouble with the Macleans if they learn Barbara is in hiding there?"

"He knows, but he is no' too worrit aboot it. He thinks Angus Maclean is too smart to risk the wrath of the church in Rome just to snatch a prospective bride from the nunnery so he can marry her off to his son. Angus knows our uncle is the abbot and that the church would soon learn of such a rash act."

"Ye do seem a mite delighted at the prospect," Colin said.

Drust grinned widely. "Aye, 'tis true enough that it is a source of delight to rankle the old dog by pulling his tail."

"There never was any love lost between Lachlan Mackinnon and Angus Maclean," Colin said. "I heard they both had their eye on the same lass at one time, and Angus lost out. There has been bad blood between them ever since."

Drust replied, "Weel, that may be, but I ken there's never been any love lost between the Macleans and the Mackinnons since the beginning of time. Bitter as gall and wormwood it is to Angus, knowing the Mackinnons belong to the kindred of St. Columba and that many have been abbots at the monastery he started. 'Twas always as damp as water on the aspirations of ole Angus."

"The two of ye are overly confident on the eve of strife. Ye should be preparing yer mind for battle and filling yer soul with iron will," Alysandir said, cutting into their conversation. He remembered when things had been that way between him and his older brother, Hugh, and how it had wounded him to be the one sent to bring Hugh's body back from where it had fallen at the Battle of Flodden Field.

He remembered, too, how he had not wanted to take the mantle of tribal chief from the shoulders of his dead brother. In the end, Alysandir had assumed a role he had never asked for and never really wanted, and at times like this he envied his younger brothers the freedom of their carefree ways and lighthearted banter, for heavy hung the mantle of responsibility upon his shoulders.

His brothers fell silent and rode on, while Alysandir contemplated how he had been only twelve years old—a peace-loving lad and a bit of a scholar—when his father had sent him to school in France. He recalled how confusing and disorienting he had found being in a foreign country, with Parisian culture so far removed from a Highlander's life.

But he had been a happy lad, hardworking and resilient, and he had taken to his studies like a duck to water. Soon he had settled in happily enough, making friends, doing well in his studies, and getting into trouble on occasion, never knowing that one day he would call upon all those experiences, trouble included, to lead the Mackinnons as their chief.

His father had wanted him to learn to interpret official documents, both public and private, most of which were couched in Latin—and learn them, he did. In addition to Latin, he also became fluent in English and French. Although Gaelic was spoken in the Highlands, Lowlanders and those of the noble classes usually conversed in Norman French, and most of them also spoke English. Years later, his knowledge of languages did open doors, as his father had said it would.

Alysandir learned to play the lute and to sing, neither of which he enjoyed. He was tutored in literature and writing, even though it was expected that he would always have clerks at his disposal. He excelled at horsemanship and the use and care of arms, as well as being educated in the behavior, skills, and qualities befitting the second son of the Mackinnon chief.

He often wondered if his father had had some sort of premonition that his second son might one day be called upon to lead and guide the Mackinnons, for if he had not had the education afforded him, he would have been ill prepared to lead and would have fallen woefully short of being the kind of leader the ancient tribe deserved. Yet, there were times like today when Alysandir doubted he was good enough, wise enough, and strong enough to be the leader his father and brother had been. So many memories; so many deaths, so much pain. Life goes on.

His face was as cold and imperturbable as his thoughts, which he knew should be directed toward more important matters, like keeping a sharp eye out for signs of trouble. In spite of the moon, the world seemed to have closed in on them, and the wind blew a little bit stronger, while the air grew a wee bit colder. There was definitely something afoot this night and he had a strong sense of foreboding.

He had never wanted more to feel the walls of Caisteal Màrrach closing around him. He longed for his brothers to be safe and out of harm's way, to know again the warm and comfortable feeling of belonging. Once inside the castle he would feel the heat of a fire drawing the seawater from his boots and hear the sound of Duff's tail thumping against his chair.

"'Tis a serious face ye be wearing." Drust said, after riding silently beside Alysandir for several minutes. "Ye have the look of a haunted man."

"We need to pick up the pace, lads," Alysandir said. He spurred Gallagher into a fast lope, not bothering to look back to see if his brothers followed. He knew they did.

A faster pace did not outrun the apprehension that had captured and held his thoughts since they left Barbara at the nunnery. He worried for her safety but for his brothers' more. It would make no sense for Angus Maclean to harm Barbara when his son fancied himself in love with her. Angus would not be so kind toward her brothers.

At daybreak, Colin stood in the stirrups and searched the horizon for a glimpse of Alysandir. Seeing none, he said, "Sometimes I wonder why he wants us to ride with him, for he canna stay be with us verra long without riding off alone."

"'Tis a part of who he is," Drust said. "Part of it comes from the role he inherited. Since he became chief, there has been a change in him. It is as if he was touched in some magical way by the same passions that touched our ancestors. So, dinna worrit if ye canna see him. He is close enough that he can see us."

"So, what are ye trying to tell me, Drust?"

"That we canna criticize that which we dinna understand."

Chapter 8

The time is out of joint;
O cursèd spite,
That ever I was born
to set it right!

—*Hamlet*, Act I, Scene 5
  William Shakespeare (1564–1616)
  English dramatist and poet

Isle of Mull
Scotland, 1515

ISOBELLA FLOATED IN A PAINLESS WORLD, THINKING SHE WAS dead and expecting her first peek of Heaven. Until she caught a glimpse of Elisabeth. Isobella frowned, feeling a bit fuzzy-headed and not certain about anything other than the fact that she did not appear to be dead. Well, that was something positive, at least. After enduring Elisabeth's fierce glare for a few seconds, Isobella did manage a weak, "What?"

Elisabeth's green eyes were full of fire. "What happened? I feel like I've been thrown out of a rocket traveling a million miles an hour." With a bewildered expression, she paused to look around.

"Are we in hell?"

"Try again," Elisabeth said.

Isobella looked around. "I'd say we're in the middle of nowhere."

"Good guess, but we might get a better answer from that specter of malevolence hovering over there."

Isobella turned her head and saw a vaporous, glowing light taking solid shape. She recognized the emerging human figure immediately. "Did you send us through a vacuum that sucked us up and dropped us here?" she asked angrily, though still a little awed that she was talking to the greatest warrior in Scottish history. "Are we still in Scotland, and if so, where?"

"Aye, ye are in Scotland, on the Isle of Mull."

"And you brought us here for a reason?"

"Aye," he said with a nod. "As bidden."

"But we didn't." Bidden? A nice, Middle English word, she thought, but not often used in the present time. "Ah, you mean because I cried back at St. Bride's when we visited your crypt?"

"Aye, yer tears reached out across the centuries to summon me. I might have been a mighty knight in the service of my king, but a woman's tears were ere my undoing."

Isobella could well believe that, but she didn't get to think upon it further, due to Elisabeth's persistent rib jabbing, which she ignored. How could she explain that this was truly the archaeological opportunity of a lifetime? Instead of digging through ruins for answers, she had her own personal history book in the flesh, so to speak.

There he stood, a bona fide knight-errant, right out of medieval Scotland's romantic past and wearing the clothes of his knighthood: chausses and a mail tunic called a hauberk and a light blue tunic, belted low about the hips. He was a handsome man, not overly tall by twenty-first century standards, but tall for the fourteenth-century male, slender with well-developed muscles, dark blue eyes, and hair of the blackest black. The legendary Black Douglas was a medieval heartbreaker if she had ever seen one.

It was all so terribly romantic, at least to Isobella, and she thought it divine good fortune that she was there. For a moment, her mind wandered off to think about what her contemporaries would give for an opportunity like this. Her sister, on the other hand, could not be charmed if Jude Law and Orlando Bloom were standing in front of them, with Patrick Dempsey and Johnny Depp as backup.

Elisabeth suddenly found her voice. "Are you really the Black Douglas? No, never mind. Don't answer that. It isn't possible," she said, her tone one of pure disbelief. "You cannot be a ghost because ghosts don't exist." She put her hand to her forehead and looked around, as if searching for help. "I don't believe this is happening. It's impossible. When people die, they stay dead."

"And yet I am here. Do ye have a better explanation?"

"All right, if you are a ghost, then undo this mischief. Take us back to our car."

Isobella took a deep breath and glanced tentatively around the narrow glen. The level stretch of ground rose to a slope at one end, rocky and choked with boulders, before dropping away to a ravine or gorge, or whatever they called it in these parts, for she could see the dark brown ridge of a mountain rising some distance beyond it. The rest of the glen was lined with a thin stand of larch trees and a thick tangle of briars that gradually thinned behind them to reveal an open moor.

"Thank you for this little excursion to Mull, but we

really need to go now. We must find a town to rent another car. We are flying home in a few days and have many places to see, but Mull isn't one of them."

"We have no cars, buses, or airplanes."

Slack-jawed, the twins stared at each other and then at him. Elisabeth threw up her arms in exasperation. "So send us to Beloyn so we can get our car."

"I canna do that today," Douglas said.

"You mean we have to wait until tomorrow?" Isobella asked.

Douglas shrugged. "'Twill be no different tomorrow."

"Then when can we go back?" Elisabeth asked.

"Who knows? Mayhap never. Mayhap when the spirit moves me."

"What kind of answer is that?"

"Never mind that," Elisabeth said, turning back to the Black Douglas. "I did not ask to come here. Why did you bring me? Isobella put her hand on your effigy, not I! You had no right to drag me along."

"'Tis no fault of mine that ye managed to stick like a leech to yer sister and now ye are here."

"Stick like a… listen, you vacuous vapor, I had nothing to do with this. I only came on this trip to keep her company. It seems to me you are the one at fault here. So tell us how we get out of here."

He looked around. "Weel, you could go that way," he said, pointing to his right. "Or you might try that way," he said, pointing to his left. "Or mayhap ye should go both ways," he said, crossing his arms over his chest and pointing in both directions.

Elisabeth threw up her hands. "I would like a straight answer for a change. One that makes sense."

"Let's back up for a minute," Isobella said. "Where can we rent a car or catch a bus?"

"Ye willna find those things here," he said.

"Why not?" Isobella asked.

His expression was rather mischievous. Isobella thought that finally they were getting somewhere. Then he said, "Ye are in sixteenth-century Scotland, and we havena such things."

Isobella gasped. "You mean *the* sixteenth century? The Early Renaissance period? Oh, Lord! What are we going to do?" She turned to Elisabeth. "Do you realize what this means? We have traveled back five hundred years to the beginning of the Renaissance."

"All I am thinking right now is how much I would love to punch you, flat out."

Isobella ignored her and turned back to Douglas. "Is Henry VIII King of England?"

"Aye."

"I knew it!" Isobella fairly jumped around, thrilled and dumbfounded at the same time. One rational thought managed to slip through and she smiled. "I guess that's one way to get rid of Jackson. He hasn't even been born yet."

Elisabeth was not looking very happy and obviously didn't give a flip whether Jackson had been born or not. "You're jesting, right? This really isn't the sixteenth century, is it?"

"Aye, 'tis the year 1515."

"Who is the king of Scotland?" Elisabeth asked, her brows knit with serious intensity. Isobella gave her an astonished look. Elisabeth wouldn't know the correct answer if it was written down on a piece of paper and handed to her. Isobella had to think hard for a moment before deciding that was when King James V was just a babe.

"'Tis the infant King James," he replied.

"Why did you bring us to Mull?" Isobella asked.

"Ye are here because ye asked to be."

Isobella shook her head. "I never asked to come here. Why would you say that?"

She saw a spark of amusement in the blue depths of his eyes. "Ye will understand when the time is ripe."

They were interrupted by the animated sounds of rolling chaos that suddenly filled the air around them. They listened to the clamor of clanging swords and the shouts of warring men. "I think we better stop talking and start praying," Isobella said, looking over Elisabeth's shoulder to stare at the warring knights.

"I hope they are friends of yours," Elisabeth said, turning toward the Black Douglas, "Could they be English?"

"English!" Isobella almost spat the words out. "You can't leave us to the mercy of those English bastards!"

A smile curved across the fine mouth of the Black Douglas. "That's a lass!"

"We need more than compliments," Isobella said. "This isn't looking good for any of us. Well, not you perhaps, since they can't run you through, but it's something we need to worry about."

Elisabeth agreed. "You're already dead. They can't hurt you. But our predicament is a bit different. Are you going to take us back or just hand us over to the enemy?"

They had only a brief glimpse of his broad smile before his image began to lighten and grow dim, before it faded completely away.

Chapter 9

In trouble to be troubled
Is to have your trouble doubled.

—*The Further Adventures of Robinson Crusoe*, 1719
  Daniel Defoe (1660–1731)
  English novelist and journalist

MORNING ARRIVED. AN UNEASY WIND STIRRED, BRISK AND chilling. The horses were restless as the Mackinnons rode on, caution their constant companion. They welcomed the full force of the warm morning sun as they left the heather-clad moorland to ride through the shadows of deep glens, surrounded by thick woodlands. A golden eagle soared, lazily gliding overhead. A large flock of skylarks flapped out of the trees in announcing their arrival. The feeling was stronger now: Alysandir felt the presence of something evil-intentioned, a treacherous presence moving about furtively, waiting in a shadowy corner, ready to pounce.

"Keep a good vigil, lads," he said to his brothers. "I have a uneasy feeling we are being watched."

"Aye, I can almost smell the Macleans." Colin looked around anxiously as he spoke the words.

They splashed across a narrow, swiftly running burn. When they reached the other side, Colin's horse began to dance and shy away, nervously chomping the bit.

The damp, salty tang of the sea hung heavy in the air. Alysandir cautiously took note of the silence in the glen as they approached.

It was suddenly still.

The birds were quiet.

Nothing stirred.

He glanced at his brothers and saw the tension in their faces and in the way they gripped the reins. He brushed away a few flecks of foam thrown from Colin's horse that had landed on his tunic. His own horse tossed his head and pranced sideways, snorting, the bit clanging against his teeth, as if anxious to be away from this place. Alysandir gave Gallagher a calming stroke and slowly moved his arm closer to his sword.

The faces of his brothers were set, grim and hard. They were ready for whatever lay ahead. Colin said, with nervous dryness, "'Twould seem the Macleans are aware that we have taken Barbara to Iona."

"Aye, they probably knew the moment we rode away with her," Alysandir said. "They were certain of it when we arrived back on Mull without her. 'Tis sorry I am that I couldna see the face of Fergus when he realized we outwitted them."

Fergus bragged oft enough that Barbara Mackinnon would be his wife, one way or another. One way was to ask the Mackinnon chief, Alysandir, for Barbara's hand in marriage, which Fergus did.

When Alysandir made the request known to Barbara, she almost spat back the words of her response, "Fergus Maclean! Troth! I would sooner marry the devil or drown myself in the Firth of Lorne than spend one day with him!"

Angus took offense at Barbara's refusal of Fergus's offer and gave his blessing to Fergus, should he decide he wanted her enough to seize her and force her into marriage. Now, Barbara was tucked safely away in the nunnery at Iona and Alysandir hoped that Fergus Maclean's desire would soon be transferred to some other bonnie lass before Barbara started to complain and make demands to return home.

"I will wager that the Macleans will have every member of their clan out to take revenge," Drust said. "We can expect to find them lurking behind every tree we pass."

"I have a feeling it willna be long afore we find just what tree that is," Colin said.

Alysandir paid them no mind. Revenge was certain because it was the Macleans' nature to settle everything with a fight. Angus was easily roused to anger and liked to incite and provoke those who did not act according to his wants and desires. Alysandir was slow to anger, and it was his way not to set himself against anyone needlessly but simply to let the varlets go on with their play undisturbed. He did not want trouble, but he would not run from it if put in his path. He protected his clan and his kin, and if the Macleans wanted a fight, they would get one, no matter how outnumbered the Mackinnons were.

He looked down at the scar on his right hand—a badge of honor, his father called it—a reminder of his first encounter with a Maclean sword. He was ten years old when the Macleans attacked as the Mackinnons returned from a visit to their uncle. During the battle, a Maclean, with sword drawn, charged Hugh. Without thinking, Alysandir guided his horse against the Maclean, causing the Maclean's thrust to miss its mark. Furious, the

Maclean had turned on Alysandir and sliced his hand in retribution. Their father had evened the score by running his sword through the Maclean.

Alysandir did not anticipate such a large number of warriors as there had been that day. Old Angus was too proud to take a large party of Macleans to deal with three Mackinnons—and one of them a novice. Alysandir and his brothers rode on, following no track and leaving no signs that they had passed. Before long, they left the cloak of trees and rode into the clearing of a glen.

Ahead of them, the peaks of Ben More rose up. The mountain's shoulders were bare now, all traces of snow having melted away. Alysandir wondered if his brothers remembered how their father had taken them to climb Ben More when they were young. He caught a flash of movement in the screen of trees just ahead.

"Have care, lads," he said, speaking softly. He said a quick prayer as six Macleans poured over the hilltop and thundered toward them. The Mackinnons drew swords, with the ringing sound of metal against metal, as they spurred their horses forward crying out the Mackinnon battle cry, *"Cuimhnich bas Alpein!"* "Remember the death of Alpin."

The Macleans, their crests clearly visible and their swords already drawn, charged into the center of the opposing threesome. Like the Mackinnons, they were in light armor—surcoat and leggings and a chain-mail byrnie over their tunics to cover the head and shoulders.

"Hold fast," Alysandir said.

The words were barely spoken, when one of the Macleans charged and rode at full gallop to crash into Colin's horse. Colin fell to the ground, somewhat stunned by the blow. Then, with a spring like a grimalkin faëry cat shooting out of the woods, Colin leapt up. He didn't have time to draw back his arm for thrust or parry, so Alysandir raised his sword, slashing his blade to meet Colin's attacker. His blow missed the chain-mail byrnie that covered the Maclean's head and drove deeply between it and the man's chin, where it pierced him just below the collarbone, sending him to the ground.

That left five Macleans still mounted.

Another rider charged Colin, who seemed to be holding his own even without a horse. Alysandir saw him deftly swing his sword to the left to push aside a blade that struck his helmet. The blow glanced against his steel mesh shirt before it slid harmlessly down his arm, where it made a slicing cut at his wrist. Colin, like Alysandir, would have, for the rest of his life, a reminder of his first encounter with a Maclean sword.

Drust was charged by one of the more skilled Macleans. A moment before the rider struck, Drust's horse made a quick turn and leap to the side, which caused the Maclean to inaccurately thrust his sword, and he hit nothing but air. Drust, meanwhile, rode toward the Maclean, fast as a young colt turned out to grass, and managed a deep, slashing cut that laid open the man's leg, causing considerable damage to the bone.

The wounded rider swayed in the saddle and rode for a few feet, barely managing to hold on while leaning heavily to the left, before he fell to the ground and landed on his back. With a quick yank on the reins, Alysandir pulled his horse into a tight turn and charged after the fallen Maclean, driving the point of his sword through the mail-covered chest. He yanked the blade free and turned back to join his brothers, never seeing the blood that spurted red. Four Macleans now. The odds were improving.

Alysandir deflected the blow from a Maclean and glanced toward his brothers to see how they fared. Stunned, he could not believe what he was seeing, for his brothers and the Macleans had ceased fighting. Not a sound could be heard on what had been, a moment before, a place of battle. The Macleans remained on one side of the glen and his brothers on the other, separated by some ten feet or so. All of them were stuck dumb, staring bewildered at something behind him.

He sheathed the mighty sword to the hilt in its scabbard and swore. Women?

He blinked to clear his vision, but there they were. Two women near a field of battle. One of them was almost naked, with her bare arms and shapely legs gleaming, slender and pale, in the morning light, while the other wore what looked like a man's light blue chausses. Why were they dressed so strangely? Where did they come from? Where were they going? Who were they?

More importantly, what were the Mackinnons going to do about them? They couldn't very well ride off and leave the women to the mercy of the Macleans. From the looks of things, the fighting was over. Alysandir glanced at his brothers, and without so much as a nod, the three of them spurred their mounts and rushed the Macleans, waving their swords and shouting the Mackinnon battle cry. The Macleans didn't wait around to see what they would do next, but quickly turned their horses around and fled back up the hill and into the trees.

Alysandir watched them leave. His victorious mood quickly turned to irritation. What was he going to do with two strumpets? He couldn't ride off and leave them to a fate that could easily end with their deaths. He looked them over, trying to decide what to do. He was bothered in a way he did not like, especially by the half-naked one with little inhibition and even fewer clothes. Who or what was she?

He had not a glimmer of an idea what to do about them. Where there was a woman, danger was not far behind. And near-naked ones were worse than slings and arrows. A near-naked woman spread the wildfires of desire, and when it came to lust, Alysandir had learned that unsatisfied was best.

As he turned his horse away, he couldn't stop himself from glancing again toward the delicate white flesh and shifted uncomfortably in the saddle. He set his spurs to his horse and wished thoughts of the near-naked lass away. Women were better left to his dreams, for the real ones were nothing but a sea of trouble.

Chapter 10

An idea, like a ghost,
must be spoken to a little
before it will explain itself.

—Charles Dickens (1812–1870)
   English novelist

THE IMAGE OF THE BLACK DOUGLAS BEGAN TO FADE AWAY
gradually, leaving the echo of his last words ringing in
their ears.

"Fear na ye."

"Please, don't go!" Isobella turned to Elisabeth.
"How can he leave us here like this?"

"With easy abandon, I'd say."

Isobella gave her sister a glaring look of disapproval,
thinking that nobody, not even a ghost, could be that
heartless. "Wait! Come back! What if we need you?
What if we're in danger? You won't be able to come
back to help us, will you? We could die out here!"

Elisabeth was already turning away from the place
where Douglas had been. "You might as well give up.
I think he is a couple of centuries away by now."

"Damn and double damn!" Isobella kicked a rock
and paced back and forth a few times. They were completely alone and defenseless against the wilds of this
primitive place.

Elisabeth was staring stupidly at something behind her, so Isobella turned to have a look and saw that where the meadow curved into a small cove, a group of men with drawn swords were staring in their direction. They appeared to have been engaged in a battle of cracking heads and running each other through.

Only now, the men were stiff as statues. Swords still drawn, they ignored the bodies strewn about as they stared directly at the women, as if frozen in time. Isobella let out a long sigh of relief. "Thank God, they are not English."

Elisabeth gave her a look that needed no interpretation. "Oh well, it is such a tremendous relief to know that if I am killed, it will not be by the bloody English. Dead is dead in any language, time period, or nationality."

Isobella wasn't listening. "Do you think they saw us suddenly appear out of nowhere?"

"Does peanut butter stick to the roof of your mouth? Of course, they saw us," Elisabeth said in a low whisper. "Look at the expressions of fearful disbelief on their faces. Right now, I'd say they are trying to decide if we are witches."

Isobella whispered, "We've landed in the midst of some kind of clannish brawl. Highlanders were always fighting someone, including family members when no one else was about. Fighting and killing was like a national sport to them."

Unexpectedly, a cry cut through the air and three of the men rushed the others, yelling in unison, *"Cuimhnich bas Alpein."*

Elisabeth glanced at Isobella. "Any idea what that war whoop was all about?"

"It's Gaelic. Probably a battle cry. All I caught was something about Alpin."

"Who or what is Alpin?"

"There was more than one Alpin, but they might be referring to the MacAlpin who was the Dalriata King of Picts and Scots in Ireland before they settled in Scotland." She said nothing more for she was thinking that whoever the three men were, they attacked with such furor that the four men opposing them turned and hightailed it into the trees.

"Do you think we should make a run for it?" Elisabeth was frowning now and looking around, as if searching for the nearest exit.

"No," Isobella replied with a shake of her head. "Men, like animals, chase anything that runs. If we made a run for it, they would think us guilty of something and give chase. And they would catch us. We would have more explaining to do than if we just wait to see what they do."

Elisabeth nodded. "I suppose you're right."

"Well, we have no idea who they are, but we need to make contact with someone. We can't stay here forever. If we hide, they will find us. If we run, they will catch us."

"And if we stay here, they will have us for dinner," Elisabeth added, "Or dessert. I don't see anyone who remotely resembles Sir Galahad among them. I will admit they do look grimly efficient."

"That is because they probably are," Isobella replied.

"How do we know which ones are the good guys?" Elisabeth paused, for the three men had now stepped out of the shade of the trees. Now they were standing in full sunlight, and Elisabeth's jaw dropped.

"Oh, my lord, I take back everything I said. Things are

not looking so bad after all." She turned toward Isobella and said, "Please tell me those are not Douglas men and our ancestors. I'm having very lascivious thoughts right now and would hate to find we are related."

With a flushed face and a dreamy expression, Isobella stared at the bodies, etched by the strength and stamina of the warrior caste. They were supreme examples of the godly mathematics of male beauty.

"If they are Douglases, it would be our luck, wouldn't it? I don't think I've ever seen three men put together any better. Would you look at those biceps," Isobella said, drinking in the sight of the slender, well-muscled upper body of the man she identified as their leader. There was something about the graceful proportion of form, the balanced turn of a well-shaped head, and the power of a warrior's body when he moved.

"They did not get those muscles lifting weights in the gym. They earned them the hard way. And have you noticed the size of those swords they were swinging? And they aren't even claymores."

Elisabeth shook her head. "No, I was imagining the size of something else when you interrupted my thoughts. Only you would look at medieval weapons when you have three demigods to drool over. I could close my eyes and grab one and come out just fine."

"Judging from the expressions on their faces, it would seem they are thinking the same about us. Either that, or they haven't eaten in a week," Isobella replied. It was good to know that Elisabeth found the male bodies stimulating—and not in a medical way. She and Elisabeth might be polar opposites, but rugged Scots were something they both approved of.

Instead of coming toward them, the men quickly disappeared into the trees. "Well, if that doesn't beat all. I know a trip through time was probably rough on us, but we can't look that bad."

Isobella smiled. "I don't know about myself, but you look as beautiful as ever." And that was true. The sun glinted off Elisabeth's neat ponytail of curly auburn hair, dusting it with gold. Her jeans had nary a wrinkle and her T-shirt looked as if it had never seen a smudge.

Isobella knew her loose hair looked wild as a milkweed pod. Her shirt and shorts were wrinkled. She was always the one who never seemed to reach an agreement with the word "neat." The last time she had been spotless was lying beside her twin in the nursery, when they had both been scrubbed to a rosy hue and dressed in identical pink gowns.

Elisabeth gazed at the place where the men disappeared. "I have to say that wasn't exactly the outcome I expected. What happened to barbaric charge and capture, or chivalrous rescue?"

Isobella shrugged. "I guess we aren't as high on the food chain as we thought. Perhaps they are still frightened by our sudden appearance. On the other hand, you may be right about them thinking we are witches. We did sort of pop out of nowhere."

"So, what do we do now?"

Before Isobella could respond, they heard a faint rumbling like thunder in the distance. She gazed at the clear sky. Where was the thunder coming from? Suddenly, she realized the thunderous sound was horses, fast approaching.

They turned in time to see four men burst out of the

underbrush and come charging toward them. Isobella wondered if they were the same four men who had been chased off moments ago, but when she saw one had his sword drawn, she didn't really care to find out. She yelled to Elisabeth, "Run!"

Isobella took off running with Elisabeth right behind her. The terrifying sound of thundering hooves grew louder as the men covered the distance between them. These men meant business, and she wondered if they had traveled back through time to be hacked to death by barbarians.

Suddenly, Elisabeth screamed. Isobella turned around quickly, ready to go to Isobella's aid, when she watched, horrified, as Elisabeth was swept up by a warrior and onto his horse.

Isobella broke into a dead run, but in her haste, she did not notice a loose bed of stones treacherously close to the edge of a ravine. As she ran across them, they slid out from under her and she went over the edge on a carpet of flying stones.

———

Alysandir might have ridden away without another thought, had they not heard the Macleans bursting out of the trees. He turned and saw them riding like banshees were after them, heading toward the clearing in the glen where the two women waited.

A spine-chilling scream shattered the silence. He saw that Colin and Drust were waiting for him to say something. He knew they were itching to ride like avenging angels, to deliver the two tarnished damsels from danger.

Beware, his mind seemed to say, not knowing whether it was a prophetic sign or his own hard heart that was reluctant to engage in a chivalrous rescue. With a heart heavy as stone and a feeling he should ride like hell in the opposite direction, he spurred Gallagher and rode toward the glen. He did not look back, for he knew his brothers followed with eager anticipation.

When they galloped into the clearing, the Macleans rode away—one rider with a woman slung over his saddle. Alysandir looked for the other woman and watched as she went sliding over the side of a crag. He turned to his brothers. "Go after the Macleans and retrieve the lass. Meet me back at Màrrach. I will go after the clumsy one."

Grinning like two buffoons, his brothers turned around, and with a touch of spurs to flanks, their horses leapt forward and broke into a fast gallop.

―⁓―

Isobella fell and kept on falling, tumbling and rolling like a tossed die, as she was battered by rocks, as well as the scratch and claw of gorse, bracken, and fallen branches. When at last she rolled to a stop, she was certain she was paralyzed, and the only medical doctor in this whole time period had just gotten herself seized. Why had she had to cry over the effigy of the Black Douglas? And where was he now?

A light breeze stirred. A few dried leaves fluttered and fell back to the ground. Then everything fell silent. She hurt everywhere, and what didn't hurt ached abominably. However, if she hurt, she wasn't paralyzed. Her thumb, especially, hurt like hell—probably jammed or broken.

Glancing down, she could see her body looked like she had run through briars or had an encounter with a giant porcupine. Dozens of scratches oozed blood. She also had that tinny taste in her mouth. And those were just her obvious injuries. She didn't even want to think about the numb places or how her insides might have suffered.

She remembered her Prada backpack and, after a brief search, was relieved to find it had survived the fall and that her arms were still wound through the straps. She removed it and absently placed it on the ground next to her, trying to come up with a plan. She rolled over and struggled to stand, but her ankle hurt too much to put weight on it.

She doubted it was broken—probably a severe sprain or minor fracture that would take eons to heal. Either way, there was nothing she could do about it. Her legs were burning like fire, and she cursed her stupidity for wearing shorts. Showing so much flesh will garner lots of points with the womenfolk before they scratched her eyes out. If she didn't end up being raped, it would be a miracle.

She put weight on her foot again, simply because she had to get out of this place before dark. She tried to take a step and fell. She gritted her teeth against the ripping pain in her ankle. While she wondered what else could go wrong, she was beginning to think Elisabeth was the more fortunate of the two. At least she didn't have to spend the night alone in a strange landscape, at the mercy of God knows what. All sorts of creatures could be lurking about—wolves, wildcats, wild boars, and the like—all probably ravenously hungry.

She didn't know where she was, and even if she did, there wouldn't be any clothing stores about and she had no money—and no one to contact even if she did. If she did find a village, they would probably murder her for looking like a harlot on hard times.

Welcome to Scotland...

A faint breeze stirred. A solitary quietness settled around her. A lonely owl hooted somewhere in the distance. Isobella shivered at the reminder that she was all alone and there was no escape. Her ankle was swelling like a yeast cake, and she could hear the rush of water from a nearby burn. Cold water would help her ankle, so she attempted to stand, fell, and decided to stay there.

She feared for Elisabeth. Would she be raped or killed, or would she spend her life in the bowels of a castle's dank dungeon? Isobella knew this time period, and the chances of Elisabeth being carted off by a sympathetic and kind-hearted band of men were about as slim as her own chances of being rescued by anyone. Here she was, the lead character in a time-travel tale hosted by a famous warrior-ghost and set in sixteenth-century Scotland. So, where were the spine-tingling feats of daring, the heroine nearly ravaged and rescued at the last moment? Where was the hero who would appear out of nowhere to rescue her?

She didn't want to die like this. She wanted to live. *Give me another chance. Give me a hero...*

A breeze stirred. Leaves rustled. A rock tumbled down the crag. She looked up and saw him astride a sturdy horse, staring down at her. The sun glinted on his armor, making him look like an avenging angel.

The two of them looked at each other for a moment, studying each other intently. Something about the aura that surrounded him said he was not a commoner, and his clothes seemed to verify that, for he wore a dark red surcoat that fell halfway to his knees and a sword that was suspended by a bandolier of leather as dark as his boots.

He pushed back the hood of his byrnie. His hair was black as sin and deliciously long. Even in the brilliant sunlight, he was a dark adaptation of the desires of her mind, for everything about him was mysterious and hard as steel, with an edge that was as ruthless and dangerous as the trenchant sword he had wielded a moment earlier.

She had a sinking feeling that he wouldn't consider coming after her from that height, even if she were dipped in gold. Would he risk rescuing her? A moot thought, for he would never make it. He wouldn't risk injury or death to him or his horse just to capture her.

Or would he?

With an expression as cold as a pagan's philosophy, he put the spurs to the side of his horse and went over the side. Was he crazy? A whirlwind came out of nowhere and stirred the branches of trees and sent debris spiraling. She heard the faintest bubbling sound of laughter, or was it simply the wind? She gasped and held her breath, and everything fell silent.

In a lightning-quick moment of decision that would give Mars, the god of war, pause, she watched him begin a death-defying descent of man and beast, straight down the near-vertical drop. The slightest slip would mean instant death, and yet he gave the horse his head, and the two of them raced faster than a torrent on its way to the sea. She was spellbound, for everything moved in slow motion after that.

Everywhere lay clumps of fern and golden prickly gorse, shapeless and deformed. Stones flew, but the Highland pony's foot was sure. Wiry, tough, and sturdy, he sailed over stumps and a fallen tree, his hooves striking fire from chips of granite strewn along the way.

For a moment, the crags in the distance echoed the thunder of his stride. Then, in what had to be the most terrifying and magical moment of her life, she watched that small, sturdy horse with fire in his eye, and the incredible, almost impossible daring horsemanship of his rider. For an instant, the rider loomed larger than life, dark and threatening as a master of the underworld. She wouldn't have been surprised if both he and his horse had sprouted wings and flown right over her head and vanished into the stratosphere.

In a heartbeat, it was over, with no sign that it had happened at all, save the dust that began to settle into the fresh imprint of hooves and the rustle of the wind that stirred it.

Chapter 11

It's true that heroes are inspiring,
but mustn't they also do some rescuing
if they are to be worthy of their name?

—*Independent*
  Jeanette Winterson (b. 1959)
  British author

IDIOTS! THE RIDE SHOULD HAVE KILLED THEM BOTH.

But it hadn't. With a slow pace, the stallion came toward her, and she leaned back a little bit further with each step that brought him closer. A lump formed in her throat, choking her with fear. Transfixed, she stared at the rider as she imagined what he could do to her.

She was frozen, unable to do anything but watch and wait. He was handsome as the devil, yet she eyed him warily as he approached her. He stopped no more than three feet away, crossed his arms over the pommel, and leaned forward, his cold gaze going over her with slow ease. Well, she had to hand it to him. There was something sexy as hell about a man dressed for battle, sweat gleaming on his forehead, his hair damp. Never did a man wear a pair of over-the-knee boots the way he did, and she was from Texas.

Under the scrutiny of his piercing gaze, she felt like an iceberg melting from the inside out. His blue eyes were sharp and assessing, and there was a brutal strength to him that could easily snap her neck in two, if he were so inclined. His face was young with un-lined features, yet she sensed an ancient wisdom, as if he had seen more than his share of the dark side of life. He was the definition of gorgeous with a chis-eled, masculine face and devilishly black hair. Even his frown was sexy as hell. Why did she feel she had seen him before?

Masculine to the core, he seemed as fierce and wild as this barbarous place. He might be a hottie, but she sensed that within he was as cold and hard as a slab of coarse-grained granite. *I'm staring into the face of his-tory*. He was a Highlander through and through. Never, ever, in a million years of excavation would she imagine this was what a Highland warrior would look like, and oh, was the real warrior better than the imagined one. The opportunity, the research that could be done here. It was a gold mine, not to mention the possibilities of extracurricular benefits. The thought left her mystified and somewhat breathless.

She tried to present a brave front and decided to break the ice. "Greetings, Sir Knight, I hope your chivalric beliefs have not been truant of late and that your code is as honorable as your knight's regalia."

He stared at her impassively, and just when she thought he wouldn't, he spoke, his words tempered with a lilting burr. "'Twould seem ye have yerself in a bit of a predicament, lass."

Lass... Oh, my, with that voice, he could make a bloody fortune in ringtones. "Yes, I'm in need of help, as you can see."

"The middle of a battle is no' a safe place for a woman. Mayhap ye should take care in the future, not only with where ye step, but with the matter of yer clothes—or the absence of them."

She lifted her head higher and met his stare until she thought her neck would get a crick in it. She really hated answering him from her submissive sitting position.

"If you plan to kill me, do it now and get it over with. However, if you're thinking to ransom me, you are wasting your time. I am alone and have no family save the sister your men kidnapped."

Isobella wasn't sure why it hadn't occurred to her before that this man with the icy stare and the manners of a caveman might actually be responsible for Elisabeth's kidnapping. The last thing she wanted was to let him see how desperate she was. She raised her chin to a lofty height.

"Where have you taken my sister? I swear, if your men harm her—"

"Do ye always talk so much and say so little?"

She sputtered, searching for something clever and gave up. "Only when I'm nervous."

"We didna take yer sister," he said, with a grudging hint of respect underlying the tone of his voice. "My brothers hope to rescue her from the Macleans."

"The Macleans? Then who are you?"

"I might be asking the same of ye, mistress, but I can tell by yer speech that ye are an English wench."

She didn't miss the way his hard stare passed coldly over her. She tried to pull the hem of her shorts lower, to no avail. Bruised legs bare and her knees knocking together in fright, she wondered what the rest of her person looked like. Not that it really mattered. What did she have to lose at this point? She lifted her chin again in the manner that always made her mother say, "That blasted Scots blood!"

A sharp pang of separation from her life and her world ripped through her. What a day of trauma it had been so far. Her home and family were centuries away, and the Black Douglas was beyond vague about their future. That revelation had been a real shocker, turned tragic the moment those ruffians rode off with Elisabeth.

Isobella could only pray they were the kind and honorable sort and would do her sister no harm. Mull was a small island and very sparsely populated in 1515. If she were to venture a guess, she'd say there probably weren't more than a few hundred people on the island. There were no towns, just castles and a few settlements. It shouldn't be difficult to learn where she was.

She wouldn't tell him any of this, however. Never expose your weakness. "I am neither English nor a wench." The whole situation was almost comical, and she bit her lips to keep from laughing at the absurdity of it. Here she sat on her bruised backside, bleeding and aching all over, in the middle of nowhere having a staring contest with an ill-tempered lout of Celtic blood, who gave her no hint as to his intent.

She shouldn't keep staring, but something about him was oddly familiar. What was it that held her transfixed? His hard, lean body? The chiseled angles of his face? The sexy burr of his speech? The daring of his ride? Or, was it the raw, almost primitive masculinity that seemed to radiate from him.

"Are you going to just sit there and stare, or are you

going to offer some assistance? We have a damsel in distress here, in case you haven't noticed."

She couldn't be certain, but she did think she saw the corners of his mouth twitch briefly—before he dismounted with a creaking of leather and a ring of rowels—as he approached her. "Get up, lass, unless ye plan to sleep here tonight and fend off nocturnal visitors by yerself."

"Do I look comfortable sitting on these hard, lumpy rocks? It's my ankle."

He raked her over with a gaze that took its own sweet time, pausing for an uncomfortably long time to give her breasts a good going-over. Apparently he had already formed a remarkably accurate picture of how she would look without a stitch on.

"I would advise ye to pay more attention to what ye are aboot. Ye are in a dangerous position, and ye have no one to protect ye. That places ye completely at my mercy."

"I am indebted to you for risking your life to ride down here, when you could have ridden off and left me to die. I am appreciative of any assistance you can give me, for I am in desperate need of help and completely dependent upon your charity."

Her eyes connected with his ever so briefly before she looked away. "I can't stand. I think my ankle is sprained, or perhaps I have a fracture," she said, then adding the Latin word, *fractura*, in case he did not understand fracture.

His brows rose, and the expression in his eyes was one of interested surprise. "Fracture? You speak French?"

So much for getting it down to his level. She nodded. "A little, but I have studied Latin, and the Latin word is *fractura*."

"'Tis the same word—fracture or *fractura*," he said.

"Either way, it hurts. I tried hopping to the burn to soak it in cold water, but I kept falling because of the loose stones. So here I am, waiting for another option to present itself. Could that be you?"

He muttered something in Gaelic, too soft and too rapidly spoken for her to catch, but the tone and the hard set to his features told her readily enough that she was already labeled a nuisance. However, she was alive, which was promising.

As he hunkered down beside her, his face was so near that she could feel the warmth of his breath brush against her cheek. She tilted her head back to watch him as he picked up her foot. She yelped with pain, which he ignored.

"'Tis swelling like a turkey cock—'tis no' broken."

"It will be if you don't stop twisting it." She yanked her foot back and tugged at her shorts.

He studied her with the sharpness of an eagle, and his stare seemed to penetrate the fabric of her scanty clothing. The way he was looking at her—a dunce could see that he wanted her—and the effect of it made her stomach tighten with desire, which was the last thing she needed right now. She exhaled with a breathy little moan that made her pray he had not heard it.

One glance told her she was out of luck in that department, for he was undressing her with his eyes as surely as God made little apples. She tugged at her shorts again.

"Yer fighting a losing battle, lass." His hand was still on her ankle, and his gaze traveled slowly up her legs. The look couldn't have been more suggestive if it had been his hand. She was trapped in his gaze, and the way he was looking her—lord, it made her feel like the only sitting duck in the pond when duck season opened. Mustering as much huffiness as she could, she said, "Surely you've seen a woman's legs before."

His eyes blazed, and a sardonic half-smile curved his lips. "Only when I was betwixt them."

The air went out of her lungs like collapsed bellows. She sputtered while searching to find an appropriate retort. The best she could do was a haughty, "You have no right to speak so. I don't know you."

"Dinna fret aboot it, mistress. Ye will know me better afore the day is oot."

Determined blue eyes met determined green ones, and for a moment it was a stalemate. He was a formidable foe; she'd hand him that much. For a disturbing moment, she couldn't speak. She wasn't much better at breathing.

His face might be a delight to gaze upon, with his high cheekbones and sensuous mouth, but his expression was permanently scowled, his stance prideful, his demeanor commanding, and she was certain laughter was a rarity around him.

"Ye do seem to have an abundance of flesh to cover with that wee fragment of fabric ye are wearing," he said, his voice like the purr of a hungry tiger.

He was both mysterious and alluring, and her heart pounded wildly as she mustered a weak dose of bravado. "If you so much as lay a hand on me!"

"Do ye ken how to play Fidchell?"

He goes from undressing me with his eyes to wanting to play a board game? "I can play Fidchell, Hnefatafl,

Tawlbwrdd, backgammon, chess, checkers, and several card games. What I don't know is whether I want to play any of them with you." He did not respond, but when had silence ever daunted her? "What does Fidchell have to do with getting me out of here?"

"Naught," he said, and grabbed her by the arm.

"Oaf!" she said as he yanked her upward, caught her around the waist, and hoisted her over his shoulder like a sack of millet, one hand still holding her arm, while the other was splayed across her fanny. "Would it be asking too much for you to move your hand and treat me like a lady?"

"Stop yer bleating. If I move my hand, *my lady*, ye will fall on yer royal erse."

Bleating? Erse? She would give anything for a quick comeback, but unfortunately since none was forthcoming, she decided to let it lie fallow, vowing her day would come. He was carrying her toward his horse when she cried out, "Wait a minute! I left my backpack," she said, pointing toward her Prada backpack.

He glanced and kept walking.

She tugged at his sleeve. "Please, I really need it."

"Impatient as the wind, ye are."

"It's all I have left."

She caught the way he stopped and looked at her and then back at her backpack with a suspicious expression suddenly etched on his face. "What is in yer pouch that has ye worrit? Dressed as ye are, I doubt ye are carting yer family jewels aboot. Or do ye have some secret ye are hiding there?"

Wonderful. She should have been more careful. The Scots were a suspicious lot, especially of that which could not be explained. And she wasn't ready to start pulling everything out and trying to explain. *He probably thinks I'm Henry the VIII's favorite spy.* She was definitely at a disadvantage with this man. Patient endurance was the order of the moment.

Riding out of this place was infinitely better than remaining here alone, and if that meant suffering the humiliation of his hand on her erse, then she would bear up as best she could. She focused upon her current state of affairs, especially the situation concerning her clothes, or lack of them. And there was little chance that other clothing would be forthcoming. The best she could hope for was to grab something to cover herself when they reached his home, lair, cave, rabbit hole, or wherever he was taking her. Aching and uncomfortable, she squirmed.

"Keep wiggling like that, and I will answer the question troubling me since I first saw ye."

"What question would that be?"

The hand moved to her bare thigh, caressing as it slid higher. He almost purred the words, "Are ye wearing naught under yer trews, lass?"

So many retorts jammed into her brain that it was deadlocked.

"Answer or dinna answer. 'Twould not be so difficult for me to answer it myself, if I had a mind to."

Her heart pounded. She trembled at the thought of him touching her. "You wouldn't dare."

"Nae, 'tis not my way to force a lass, unless persuaded." He lowered her to stand next to his horse. She leaned against the saddle for support. "Ye are in no position to bargain, lass. If I decided to take ye here and now, no one would stop me. If I rode off and left ye here, no one would come to yer aid. Ye could die oot here, and no one would bury ye. Yer puir bones would end up being a wee morsel for the wild animals that roam aboot. Like it or no', ye are at my mercy, and yer survival is dependent entirely upon me. That should sweeten yer mood and add a musical sound to yer squawk."

He was a man who lived by his wits and the edge of his sword. He seemed to be on the brink of violence, as if the power held in check within him was done so by a very thin thread. A man like him was at his most danger-ous when he seemed to be cool and dispassionate—like a rattlesnake before it strikes.

"Are you trying to frighten me?"

"If I was, 'twould seem I succeeded. Fear robs the mind of reason."

The soft cadence of his words melted everything in-side her, including her resistance. "And what makes you think I have lost all reason?"

"If ye were in possession of good judgment, ye wouldna be out here, and not dressed as ye are, for it robs a man of all rational thought and replaces it with a desire to touch ye."

"There is a reason for my being dressed as I am, and it isn't as it seems. You should be careful of being pre-sumptuous or making swollen claims when you have nothing to back them up."

He seemed to be waiting for her to say more. She remained silent rather than risk his leaving without her.

"Ye have nothing further to say on the matter?"

"No, I have nothing further to say."

"Ye surprise me. Mayhap I mistook ye for a lass with

spirit; a woman with more fight in her. Ye give up too easily, lass."

She lifted her chin. "You misjudge both me and my motives."

"Weel, yer no whore," he replied.

She gasped. All the blood seemed to run out of her. She felt limp, washed out, and exhausted. "I'm not afraid of you."

He laughed. "Mayhap ye should be. The eve is young. It's a long way to anywhere from here. Around a near-naked lass, a man can get thoughts he canna always control, especially with the hunger that builds in his bluid after a battle. Ye should be careful. I have been without a woman for a long time."

"I can certainly understand why." She decided then and there that, rescue or not, she did not like him. He must have been born in a barn. He was proud, crude, and arrogant. Who did he think he was, Genghis Khan? She knew he was baiting her and decided that, for the time being, the wisdom of the moment was to retreat.

The iciness seemed to vanish from his eyes as he said, "'Tis a fault of mine to be presumptuous and persistent. Ye have naught to fear from me, mistress."

Perhaps there was a grain of humanness in him after all. She was confused. In a short period of time, he went from Ivan the Terrible, despot and barbarian, to the archangel Michael, the slayer of dragons and weigher of souls. She gazed at the powerful hands that had gracefully wielded a sword a short while earlier and examined her ankle with surprising gentleness.

"'Tis getting colder, and yer nose is as shiny as a hedgehog's. I'll not have ye turning sick on me."

Now he was being nice, just when she had decided he was an ogre. *Well, you aren't exactly a good judge of the male character now, are you?*

Chapter 12

*I have yet to see any problem, however complicated,
which, when you looked at it in the right way,
did not become still more complicated.*

—Poul Anderson (1926–2001)
 U.S. science fiction writer

SHE WAS A STRANGE TALKING WOMAN WITH A FAIR FACE AND
a heavenly body that kept diverting his thoughts. He
was a man of strong desires and in his prime, but what
he wanted now were the answers to a lot of questions.
Judging from the way she clamped her lips together, she
was through talking.

There was something achingly real about her resistance. He shouldn't have frightened her. He looked at
her hair, rich as sable, the fair skin, and the green eyes
that watched him with disdain and suspicion. Was it
possible that this woman was truly an innocent? Why
did he keep having the feeling, incredible though it
was, that she was a novice and not really conscious
of how serious things were, as if she had been locked
away in some tower for most of her life and just
recently escaped.

She was a strange one, and he intended to find out
who she was, where she was from, and why she was
here, dressed or undressed as she was. She wasn't a Scot,

but he could not place her accent. She spoke English, but he did not believe she was English or Irish. Nor was she French, Belgian, Norse, or Spanish, or of any other blood that he could think of.

He knew she was afraid and went to great lengths to hide it, which was admirable although ineffective. While he had to admire the false bravado, he detected a sadness in her—in spite of her defiance and daring—that made him want to know her story.

He studied the tightly held mouth and the distrustful gaze she directed his way and fought the urge to laugh. Didn't she realize he could have snapped her lovely neck with one blow if he had desired and that he was not doing so because she had backed him down? He did not point that out, preferring, for some unknown reason, to hand her this small victory. It would be easier to learn what he wanted to know if he stopped scaring her.

At the present, he only knew two things about her: She and her sister had appeared in the glen suddenly without a horse or an escort, and she was not a Scot. While he didn't think she was from England, he did not rule out that she could be a spy sent by the English. Whatever she was, she was more likely to reveal herself if she was comfortable around him.

"Ease yer fears and dinna worrit, mistress. Ye are safe with me. 'Tis not my way to harm a woman. Ye need help and I am the only one aboot, so that puts us together, does it not? Yoked by the fates, we are, and ye have no choice but to come with me, for I canna leave ye here at the mercy of the elements or the unknown."

She looked immensely relieved, but he also heard her swallow with a gulp, just before she asked softly, "What are you going to do with me?"

He fought the urge to laugh and replied, "Nothing as vile as ye are imagining. It grows colder, and ye wouldna last the night out here dressed as ye are. The temperature goes down with the sun. In life, as it is with a sea voyage, it is oft necessary to lose sight of the shore for a long time. Ye will come with me."

He returned to the place where she had dropped the strange-looking satchel. What was so important about it, he wondered. Did it contain clues to her identity? Why was she here? Who had sent her? As he pondered those questions, he came up with one more: *And just what am I going to do with her?*

While his back was turned, she seriously considered jumping on his horse and riding off. But she had no place to go, no survival skills for sixteenth-century Scotland, and she wanted her backpack, so she waited. Instead of handing it to her upon his return, he tucked it into a leather pouch hanging from his saddle.

"I can hold it," she said.

"It is safer where it is and less likely to get wet if it should rain." He removed a flask from the pouch and handed it to her. "Have a nip or two o' this. 'Twill make the journey easier and ease the pain of yer ankle."

"What is it?"

"'Twill warm yer insides."

I ask what it is, and he tells me what it will do? "Was that an answer?"

He actually smiled, but it was so brief that she wondered if she had really seen it. As for answering her question, he shrugged. "'Tis something to ease ye. 'Tisn't a declaration o' war."

"Well, I always say that necessity drives away common sense." She reached for the flask and upended it. After several quick swallows, she was certain her esophagus and everything below it were blistered. She gasped, choked, and then coughed.

"'Tis better, aye?"

When she could talk again, she whispered, "Only because it could not be any worse. You said it would warm my insides. You didn't say it would set them on fire so I could feel them disintegrate. What was in that flask?"

"Mead."

"Mead," she repeated, feeling positively thrilled. Just knowing what it was made her forget the burning in her plumbing from throat to toenails. She once studied the ancient Celts and recalled their celestial nectar they called the drink of the gods. She always wondered what the mead of old would taste like.

And now she knew. The moment was star-spangled and one of those rare, almost poignant times in life when one experiences something so profound that it produces strong feelings of inspiration. She was thrilled and didn't mind that she wasn't sipping from an ancient Celtic drinking horn, trimmed with silver. People in the twenty-first century would kill to taste what she had just swallowed.

She closed her eyes so she could relish the earthy flavors that danced around her mouth, jubilant, savory, and warm. She gave him a tentative smile while contemplating a generous hug. "I always wondered what mead tasted like, and now I know."

He said nothing, but he was certainly looking at her in an odd way. She knew she had a glow of childish wonderment on her face, but she didn't care. It was such a special moment for her. What her professors wouldn't give to be in her shoes. She wished she could turn back the clock and run screaming into one of her college classes, shouting, "Come quick! I have tasted history!"

She wished he didn't have that sensual mouth with the yummy full lips, or the proud curve of an aristocratic nose, not to mention the powerful body that was deceptively lean and tapered. At five feet, six inches, she wasn't short by any means, but she knew he would tower over her by a good six inches, perhaps more, which meant he was exceptionally tall for a sixteenth-century male.

She tossed her head to throw the curling tendrils of hair back over her shoulders. She wished for a scrunchie to hold it and tried to remember if there was one in her backpack. A haircut would do, but beauty shops were on a growing list of things she would have to learn to do without. Gad! She couldn't begin to dream up a likely substitute for a toothbrush. Rubbing her teeth with a cloth simply wouldn't do. And shaving her legs with a knife? She did not want to go there.

He reached for her and caught her up into his arms. He leaned his head close and said with a husky whisper, "Put your leg over the saddle."

"I know how to ride." She started to mention that she was raised on a Texas ranch, but neither word would be in his vocabulary and she wasn't up to a lengthy explanation. She threw her leg over the saddle and swallowed hard when he removed his surcoat, left wearing only his mail hauberk and the shirt beneath.

He pulled the tunic over her head and tucked it around her bare thighs. She was certain that if she was standing, it would fall almost to her ankles. Relief washed over her. If she had been the Pope she would have canonized him on the spot. "Bless you, Sir Knight."

The corners of his lips lifted into a bona fide smile. Apparently, some humor transcended time. Such an odd thing really to pop into her head, but it was a comforting thought and all the angst flowed out of her. People were people after all, no matter the time period, for it stood to reason humor was not a modern invention.

She rubbed the fabric of the tunic that covered her legs, bathed in the warm feeling of knowing everything necessary was covered. "You have no idea how glad I am to have this."

"Ye have no idea how glad I am to see ye covered."

There was something oddly familiar about his husky voice, but the thought vanished. She smiled. "A compliment and a truce of sorts." She turned toward him and asked, "Does that mean you find me a distraction or a burden?"

His gaze was cool and measuring. "Ye are a distraction, mistress, and one I do not need." The saddle leather creaked as he mounted behind her. He caught up the reins and clucked to his horse, who tossed his head a couple of times, and they began their journey to wherever he was taking her.

When they reached the fringe of trees, she was charmed when he slipped his left arm around her and transferred the reins to that hand so he could shield her face from the low hanging branches. "My name is Isobella," she said, and waited for him to introduce himself.

"And the rest of it?"

She hesitated. Should she give him her last name? It was possible he wasn't any more enamored with the Douglases than he had been with the Macleans, but since no other name came to mind, she had no choice but to tell him the truth. "Douglas," she said. "Isobella Catriona Douglas."

"Humph."

Humph? That's it? Just humph and nothing more? She glanced down at the powerful thighs pressed against hers, and she was tempted to poke one of them with her finger, just to see if it truly was as hard as it looked. "Would that be an approving humph or a disapproving one?"

There was no answer to that question, but it did not matter, for she was already warmed by the knowledge that he came from a bold and hardy race of men, descended from brave and warlike ancestors filled with passionate affection for their native land—their Highland mountains, the burn-filled glens, and the heather covered moors. They were tightly bound together by their tribes or clans, and distrusting of strangers.

They rode on, through the thick growth of brush and trees, broken by an occasional clearing. Not once did they come upon a road, a trail, or even a path, and she realized how primitive her surroundings truly were. The reality of sixteenth-century Scotland was vastly different from the version she had acquired in books.

"You did not tell me your name. What should I call you?"

"Alysandir."

She waited for him to say more, but when the silence stretched on, she decided "Alysandir" was all she was getting. He was precisely the kind of man she had spent years studying about. But he was flesh and blood. She was bewitched by the man, who he was and the time period in which he existed. Everything appealing about him was natural and masculine because he was of the warrior class, not because he lifted weights and wore sleeveless T-shirts.

Sex appeal stuck to him like he bathed in it and forgot to dry off. He seemed relaxed, but there was an alert tenseness to his powerful body, for even as he spoke with her, he was acutely aware of his surroundings. He heard every sound and saw every movement. His guard was never down. She felt safe with him and prayed Elisabeth could say the same. And where was that reprobate, Sir James Douglas? *I hope you are protecting Elisabeth and plan on getting us together.*

"Are ye weary, lass? Do I need to stop so ye can rest?"

"If you can make it, I can make it." She felt the rumbling of chest muscles against her back that indicated he found her comment amusing. She would show him that she meant every word of it. They continued on for quite some time before they stopped by a narrow burn that was nothing more than a thin streamlet of water winding its way around moss-covered rocks. He dismounted and lifted her from the saddle, but he did not let her stand. Instead, he carried her to the bank and bathed her foot in water so cold she gasped. "It's freezing!"

"Aye, 'tis good for yer ankle." He withdrew a kerchief from his mail shirt and, wetting it, handed it to her with instructions to wash the dirt from her face. "Ye look like a street urchin," he said, before he gathered her back into his arms.

He did not move for a moment, studying her face. "Yer a bonnie lass, and ye've a face that makes a man think of naught but wanting to kiss ye and see where that leads."

"I can save you the trouble by telling you where it would lead. Nowhere," she said, feeling light-headed from the throbbing of her heart. Sure, she would love to kiss him until his lips were numb. Who wouldn't? She was attracted to him, and she was snared in the moment until he chuckled and carried back to his horse. Once she was mounted, he handed her the flask.

"Is this for my ankle or to loosen my resolve?"

"It can be for whatever reasons ye want it to be, or for all of them, but ye needn't worry that I will take advantage of ye. A loose-limbed, slack-tongued woman in my bed holds no appeal."

"Good. I will work on becoming both," she said and upended the flask, torching her insides for the second time that day. She would have toppled from the saddle had he not mounted behind her and wrapped her in his arms. When she found her voice, she said, "Thank you. I have a surplus of bruises already."

His dark face was expressionless. "'Tis the splendor of a sudden impulse." They rode silently for some time, and she was on the verge of falling asleep when they passed beneath a tree and startled a linnet into flight. Still drowsy and relaxed from the mead, she thought about her parents and younger siblings. Did they know their daughters had disappeared?

They continued on as the red ball of sun dropped lower and the air grew colder, and she was thankful for the warmth and protection of the man who held her close. The peacefulness of this place surrounded her as they rode out of the trees and into a long, narrow glen dotted with prickly gorse. She felt her eyelids growing heavy.

They had no more than entered the glen when the ears of his horse pricked forward and the animal started to snort and dance sideways, tossing his head.

"Have a care, lass. Put yer hand around the pommel and hold tight."

Chapter 13

He was a verray
parfit gentil knyght.

—*The Canterbury Tales*
  Geoffrey Chaucer (1343?–1400)
  English poet

THE LAST WORD HAD YET TO DIE AWAY, WHEN TWO HAWK-like men burst forth from the stand of trees at the other end of the glen. They raced toward them, hooves thundering at breakneck speed, their mighty swords drawn, twisted grimaces on their dark faces. Her heart hammered furiously. Dear God! They would be cut down like ripe corn. She suddenly felt herself grabbed about the waist and rudely dropped to the ground.

"Stay there and dinna move, no matter what happens."

Like she could go anywhere with her ankle throbbing like a drum and prickly gorse jabbing her in the backside.

Alysandir let out a bloodcurdling war cry and spurred his horse into a dead run. What happened next would be forever imprinted upon her mind. With her heart pounding triple time, she watched how his magnificent little stallion held a straight course, throwing up clods of turf as they raced across the clearing.

It was two of them against one of him, and she realized he was all that stood between her and bloodthirsty marauders in search of booty. She didn't like thinking of herself as a battle prize, and she could tell they would not be as chivalrous as Alysandir. She held her breath and thought of covering her eyes, but she had to watch no matter how bloody it became.

Alysandir dropped his reins to dangle free as he drew the huge sword and held it in both hands, high over his head. He rode between the two men, slashing first the one on his right, with a full stroke that sliced across the stomach, and then to the left. The second brigand's roar was reduced to a ghastly gurgle as the great blade sheared with a deep hack between his neck, shoulder bones, and ribs.

Blood spurted and sprayed everywhere, covering the silvered blade of Alysandir's sword and dulling the shine of his mail shirt. Both men toppled to the ground while their horses kept running.

As easily as a scythe cuts wheat, he had stopped the attack, which lasted only a few minutes. It could have been a scene from an epic film. Except that this was not a movie but the real thing, with a Highland warrior-knight doing what he was bred to do. In her time, this would have been considered barbaric, criminal even. But he was of another era when people lived by a different code and when a good horse, a keen eye, a strong arm, and a deadly sword meant the difference between life and death.

She rose to her feet awkward and wobbly as a newborn foal, not thinking about her scratches as she watched him, her mouth still dry and her thoughts in a jumble. She hoped he would not, in the aftermath of battle, forget he had tossed her into the briar patch and ride off into the sunset without her.

He leaned forward, caught up the reins, and turned his horse around in a tight arc. Without ever slowing, he thundered back the way he had come, transferring his sword to his left hand as they galloped at break-neck speed toward her. She was terrified he did not see her and that his horse would cut her down like a scythe to grain.

At the very last moment, the horse veered slightly to her left and Alysandir leaned down, almost touching the ground. Without realizing she did so, she lifted her arms, her gaze never leaving his face as he swept her off the ground and up into the saddle before him. His sword came to rest across her lap, and the blood upon it still ran warm as it trickled down her leg.

He did not slow down until they approached the thick stand of trees just ahead, and only when they were swallowed into the screen of dense growth did he slow Gallagher to a walk.

In college, she had written a paper on "The Warrior Mentality," and she recalled that warriors, as well as modern-day soldiers and athletes, could become so "super-charged" with rising hormone levels during a battle that they could actually go into trances. They could enter into a kind of altered consciousness—so that their sense of pain was subdued and their sense of well-being highly elevated. They were often highly charged in a sexual way as well...

"I am sorry ye were witness to that," he said. "'Twas an inescapable encounter."

She nodded, thinking for a moment before she said, "Sometimes it is impossible to escape from danger, no matter how badly we want to."

"I am no' as barbaric as I seem. There was naught I could do to prevent the outcome."

"I know," she replied. She decided not to tell him she would never be able to wash the stain of what she witnessed from her mind. Yet, in spite of the horrific scene, she did not think killing came easily to him.

"Ye are a wise lass, and ye dinna seem to have a fondness for complaining. 'Tis no' an ordinary thing to discover in a woman. How come ye by it?"

"There are so many things to complain about in this world that I find it difficult to choose just one." She turned slightly to see how her attempt of humor went over with him. She was pleased to see the slightest uplift at the corners of his mouth.

He gazed at her curiously. "Would that I could carry with me such a clean conscience."

"I've heard it said that conscience is a more expensive encumbrance than a wife or a carriage," she said, without telling him that was actually a quote by an eighteenth-century author, Thomas de Quincey. When he did not say anything, she continued, "I know you don't like killing, and it is obvious that you wrestle with devils each time you must take the life of another. Be careful that you do not overthrow more than your enemies."

"Ye speak not words but thoughts and wisdom. 'Tis not the way of an ordinary lass. It makes me wonder if ye are an angel sent to change my warring ways, for ye did appear suddenly in the midst of a battle. Are ye a messenger, a spirit that protects and offers guidance? From whence came ye, mistress?"

She wasn't certain if he was serious or teasing her. But, she knew she had to change the direction of things quickly. "I am no spirit but a woman born of an earthly father and mother, and mortal enough that I felt the prick of briars when you tossed me on my erse in the bracken."

That actually produced a chuckle, and she almost swooned with relief. He did not speak of what happened again, but that did not mean he had forgotten it. She did her best to ignore the fact that blood, recently flowing in human veins, was now drying upon her legs. Silence, she decided, wasn't half-bad, for it gave her time to take in the stark beauty of the hills lined up beneath the fading blue sky and the hidden hollows of the moors.

They had been riding for quite some time when they approached another burn, this one larger and slower flowing than the previous one. Bordering it were spiny clumps of yellow-flowered gorse and weedy fronds of green bracken, as dense as thickets. The nearby hills seemed gaunt and inhospitable, their gorges littered with rocks, reminding her of the place where she had fallen.

Alysandir drew rein and dismounted. He placed his sword on the grassy slope before he turned and pulled her from the saddle and into his arms. He stood looking down at her for a moment and then, without speaking, carried her to a boulder close to the gently flowing water.

He set about unsaddling his mount before he led Gallagher to the burn to drink. Alysandir rubbed the pony down with dry grass and then dropped to his haunches beside the water and washed himself in what had to be freezing water, for the air temperature had to be hovering around 60 degrees.

There was no conversation, and she was beyond thrilled to have this rare opportunity to watch a warrior of old, for this was history in the making, and she was in the midst of it. Speechless, she observed how he ministered according to the code of chivalry and viewed the sequence of his priorities: first the damsel, then his horse, and his own needs last.

He rinsed his sword and used sand and grass to clean the dried blood from the blade. She observed the beauty of the motions as he performed each task. She had a feeling those hands would stroke a woman's body with the same practiced ease and mesmerizing skill, and the thought made her mouth dry. By the time he replaced the sword in his scabbard, his horse was grazing nearby.

She watched him walk to the edge of the burn, where he removed his bandolier and dropped it to the ground. Then he removed the chain byrnie and washed as much blood from it as possible before he placed it on the grass to dry in the sunlight. He pulled the shirt he wore beneath the byrnie over his head and she swallowed hard. She admired the finely hewn muscles of his back and the powerful forearms. The next moment, she was shocked into stupefied silence when he removed his boots and started to unhitch his chausses. She should have looked away.

It was an intensely sensual moment, and she felt lost in it. She wanted to touch him, to know the scent and texture of his skin, to feel the muscles of his warrior's body, to discover if he was real. She had not realized he was watching her. Their gazes locked, and he made no move to break the visual connection—waiting for her to do what any lady would do and look away, but she was frozen in place and her body did not seem to speak the same language as her mind.

She thought she saw the faintest hint of a conquering smile, just before he gave her his back and peeled the tight trews away from his body. And there he was, naked as a needle, and she was forced to stare at his bare backside with the driest mouth and wickedest thoughts imaginable. It was a stunning display of male anatomy, and, to her way of thinking, if he didn't mind baring it, she didn't mind looking.

It sure beat R-rated movies, for none of the actors in them could compare to the beautiful specimen standing before her. She was amazed, actually, that she did not have one shred of embarrassment as she checked him out, stem to stern.

"Thou strong seducer, Opportunity," as the English poet John Dryden had written. She was seduced, all right, and if Alysandir had so much as crooked a finger in her direction, she would have crawled, if need be, to get to him. There he stood, as magnificent as creation, as perfect as Adam, as beautiful as Lucifer before the fall.

When he entered the water, she was still captivated by his beauty. Everything about him conveyed power and stature. His was a body full of life and passion, and she could feel it reaching out to her. She longed to go to him, to strip as naked as he, and join him in the burn.

And freeze your erse off. What are you thinking?

He waded further into the frigid water and washed away the blood with wet sand. Gawking like a simpleton, she could not look away as he waded back to the bank. He was exemplary of a warrior at the peak of his virility, and every feature, down to the most insignificant muscle, was the standard by which others should be compared—from his commanding brow and Roman nose to his well-defined chest and stomach muscles, down to his shamelessly uncovered—she quickly turned her head away.

She would retain forever the memory of his potent and boldly naked form. She closed her eyes and listened to the sounds of him dressing, relishing the heat that the sight of his wet-slicked body sparked within her. She was overwhelmed with feelings she had never experienced before—sensuality, lust, and desire. His body left her breathless and craving more.

"'Tis safe to look now."

She expected to see him dressed in his trews and chausses, not with his body gleaming and his plaid wrapped low around his slender hips. Fascinated, she watched him walk toward her, and she fervently wished he would drop the plaid... no she didn't. She was her own worst enemy, and she was beyond thankful when she found her rational voice.

"Why aren't you dressed?"

He threw back his head and laughed at her. "To keep my clothes dry," he answered, and swept her up into his arms. Pure instinct sent her arms curling around his neck. His skin was cool and damp, and he smelled clean, like the air after a rain. She had to resist the urge to touch his chest. She sighed, thinking this was like a dream or something out of a movie, only better.

He turned and carried her toward the burn. "You aren't going to drown me, are you?"

He paused and gazed down at her upturned face. "Not with water, but I'm tempted to pour a little more mead down yer throat. With yer mouth gaping as long as it was, it has to be… parched."

She became suddenly conscious of the fluid movement of his body against hers and the press of her hipbone against his battle-hardened muscles. Her arms were still around his neck, and her head found a resting place in the cove of his shoulder. She had not realized until this moment, when she felt safe and comfortable in his arms, just how very weary she was. After all, it wasn't every day that she traveled five hundred years.

He stopped and slowly lowered her until her feet touched the ground. "What pleasures ye, lass?"

Everything you're doing, so far. She wanted to tell him that whatever she found pleasurable was illegal, immoral, or fattening, but she decided to temper her words to the time period and hope for a little sensual indulgence. "Oh, books, fruit, music…"

He cut the list short when he threw back his head and laughed heartily, and she wondered why she had the feeling it wasn't something he did frequently. She looked at the dancing water and shivered with anticipation. "It looks very cold."

"Aye, verra cold, but there are ways to warm ye quickly once ye are oot."

She didn't doubt that for a moment. She decided not to tell him the wild imaginings going on in her mind. "How many ways are there?"

"An infinite number, lass… numerous as the stars in yer eyes."

She understood how a flower must feel the first time it unfurls its petals.

"'Tis good ye are no' a coy lass, I am warmed by the bloom of desire in yer eyes. Do ye prefer to remove yer clothing and bathe yersel', or do ye want to leave some o' yer clothing on and let me wash the blood off of ye?"

Well, if that isn't the proverbial between a rock and a hard place, I don't know what is. "That doesn't sound like much of a choice to me."

"'Tis borne of necessity, lass, for ye canna stand on yer own, so either way, I will have to help ye. Soaking yer ankle in the cold water will ease the pain and help the swelling." He pulled the surcoat over her head, and she felt a cool waft of air wrap itself around her.

"What if you put me on that flat boulder jutting out over the water?" she said pointing, "I can sit there and soak my foot. Do you have some sort of cloth or a kerchief I can use to wash off the blood?"

"Aye," he said and placed her on the rock, his surcoat beside her, and then fetched a cloth from his pouch.

By the time he returned, she was shivering from the cold, but it did ease the pain. He wet the cloth and bathed her face. She had never known face washing could be so sensual, and when he paused long enough to trace the shape of her lips with his thumb, her pounding heart kept tempo with her shallow breaths. Inside, everything felt warm and liquid. He attended to a couple of scratches on her arms and wiped the dried path of blood from her legs.

She would never have believed something so innocent could be so arousing. To have a man touch her like this—there was something undeniably sensual about it. She leaned back on her arms, her head back, her eyes closed, until she suddenly became aware that he was no longer washing her legs. His hand was resting warmly on her left thigh.

She opened her eyes and saw that he was watching her, but nothing in the clear blue depth of his gaze gave any hint as to what he was thinking. But his hand was warm, his touch light, and it was terribly erotic.

"I think you've gotten it all," she said, her voice low and breathless. "My ankle is feeling better, but my foot is going to freeze." She pulled her foot out of the water and felt everything turn liquid inside as he began to dry her foot with his plaid. Afraid it might come unwrapped and fearing her reaction, she squeezed her eyes shut.

His hand stilled, and its warmth seeped into her skin. "Have ye never seen a naked man before today, lass?"

"I saw Michelangelo's David." *Isobella, you're an idiot!*

He studied her closely. "I am beginning to think ye havena the wit to be a spy."

She was frantically searching for a way to respond when his horse saved the day by coming up to Alysandir and giving him a shove with his nose. Alysandir picked up the surcoat and pulled it over her head and carried her back to her previous perch before he gathered his clothes and disappeared. While he was away, she put on her shoes. A pair of athletic socks had never felt so good.

He returned a short while later. "What ye witnessed earlier was brutal, and I ken I have washed away only the bluid and no' the memory. Ye fear me now, no?"

She crooked her head to one side to better look at him. "No, I don't, but I am in awe," she said, with sincere honesty. "It was both the most spectacularly beautiful thing I have ever seen and the most barbaric."

She saw the pained expression in his eyes and knew

that whoever the dead men were, killing them was not something he wanted to do or enjoyed. To the contrary, it seemed to have subdued him considerably. He was not only a man of courage but also a man with a noble conscience.

For the first time in her life, she understood the true meaning of the word "hero." It wasn't an NFL player or a rock star, a narcissistic CEO or an actor with an inflated sense of self, and it certainly wasn't a foot-long sandwich. Alysandir was simply a remarkably brave man who had committed an incredible act of extraordinary bravery, a man of great courage and strength of character who gladly risked his life for others without consideration of the danger to himself or thought of reward. And when killing was necessary, he did not take pleasure in the act but carried the burden deep inside where others could not see.

"Who were they?"

"Puir Highlanders driven to rogue thievery out of desperation."

"Because warfare is all they know." She said the words without thinking. When she glanced at him, she saw his surprise and some sort of understanding passed between them, although neither of them addressed it.

"Aye," he said at last, 'Tis all they know and the only way they have to survive."

Killing was a way of life here. She recalled that the ancient Greek geographer Strabo had written that the Celts were "madly fond of war, high spirited, and quick to do battle, but not of evil character." Warfare was one of their major pastimes, and if an enemy did not present itself, they were content to war with each other.

Naturally, it would be even more manifest when they were faced with starvation.

"I know you had to kill them, and I'm glad that you did not enjoy it," she said.

"Aye, kill them or let them kill us. That is the way of it. Kill or be killed. There is no midpoint, mistress. Had they killed me, ye might have been spared, but if ye were, ye stood a good chance of finding yersel' flat on yer back. Either they would have kept ye to use fer their own pleasure, or they would have bartered ye to be used by another."

Survival of the fittest. "That possibility entered my mind. I do not judge nor do I criticize what you did. I know it is part of the way of life you lead here."

His gaze penetrated deeply, warming her. "Ye are a strange lass and far more accepting than most. Although it is rare for a woman to witness such as ye did, it is rarer still to find one who is not horrified or one capable of accepting it as a way of life."

"Yes, I would imagine most women would not consider that a form of entertainment."

"I do not know that last word."

"Entertainment… it means amusement, as in seeing a play or playing music."

He said nothing as he dropped down on his haunches and picked up her foot. "'Tis a strange shoe ye wear."

She glanced at the North Face cross-trainers and said, "Yes, I suppose it is."

He lifted his dark head, and their gazes met and held. Without a word, he turned to rummage through the bag attached to his saddle and withdrew two round things that looked similar to a biscuit.

"Will ye have an oatcake?" he asked, and offered one to her.

A distrustful look settled over her brow. "Persephone was dragged into the underworld for eating just a pomegranate seed."

He chuckled. "Aye, 'tis true, well enough, but there are no seeds in my oatcake and I find myself far too weary this day to drag ye any further than to put ye astride my horse." He offered it again. "What say ye? Starve or eat?"

She held out her hand, thinking she would soon take a bite from history. *Blaah!* It tasted exactly as she had imagined it would, only worse, like cardboard—really old, musty cardboard with a hint of leather. She refrained from asking just how old the oatcake was, but it did hold the hunger pangs at bay.

Later, he saddled his horse and she found herself surrounded by his warmth as he gathered the reins and mounted behind her. This time, when his arms came around her, she knew she was in the hands of a very brave man, more than capable of protecting her.

Before long, a thin grey cloud of water droplets gathered and a fine, white mist floated down upon them. He stopped long enough to take a plaid from the back of his saddle and to hand her the mead flask. "I know, have a nip. It will warm my insides."

His eyes gleamed, calm and blue as a tranquil sea. "'Tis a good memory ye have, mistress, when it suits ye." He mounted, put the plaid around himself like a woman's shawl, and then brought the edges forward to wrap around her, tucking the edges beneath his powerful thighs.

"We are one now, lass," he whispered with a warm breath brushing her ear. A melting of warm desire enveloped her. She had no idea a Scot five hundred years in the past could, or would, be so seductive. She was becoming way too comfortable with him, so she stiffened and said in a rather prim voice, "We are not one, for we are halves of two different fruits."

His laugh was beautiful, and her body was warming both from the heat generated by their closeness and her occasional hefty gulps of mead. She could see herself throwing caution to the wind for a little Highland fling. She almost unseated herself with the thought, and she would have fallen if he had not had the quickest of reflexes and grabbed her.

"Careful, lass." He breathed the words against her skin, and she melted against him as the slow ache of desire quickened the blood warm in her veins.

The mead had to be doing this for she had already decided to swear off men. And the Black Douglas whipping up this time-travel scenario made any kind of a dalliance dangerous territory—at least until she knew what was going on. She wondered what kind of game her mercurial ghost was playing. She felt like a feather "for each wind that blows," as William Shakespeare had written. She wished she knew more about the rules of time travel—where was theoretical physicist Michio Kaku when she needed him?

Here she was, escorted back in time by a ghost who probably had his own set of rules. When the Black Douglas spoke vaguely about returning them to their own time, was he toying with them or didn't he know the rules either? Well, there was nothing to do in the meantime, other than make a life for themselves here.

She put her hand to her head and massaged her

temples, where a dull throbbing had begun. She decided to enjoy her time here by taking advantage of the educational aspects and archaeological opportunities she would find. Scotland had a long and enriching history involving many tribes, clans, and cultures.

She would have countless opportunities to excavate and write a few reports on her findings to be left for posterity. If one had to travel back in time, this was a great place to have landed. But she wondered why the Black Douglas brought them here to this time period. He was up to something, and that made her feel like a chess pawn. *Wonder and imagine all you wish, but he won't reveal anything until "the spirit moves me."*

"'Twould seem the mead is having an effect upon ye, Isobella Catriona Douglas."

The way he said her name flowed over her like a massage with warm oil. *Everything about Scotland is having an effect upon me… especially you…*

"You told me your first name, but you have yet to give me your last name. You do have one, don't you?"

"Aye."

She knew Scots were very private people and not at all like Americans, who had a natural propensity for telling everything about themselves to total strangers. But, what was the harm in knowing his name?

"Mackinnon," he said at last. "Alysandir Mackinnon of Caisteal Màrrach on the Isle of Mull."

Mackinnon… Oh, lord, did she know that name! It was one of the oldest Celtic tribes and used the wild boar on its crest. "And you have always lived here."

"Aye, I was born here and here I remain, like my ancestors afore me."

"And who is the laird or chief of your clan?"

He didn't answer. "I take by your silence that you are the chief."

"By chance, not choice."

She caught the sadness in his words and understood he had assumed the title because someone dear to him had died. "We can shoot the arrow, but we cannot control where it lands," she said. "Some of the world's greatest men were forced into the very thing that made them great."

He nuzzled her neck and breathed the words, "Yer wisdom warms me."

She was in way over her head and didn't know how to extricate herself. So she yawned and gave in to the sweet warmth of honeyed mead. That and the rhythm of the horse, the exhaustion, and the strong arms around her were all comforting, and she was ushered into silence by her last conscious thought. *I do like that mead, almost as much as the Scot who gave it to me.*

And liking either of them too much would be very dangerous.

Chapter 14

The Hero can be Poet, Prophet,
King, Priest or what you will,
according to the kind of world
he finds himself born into.

—*On Heroes, Hero-Worship, and the Heroic in History*, 1840
   Thomas Carlyle (1795–1881)
   Scottish historian and essayist

THE MIST HAD BURNED AWAY BY THE TIME SHE AWOKE, NOT
certain where she was. Then she saw the tanned hands
careless on the reins in front of her, felt the warm strength
of arms that held her, and heard the name that quietly
rode into her consciousness. Alysandir Mackinnon.

He had slowed his horse to a walking pace now, and
she wondered if it was to allow her to sleep. Neither
of them spoke as they rode over rocks dappled with lichen, scattered between puffy tufts of heather. Nearby,
a curlew gave warning, and when they passed, it went
flapping out of a tree, leaving only chirping meadow
pipits and greenshanks to do the scolding.

She took in the silvery boles that rose like columns
into the lofty branches of a grove of beeches, where a
gleaming ray of the descending sun had come to rest
upon a white trunk. Beyond the grove stretched tracts
of brown heath and brilliant whin, with a holly brake

interrupting the scene now and then. It was rough country and hauntingly beautiful.

She was wondering if they were going to ride all night when he guided his horse toward a place where an outcropping of stone formed a semicircle around a small clearing. She could hear the music of a waterfall and saw the burn nearby, as it tumbled over timeworn stones. She recalled that in Scotland, one was never far from a burn.

The spongy, damp earth cushioned the sound of hoofbeats. The evening was unnaturally quiet, the light penetrating the trees insubstantial. A breeze seemed to come out of nowhere to float eerily through the pine trees, creaking the branches it passed through.

He pulled his horse to a stop and dismounted; only this time, when he lifted her in his arms, he did not carry her anywhere. Instead, he lowered her to her feet, not releasing her but holding her close while he searched her face with a steady gaze that also probed the depths of her eyes, searching, asking. It didn't take a PhD in psychology to know that he wanted her. She swallowed audibly and looked away, fearing that he might see the same acute yearning for him in her eyes.

"Why are we stopping?"

It was unnerving the way his eyes, his words caressed her, sparing nothing and sending an eddy of pleasure rippling throughout. She supposed she deserved that for unashamedly gawking at his nakedness earlier. She found herself wondering what kissing him would be like and gave herself a mental slap.

Letting him know she desired him would be foolish,

for he would act upon it and a loose woman could end up the castle whore, so she gave him a seraphic smile. Then she lifted her chin and looked him in the eye, letting him know that if he tried to force his attentions upon her, she would not be receptive to such overtures. She narrowed her eyes as if to say she would not give up without a fight.

"*Vae victis.* Such bravery, but wholly unnecessary. A man can desire a woman without raping her."

His words were powerful and the caress on her face infuriatingly gentle. He stroked her cheek and then gently lifted her chin with the curve of a forefinger. The humid breath of the wind caressed her face as tenderly as did his gaze when she looked at him.

Vae victis, woe to the conquered. If he only knew she was conquered already. But she did not have to let him know that. She sighed, thinking the golden tint of late afternoon did nothing but enrich the warm tones of his skin, the high cheekbones, and the silvered gleam in the depths of his blue eyes.

"What would ye say if I said I wanted to kiss ye?"

For a moment, she stared at him blankly, but then his words sunk in and she said, rather flippantly, "I would have to say no."

"Then I willna ask," he said and drew her more tightly against him.

Her insides felt like they were floating, and her heart had already risen to her throat, rendering her speechless. *No, this can't be happening.* She twirled around with silent dignity, intending to walk dramatically down to the burn to break the spell. In her haste, she forgot about her ankle and proceeded to tumble over the gnarled root of a tree, rolling a couple of feet and landing on her side in a thorn bush. At first, she didn't think she was hurt. Then she howled in pain. *"Yeowwwww!"*

He stood in place, observing her. He said calmly, "Bad choice. The cure was worse than the poison. Kissing me would no' ha' been so painful."

In spite of her pain, she laughed, but she stopped when she learned a valuable lesson: In the pain department, thorn bushes rank considerably higher than bracken. Her left side bristled with thorns from hip to ankle, and she felt as though she had been stabbed with a million needles.

She knew she was becoming a great deal of trouble and wondered if he was contemplating riding off and leaving her. When she glanced up at him to get some inkling of his thoughts, he shook his head and dropped down to survey the damage.

"Apparently ye were never told that a gorse bush is to be avoided. 'Tis a valuable lesson ye have learned today, and ye are fortunate the thorns are only on yer left leg. I need to put ye where ye willna get into more trouble." He reached for her, and she pulled back. "Be still. Do ye want to push the thorns in deeper?"

She leaned back. "Aren't you going to pull them out?"

"Nae. I will see to my horse and make camp first."

Her mouth dropped faster than a ripe fig. He was going to see to his horse? And leave her sitting here pricked with a million thorns?

"When I have a fire going, I will boil some water to bathe yer leg. The hot water will make the thorns easier to pull." He turned to remove the flask of mead from his pouch and tucked it into his tunic. He lifted her carefully, carried her to a ledge hewn from a large rock, and sat her down gently.

He was like no man she had ever met. It was not simply because he was from another century that was wild, passionate, and untamed. No, it was more than that. He did not try to impress her or pelt her with sexual innuendos or play games. And he didn't seem to define his masculinity through aggressiveness. His virility and courage were as natural to him as his horsemanship.

He removed the flask and handed it to her. "Drink some o' this while I see to my horse." When she took a sip, he turned away. He returned shortly to wrap the upper part of her body in his plaid, and she wondered how many women had received such. She drank more mead, thankful once again for its numbing warmth.

As he unsaddled his horse and rubbed him down, she sensed a bond between the two of them, for the sturdy hobbler responded to Alysandir's slightest command. Once the horse was cared for, Alysandir gathered wood and kindling to start a fire.

She took another drink. "Aren't you going to tie your horse?"

"Nae."

"Why not?"

"He willna leave."

Alysandir used a tinderbox to coax smoking leaves into a fire, adding small chips of wood taken from the interior of a fallen log to bring the emerging flame to life. He added a few logs, and soon the fire blazed. She could feel its warmth reaching out to her. She had never thought to consider a wool plaid and a smoky, peat-smelling fire sheer luxury, but she did at this moment.

She shuddered to think what she would be doing now, if he hadn't come along. She pulled the plaid closer and noticed he seemed amused.

"Ye have the look of a wet cat aboot ye."

"You don't look too impressive either," she shot back, feeling a bit miffed at her bedraggled appearance when he, even battle weary, looked absolutely sumptuous. Oh, fiddle. She was so tired she couldn't put two thoughts together. The oatcake she had eaten earlier did nothing to stop the awful gnawing in her stomach, and her leg throbbed with each pulse of her heart.

What I wouldn't give for a hot bath and a warm, soft bed about now. She sighed, imagining the fragrance of crackling clean sheets and skin scented with rose soap. What she settled for was another nip or two of mead. *Can one become a mead alcoholic?*

She watched him carry a few things from his pouch to the fire, and she marveled at watching a real knight set up camp. It was so much better than one seen in a high-budget film. *I wonder what he'd think if he saw* Braveheart? *Laugh his head off, probably.*

She watched him carry a tin of water from the burn and place it on the fire. While it heated, he came toward her. "I will need my plaid to carry the water over here."

Her eyes narrowed suspiciously. "You aren't going to pour boiling water on my leg, are you?"

He gave her a look that said how stupid he thought that question was. "Lie doon, lass."

She smiled, feeling a bit giddy as she obeyed, and stretched out on the stone, gasping at the brittle slap of cold against her skin. "Hurry. I'm freezing."

"'Tis to be expected when ye go about naked as a

shorn sheep." He rolled up one end of his plaid and poured the hot water over it, then quickly arranged it over the length of her injured leg. She raised her head, yelped, like a kicked dog, and lay back down. A moment later, she said, "Ahhh, it's nice and warm."

"'Tis the mead what warms ye. Lie still, for it will soon cool. I must work quickly." He peeled part of the plaid back and began to pull the thorns.

She gritted her teeth and squeezed her eyes tightly together to ward off the pain, determined to show how Texas tough she was. After what seemed hours, she raised her head.

"*Ouch!* This is taking forever. How many... *ouch!*... more are there?"

"I ken there will be aboot as many as were poked into yer skin," he replied.

"Can you translate that into an *ouch!*... number?"

"Mayhap ten or fifteen."

"I'll be dead by then." She closed her eyes and grimaced with each thorn, howling with the extraction of a few of them.

"Pain can be a guid thing."

"How so? *Owwww!* Are you doing *owwww!*... that on purpose?"

"Nae. That one was in deeper than the others. It was the last one."

She let out a long breath. "Thank God." She opened her eyes. "How can pain be good?"

"It can teach ye a lesson. 'Twould be safe to say ye willna fall into a thorny gorse bush again, now will ye?"

"If you are trying to learn how to be humorous, you've a long way to go." She rose up on her elbows.

"I might have known you would find another way to poke me."

"Of that ye can be certain," he said, laughter dancing in his eyes. "I anticipate the moment."

You idiot! Her head fell back and cracked loudly against the stone. "*Owwww!*"

"Yer twin... is she as clumsy as ye?"

"No, and not half as entertaining either."

"Humph!" He picked up the plaid and carried it back to hang near the fire.

She was feeling a bit tipsy as she watched him fill the tin again and set it on the fire to boil. He added a few leaves, which she assumed were tea leaves or something akin to them. She was shivering by the time he poured some of the steaming liquid into a small tin cup and handed it to her.

"'Tis herbs that will give ye strength and warm yer insides," he said, and handed her another oatcake.

She wouldn't have to worry about gaining weight here. She wondered how a warrior such as he could wield a heavy sword and maintain his stamina on herb tea and oatcakes. He stood a few feet away, his feet wide apart and thumbs in the waist of his chausses, with a serious expression on his face—and he looked sexy as hell.

"Is something wrong?" she asked.

He checked the plaid and, finding it dry, folded it. "Nae, ye didna do anything, if that is what ye mean, but ye willna like what I am aboot to say. I have only one plaid, and that means we will have to share it for the night."

How convenient. She was too tired to even consider arguing the point. "Fine. Just make sure that is all you intend to share, for I warn you, I will resist."

He smiled wickedly. "A woman who resists is a woman won, and her passion is equal to the fervor of her resistance."

"You will realize in the morning just how wrong you are about that."

He tossed the plaid on the stone ledge and stepped closer. Cupping her chin, he lifted her face until she had no choice but to look into his eyes. She was captivated by the overpowering gentleness she saw there, the softness of his touch.

"Ye are afraid of me? Afraid I might harm ye?"

She intended to say something trivial but stopped herself. His magic closed off any means of escape, just as an enemy surrounded a fortress. She had nowhere to turn. Truthfully, she wasn't sure she wanted to. He was too overpowering in a gentle way that reached out to surround her like a warm blanket.

She couldn't lie to him. It did not seem fitting for the time, the place, or the man, and she was just a little scared to have this feeling and not know where it came from or what had caused it. She trembled, but from his nearness, not the cold. She yearned for him to take her in his arms and kiss her until she could not bear it any longer. After all he had done for her, he deserved honesty.

"I'm afraid of what might happen when I'm around you. I'm afraid of what I might do. You are a threat to me... a threat I do not understand. I feel you could surround me with your strength, so much so that I could no longer breathe."

She turned her head away, feeling a mixture of shame, embarrassment, relief, and dread. She could not continue talking. She had said far too much already. Her fences were down, her defenses penetrated. She felt vulnerable, exposed, and open to attack.

"I don't know why I'm babbling like this." She put her hand to her head. "I'm so confused right now and tired. Please, forget everything I said."

"A compelling thought but fruitless, for those are words I canna forget. Not now and mayhap never." He reached for her and folded her in his arms. She swayed against him, her resistance easing.

"Don't pay any attention to me. The mead is making me say and do things I shouldn't."

He chuckled. "Aye, I ha' reached the same conclusion." With a kiss to her forehead, he said, "My horse needs to rest, and so do I. We will ride again afore daybreak."

She smiled and felt like she was floating in a vat of warm chocolate. She was exhausted and the mead-chocolate-Alysandir combo made her relax. After all, the last time she'd slept was five hundred years from now. She watched him spread his plaid on the ground in front of the boulder. A moment later, she was on the ground wrapped like a cocoon in the plaid. When he joined her, she thought he would turn his back to her, but instead he took her in his arms.

"Are you going to make love to me now?"

"Do ye wish me to?"

Oh, yes. "I refuse to answer that because it might implicate me."

"If it will ease yer mind, when I make love to ye, it willna be the mead talking."

She sighed and closed her eyes. "Thank you for being a gentleman and not taking advantage of me."

"I didna say I wouldna take advantage of ye."

The man scent of him and the warmth of mead in her veins caused her resistance to recede.

"I will take that kiss now." Before she could sputter, his mouth was on hers, feather-light. She was unprepared for the rush of feelings created by the touch of his lips upon hers, full and searching, his tongue touching hers, probing, encouraging. The sensation was addictive, carrying both promise and fulfillment, and it settled around her like a cloud of opium smoke.

The touch of his hand at her throat sent a wave of dizziness over her. The words whispered against her cheek made her yearn for more, and she feared he knew that inside, she was a quivering mass of craving desire and aspiring hopes. He lifted his head, his lips brushing against hers again and again, and she felt as if she had been blessed by angels, smiled upon by the gods, exalted and raised to angelic heights.

She sighed blissfully and felt his smile against her cheek. He drew back to study her face in the dying light of the fire, and she wanted to yank him back to kiss her again, but longer this time.

Her breath caught, and she felt the beat of her pulse hammering against her throat. She knew he was going to kiss her again and that it would be a real, toe-curling kiss, the kind she always dreamed about and never had. When his lips claimed hers again, she was undone. His arms came around her, and the world seemed to fall away until there was nothing but the two of them.

She inhaled the scent of him, and something warm and liquid spread through her, more powerful than the mead she'd had earlier. This was the real thing, and it suffused through her veins until she was sure he could hear them hum and vibrate like the strings of a well-played harp. She was on fire, burning for his touch.

"I have wanted to do this since I first saw ye across the meadow wi' yer legs gleaming in the sunlight, but dinna worrit. I will have ye, but not tonight." She almost cried out when he pulled back and placed a gentle kiss against each of her eyes. "Sleep now. The morrow will come early, and I wouldna have ye traveling in an overly weary state." He kissed her eyes again, her nose, her cheeks, and her lips. "Fear not. I will protect ye."

And she knew he would.

She realized suddenly that she had no idea where they were going. She had assumed, of course, that he was taking her home with him, since his brothers would be bringing Elisabeth there when they found her. But she wanted to be sure.

"Where are you taking me?"

"Caisteal Màrrach."

"Is that your home, or are you leaving me elsewhere?"

"Ye are wi' me, lass. I keep what I have. Caisteal Màrrach is my home and where ye will reside."

She sighed and closed her eyes. Alysandir turned, giving her his back so he faced the fire and the open glen. His sword lay beside him, while a few feet away his horse grazed quietly. She felt warm, peaceful, protected, and safe knowing this man would not harm her, that he would give his life to protect her.

Sometime later, she felt his hand take hers. He pulled her arm around his chest, tucking her hand in his and cradling it against his heart. She melted against him like a double-dip cone dropped on the Galveston seawall in 105-degree weather. She sighed blissfully. Later, when she had time to analyze his gesture, she might think it a signature move that he used with the many women he'd bedded, but now, she was warmed by the tenderness of it.

It seemed a moment later when she felt something nudge her leg. A voice cut into her consciousness. "Lass, wake up. 'Tis time to go." She opened her eyes to mere slits in time to see the toe of his boot coming to nudge her again. "Make haste, lass. We canna abide here any longer if we are going to reach Màrrach before dark."

She moaned and hoped this was a dream, but when she was nudged a third time, she knew it was real. "Up wi' ye now."

Surely that was a jest. It was so dark that the moon had already gone to bed and the sun was still asleep. She closed her eyes and fell right back to sleep, only to be roused a while later by the nudging of his boot, more firmly this time. "Either ye get up, or I will undress and join ye there."

She sat up quickly and remembered her accumulation of wounds. She saw the crackling fire and was about to say something grumpy when she heard a noiseless whisper creeping through the trees, rattling the branches, and filling the empty spaces deep within her. *Damn you, Black Douglas! What are you up to?*

Alysandir handed her a cup of something fresh from the fire and she drank it, not caring what it was. It was hot, and that was enough. She noticed that he was eating something.

"And my oatcake is where?"

She didn't care if she sounded like a shrew. She was

grumpy and sore as hell after her falls and run-ins with gorse and bracken. Her wounds, along with a certain family ghost, were irritating as hell.

Without saying a word, Alysandir tossed her an oat-cake. She caught it in mid-air and ate it quickly. Soon, they were riding again and she was lulled back to sleep while strong arms held her as safe and securely as they had done the day before.

When she awoke, the sun was a brilliant orb over-head. It was a good omen. They rounded the top of a gently sloping hill and then continued down the other side until his horse stopped in the middle of a noisy little burn, his fetlocks awash and flanks wet. Alysandir relaxed his hold to slacken the reins. His horse stretched out his neck, stirred and splashed the water with his nose, and then drank deeply.

"Does your family call you Alex?"

"Nae."

He turned in the saddle, listening, with the palm of his left hand resting flat upon the crupper of his horse. Isobella held her breath, listening, too, but all she heard was the murmuring burn where the water ran over the rocky shallows and the gentle, sucking noise of the horse and the splash of water when he pawed.

"Are ye tired, mistress?"

Their gazes met and held, and a shiver rippled over her.

"More stiff than tired."

His horse tossed his head a couple of times, jingling the snaffle bit, and then responded when Alysandir nudged him with his spurs and they crossed to the other side. When they stopped, Isobella leaned forward and rubbed the horse's mane. "Ye like horses," he said.

"Love them! I have a horse of my own, a gelding named Morrigan."

"Morrigan, the Celtic god o' war? This is a fashionable name for a horse where ye are from?"

She smiled. "Not really. It's a name that appealed to me when I read a book about Celtic deities. And your horse? What is his name?"

"Gallagher."

"And in Gaelic?"

"*Ó Gallchobhair,* and it means "foreign helper."

Foreign helper. Warmth suffused her, and she considered his horse's name to be the second good omen since meeting him. But then, he could mesmerize her by counting horse droppings, for there was such beauty in the Scot tongue and the *beautiful lilt of Gaelic that he spoke*. She could almost feel his essence reaching out and touching her, for his sense of belonging and family pride resonated with each word, and she knew what it was to envy the strength of kith and kin. His family had lived on this island for centuries.

His roots ran deep and strong. And what of her roots? Thoughts of her own family sliced sharply into her heart. How could she bear never seeing her family again or riding Morrigan or laughing with her girlfriends? And Elisabeth. Were they all lost to her now, too?

She felt tears prickle her eyelids, but she quickly brushed them away and focused on how fortunate she was to have landed smack in the middle of an archaeologist's paradise. She glanced at Alysandir, who had ridden into her life and saved her.

"Thank you for coming to my rescue. Things were looking very grim before you arrived."

"Ye have no assurance yer situation will improve now that ye are with me."

She smiled to herself. *Oh, Alysandir Mackinnon, I know all about your family name, your code of honor.* Even the blood racing through her veins seemed to be humming with excitement that she had been found by this remarkable knight and no other. It did not occur to her until much later that perhaps this was what the Black Douglas had had in mind all along.

Chapter 15

An ally has to be watched
just like an enemy.

—Attributed to Leon Trotsky (1879–1940)
  Russian revolutionary

ALYSANDIR CAUGHT THE AMBROSIAL SCENT OF HER HAIR and smiled at the crooked part. Like her face, her hair was beautiful, in spite of its unruly state, and he was glad she did not bind it with cords of blue or ribbons of a rosy hue. They suited her, these wild and rebellious curls flowing in no logical order. He imagined her in a low-cut, tightly laced corset of green, with her hair tumbling down her shoulders.

He leaned closer and inhaled the fragrance that curled around him like a courtesan's arms. Saint Columba, how he longed to thread his fingers through the mass of it and to hold her fast, bound to him while he ravaged her sweet mouth again and again before he entered her. In truth, he had thought of little else since their meeting.

Like the sphinx, she was an enigma and a mystery to him, quite the most unique woman he had ever met. She appeared naïve, lush, lovely, and so appreciative that he regretted he could not trust her. But innocent women of her ilk did not wander around glens unprotected, unless they were intentionally placed there for a purpose. What was hers?

He could not help his suspicions. In the first place, she was a woman. Secondly, she had not revealed where she was from or how she and her sister had ended up in the middle of his quarrel with the Macleans. At one time, the sacred belief that people were innately good had existed in his heart, but actions can quickly shatter faith. He had learned the hard way that those who appear the most innocent are often the most suspect.

The greenness of his youth was gone. Trust and confidence were now plants of slow growth within the bosom of an older and wiser man. God help him, but he knew in his heart that he dared not trust anyone save his brothers. *The axe forgets, but the cut log does not.*

He knew she was no common whore, but would she soon offer her body to hide her true purpose? It angered him to think that she had been thrust into the hands of a stranger, risking her life, to accomplish a goal. If this be true, then she was naught more than a pawn—a beautiful woman being used for the advantage of those she served. Or was she forced into such to protect her family?

Nothing would save her but the truth. But God help her if she took him for a fool. Now wasn't the time to question her, but once they reached Màrrach, things would be different. Be she spy, witch, or maleficent, he would know her story.

"Do you think your brothers will find my sister?" she asked, breaking into his thoughts.

"Aye, they willna come home until they do, unless, of course, the English have taken her. If so, my brothers will return with the news and not yer sister. But dinna worrit. 'Tis difficult, but no' impossible to steal her back from old Angus Maclean."

"I would hate to think anyone could lose their life trying to rescue her. Elisabeth would abhor such action."

"When dealing with Angus Maclean, one must always use guile and deception. When entering the den of the fox, 'tis best to play the fox."

She said a quick prayer that the English would be far away from wherever Elisabeth was and that her twin would not be hostile toward the Mackinnons when they rescued her.

Isobella breathed deeply. "Where are we, exactly?"

"Why," he asked, stroking her cheek with the back of his hand. "Do ye need to get word to someone?"

She fought the urge to melt against him. "No, of course not."

"Then does it really matter where we are? Wherever I choose to take ye, whatever I choose to do is far better than yer prospects afore I found ye." He guided his horse around a boulder and headed in a new direction. "'Tis a strange manner of dress ye are wearing, lass. It doesna cover much and leads the thoughts of a man astray. Why is it the fashion for ye, while yer sister was dressed differently?"

"It was a quirk of fate that we made different choices yesterday," she replied and hoped he had no more questions.

"Ye are a strange lass with a strange way of talking and a strange manner of dress. If ye are not English, then where is yer home?"

"America," she replied, thinking he had never heard of it. She felt an immediate stiffening of his body.

"Ye canna be from America, for according to the Spaniard Juan Ponce de León, there are no people there but tribes, and there are no towns or villages. It is said also that he did not find the Fountain of Youth. So, tell me, mistress, where do ye call home, for it canna be America."

Damn Ponce and his big mouth! "Truly, I am from America, but not the same America of Columbus or Ponce de León." She decided not to add that her America was in the twenty-first century.

This time, his body went rock hard and the muscles of his arms flexed powerfully. 'Tis a dangerous game ye play, mistress. I think ye are spying for the English."

She was shocked. He had been so nice to her. Did he really think she was a spy? "I am not English! My ancestry is Scottish, Italian, and Irish. And I am not playing a game."

"Ye are no' telling me the truth, either."

"I haven't told you *all* of the truth, but I haven't lied."

"Then tell me the rest of it."

"I cannot. Not because I don't want to tell you or that I am hiding something. It's a long story, and I am quite weary. I would rather wait for another time and place to tell you because you will have many questions and I am not up to answering them. I am not being evasive, but it is an incredible story. However, I can assure you that every word of it is true. I know this because I have difficulty believing it myself."

"Is that yer way of saying ye are no' a spy?"

"I'm not a spy."

"Who brought ye here?"

"You would really find that preposterous and…"

"I speak Gaelic, English, and French, but I dinna ken the word 'preposterous.'"

She knew that had to mean the word came into use after 1515. Being here was getting more complicated by the minute. "'Preposterous' means absurd, unbelievable, exaggerated, and outrageous."

"'Exaggerated' I dinna ken."

This communicating thing was going to be her undoing. "But you do understand 'absurd' and 'unbelievable.'?"

"Aye. They are words that describe much I have heard ye say. Am I to believe ye came here from America by magic?"

She nodded. "Actually, that is very close to the truth."

"And did ye wish to return?"

"I do not know if that is an option available to me."

"'Option' I dinna ken."

"It means choice, as in I do not have a choice about returning." She didn't want to mislead him, but she was afraid he might decide to toss her on her duff and ride on without her if she talked about time travel and a mischievous, meddling ghost.

She caught a glimpse of the russet hindquarters of a deer as it broke cover and darted across the track in front of them. Everything began to weigh down upon her again. She understood his doubt, disbelief, and distrust. She did not blame him. He really couldn't trust her. She could be anyone, even someone who threatened the security of his family.

Isobella, you are an idiot! How can you possibly expect to pull this off? It's a lose-lose situation at best. If she didn't tell him the truth, it was into the dungeon; if she told him, he would not believe her, ergo the dungeon. Either way she lost. Not the best place to be when up against a warrior on his own turf.

"You have been kind. You deserve an answer, and I promise to give you one. Right now, I am hungry and tired from an unbelievably long journey. I ache all over. I'm in a strange place with strange people. I miss my home, my family, my friends, and the life I had. I am worried about my sister. If you don't want a crying woman on your hands, you would do well to change the subject."

He put his hand on her thigh and rubbed gently. "Not with your hands, Lancelot. I was thinking more along the lines of conversation."

He spurred his horse to a faster pace. The silence settled around them like an opaque veil, and the world seemed cold and dull and without luster as he became impervious to her.

She must have fallen asleep, for sometime later, he said, "Wake up, mistress. We will be there soon."

Her mouth was suddenly dry with anticipation as she caught her first glimpse of a castle still some distance away. Its outline was sharp and clear in the fading light of a summer day—a mammoth in granite, dark, threatening, unfriendly, and unknown.

Your fate sits upon those dark battlements, a ghostly voice whispered in her ear, and Isobella shuddered at the thought.

Chapter 16

Don't let us make imaginary evils,
when you know we have so
many real ones to encounter.

—*The Good-Natured Man*, 1768
  Oliver Goldsmith (1730–1774)
  Irish-born British novelist, playwright, and poet

Isobella inhaled the fresh scent of salt water and viewed the Gothic castle rising out of the summit of a rock, whose base lay submerged in the cold depths of the Atlantic. It was worthy of reverence and commanding of respect by virtue of age, dignity, and the secrets of bygone centuries contained within.

It was the ancestral home of Alysandir Mackinnon, descended from the tribal chiefs who came before him, proud, ambitious, protective, and revengeful, who had lived here during a time of feudal greatness. She found herself in awe at the stories the castle could tell and felt the distress of tears, long dried, that had been shed there. Little wonder that the gargoyles frowned down from battlements secluded in shade.

She sensed a warm heartbeat within this fortress that shimmered in the hazy glow of the last remnant of evening, for it was like something out of a fairy-tale. She found herself wondering what it would be like in the cold and stingy grey light of winter, snow lying icy and deep on its stones. The sun melted into deep purple and red on the horizon, and she felt as insignificant as a shadow. She grieved inexplicably for her lost past, the uncertain future, and the knowledge that her life was no longer her own.

Yes, as the voice had told her, her fate lay within the hard, granite walls of that dark stronghold and with the people who lived there. Would they be accepting or rejecting, filled with envy and distrust? She felt an unexpected tightness in her throat and knew she had to redirect her line of thinking, so she started talking.

"Is that your home?"

"Aye, 'tis Caisteal Màrrach, or Màrrach Castle if ye prefer the English pronunciation over the Gaelic one."

"It's a beautiful name in any language. It has an almost magical sound to it. Màrrach," she said, and let the sound of it penetrate her psyche like an aromatic balm. "What does it mean?"

"Màrrach is an enchanted castle that keeps one bound by a spell, usually with a labyrinth, a maze of passages."

Spellbound in a maze of passages. That should go well with my current state of affairs, wandering through centuries like a celestial nomad.

They passed under the whispering foliage of a towering beech. Then they were suddenly clear of the trees. She caught another shadowy glimpse of the towering, grey fortress looming in the distance just as they passed by a fringe of dark pines and rode into a clearing, leaving behind the scent of rooty dampness that had clung to the woods.

Overhead, she heard the cry of birds and she watched them circling high above, majestic and unfettered. She envied them their freedom.

"Eagles," he said.

Startled, she waited for the rest of his sentence and realized that, to him, that was a sentence. She didn't know why she found the idea amusing, but it lifted her mood slightly.

"The entrance to Màrrach lies thither."

Thither... she sighed at the sound of the word riding upon the rhythmic waves of his Scots burr and once again felt herself seduced by his history. 'Impenetrable' was the first word that came into Isobella's mind as they rode close enough for a more critical inspection. She imagined herself sitting in the sun and describing it in one of her journals and hoped she would have the opportunity to do so.

Màrrach Castle was a large, fortified structure built on the quadrilateral plan, with curtain walls about eight feet thick and thirty feet high. Corbelled battlements and square turrets seemed etched in black against the blue sky, which caught the sun while everything below lay dark and gloomy.

The castle possessed three square towers. The entrance was wide, with a portcullis protected by iron bars that rose with an intimidating creak to grant them passage, just like something out of the movies but more powerful. How sad to think that in her future time, this beautiful fortress might be in ruins, like so many others of this time period.

"It's rugged but beautiful," she said. "You must never grow tired of seeing it, of knowing that you are home."

"Aye, 'tis receptive as the open legs of a warm and willing woman."

A thickness seemed to lodge in her throat, and she was left to think upon his words as they rode through the open gate in the wall of enceinte. They continued on past the guardrooms that flanked the passageway through the keep and into the courtyard, to stop at the donjon. Here, beyond those massively carved and iron-studded doors, a new life awaited her. She lowered her head and said a quick prayer for her safety and that of her sister.

Someone spoke, and Alysandir replied with a chuckle of amusement. "Nay, she isna dead. 'Twould appear that the wee lass has frightened herself into a stupor."

Laughter erupted. He dismounted and leaned against his horse, gazing up at her in a questioning manner as if he would find what he searched for written in her eyes or etched upon her face.

"And now, Isobella Douglas, from a place unknown, we will soon have the truth. Are ye a witch, a mortal, or a mixture of more desirable elements than simple flesh and blood?"

She smiled tentatively as she replied, "I am a simple mortal with no hidden talents or magical powers."

"Are ye now? Ye are in the land of faëry, and I think ye are an imaginary being in human form, clever and mischievous, or mayhap something more dangerous, endowed with a body that softens a man's brain and hardens another part of him that it shouldna. Yer face is full of innocence, yet yer speech is odd and yer words hard to swallow. Will ye be true to yer word and reveal the truth, or will ye spin a silken web that leaves me wandering in a boscage unable to find my way oot?"

Each word he spoke tore at her conscience. She glanced away, unable to withstand the heat and fire in his gaze. He was a man of superior intelligence, educated, intuitive, wise, and full of distrust for anyone not of his ilk. She had to be very careful how she answered his questions.

She shuddered when she saw the sky had dulled to a wash of deep, blood red, the last glow from the sunken sun marred by a wisp of black cloud, dark as a blot of ink upon her future. She could not hide the woefulness in her words.

"I am at your mercy, for if I prove false, your dungeon will prove worthy of my deception."

A grim smile crossed his features, and she shivered in response. When he spoke, there was an edge of distrust to his voice that she would have been foolish to ignore.

"Though she should prove false, 'tis not my way to tether a woman. However, ye should be aware that I am the law here and I am within my power to do with ye as I please. That includes giving ye to my men for their pleasure or locking ye away in the dungeon if I so choose. All I ask of ye is honest candor and the answers ye promised to give me. It would be in yer best interest to speak the truth."

He gave her a stark and forbidding look. "Do ye understand?"

"Perfectly."

"Would ye like to dismount now, or are ye unable to move?"

"That all depends on what you intend to do with me if I do. Would I fare better taking my chances in the wilds of Mull alone?"

He probed the depths of her eyes with a look she absorbed like a warning. "Ye are safe wi' me, mistress, as long as ye do not take me for a fool."

She was more than glad to stretch her cramped legs as she slid from his horse into his open arms, and she turned to face the unknown fate that awaited her within the ancient walls of Màrrach Castle.

Chapter 17

I have learned to live each day as it comes,
and not to borrow trouble by dreading tomorrow.
It is the dark menace of the future
that makes cowards of us.

—Dorothy Dix (1861–1951)
   U.S. journalist and writer

SHE FORGOT ABOUT HER ANKLE UNTIL SHE PUT HER FULL
weight upon it. She would have gone down if Alysandir
had not caught her against himself. He did not release
her but continued to hold her, her body perfectly aligned
to his, and she felt as if she were melting into him. Here
she was again, imprisoned in his arms, lost as a fledgling
fallen from the nest.

Early Renaissance life was going on all around her,
laundry being done and chickens plucked. Children
were being fed, candles made, fireplaces cleaned, herbs
bundled, bedchambers aired, and vegetables brought in
from the garden while a visitor from the twenty-first
century stood in the courtyard.

A flag flapped from a tower high above them, and
it serving as a reminder to Isobella that her idyll with
Alysandir was over. She was about to pull away from
him when she was overcome with a strange enchant-
ment. Overhead, the sky was darkened by a mass of

shifting, vaporous clouds and dense black fog. She wanted to cry out, but no words would come as brilliant flashes of light hit her eyes.

Fear na ye.

She cast a quick look in Alysandir's direction and realized she must have been the only one who saw the darkened sky or heard the deep, booming voice of the Black Douglas.

About time you paid me a visit, you one-man disappearing act. Are you going to leave me here? Where is Elisabeth? Aren't you going to help them find her? What are you planning? I have a right to know. I want some answers. I want something besides silence.

Silence is an answer.

She gave a start. What kind of answer was that? A one-size-fits-all reply, like a chair that fits all backsides? A whirlwind stirred up a little cloud of dust that faded just as quickly. She shivered as if a cold rain had washed over her. She opened her eyes. Alysandir was staring at her.

"Why are you looking at me that way?"

"And how am I looking at you?"

"Like I'm a piece of bread and you're trying to decide which side the butter is on."

He gave her a ghost of a smile. His finger traced the line of her cheek. "Ye are pale as an evening primrose. Are ye afraid or hiding something ye fear to tell?"

"I am apprehensive. That is all."

"Yer ankle pains ye?"

"No, I took a moment for some self-encouragement. It isn't easy to walk into a strange place where you don't know a soul. I was trying to summon my courage and hearten myself to what lies ahead."

She realized how very fragile her situation was. If he turned his back on her, no one here would dare lift a finger on her behalf. Comfortable or not, her very life depended on him alone. Numb, she looked away, not wanting him to see what her eyes could tell him. She knew fear now. Real, aching, paralyzing fear.

He whispered softly, "Beware of fears in borrowed feathers, appearing as counsel and see danger in everything."

Trembling, she turned and their gazes met. He cupped her chin. "Fear 'tis not always a bad thing. 'Tis never present when all hope is gone."

Her heart pounded. Did he have a sixth sense? His powers of perception went beyond the ordinary. He seemed to know her thoughts as soon as she had them. She had never known anyone so discerning. How could this man from another time and place understand her with such acuity? How did he find words that were as soothing and warm as a balm of fragrant oil? How could the warrior live in harmony with the poetry of a man who could soothe her with mere words?

His voice held grudging respect, and his hand came up to cup her cheek, soft and comforting. "Dinna worrit aboot their reactions to ye or what they will be thinking in their silence. They will be curious and mayhap they will stare at ye, but they willna raise a hand to harm ye nor say a baleful word against ye."

He tossed the reins to an approaching groom, caught the shoulders of the surcoat, and gave it a shake or two. It settled into place as it fell to her ankles. The amusement in his voice was frank and undisguised.

"Ye do look like a street beggar," he said cheerfully.

"But dinna worrit, for no one will suspect that beneath the surcoat ye are wearing naught but a wee fragment o' cloth that barely covers yer particulars."

She shoved his hands away, which made him laugh. In spite of her hurt and humiliation, she suspected he had inflamed her ire intentionally, for her apprehensions burned away in the heat of her rage. It would be easier to face the scrutiny to come with an angry sort of pride and her head held high than to be led inside mewling and sniveling in subjection.

Alysandir laughed and swept her into his arms and carried her forward with confidence and a long stride. She focused her attention on the intricate carvings of griffons—the ancient, medieval creatures with the head, talons, and wings of an eagle and the hindquarters of a lion—over the doorway.

Not as ornate as the Byzantine ones she saw at St. Mark's Basilica in Venice last summer—make that centuries from now. It gave her a dash of optimism to be greeted by griffons, the protective symbol of strength and vigilance, in spite of the twisting vines of thorns that coiled around them.

Her arms clung to his neck tightly as he carried her through the heavy doors into the massively walled penetralia, the innermost sanctuary of the castle. She was well aware that she was an alien intruder being hauled into the stronghold like a sack of barley. As if sensing her unease, his lips curved into a smile.

"Dinna worrit if ye should find yerself fraught with fear. I am sure I can find a way to divert yer thoughts and to give ye something else to think aboot now that we are home." He spoke with surprising cheer.

"I am sure you can," she said, but her mind was focused upon that one word.

Home. The word reverberated inside her skull like a ricocheted bullet. She had not considered that Màrrach would become her home, and the realization of it shocked her. But where else could she go? She had no money, no friends, no family or connections. Mull was sparsely populated with probably no more than a thousand or so people. There were small settlements but no towns. Other than the monastery and convent on Iona, castles and clans were the center of gravity for those who lived here. But the truth was that she suddenly felt safe.

"Ye have had plenty to say, but now ye fall silent. Are ye afraid?"

"Uneasy would be a better word." A murky darkness surrounded them, illuminated only by torches flaming from the stone walls. Her eyes had not yet adjusted to the dim interior, and by the time they approached the door to the Great Hall, she could still barely see into the room, which was lit only by fat, tallow candles guttered in sconces along the walls. The moment they entered, the murmur of conversation died away.

She glanced around and saw that every eye was on her. Even the fire in the fireplace seemed to cringe and withdraw its light. She felt like a waif as he carried her further into the hall. Here she was in a medieval castle in Renaissance Scotland. Under different circumstances, she would have given more attention to her surroundings and taken note of the tapestries, heavily carved furniture, and the vaulted ceilings decorated with shields that they passed.

Instead, her attention was drawn to the sight of at least three dozen people who stopped eating to stare at her. She knew that behind their stunned gazes loomed many questions. She could almost hear them asking, Who is she? Why is she here? Why is she wearing the red surcoat of Alysandir Mackinnon? And what does she have on underneath it?

With cowardly hope, she prayed the trip through this hall would be a short one and that she never had to experience humiliation such as this again. Never had she felt so undressed, unwelcome, or insignificant, and she doubted this was likely to change.

"Was this necessary? Did you have to parade me in front of everyone like some captive slave?" she whispered.

"I brought ye here because it is better to let them see ye in my arms and holding yer head high enough to strike the cobwebs on the ceiling than for ye to be led with a chain through an iron collar, submissive, defeated, and trembling with fear."

"I am surprised they make such an effort to stare. One would think they would be accustomed to the public display of your captives." She lifted her chin a bit higher, determined to give him, and them, the cobweb-striking pride he described.

"My captives don't make their first appearance wearing naught but my surcoat. That usually comes after I have bedded them."

Her indrawn breath sounded, even to her own ears, like the wheeze of a winded horse. "I wouldn't sleep with you for all the bells in Edinburgh."

"'Tis a moot point, mistress, for ye slept with me yester eve."

That sent a warm flush of blood racing to her cheeks, made redder by the sudden bark of his laughter. She looked down, thankful for the surcoat, in spite of how it must look to them. It would have been worse, much worse without it.

"I'm too tired to bandy words with you." The only thing that was truly inviting about being in the Great Hall at a time like this was the succulent scent of food. That and the warmth emitting from the fire that blazed in the fireplace as they passed. What she wouldn't give for a hot shower, a razor, a toothbrush, a bottle of fragrant shampoo, a large Mexican martini… no, make that two… and some honest-to-God privacy.

"Fret not. 'Twill not be long now, lass." Alysandir shouted a few words in Gaelic, and two women about her age left the table and hurried toward them. A few more words of Gaelic, and he carried her from the room, the two women following close behind as he barked what she assumed were orders, and then they turned away.

"My sisters will be in charge of finding something more suitable for ye to wear, and they will send Mistress MacMorran to yer room. She will to see to yer ankle and to a bath fer ye. Once that is taken care of, a servant will bring ye something to eat."

Before she could respond, he said, "I didna mean to humble ye by such a display, but it would have been a long time if we waited until everyone left the hall. With yer ankle ailing ye, 'tis better to get ye to a place where ye can rest."

When she did not respond, he said, "Be of good cheer, lass. The worst is over," as he carried her from the Great Hall into the corridor. Relieved, Isobella let her head flop against his chest and closed her eyes, listening to the sound of his footsteps, the ring of his spurs against the stone floor, and the low whispers that followed them.

"Ye came out with yer head intact."

"Only because I was in your arms. Had I been alone, they would be mopping the floor with my blood about now."

He laughed. "So brave a mouth, so faint a heart."

She felt a flash of anger. "So quick to pass judgment, but then, the fox is always comfortable in his own den." She sighed wearily.

"Tired, are ye?"

"Yes. I am tired of thinking, talking, and worrying. I don't think I can link two words together."

Her head flopped against his shoulder again. She found comfort in the familiar sound of his breathing. With her arms around his neck, she could feel the hard coil of the muscles of his shoulders and she understood what it was like to feel safe. Yet she could not help wondering: now that their time alone had come to an end, would she become one of dozens of castle-folk who lived here, rarely catching a glimpse of him?

He stopped in front of an arched door, beautifully carved and heavy. *He will deposit me in this room and leave, and that might well be the last I will ever see of him.*

He paused just long enough to nod at a sconce on the wall. "Remove one of the candles," he said. She did as he asked. He pushed the door open with his foot and carried her into the dark room, their way illuminated only by the light coming from the hall and the candle in her hand.

"'Twill be yer room, mistress," he said, and kicked

the door shut behind him. He paused while she lit a taper and took in the sight of the dim room. Then he carried her to the bed. He stopped beside it, but he did not put her down. Her heart pounded thickly in her throat, and his heart pounded wildly under her ear.

She gave him a questioning look. "Do you intend to hold me while I sleep, or are you going to put me down?"

"'Tis a tempting thought surely."

"I would think that coddling a lass while she slept would be beneath the dignity of the chief of Clan Mackinnon."

"That," he said, "all depends upon whether I deem it worth my while."

"Put me down. I'm too tired to bandy words at the moment. Trust me. There is nothing you could do to me at the moment that would be worth the time that it took to do it."

For a moment he did not seem to understand what she said, and then he laughed. "I wouldna be so certain of that if I were you."

She wasn't certain about it either, but she wouldn't let him know how his nearness disturbed her or how the warm touch of his breath upon her skin brought back memories that were best left forgotten. She did not want to remember what it was like to lie next to him or to recall the feel of his arms around her, the melting into him at the touch of his lips upon hers. "Think of me as a cold, stone statue in your arms and drop me on the nearest bed."

"Seems I've captured a lass who canna resist having the last word."

A hot retort formed quickly in her mind. She opened

her mouth and noticed the laughter gleaming in his eyes. She quickly clamped it shut.

"Take care," he said. "Ye havena no idea how close I am to tossing ye on that bed and joining ye there."

He had no idea how she wished he would do just that. He was so real to her now and had become a part of her life in such a short time. Would he also be part of her future? Or would his noble existence be nothing more than a memory, a whisper from the past? They were pieces on a chessboard, and the game had yet to be played. Would she be a captured pawn or a queen?

Only the ghost of the Black Douglas knew the answer, and he was being very close-lipped.

Alysandir was fighting a few battles of his own. One of them was the urge to place her on the bed and strip away her strange clothing, piece by piece, kissing each newly exposed bit of skin he uncovered. Saint Columba! He had thought of little else since meeting her. He had to hold his yearning for her tightly in check, now that he was in her bedchamber.

He wanted, nae, he needed to know her story—how she came to be in Scotland, who she was, and whether he could trust her in his home among his family. Only then would he dare to make love to her, slowly at first, then wildly and passionately until she cried out his name and begged him not to stop. By that point, he would not want to.

He glanced down at her face and saw the softly glowing fire of desire in her eyes. She made a little noise deep in her throat, and he knew that she was under the same spell as he.

"I think you should put me down now."

She breathed the words against his skin, and he thought she was the loveliest lass he had ever encountered. He wrestled with himself, yet he knew the man in him had to step away and defer to the clan chief.

He lowered her to her feet beside the bed, and this time she remembered not to put weight on her injured foot. "Sit down."

"Ahhhh…" She sighed as she sank into the delicious softness of the bed.

"Move back."

She frowned, gave him a suspicious look, and scooted back.

"I only want to examine yer ankle, naught more."

She lifted her head to see how her ankle fared. It was horribly swollen and had a bruised, purplish tint.

"'Tis a nasty twist ye gave it," he said.

"You should see it from my side. It hurts worse than it looks," she said, not bothering to hide her grumpiness. She was tired, dirty, hungry, and separated from her life, her family, her home, her country, and her century. Her ankle hurt like hell, and she felt like the world was closing in on her. She stole a look at him, and desire coiled in tight knots inside her. Her breathing was erratic.

Did he have to be so damned desirable and the living reality of what she had imagined? He packed so much ammunition that she knew she would be a goner if he ever decided to use it on her. How could she resist him? Why would she want to? *Danger*, her mind warned. Panic swept over her and she felt stricken, knowing escape was impossible. She was praying for a diversion. She got one when he twisted her ankle again.

"Ouch!" she cried out.

He rolled up a blanket and propped her foot up on it. "'Twill ease some of the throbbing."

"It wasn't throbbing until you tried to twist it off!"

"Elevating it will ease the pain."

"It hasn't done much to ease it so far."

He made a disinterested shrug. "I will have Mistress MacMorran make a poultice for the swelling."

"Have her make one for your swelling confidence, while she is at it. And I don't want a poultice."

"What have ye against a poultice?"

"As long as it isn't amulets, charms, snake tongues, hot irons, or leeches, I'm okay with it," she said, and wondered if anything from this period truly was beneficial. They had no antibiotics, but she recalled they did rely heavily upon roots and herbs and garlic. She recalled Elisabeth telling her that, strange though it was, antibiotics were not effective against viruses, but garlic was. And that was about as far as she could go with this.

"I dinna understand the word 'okay.'"

She was startled out of her reverie. "It means something is all right, or that you approve of it."

"So ye willna allow amulets, charms, and such?"

"No, I don't want those things."

"Why?"

She started to say, "Because they are ineffective" but decided he would not know the word "ineffective."

"Because they do not work."

He gave her close scrutiny. "Ye have used them then?"

"No, I haven't," she said hastily.

"Then how do ye know they dinna work?"

She was too exhausted to delve into that now. "I have been told so by those who have tried those remedies."

She glanced down at his hand on her ankle. She felt her face warming. He must have realized where his hand was about the same time she did. Before she could say something, he pulled his hand away.

"Ye have a way of coming between a man and his good judgment, mistress."

"Well, perhaps that will change now that you have me here in your castle. An object in possession seldom retains the same charm that it had in pursuit."

"Ahhh, a learned woman who can quote Pliny the Younger," he said. He stood and gave her a look that made her debate whether to raise her foot and invite him back to hold it again.

"Dinna fret. I am harmless as a setting hen at the moment and too tired to be much of a threat to ye. Mistress MacMorran will be along to minister to ye better than these rough hands," he said, and with a nod, he departed.

She fought the urge to call him back. Rough hands sounded wonderful to her, but he was gone and seemed to take with him all the light and warmth. She was left with the gloom of a cold and unfamiliar room. When she heard the door click, a stony weight settled over her.

She remembered her sunny yellow room at home, with the French doors that opened to a veranda, the sound of music coming from Elisabeth's room next door, and the sight of the Blanco River flowing slowly. She closed her eyes and could almost smell the aroma of her father's barbecue and hear the laughter of her younger siblings dancing and chasing each other around the pool, and she wondered if she would ever dance or laugh again.

Thankfully, she did not have very long to devote to melancholy before the door opened and a middle-aged woman, with kind eyes the same color as her grey hair, came into the room. One glance at the pleasant, motherly face, and Isobella's spirits lifted. "Are you Mistress MacMorran?"

"Aye, mistress, indeed I am, and ye are Isobella Douglas, newly arrived upon the Isle of Mull from parts unknown."

"Guilty on all counts."

Mistress MacMorran looked around the room and made a clucking noise with her tongue. "'Tis colder than St. Mary's Loch in here, and I see a fire has not been laid in the fireplace." She clapped her hands on her hips, her elbows jutting out like tumped-over pyramids. "I will see that it is taken care of immediately, so dinna worrit aboot it."

Isobella looked around. The room was dreary, sparsely furnished, and eons away from home, but she would make do. *If my ancestors could stand it, I can, too!* She forced a smile she did not feel and said in the most cheerful voice she could muster, "You have no idea how wonderful a fire sounds."

"'Tis the dampness that comes in with the mist at night that makes the chill greater," Mistress MacMorran said, placing her stout hands on her hips again. She gave Isobella a good going-over, her gaze coming to rest on the throbbing ankle. Her caterpillar-like eyebrows rose in silent study before she finally said, "Weel now, 'tis a fine looking bit o' damage ye have done to yersel'. Does it pain ye greatly now?"

Isobella nodded, as tears welled in her eyes and began to slide down her cheeks.

"Och! Ye puir lassie, dinna ye worrit none. I will have ye up and aboot in no time. A good soaking in a hot tub will work a miracle, and a brisk rubbing wi' a few herbs and oils will have ye feeling better soon." She paused. 'Tis a certainty that ye will be needing some more appropriate clothing to sufficiently cover all yer… charms."

The longer she talked, the more Isobella cried. She couldn't help it; exhaustion and anxiety had taken over. But it wasn't exactly the first impression she had wanted to make. Mistress MacMorran removed the blanket Alysandir had placed under her ankle.

"This will do to cover yer hiddens for the time being." She covered Isobella and said, "Ye will be needing yer food on a tray, for ye canna go hopping on one foot doon to the hall fer yer repast."

With that, she turned and departed, leaving Isobella to laugh at the use of words like "hiddens" and "charms" for her private parts. But, the laughter did nothing to lift her sagging spirits. A short time later, a pile of clothing walked into the room on two human legs, followed by two more legs carrying a few more garments.

A lovely, smiling face surrounded with dark, glossy hair peeped over the top. "I am Alysandir's sister, Sybilla," the young woman said, and with a great heave, she dumped the load of clothes upon the side of the bed Isobella did not occupy. "This is my younger sister, Marion," she said, and Marion dumped her load next to Sybilla's.

Sybilla had very fine hazel eyes and a beautiful face framed by sable brown hair that hung in one long braid down her back. "'Tisn't much," she said, "but 'twill fit ye, I think." She gave Isobella a good going-over from head to foot. Sybilla pulled a garment from the pile and laid it out on the bed next to Isobella. "'Twill do for a sleeping gown."

Isobella looked it over and decided it did indeed look like a nightgown, made of fine white linen and trimmed with a thin edging of lace.

"Thank you for your kindness. I will have a care with them." There was a moment of awkward silence, then, "I'm Isobella Douglas."

She smiled at Marion, who stood quietly to one side, her blond hair in curls, her grey-blue eyes looking at Isobella with great curiosity. "I do hope we will become great friends. I find I am much in need of feminine company."

"Alysandir said the Macleans took yer sister," Marion said.

Isobella nodded. "Yes, and I hope your brothers return with her soon."

"Yer speech is strange," Sybilla said. "Ye are no' English?"

"No, I'm not." She hoped Sybilla wouldn't question her further. She did not want to alienate her new friends. "I apologize for my appearance. I know I look a fright. I hope to change that soon."

Sybilla smiled and said, "Mistress MacMorran will put yer other things in the trunk, and she will be back to aid ye with yer bath since ye canna walk."

Well now, things were definitely looking up, so she thanked Sybilla and Marion. "Please come back to visit me. Often! With my ankle this way, I fear I shall not be able to leave the room for a few days. I would love the pleasure of your company."

Marion said, "I think ye are verra bonnie, and I ken Alysandir thinks so, too." Her face turned a lovely shade of pink, and Sybilla laughed. "We will leave now, but we will visit ye again."

"That would be lovely," Isobella said, thinking the wind must have changed directions, because a delicious smell drifted into the room and she realized just how very, very hungry she was. She was hoping she would be getting something to eat soon.

As if by magic, Mistress MacMorran entered with a large tray in her hands. Isobella eyed the tray and saw something that looked like chicken, a green vegetable she did not recognize, and some fairly dry, crusty bread. She devoured everything, including the bread, which was divine with a swath of butter and a little honey.

Soaking her ankle in the tub did help, and so did the comfrey poultice Mistress MacMorran put over it after Isobella bathed and returned to bed. She glanced to her right and saw that a demijohn of water had been placed on a small, wooden table next to her. She turned her head back to Mistress MacMorran, who was pouring a cup of something dark and red. Isobella eyed it suspiciously.

Watching her with sharp eyes, Mistress MacMorran said, "'Tis cherry-bark tea. Drink it doon, lass. 'Twill ease the pain and help ye sleep," Mistress MacMorran picked up the tray, peered into the goblet to be certain it was all gone, and turned away. She paused long enough at the door to say, "I will come by to see how yer ankle fares on the morrow. Will ye be needing anything else now?"

"No, nothing, thank you. You have been so very kind," Isobella replied. She was the most comfortable she had been since she arrived on Mull.

So why did she wish she could sprout a pair of wings and fly away?

Chapter 18

The mountain sheep are sweeter,
But the valley sheep are fatter;
We therefore deem'd it meeter
To carry off the latter.

—"The War-Song of Dinas Vawr"
  Thomas Love Peacock (1785–1866)
  British satirist and novelist

THE NEXT AFTERNOON, ALYSANDIR PACED THE ROOM
before he stopped in front of the fire, his hands clasped
behind his back. Behind him, his brothers Gavin, Drust,
and Colin were gathered. They had returned to Màrrach
moments earlier without Isobella's sister. Alysandir
paused to search their faces. "So ye never found the
Macleans after they took the lass?"

"Oh, aye, we found them, along with aboot sixty of
their clansmen," Drust said. He was seated on a straight-
backed settle, his legs stretched out toward the fire in
front of him.

Colin seemed to be waiting for one of his brothers to
say something, and when none did, he said, "Alysandir,
ye might have figured out a way to retrieve the lass
without a scuffle, had ye been there, but the two of us
couldna find a way that would allow us to return home
with both our heads attached to the rest o' us."

Alysandir stared into the fire and thought a moment. "Do ye have any idea where they were going to take her?"

"Aye, we followed them," Drust said, then added, "at a distance, of course. They rode right back to Duart Castle, bold as lions and in a verra relaxed way, confident that if we did follow, we wouldna be so foolish as to try and rescue the lass."

"Ye are no thinking of rescuing her from Duart, are ye?" Colin asked.

"Nae, I value my head as much as ye do. 'Twould be a difficult undertaking, for Duart is a formidable fortress, built to withstand attack. Bartering willna work either, although I know that if I offer to arbitrate for the lass, ole Angus will be most agreeable."

"Then what are ye waiting for?" Gavin asked.

Drust's face grew intent. "Think, Gavin. What do we have that Angus Maclean would demand as a fair exchange for the lass?"

Gavin frowned, his dark blue eyes seriously considering his choices. "Ye mean Barbara?"

Drust nodded. "Aye, he would be more than willing to exchange our sister for Elisabeth Douglas, and I'd wager my life on it."

"What will we do, then?" Colin asked softly as he looked from brother to brother.

"I will have to think upon it," Alysandir said. He glanced at his brothers and smiled at the way Gavin was impatient with expectancy and eager to become a part of the discussion, in spite of his younger years.

Drust studied Alysandir's face. "What will ye tell the sister?"

Alysandir shrugged. "I willna tell her anything right

away. She will no' understand why I dinna ride out in the morning to fetch her sister. She will have questions, and she will want answers I dinna have. Ye ken that Duart is a castle that has never been penetrated. Maclean will be prepared and ready for us.

"A daring attack would be foolish and costly with Mackinnon lives, and it is doubtful that we would have the lass even then. Attempting a rescue without a plan is equal to love withoot strategy. Planning is everything." He paused and said with a grin, "Of course, the simplest solution would be for Barbara to change her mind aboot Fergus."

Colin let out a whistle. "Ye are no' going to tell Barbara to marry Fergus Maclean, are ye?"

Alysandir tried to hide his amusement. "Does anyone tell Barbara what to do? And no, I'm not going to tell her to marry him, but I do want to see how she feels aboot it after being at the nunnery this past week. There was a time she fancied Fergus, and if time has brought back that feeling, then the task is an easy one. If she is still adamant aboot not wanting to wed him, then I must come up with a solution."

"What have ye found out aboot the sister? Ye mentioned when we arrived that she hurt her ankle in the fall doon the crag. Is it healing?" Colin asked.

Alysandir nodded. "Aye, 'tis better. 'Twas a nasty tumble she took, and her ankle, though not broken, was dangerously close to it."

"Did she tell ye her story?" asked Drust.

Alysandir shook his head. "Nae, she has yet to speak o' it."

Drust's brows rose and he looked at Colin, whose face

also wore an expression of surprise. "And ye havena pressed her?" Drust asked.

"Nae, I havena."

"Why?" his brothers asked in unison.

"I was hoping the two of ye would return with her sister and I could question Elisabeth aboot it before I heard Isobella's account."

"Ye smell a rat, do ye?" Colin asked.

Alysandir shook his head, conscious of his brothers' gaze upon him. "Nae, but that doesna mean there isna one aboot."

"Ahhh," Drust said. "Ye are going to play the fox."

Cool as a cathedral, Alysandir smiled and turned toward his desk. He poured himself and his brothers Drust and Colin a dram. He handed each of them a silver goblet, and then seeing the disappointed look on Gavin's face, he smiled and poured another one. He extended it toward Gavin and said, "'Tis aboot time ye rid yer face of that goose down."

Gavin jerked his head, tossing his sandy brown hair back and out of his eyes as he sprang to his feet, which set his brothers to laughing. He ignored their teasing jibes. "Ye mean I can shave?" he asked.

The brothers raised their goblets in salute. "Aye, 'tis a man ye have become, Gavin, so shave away, unless ye need us to help ye with yer scraping," answered Alysandir, and a round of laughter erupted when Gavin's face turned as red as a newly bloomed rose.

After a round of teasing, the laughter died down. Alysandir waited to see what his brothers would say. Drust looked thoughtful as he swirled the liquid around in his goblet. He took a sip. "Ye know, Alysandir, that the longer ye wait to tell the lass aboot her sister, the more awkward the spot ye are in. What if she learns we returned afore ye tell her?"

"There are times when one must temper good judgment with silence and, when that doesna work, add in a little deceit. 'Tis a blessing of sorts that she isna oot and aboot right now, due to her ankle. Hopefully, I will have a plan laid soon."

Drust shook his head. "I hear that thin ice ye are walking on cracking under yer feet."

Alysandir went back to the fireplace and placed his goblet on the mantel. He took up the poker and gave the logs a poke or two, enough that sparks swirled about and the flames were fanned to life. When he picked up his goblet and turned back to his brothers, he saw they were grinning at him.

"What mischief are ye aboot, or have ye no told me the entire story of yer encounter with the Macleans?

"We were wondering the same aboot ye," said Drust.

Alysandir regarded his brother with narrowed eyes. "What do ye mean?"

Colin was grinning widely. "Weel, ye havena told us aboot yer journey back to Màrrach with such a bonnie lass. How fared ye with her for two days and one night? Did ye roll her up in yer plaid with ye?"

Alysandir answered coolly, "And if I did?"

Drust looked at Colin and slapped him on the back. "I told ye so. Now ye owe me yer blue velvet doublet."

Colin scowled at his brother and then said, "I have an idea how to solve the problem with the two lassies. If we canna snatch the one lass from under the Macleans' noses at Duart, then we can give them the lass we have here. The lassies want to be united, and I'll wager they dinna care if it is at Màrrach with the Mackinnons or at Duart with the Macleans. Then ye willna have to worrit aboot Isobella discovering we are back or how ye can rescue Elisabeth."

Drust turned back to Alysandir, his grin flashing over the lip of the goblet. "That sounds reasonable and by far the easiest way I've heard yet. We simply give them the one we have. The sisters will be together, and that will be the end of that."

A long silence followed, while every eye was upon Alysandir. When he did not respond after some time, Drust glanced at his brothers and then asked, "Alysandir, ye are no' against Colin's idea, are ye?"

"Nae, I am not against it, but neither am I for it. Therefore, I'll not act upon it."

"Why canna ye act upon it?" Gavin asked. "'Tis the perfect solution."

"Aye, 'tis perfect all right, save for one thing," Alysandir replied, sounding quite amiable.

"And what is that?" Colin asked, itching with curiosity.

Alysandir lifted his goblet, finished the liquid inside, and then said with a dismissive tone, "Mayhap I have discovered a more attractive reason for keeping the lass here."

After his brothers left, Alysandir thought upon his last remark. Isobella had him thinking about things he had not thought about for a long time. He thought about his response to Colin's suggestion. He poured another dram, telling himself it wasn't because he needed it to help resist her. He was past that already.

He desired the lass, and at the same time, he wondered why he didn't make things easier for himself and send her packing to the Macleans as his brothers had suggested. He had enough trouble at the moment without dragging back more in the form of a woman who made his blood run hot.

Suddenly, Drust walked back into the room. After one look at Alysandir, his eyes were alight with humor. "'Twould seem ye are having a bit of a disagreement with yerself. Let me see. It wouldna have to do with that fire-haired lass wi' the emerald eyes, would it?"

"Did ye come back in here to add more dross to the weight of my growing mountain of problems?"

"A growing problem for ye, is she?"

Alysandir did not say anything, but that did not deter Drust. "Weel, that will bear watching, for 'tis obvious that Alysandir, the man, wants her to warm his bed, but she isna the sort of lass to go for that sort of thing. And Alysandir the chief of Clan Mackinnon, willna trust her because he doesna ken if she is a spy. The truth is, he canna trust any woman again.

"Desire and duty. Those are the dilemmas he faces. Mayhap he will find a way to have both the truth and the lass in his bed. Of course, she might refuse to tell him what he wants to know and he canna bring himself to bed her unless she does. 'Twould seem ye are sitting on the sharp horns of a predicament, and all yer alternatives are unsatisfactory ones."

After a long spell of silence, Drust continued, "'Tis not the worst thing in the world for ye to marry again, Alysandir. 'Tis no yer fault that it didna work out before. Ye shouldna let it trouble ye."

Alysandir gave Drust a hard look. "Do I seem troubled?"

Alysandir's voice was almost jovial, but Drust knew his brother well. "Aye, brother, ye do at that, and ye only get that look when it's aboot a woman... or the lack of one."

"Ye should be concerned aboot yer own unmarried state and not mine."

"I know it is difficult to bury the past, but ye canna let what happened before place a shadow upon yer future. Ye are too young to be bitter. Ye have to bury it. If ye did, ye could find love again."

"Love!" Alysandir almost spat out the word. "Och! The last thing I want is to be yoked together with a woman like a pair of Highland cattle. I am done with that, and keep yer thoughts on yer own unmarried state and off of mine. Love is no longer a reality or a desire. I am finished with love, finished with women, and sick of being burdened with both. Love with a woman is impossible."

A log in the fireplace fell with a loud crash and sent a shower of sparks scurrying into the room and across the stone floor. A stand holding a book given to Alysandir by his uncle fell over, and the book landed face up and open.

Drust righted the stand and picked up the large book. He was about to replace it when something caught his eye and he began to read, "'Love feels no burden, thinks nothing of trouble, attempts what is above its strength, pleads no excuse of impossibility,' and the words were meant fer ye." Alysandir looked at Drust with an odd expression. "Read it again," he said, and Drust did.

Alysandir frowned as he looked at the book in Drust's hands. He tried to remember what book it was, but it had been resting in the stand so long without him taking any notice of it that he could remember nothing.

"What book is that? Whose words are those?"

"They are the words of Thomas à Kempis, a German monk and writer. It was written in the early fifteenth century. It would seem he had some words to say to ye." Drust laughed. "Och! 'Twould seem ye are no' so finished with women as ye thought, for as it says, love pleads no excuse of impossibility. 'Twas no accident."

Alysandir shook his head. "The wind blew it over."

Drust laughed. "Say what ye will. I know what yer life has been like. But there are good women in the world, Alysandir, and a good number of them can be trusted."

"I am no' a bitter man but a cautious one. I depend upon no one but myself and trust no one but our uncle and my brothers. My life has been handed over to leading the clan."

"Aye, and ye are fearlessly devoted, for ye have neither dread nor fear of death. 'Tis yer disregard for yersel' that makes ye a dangerous man, for ye will call any man's bluff. 'Tis true ye once married for love, but ye locked away the memory until ye canna recall what it feels like to be in love any more than ye can remember the face of the woman who left ye. Mayhap that is also why ye canna stand the sight of yer son."

Drust's words brought back memories, and Alysandir recalled a point when he had felt the joy of life and living. But that had all been wrung out of him, and he was left with nothing more to give. He slammed his hand down. "Do not speak of them again. They are dead to me."

"Saying doesna make it so. Ye vowed never to allow a woman close enough to betray ye again, yet something within ye hungers to pleasure a woman ye love. Deny it all ye wish, but I know ye keep the beast chained. Whether out of fear or regret, I doubt even ye know."

"Perhaps some men were not meant to be married or to love anyone."

"Aye, just as ye never expected nor wanted to be chief of the Mackinnons, but once the responsibility was on yer shoulders, ye became a fearlessly devoted leader. Ye are dedicated and focused upon being a good shepherd to our clan.

"Ye did not strive to have their adoration, or praise, in a kingly fashion like Argyll. Rather, ye wanted them to feel confidence in yer ability to guide, and secure in yer protection as they went aboot their daily lives. Ye are a strong man, and ye meet yer destiny face to face without wincing."

Drust knew him better than he had thought possible, Alysandir mused silently.

"I know ye have a burden to carry," Drust said. "Just as I know that since the death of James IV, ye have had to learn how to avoid the wrath of that pompous Regent John Stewart and how ye worrit aboot his oversight for the infant king James V. I ken what it must be like fer ye to be always on guard and judging the powerful earls, like Argyll, and holding yer own against them. And there is always the constant threat of England, which is far greater than the feuds amongst the clans."

Alysandir bet Drust did not know about the rumors

THE RETURN OF BLACK DOUGLAS

that England was now using female courtesans—and from time to time, ladies of high rank—to extract information from unwary Scots. He decided to keep that bit of information to himself, even as he wondered if a pair of them had reached Mull.

"So, what do ye intend to do with the lass?"

Alysandir would not deny the possibility of anything concerning Isobella. "I intend to watch her as closely as an enemy."

"Mayhap ye will be the lion what lay doon with the lamb, as our uncle said. The lass seem harmless enough."

"Aye, the lion would lay doon with the lamb," Alysandir said, "but I doubt that the lamb would get much sleep."

Drust laughed, and Alysandir looked down at his empty goblet and considered filling it again. But he had tried that before, and he learned it was a temporary cure. Once he was sober, the problems that sent him to drink in the first place were still there. He slammed the goblet down and slumped back into his chair, wondering if all of this would ever end.

He rarely admitted it to himself, but he knew that deep in the innermost part of him there still existed a remnant of the man who wanted the love of a good woman. Now the question seemed to be: Was the fear of pain greater than his desire? What would he risk to allow a woman into his life again? He glanced at Drust.

"Don't ye have something ye need to see aboot?"

"Nae, I would rather watch ye squirm and apply all yer logic to a situation that ye dinna have any control over. Ye want the lass, but ye dinna want to admit it. So, let the lass go to be with her sister. I will accompany her to Duart, and ye will be done with it. Ye canna win if ye keep her. She is different from all the rest. Ye have only met her and look at what it has done to ye. Let her go."

Alysandir slammed his hand down upon his desk. "She stays! And ye'd best find something that diverts yer attention or I will send ye to Iona to spend some time praying with our dear uncle."

The sound of Drust's laughter followed him from the room. After he was gone, Alysandir hurled the decanter across the room. The sound of the glass falling was as musical as the sound of her voice. He pulled his mind away from Isobella, the desirable one, and concentrated on Isobella, the woman he did not trust.

All war is based on deception, therefore when capable, feign incapacity, and when active, appear inactive. He now wondered if her ankle truly was as bad as she let on. True, it was swollen, but that also would be the perfect cover.

Isobella was his captive. She could not be trusted, and until she proved differently, she would be his enemy. He thought of the dream he had had the night before Isobella appeared in the glen, imagining her as the willing fantasy lover he craved to see again. He ached to have her in his bed waiting to be delighted.

He hadn't cared who his fantasy lover was or where she came from. She hadn't asked for promises he could not keep or vows in which he no longer believed. He wished Isobella had come to him like that with no mystery, no secrets, just smoldering passion. Impossible, of course, but perhaps that was the purpose of the dream after all. He hoped Isobella would drive him as wild as the fantasy.

He did not know if he could trust her. But he did want to bed her.

Chapter 19

Can I see another's woe,
And not be in sorrow too?
Can I see another's grief,
And not seek for kind relief?

—"On Another's Sorrow," 1789
   William Blake (1757–1827)
   British poet, painter, engraver, and mystic

THE NEXT MORNING, ISOBELLA HEARD THE RATTLE AND clank of armor and the nickering of horses coming from the courtyard below. She had learned from Marion the day before that Alysandir and his men were leaving on a hunting trip.

She was still fretting about Elisabeth. It had been a week since she was captured, and still there had been no word about her sister or Alysandir's two brothers. She would have to be patient. If his brothers were anything like Alysandir, they would do their best to find Elisabeth. The only good thing that had happened was that her ankle was healing and she could walk on it with the slightest limp.

She was sitting in the solar with Alysandir's sisters, Sybilla and Marion, who were becoming her good friends. She was beyond thankful for their companionship and help, for she would have been bored out of her mind and sick of her room, were it not for them.

Coming to the solar to sew with them had become a daily occurrence. Today, they undertook the impossible task of teaching her to embroider. They were working on valances in tent stitch. She watched them quietly stitching with a precision she would never be able to attain.

After about fifteen minutes, she was still trying to get a bit of wool yarn jabbed through the eye of her needle. She glanced enviously at the sisters' canvases, with their elaborate tendrils of fruit, colorful and exotic flowers, and brilliant foliage winding around tree trunks, and let out a sigh of defeat.

"There seems to be an awful lot of yarn for the wee eye of this needle."

The sisters laughed, and Sybilla said, "It takes a lot of practice."

"I don't think I will live long enough to learn. Perhaps I should try stable mucking."

When the laughter quieted down, Marion said, "Perhaps ye could read to us while we embroider."

Isobella shook her head. "My Latin is best read silently. My Gaelic vocabulary is miserably inadequate."

"Alysandir has a few books in English in his library," Sybilla said.

Isobella had replied that she liked the idea when they heard a loud commotion coming from the courtyard, followed by the clatter of horses' hooves, and the ring and jostling of bridles and equipment.

Sybilla sprang out of her chair and hurried to the window. "Alysandir and our brothers are coming through the gates now," she said. Marion and Isobella joined her to crowd around the window for a look. Isobella

recognized Alysandir as he pushed back the hood of his
hauberk and the sun drew out the richness of his hair,
dark as the wood of the ebony tree.

About that time, another horse snorted and danced
sideways, bumping into Alysandir's horse, which
reared, pawing the air with his forelegs. Alysandir acted
with swift confidence to bring his mount under control.
Gallagher was a lot like his master, for both possessed
latent strength and a capacity for violence. The way the
two of them worked together was quite a magnificent
sight to watch.

"Alysandir is a fine horseman," Isobella said. He was
about to dismount, and she stepped upon a stool to get
a better view. Just as she did so, he glanced toward the
window and nodded in her direction.

Sybilla gasped and brought her hand up to her chest
with open-mouthed amazement. "Did ye see that?
Alysandir nodded at ye. I havena seen him do that before."

Isobella did not want to be singled out, so she replied,
"He was being courteous."

"Nae. He recognized ye in front of all and sundry,"
she said, with a shy smile that made her lovely grey-
blue eyes shine as brilliantly as the golden locks of hair
braided on top of her head.

"I don't know why. I've been nothing but a thorn in
his side."

"That isna what Alysandir said," Sybilla replied. "He
was most full of praise aboot ye."

Isobella glanced at Sybilla, who smiled inno-
cently, which was her way of letting their visitor
know that was all she was going to say on the subject.
Isobella was thinking that some handsome knight like

Alysandir should be nodding at Sybilla. Her lovely sable brown curls brought out the vivid golden color in her hazel eyes.

"I see Colin and Drust. They must have met up with the hunting party," Marion said, then added softly, "Oh dear." She turned to Isobella. "I am sorry but I canna see any sign of yer sister."

Isobella frantically searched the bailey, but there was no sign of Elisabeth. She could not hide her disappointment. "If those English bastards have taken her!"

Sybilla put her arm around Isobella's shoulders. "Dinna fret. Alysandir willna give up. They will find her. Alysandir knows Angus Maclean is a shrewd old fox. He will find a way to rescue her."

"We should put away our sewing for today," Marion said, rising. "It is almost time for supper."

Isobella hurried to her chamber to find a dress. Choosing one wouldn't be a difficult decision since only three dresses graced her trunk. A seamstress had taken her measurements and fabrics had been chosen, so her sparse wardrobe would soon be adequately replenished. Not wanting to draw attention to herself, she chose the deep blue gown, without ornate trim, over the ruby silk.

She was a bit apprehensive about seeing Alysandir at dinner. They had not had much contact since her arrival. Yet she knew he would not wait forever to hear her story. After her bath, her skin was baby soft and just as pink, and she smelled faintly of heather. She took extra care with her hair, twisting it into a bun of sorts, and missed the big mirror she had at home. She eyed the small hand mirror and reminded herself that by sixteenth-century standards, she was most fortunate to have even that.

With trembling hands, she slipped the blue silk over her head and was grateful when Sybilla and Marion came and helped her with all the buttons. When they entered the Great Hall a few minutes later, Marion and Sybilla lagged, leaving Isobella to make her entry alone.

The moment she stepped into the hall, everyone stared and all conversation died away. Across the room, Alysandir heard the whispers and then the silence. He looked up and saw a beauty walk into the hall with his sisters not far behind. She looked familiar, and then the realization hit him with the swiftness of a striking sword.

"Is that Isobella?" Gavin asked.

"Aye. Every desirable, beautiful inch."

"'Twould seem ye are the envy of every man in the hall," Ronan said. "I can certainly see why."

"Do not take a fancy to the lass," Alysandir warned.

Ronan laughed and slapped his brother on the back. "Not to worrit. I value my life too much."

Alysandir swallowed, his hand almost crushing the silver cup in his hand. He knew the beauty was Isobella, but his mind could not seem to accept the idea. All he could think was, it had been a good thing she wasna dressed like that in the glen because he wasna certain he could have kept his gentlemanly manners.

He saw her uncertainty and knew she did not know what was expected of her or where she should sit, but having him come to her rescue would do her more harm. Thankfully, Marion and Sybilla appeared, and flanking her, they accompanied her rest of the way.

He had never seen a dress fit a woman so well. He

had not thought about it, but now he could see that she was well blessed where she should be, filling out the bosom of her dress and leaving plenty of enticement above the décolletage. There wasn't a ripple or a loose place anywhere. The dress almost looked like it had been painted on her.

She carried herself like a queen,: graceful, regal, and dignified. She was all woman and every inch a lady, and he had never seen her equal, not even in Paris. He was thinking she would make the perfect mistress, but at the same time, he wondered if she would accept such a role. Beautiful, arousing, and complicated meant nothing but trouble.

Isobella took the seat, while Alysandir watched her from across the hall. She found it a bit disconcerting, but by the time supper was over and the tables were cleared, he was no longer there. The experience became rather like performing a play with no one in the audience.

In his absence, she was lighthearted and gay, and although she would have loved to join the dancing after the meal, she did not want to stress her ankle, nor was she ready to draw unnecessary attention to herself. Instead, she engaged in conversation with members of Alysandir's family and a few of the bolder clan members who came to meet her, curious about her strange speech and sudden appearance at the castle.

At one point, Drust rescued her. "We must let the lass rest," he told the others. "She has done naught but answer questions fer the past week. 'Tis a wonder she doesna have crossed eyes from all of it."

"Oh, but I do," she said and crossed her eyes and joined in the laughter.

During the ensuing lull, she studied the hall, especially the murals, which were painted in vivid, prime colors to depict heraldic, religious, and historical themes. Carved stone corbels bore the arms of the Mackinnons including those through intermarriage. The huge fireplace, with its stone-carved lintel, depicted the face of the ancient Celtic green man, leaves sprouting from his head.

Above the lintel was an overmantel hung with a shield bearing the chief's crest. The flagstone floors were thankfully bare, free of reed mats or the flowers and herbs typically scattered over the floors during this time period.

This was Renaissance Scotland on an evening very removed from her time. It was an historian's dream come true, experiencing this race of hardy people living in a stern and sometimes comfortless manner, always mindful of a neighboring realm that was richer, larger, and more powerful. They lived amid jealous kings and betrayals among powerful families, all vying for control and position.

It was a place of myth and mystery, a place of mountain tarn and moors, of mist-shrouded crags, soaking rains, and never-ending jealousies and feuds between warring clans. And yet, they were a resilient race, strong, robust, hard-headed, quick to draw a sword, resolute, family oriented and distrustful, yet oddly accepting of a stranger in need who was very far from home.

Drust said something to Colin, who replied louder than he should have. "Nae, I wasna born under a lusting planet."

Everyone laughed, and Isobella's head went back as her hand came up to her throat. As she caught her breath, she discovered that Alysandir had returned. He was deep in conversation, which gave her ample time to study him. He was absolutely the sexiest man she had ever seen. And wasn't he just the epitome of elegance in his velvet doublet and white shirt, with his hair neatly tied back?

Then their eyes met, and he gave her a slow grin. She smiled and looked away, for she was growing weary and she had sipped at least two glasses of wine. When Sybilla whispered that she and Marion were leaving, Isobella responded quickly that she would go with them.

Once she was in her room, she undressed quickly and settled herself comfortably in bed. She was barely asleep when a violent storm blew in from the Atlantic. She opened her eyes and yawned, thankful she was safe, warm, and dry, and then fell asleep again. She slept soundly until a sudden crash of thunder jerked her awake. Another ear-splitting boom followed, louder than the one before.

She listened to the roar of wind and the explosive leaps of thunder that rattled the crags in the distance while jagged flashes of lightning ripped across the sky, filling her room with light. Wind roared down the chimney and fanned to life a small blaze, which she welcomed.

Strange though it was, she conjured the memory of the heat emanating from the Mackinnon's body the night they had slept together in the glen, wrapped in his plaid. She sighed when she remembered the way he had taken her hand and held it against his chest.

A fool's counsel from a wise head…or is it wise counsel from a fool's head?

Her eyes popped open, and she looked around the

room. She saw nothing, but that did not mean the Black Douglas was not there. Was he trying to warn her? Or was he trying to play the court jester? Where was he?

Now you see him; now you don't.

"I know you are here, so you might as well show yourself."

"I have been here for some time."

She whipped her head around and saw him, a shadow in the dark corner. "Sir James, have you misbehaved and been confined to the dark corner by the gods?"

"'*Far an taine 'n abhainn, 's ann as mo a fuaim.*'"

"I am supposed to understand that?"

"Where the stream is shallowest, greatest is its noise."

"I have asked you to visit me many times and you've never come, and now when I am asleep you pop up."

"A little neglect may breed mischief."

"Mine or yours?"

He laughed. "If this poor ghostie ha' offended."

"I am not going to ask you about Elisabeth."

"Then I will tell you that she is well, but then I could be speaking falsely."

"When are we going back home?"

"Did I say ye were ever going home?"

Her heart seemed to stop beating. "But, you said— you cannot mean to leave us here."

"Ye make insufficient conclusions from sufficient premises."

"I didn't say anything."

"Did I say it was now?

He gave her a Mona Lisa smile and vanished.

She was glad he had come, if for no other reason than to know he had not forgotten about her. She stared at the uncovered window, watching the lightning flash bright as the beam of a lighthouse. She wished someone had had the forethought to draw the tapestry. When the next slash of lightning illuminated her room, she decided to close it herself and made her way to the window.

Her attention was drawn to the figure of a man. She frowned, for she was certain it was Alysandir standing there, wrapped in the fury of the wind and swirling mist. He was staring out over the vast darkness, toward where the battered shores of Mull met the waters of the Atlantic.

What was he doing standing on the battlement walk in the midst of a storm? Was a ship running aground? Lightning flashed. She saw his head thrown back while rain pelting his face. And then she had a horrible thought. Was he contemplating suicide?

A storm such as she had never seen was setting in, and still he did not leave. She didn't know what to do. She couldn't tear herself away from the window. There was something achingly sorrowful, even dangerous about his dark figure and the agony she sensed that had drawn him to the water. Another serrated flash of light split the night sky. And at that moment, he turned to look at the window where she stood.

They remained as they were, each staring at the other for a moment or two, before he drew together the cape that whipped wildly about him and turned away. Then, he did something that made her heart stop. Instead of turning back to the castle, he walked closer to the edge and leaned out over the embrasure.

Terrified he was going to jump, she grabbed her cape and hurried down the stairs, rushing past two surprised guards and a drowsy hound before she reached the door that led to the parapet wall.

Alysandir felt the yank on his arm and turned to see Isobella standing beside him, wild-eyed, as she tugged on his sleeve.

"Don't do it! Nothing can be bad enough for that. Once you jump, there will be no going back."

Alysandir stared at her, not understanding her gibberish until he saw the terrified expression on her face just before she threw her arms around him. She looked pleadingly into his eyes and said, "Please, I beg you. Don't jump!"

Jump? He was about to laugh outright, or at least chastise her, and then order her back to her bedchamber. But something about the desperation in her voice touched him and gentled his spirit. He looked down at her upturned face, and the blood began to run thick and heavy in his veins as an aching need for her gripped him low in his belly.

Her braids had come undone, and her hair fell in a wet, tangled mass down to her waist. Water ran in streams over her face, causing her eyelashes to clump together, but her trembling mouth, so soft and full, was his undoing.

With a muffled oath, he took her in his arms and crushed her against himself, consumed with dark, primal lust. Her mouth tasted sweet and lushly potent, and he was consumed by an aching desire to know what it felt like to be inside her. He wanted to absorb her into himself, to possess her in a way that she would never be able to forget. Nor would she want to.

Her slender arms were clamped tightly around his neck. In spite of the two cloaks between them, the hard press of her body inflamed him. He kissed her again as all about them rain poured down and the wind blew.

Her mouth was wild and hunger-laced and equal to his wild craving. She was achingly beautiful with her lips swollen from his kisses, and he could see desire burning deep in her eyes. Was he dreaming? Was this the woman of his wild fantasy? Was she his dream lover? Or was this truly Isobella he held?

Mayhap she is the granite crag upon which thou will wreck…

For a moment, her image seemed to blur before him. Whichever she was, she was here in his arms, and he did not care if she was a fantasy or not. He wanted to devour her with more than just his eyes and taste more than her lips.

"Come inside," she pleaded. "We can talk about it."

Part of him wanted to turn away and leave her. Part of him wanted to carry her back into the castle and make love to her until the sun was high in the sky. No part of him wanted to talk. "I want to do more than talk, lass," he said, and he swept her up and into his arms.

He carried her inside, his body hard and throbbing with desire. He wanted to fill her with himself and spill his seed in the bed of her warmth. Her delicate arms were still wound around his neck, and she laid her head against his chest until he pushed the door to her room open and carried her inside. She lifted her head and looked around. "I thought we were going somewhere to talk."

"We are somewhere. We can talk here."

She lifted one eyebrow so doubtfully that he wanted to laugh. But he held the urge in check, for his desire to bed her superseded all. The humor drained away. He lowered her to her feet in front of the fireplace, surprised to see the fire still blazed so far into the night, something he accepted as a boon.

Firelight adored her face and tinted the copper spirals of her wet hair with the brilliance of rubies. He closed his eyes and imagined her standing thus, the golden glow of the fire upon her naked skin, and wearing naught but his mother's ruby necklace. He would bathe her in the nectar of brandewijn and make himself drunk on the taste of her velvety skin.

The bottle he had sent to ease the pain of her ankle still stood upon the tray near the bed. He filled a goblet from the bottle, and when he turned toward her, he was breathless at the sight of her. Her cape had fallen open to reveal a nightgown the color of the sun—pale and amber—the damp fabric draping her damp body and flirting with her hips. He drank deeply, wanting to warm his blood and stoke the fire in his loins.

His head felt light and his body hot. He frowned and gazed down at the goblet still in his hand. He did not drink enough to be drunk, and he wasn't dreaming. Yet the lines separating what was real, what he dreamt, and what he desired had disappeared. All was illusory.

He could not go back to his life as it had been before. Her coming had changed that. It was not her fault, nor was it his. It was not the fault of desire or the lack of it. It was not the fault of having a woman in his life or having none. The fault lay with this woman, because she was different.

She filled his thoughts by day and tormented his sleep at night. He desired her, and the yearning rose in him as the sap rises in a tree. He wanted that part of her that was warm and naïve, kind and curious, considerate, and full of empathy. He welcomed her lightheartedness and her laughter and the companionship he had with her. He enjoyed her odd way of expressing herself and, yes, even her outspoken ways. But he did not want to.

"Ye came to me on the parapet. Was it to tempt me?"

"It will take me the rest of the night to dry my clothes and hair and to warm my body—a little extreme for sport. I thought you were going to jump. I wanted to prevent it if I could."

He almost laughed, until he saw the way her eyes glistened as she drew the cloak tightly about herself and turned toward the fire. "I think you should go now. It will be daylight soon. I need to dry my hair and get out of these wet clothes."

"And would it have bothered you if I had jumped?"

She whirled around, her eyes flashing angrily. "Of course it would! I am not a hard-hearted wretch! You saved my life. I owe you a tremendous debt. How could I hope to gain anything by your death when you have treated me with every kindness and sheltered me in your home?"

"Those are the only reasons?"

She shrugged. "I like you. You are brave and strong, yet your heart is kind, your manner gentle, and your heart pure. You have a great future ahead of you. Your clan and your country need you. And I am indebted to you. Why would I want to watch you jump if I could prevent it?"

He gazed down into her upturned face, mesmerized by her eyes, huge and luminous, and he felt another little part of him open to her. Looking into her eyes was like staring into a clear loch, for beneath the surface there was nothing he feared, nothing that troubled him or made him distrust her.

"And if I wished to collect upon the debt ye owe me this verra night? What would ye say?" He fought against the dizziness of desire. Och, he could take her right now, standing up, on the floor, straddling her in the bed, tupping her backed against the wall.

He took her chin in his hand and tilted her face and saw that her expression was watchful, almost fearful. The lamplight filtering through her long lashes left a fringe of a shadow upon her porcelain cheek.

There was honesty in her eyes, and he knew her capable of telling the truth, yet something did not sit well with him. It was like a burr that pricked at him each time he moved, a reminder that he needed to dig deeper, to find the real reason she was here. And therein lay the crux of the matter.

He wanted to learn the truth, but he wanted her to tell him because she wanted to, not because he forced it from her. "Ye have naught to fear from me." He wanted to be close to her on this night. He needed her warmth, her softness, her understanding, her tolerant manner to make him forget the women in his past, if only for a short while.

She studied him with eyes green as the mossy stones in Macquarrie's burn. He needed no further prompting, for simply talking to her turned him to stone. His thumb stroked the fullness of the mouth he had wanted to kiss since she walked into the hall tonight, wearing the gown that fit every supple inch of her.

His mouth slid over hers in a hard kiss that grew more demanding as he felt her arms go around him. She groaned, and his body leapt in response. His hand covered her breast, and he felt her softness through the thin fabric of her gown. He pulled away from her and whispered Gaelic phrases in her ear.

"Let me make love to ye."

"No…"

"Aye," he said, and his hand lifted the damp gown so he could touch her smooth skin. Her softness made him groan. He touched her gently, insane with wanting. "Ye are denying what ye want, and yer body is the proof."

"It isn't the first time my body and my mind did not agree." She pushed against him. "I can't."

He wanted to teach her to make love with him and to him, to bring her pleasure and to show her how to bring pleasure to him. He knew it would be perfect between them, and he would give her anything she desired…

Except marriage…

He pushed the thought aside. His hand trembled when he lifted one copper curl and rubbed the damp, silky texture between his fingers. "So lovely to look at. So desirable to touch. So impossible to trust."

Her look of confusion turned to shame and remorse, born of a brief moment of pleasure. He sensed the sudden shift, the cool withdrawal. She wasn't going to give in to him now. What kind of sorceress was she? For she tempted him even with her denial.

Chapter 20

A primrose by a river's brim
A yellow primrose was to him,
And it was nothing more.

—*Peter Bell*, 1819
  William Wordsworth (1770–1850)
  English poet

ISOBELLA'S FIRST IMPULSE WAS TO SLAP HIM, BUT SHE KNEW his actions were partly her fault. He kissed her, and she kissed him back. Her arms went around him, and she groaned low in her throat. She did nothing to stop him when he put his hand on her breast. She was ready when he touched her. He knew exactly what that meant, and he was right. She had gone to him in a thin, linen nightgown and ended up here in a candlelit room, with Mr. Darcy peering down at her in his wet shirt. She had let him think that he could come to her room and she would melt against him.

But now his words stopped her, and his next question was the one she feared the most. "Who are ye? Ye appear suddenly out of nowhere and willna tell me from whence ye came. Ye wear strange clothes and speak English with an unknown accent. Ye and yer sister were alone with naught a possession but yer satchels.

"Ye act cold and withdrawn one moment, then ye melt

in my arms when I least expect it. Ye can bare yer heart to me one moment, only to be shrouded in mist and mystery the next. I find ye so beautiful I ache and so full of suspect I want to lock ye away. So tell me, mistress, who are ye and why were ye spying on me from the window?"

His voice was thick, and his finger stroked her cheek. "Did ye find out what ye wanted to know? Will ye send word to someone that I am here at Màrrach? Will there be hell to pay when I leave here on the morrow? What is the real reason ye are here?"

She was flabbergasted. "I don't know what makes you think I am a spy," she said, and that much was true. Spying on him was absurd, but he had no way of knowing that, and she wasn't ready to tell him. Not until they found Elisabeth.

His hands came up and closed around her neck. His thumbs stroked the hollow of her throat where her blood pounded. Her eyes never left his face. Her body trembled from fear, and yet something about him made her hope for the best. He could snap her neck with ease, or he might decide to press his thumbs just a little bit harder and harder still, until her lungs screamed for air.

She looked away and closed her eyes. Her heart cracked like the shell of an egg, and disappointment flowed swiftly throughout her body. She was so attracted to him. She had seen him as her ideal, her Mr. Darcy. But the real Mr. Darcy would never have made her feel so cheap or so insignificant, so capable of bringing him harm.

The beautiful iridescent bubble of her romantic notions, nurtured for a lifetime, suddenly burst and left behind a cold emptiness. Nothing mattered now except finding

Elisabeth and asking that interfering Black Douglas to do his best to send them back to their time, and failing that, at least to help them get far, far away from here.

"Have ye found what ye came here for? Are ye an English spy? Tell me. Are ye?"

"How could you accuse me?"

He stroked her cheek and cupped her chin, lifting her face so he could see her eyes. He searched the depths for an uncomfortable length of time before saying, "The fairest face, the falsest heart."

Pain turned to anger, and she shoved his hand away. "You dare to call me false-hearted when you have nothing to base that upon? Am I not innocent until you prove me guilty? Where is the evidence of my duplicity?" She glanced away. "I am not the monster you make me out to be. I am innocent, and you are wrong to persecute me unjustly. I am telling the truth."

His gaze didn't waver. "Ye could also be lying. Ye could be a spy. Ye could be many things, and until ye can convince me otherwise, ye are, at present, someone I canna trust."

She drew back her hand to slap him, but he caught her by the wrist.

"I wouldna advise that," he said coldly.

He jerked her against him. "Let me see what wiles ye would have used to wheedle the information from me. Ye have the mouth of a courtesan, so use it." His mouth came down upon hers, hard. He kissed her with arrogance, abandon, and so much anger that it made her lips numb. He drove his tongue into her mouth again and again, while his fingers dug into the skin of her arms and then moved up to her hair.

He broke the kiss, and his hands covered her ears as he held her head in place so she could not move it. He wanted to master her, to show her he could control her and bend her to his will and that he could force his kiss upon her whenever it suited him.

But she saw the sadness in his eyes. Yes, he knew he could force his kiss upon her, but he would never, ever force her to kiss him back.

He released her, and she wiped her hand across her mouth. "You provoke me and think that will make me meekly submit? You will never bend me to your will like that."

Alysandir was breathing hard, whether with passion or fury, she was not sure. "I think it is time ye told me the truth, mistress, and end this suspicion between us once and for all."

She sighed wearily, wishing she knew how to get them off this merry-go-round they seemed doomed to ride in circles for forever, it seemed. "I am not an English spy or any other kind of spy. I do not know the first thing about spying. I did not come here for any reason, and if you really want to know, I'm not sure how I ended up here."

A fool will try by force or skill, but ne'er can bend a woman's will. Alysandir leaned his head back and closed his eyes and tried to still the wild rushing of his blood.

Isobella saw the thick veins in his neck and listened to his rapid breathing and knew he fought a war within himself. In the shadowy glow from the tapers in the candelabra beside him, he looked like a being from the netherworld with his wet hair and flexed jaw muscles. When he opened his eyes, she saw such pain and despair that she immediately thought of Dante's words, "Abandon all hope, ye who enter here," and she wondered what could be so terrible that it tormented him so.

She had no answers, but she knew the cause was more than simply suspicion. There was distrust in his gaze, yes, and it was aimed at her, but she wasn't the one who had earned it. She knew now that, without a doubt, at some time in his life a woman had hurt him so deeply that he seemed to have difficulty drawing the line between them. What surprised her most, though, was that instead of firming her resolve, his emotional scars actually softened her feelings toward him.

The power emanating from his tense body enveloped her. She recalled him riding between the two thieves, sword held high as he slashed right and left and killed them both. He was not a weakling she could toy with or put off for very long. Besides, toying with men had never been her forte.

Even now, she could feel herself drawn toward him, moth to flame, possessed and consumed. She inhaled deeply and looked away, but that did not release her from the bondage of his gaze.

"You should go now. I am tired. I am exhausted mentally by you, from thinking about my sister, all of it." She turned away from him and went to sit on the bed. She stared at the hands folded in her lap. Instead of turning away, he joined her.

"Lovely Isobella, beautiful and mysterious, I yearn to make love with ye. Why do ye resist so?"

She turned her head away and thought of the man in her dream whose gentle touch had made her respond without fear, without distrust. Why couldn't Alysandir be that man? She felt hopeless. She would never be able to convince him of her innocence, and it seemed pointless to try. She sighed wistfully. Did it really matter?

She did not belong here. This was not her time. These were not her people. She had a home, a family, and a country that lay centuries away. She could not give her heart and fall in love with a man who only existed in the past, any more than she could give her heart to a man who suspected the worst of her—a man who branded her a spy before he heard her story. It pained her deeply to realize Alysandir wasn't the romantic hero she had pegged him to be. In truth, he was no more attainable than her romantic dreams of Mr. Darcy.

"Ye canna win, lass. There is no escape from Màrrach, and if by some miracle ye were able to do so, ye would not survive long out there alone."

Why? Why was she here? Why was this happening to her? And where was that sovereign of insufferables, the Black Douglas?

Isobella stared blankly at him. "At least I would have a chance out there."

He remained silent, his gaze hard and unsympathetic. She was caught completely off guard when he lifted his hand and gently stroked her cheek with his knuckles. "Ye are a comely lass, and that will serve ye in far better stead than resentment and anger."

Then he stood, and she watched him cross the room in a few short strides. He took the silver goblet from the mantel and poured a generous amount of brandewijn. He carried it back to her. "Drink it doon."

Her hand trembled as she reached for the goblet. "It isn't mead."

"Drink it doon!"

She did as he asked without saying anything. When she had finished, she handed him the goblet. "My throat is on fire. What else must I endure before I can sleep?"

"And is it so bad… to be here with me?"

"There have been moments…" She let the word drift away.

"Moments?"

"Yes, brief ones, when I forget your distrust and your anger and find myself liking you, but then you turn on me and become cold and accusatory. I remember what I have been through and how much of what has happened to me is something that I cannot understand or control.

"My heart is heavy. I wish I could go home, but I fear that option will never present itself to me. When I first met you, I trusted you enough to go with you. I thought you would help me. I thought you were different. I thought you were nice. I was wrong."

His face came closer until his lips were warm against her cheek and then her throat, while, at the same time, his hands went around her. He pulled her close and held her tightly, as he whispered against her hair, "I am nice."

Whatever it was she had drunk, it must have been working, for she couldn't seem to muster an ounce of resistance, and her brain completely deserted her. Oh dear, now he was kissing the curve of her collarbone and moved back to the hollow of her throat.

His lips were soft and warm, and for a moment, she forgot who she was. Just for a moment. Then it hit her. She was kissing a man five hundred years her senior. Talk about an older man. But a kiss was a kiss in any century, and he was good at it, very, very good.

She moaned, low in her throat, and he responded by pulling her closer. Her arms came up of their own accord to slip around his neck. Her heart pounded wildly. She had trouble breathing. She felt her resistance fading.

"Why are you doing this to me?"

"I wish to God I knew. I am trapped in this eddy along with ye," he said, lying down beside her and nuzzling her ear. He pulled her close and buried his face in the smooth slope of her neck and shoulder, drawing her against the hard length of his body. He placed soft, gentle kisses along the line from her shoulder to her ear and then plunged his hands into the thick coppery strands of her hair.

She moaned and he kissed her, whispering words against her throat. "I canna think when I am with ye. I am like a wild animal pacing in a cage and ye are on the outside. I want ye until I ache, but I canna do anything aboot it. And still I yearn. I ken ye dinna feel the same aboot me and that I should leave ye be. I dinna want to drive ye away, and yet I canna let ye go."

Her voice was low, pensive. "When I was little, someone brought a small wildcat to my father. Its leg was broken in a trap. After my father set the leg, I cared for the animal, feeding and soothing it as best I could. I came to love it, and when my father said it was time to let it go, I cried and begged him to let me keep it.

"But, he said, 'Isobella, you cannot tame something that is wild. You cannot keep it from being what it was born to be. Its life is out there with the other wild creatures like it. To keep it here, in a cage, would please you, but it would be nothing like the life he deserves. Sometimes, caring for something means letting it go.'"

"I dinna want to tame ye, Isobella, and I dinna want to force ye to do something ye dinna want to do or to be what ye dinna want to be. But I am a man and I desire ye and I ken ye have some feeling for me. I willna force ye, and I willna stop trying to persuade ye. But if ye say no, I will stop. 'Tis fair, no?"

"And if I ask you to let me go?"

"'Tis a moot point, for ye have nowhere to go. In case ye dinna ken, Mull has few settlements and five clans who live here. Our castles are the center of our lives and our means of protection.

"'Tis not like Paris or London, where ye can hire someone to drive ye to another place. We have no roads, no towns. A woman traveling alone would be beyond dangerous. Aye, I could take ye where ye wanted to go, but what would that solve? Even if ye went to live with the Macleans, I ken ye would come to regret it and wish ye were back here."

"I would not, for Elisabeth would be there with me."

"I have said I would find yer sister and bring her here, and I will honor my word. 'Tis no simple matter and will require planning, imagination, and cleverness, for Angus Maclean is a wily old fox who takes great pride in rejecting each offer I make. Can ye no' be patient, lass?"

She had no comeback, for she knew one thing about Alysandir Mackinnon and that was he spoke the truth.

"Is it fair enough?" he asked.

"'Tis fair, yes," she said, mimicking him, then followed it with a weak smile.

"Keep looking at me like that, and I'll change my mind. Forbidden fruit tastes sweetest."

She did not say anything. She couldn't. She wasn't too experienced in sexual matters. Plenty of guys had tried to put a move on her, and plenty had tried to persuade her to have sex, but she had never had sex with anyone until she was engaged. She'd wasted it on Jackson, thinking herself in love with him and too naïve to see that he was nothing but a womanizer.

And then Alysandir comes along. He pushed her back and rolled on top of her. "Ye know what I think? I think ye dinna know what ye want. I think ye want to mate with me but yer afraid to admit it." He kissed her nose. "I did say I would do my best to persuade ye."

"It wouldn't take much," she said and closed her eyes.

"Isobella, look at me," he said, kissing her face.

Her eyes opened. "Why?"

He nuzzled her neck and whispered, "Because I want to see in yer eyes what it does to ye when I touch ye like this." He drew one finger over her lips and down her throat to her chest and then between her breasts.

Her breathing quickened.

"I want to see what it does to ye when I kiss ye here."

He followed the same trail his finger had taken a moment before, only this time he pulled the tie at her neck and pushed her gown apart. He kissed the crowns of each of her breasts.

"I want to see what it does when I move like this." He pressed his hips against her, and God help her, she began to breathe heavily.

"Ye belong to me," he said, whispering the words against her mouth, "only ye refuse to admit it, even to yerself. But ye will. One day, ye will."

Was it his voice that made her feel groggy and stupid?

Or was it the drink he had given her? Shivers rippled across her. She felt hot at every point where they touched.

"Yer face can drive a man wild with wanting. I have thought of naught but lying with ye like this." He lifted his hand and pushed her damp hair back away from her face, and then he lightly traced the outline of her lips with his finger, stroking, teasing, driving her pulse wild, and set her heart to beating triple time. She studied his face intently, the dark eyebrows, the long, black hair, the full lips, the flare of nostrils, the eyes dilated heavily with desire.

He kissed her throat, whispering words in Gaelic, throwing her heart and her mind into utter confusion. He kissed her shoulders, his breath rapid and hot in her ear when he took the tip of her lobe between his teeth.

His touch sent ripples of intense desire over her, wave after intense wave, until she moaned. He took the sound of it into his mouth with a kiss so gentle that she felt she could cry. How did he know how to tear down all her defenses and leave her mindless with desire? She wanted him, so much she could not think of anything but feeling him inside her.

If he had opened his trews and pressed against her, she would have opened her legs and welcomed him.

And he knew it.

Yet he did not stop kissing her. It was delicate, elusive, his tongue cunning and skillful, teasing, tasting, flirting with her, then penetrating deeply and thoroughly. When he finished, she knew without a doubt that she had been kissed thoroughly by someone who knew an awful lot about kissing and must have devoted a great deal of time to practicing it.

When he broke the kiss, she sighed and went limp. Then she felt him shaking. It was nothing more than a low rumbling, like thunder rolling over distant hills.

The bastard was laughing. At her!

She wanted to hit him. She doubled up her fist and would have connected with his arrogant nose, if he hadn't grabbed her arm. Embarrassment oozed from every pore, and she squeezed her eyes shut so she did not have to look at the triumphant gleam in his eyes.

"Ye canna deny it. Ye wanted me to kiss ye like that. Ye want me to kiss ye like that again. I could feel it. Ye can fight me with yer words all ye like, but yer body does not lie. I dinna know when it will be, but fair Isobella, I will penetrate yer defenses and yer maidenhead, and ye willna say a word to stop me."

It was her turn to laugh.

"Why do ye laugh?"

"You can penetrate my defenses but not my maidenhead. I am not a virgin, Alysandir. I know it is very important to you for a woman to be a virgin, but that is not so where I come from. There was only one man, and I was to marry him."

He did not say anything. That did not bother her, for she knew he would, after he had time to think about it.

"What happened? Why didna ye marry him?"

"A week before we were to marry, he left and went to another country with another woman. And now I am here, and he doesn't cross my mind at all. He never made me feel like you do when you kiss me."

She waited, and when he did not speak, she knew she had her answer. She tried to push him away, but he remained on top of her.

"I know it is important to you to be the first man to lie with a woman. That is why I told you. I cannot lie to you, Alysandir, no matter what you think." There was melancholy in her smile. "I think you should go now."

She gazed into the warm liquid of his eyes, his hair drying with a touch of curl, the look on his face confident but with a surprising hint of vulnerability that made her realize once again that he wasn't all hard and conquering. It pleased her to know she had enough control that she could hurt him if she so chose. Except she knew that he had been hurt enough.

He kissed her nose and rolled away. One moment she could feel the hardness of him, and then the next moment it was gone. He stood over her looking strangely warm and beautiful—angelic almost, all tousled and bathed in the golden light of candles and a dying fire. She fought against lifting her arms to him and inviting him back, for already the place his body had warmed was growing cold.

"I will miss you," she whispered before she could stop the words. She was praying he hadn't heard her when he threw back his head and closed his eyes, the cords in his throat standing out.

Then he turned and walked to the door, pausing just long enough to look at her one last time. Then without a word, he was gone, and she was left with the memory of what could have been.

Chapter 21

There are two gates of Sleep,
one of which it is held is made of horn—
and by it real ghosts have easy egress;
the other shining fashioned of gleaming white ivory,
but deceptive are the visions the Underworld
sends that way to the light.

—*The Aeneid*, Book 6 (19 BC)
   Virgil (70–19 BC)
   Roman poet

ISOBELLA FELL INTO A DEEP, FITFUL SLEEP, TOSSING AND twisting, tormented by nightmares. She was running down a long, dank corridor that was dripping with spider-webs and followed by the heavy breathing of a red-eyed fiend lurking close behind.

"No!" She screamed, sitting straight up in bed and looking around the empty room. Embers still glowed faintly in the grate. Wet with perspiration and still breathing hard, she assured herself it was just a night-mare and nothing more. She frowned as a suspicious look settled across her face and she thought of the Black Douglas.

"You did this," she whispered. "You brought me here and abandoned me, and I don't know why." The words sounded small and forlorn even to her.

She closed her eyes, hoping for a few hours of peace-fulness instead of more wild adventures in strange, frightening places. Eventually, she fell into a deep sleep, lured by the ghostly music of a bagpipe. The tapestry at the window billowed out and a great wind blew into the room, and then everything grew still. A sweet fragrance surrounded her, and she saw that the candlestick on the bedside table had fallen over. She stared at it, puzzled. Was this a dream, or was it real?

She could not tell the difference.

She could hear herself speaking, but the sound seemed to come from far away. "I know you are in here, and I wouldn't show my face either, if I were you. How could you do something like this? And to a Douglas… I thought you were our friend, a member of the family, a chivalrous knight, and beloved protector. Well, something has cer-tainly gone wrong, if this is your idea of being a protector. I have never felt so alienated in all my life."

She looked around. She knew he was here, although she couldn't see the faintest hint of a green vapor. "Are you afraid to show your true self?"

The room began to spin, and she would have smiled if she had the energy, for even a man's ghost would spring to action when his masculinity was insulted. The spin-ning stopped and everything stilled. The faintest wisp of green vapor finally drifted through the open window.

"Go ahead, slink into the room and offer me your lame excuses."

The ghost bubbled up at the foot of her bed, nothing more than an obscure shadow, glowing with light. She watched it become a glittering haze and then, at last, a solid shape in the figure of the Black Douglas.

"I dinna slink!"

She was shocked by his sudden appearance. All tall and powerful, with a scowl on his face. She couldn't think of anything to say, except "Am I dreaming?"

"Do ye wish to be?"

"No."

"Then ye have yer wish. This is reality, lass, and no dream, for I am here in all my ghostly splendor."

She burst out laughing. He was so—human sometimes, but she had questions and he had answers and she wanted them. "Could I have a moment of your time for an interview?"

"Mayhap, if ye dinna ask any questions."

She frowned. *How can I have an interview without any questions?* "Where is my sister?"

"Dinna worrit. She is safe."

"Where?"

"Ye will ken when the time is ripe."

"It is easy for you to be nonchalant. You aren't the one who has been rudely thrust among strangers."

He grinned wickedly. "Strangers, are they? 'Twould seem ye are doing quite a bit to make yersel' friendly wi' some o' the inhabitants of Màrrach—one in particular."

"Have you been spying on me? That's quite ignoble of you. It should be against the rules of ghosting."

"Mayhap, but there are few enjoyments left for a ghost. 'Twould be a dastardly thing to rob me of the memories it evokes, but have no fear. I dinna invade yer most private moments."

Now she felt like a heel. "Why did you yank us back in time without asking if we wanted to come?"

"'Twas yer fate. Mayhap it was not."

Talking to him was like talking to an oracle. "My fate? Who told you that?"

His eyes gleamed, and she felt warmed by the glow. "That is a secret ye canna have an answer to."

"When can we go home?"

He shrugged. "Today, I have no answers."

"Why not?"

"Because I have only questions."

She counted to ten. "That doesn't make sense."

"Aye, and there ye have it."

"That isn't fair!"

"I dinna make the rules, but I do obey them."

Up went her brows in surprise. "You have rules?"

"Aye, there are rules for everything in the universe."

"But you're a ghost, aren't you? You come and go at will."

"Aye, 'tis true that I am, well enough, but I am no' God. There are some things I dinna ken and some things I canna do. Like ye, I have my limits."

"Well, I find that depressing, and for your information, I'm having a miserable time here. They aren't being very nice to me."

He laughed. "'Twould seem I would have to disagree wi' ye, lass. I seem to remember Alysandir going out of his way to be accommodating, and he might have been even nicer to ye if ye hadna done yer best to cool his ardor."

She gasped. "You were spying on us? That is ill mannered and uncivilized. Have you no shame?"

"'Twasn't spying, but I have a way of knowing what happens to ye."

"Is there anything I do that you don't know about?"

"Not verra much, but dinna worrit aboot it. Bide yer

time, lass. Have ye nae heard that Rome wasna built in a day? These things take time, ye ken."

She eyed him suspiciously. "What things?"

"Ye will—"

"Know when the time comes. Is that the only response you have?"

"Aye, for now."

"Were you this hard on Meleri?"

"I fear she would tell ye it was so."

"And did she complain about it as I do?"

"Aye, she did, and it seems the family trait has been passed doon to ye remarkably intact."

"Was she ever angry with you?"

"Aye, most of the time."

"Were you friends?"

"The best friendship has to offer, in spite of her tendency to ask too many questions, a lot like ye."

"Maybe I inherited that from her as well."

He grinned. "Mayhap ye did."

"What kind of questions were they? General? Specific?"

"Weel, she once asked me what I liked aboot being a ghost."

"What did you tell her?"

"That ye never have to open doors and yer feet never ache."

She laughed. "Did she accuse you of things that were not true?" she asked.

"Aye."

"Such as?"

"She liked to think I had affections for the Countess of Sussex and that it was the reason why the countess's Van Dyke portrait was never found."

"Did you have affections for the countess?"

His eyes were twinkled merrily again. "My time is up, and I must leave ye now."

"You aren't going to help me, are you?"

"'Tis not always smooth sailing. Life is riddled with doubts. Truth will come to light. 'Twould be better if ye stopped fighting it. 'Twill be over soon."

"It is not my way to surrender."

"Conquer or capitulate. It is the end result that counts."

She felt lost in a cloud of gloom. "I think I will die in this place."

He had the audacity to laugh. "I will remind ye of that one day."

"It better be soon," she said glumly. "My days are numbered."

"Be of good cheer, or dinna be of good cheer. That is for ye to decide." He stepped closer, removed his gauntlet and placed his hand along the side of her cheek. It was an odd sensation for he was still a ghostly form, yet she could feel the warmth of his hand.

"There are answers aplenty, and whys and wherefores abound, but naught are forthcoming at the present. 'Twill not be long now, lass. Have faith, and remember anything is possible if ye believe. Go back to sleep and dinna think too much aboot that which ye canna change.

"I didna bring ye back to torture ye, and I didna separate ye from yer sister to bring harm to either of ye. Mayhap there will be some trial by fire, and ye will come out the better for it. The future suffers no threat, even when the present is unbearable. Rest now, and dinna worrit that ye canna remember everything when ye awake."

Later, when she did wake up, she had a vague sort of assurance that he had been there in her room, but some of the details were fuzzy and nebulous, like one feels when awaking from surgery. It was as if she had been there, but she really hadn't. And she had a warm feeling that Elisabeth was being well cared for in a situation similar to her own. Or was that just because she wanted it to be true? *Anything is possible if you believe*.

But then, the opposite is also true.

When she went down to breakfast the next morning, she made two discoveries: Alysandir had gone hunting for several days, and she had no appetite.

Marion asked why she wasn't eating.

"My throat feels raw. I'm just not hungry."

"Ye should lay doon. 'Tis an illness aboot that has affected many in the castle. It willna last overlong. I will tell Mistress MacMorran to keep a watch over ye."

Isobella returned to her room and went to bed. She slept until Mistress MacMorran carried a supper tray in to her and said, "'Tis a nice, thick broth to give ye strength and some cold milk to ease the burning in yer throat."

Isobella thanked her and ate a little broth and drank all of the milk, which felt wonderfully cool. Then she slept. She vaguely remembered Sybilla and Marion coming by and Mistress MacMorran bringing her a tray, of which she ate little. By the third day, she felt wretched and wondered if she was dying. Was it her fate to come back five hundred years to die in a foreign land among strangers? Or if this was not death, then perhaps insanity? That was possible. Nothing made sense anymore.

She had a vision that she was back home on the Blanco River. She and Elisabeth were young girls again, swinging on a rope out over the water. When they let go of the rope, they fell with a splash into the cool, clear river. Laughing hard, they swallowed a bucket of water, only to stagger out and swing again.

She could almost feel the water, so cool, going down her parched throat... She swallowed and then frowned when she felt something press against her lips. Her mouth tasted sweetness, but it wasn't water. It was something almost as delicious as a Mexican vanilla cone at Amy's Ice Cream in Austin.

"Drink a little more, lass... verra, verra slowly now."

A male voice, vaguely familiar. Gradually she became more aware, but her perception was still fuzzy. *What is he feeding me? Is it poison?* She turned her head away and slapped at his hand.

"Why are you trying to poison me? Can't you see I'm dying?"

He chuckled. "Nay, lass, dinna worrit aboot dying. 'Tis only a sickness that comes every year. 'Twill no' kill ye, even if it feels like it will."

She was surprised that she could not remember how long she had been ill, for each day seemed to bleed into the next. What was it he had said? A sickness that comes every year? Body aches, stuffy nose, fever, chills, sore throat, headache. *All I have is a Renaissance version of the flu?*

"Drink this. 'Twill make ye feel better."

"What are you giving me?"

"Milk and honey. 'Twill nourish ye back to health."

He shoved the cup at her again. "Drink it doon, lass."

She opened her eyes, and the blur of his face sharpened. "Gavin," she said. He pushed the cup against her lips. She had to drink it, drown in it, or end up wearing it. After three gulps, she turned her head away.

"I am Grim, Alysandir's younger brother," he said proudly. "I am the ninth of twelve bairns. Gavin and I are twins, but he is number eight because he was born first."

Grim, she thought. Boy, did they ever misname him, for a happier, jollier looking guy she had yet to see. He had Alysandir's dark coloring, but his eyes were a silver-blue.

"Ye are feeling a wee bit better now."

"A wee bit," she said. "Has Alysandir returned?"

"Nay, he hasna."

"Why are you here instead of Mistress MacMorran or Sybilla and Marion?"

"They are sick wi' the same thing that ails ye. Many in the castle are sick. Those of us who are well are helping oot." He stood and smiled down at her. "Rest now. Ye will be feeling more like yersel' on the morrow."

Isobella nodded weakly. "Thank you, Grim."

She was asleep before he was out the door.

Two days later, she was feeling good as new and wanted nothing more than to be outside. She yearned to feel the sun upon her skin and to inhale the fresh air blowing in from the Atlantic.

After a breakfast of smoked haddock and a poached egg, she walked toward a wild grey-blue sea beneath the rosy fingers of a grey-blue dawn spreading above her.

She was accompanied by the sound of a narrow waterfall spilling out the rocky crag of old, moss-covered stones at the base of Màrrach. She paused to study the wide crescent beach of white sand that began at the base of rocky outcroppings and extended as far as her eye could see. Until it seemed to melt into mist and tall beach grass.

The sky was growing lighter now, and her feet sank into sandy heather. Shorebirds, angry at her intrusion, cried out and flapped away, swallowed by the sky. She watched them go, as she recalled a story of how the ancients had believed that when one's parents died, there was nothing between the child and the sky.

She felt as if she had been hurled back to a time when the earth was new and unspoiled. She felt peaceful and at home, as if it was a place she had once known and left behind. Were her ancient Celtic ancestors calling her home?

She was filled with a wild sort of freedom, and had it not been for her caution over her newly healed ankle, she would have left the grass and run down the beach, searching for the throbbing heart of this magical place. Perhaps, like Alice, she would fall down the rabbit hole, down, down, down to the beginning of time.

Had she entered another dream?

She stood on a hill and looked out over the sea, and spotting a boat, she thought of how Odysseus must have felt, so enchanted that he did not return to Ithaca for ten years. Here she stood—the sentinel, with one foot in the past and one in the present. How like a book life is, she thought, where one turns the pages that turn into chapters, and the preceding pages hold clues to all the ones that follow.

Quite by accident, she stumbled upon an ancient burial site and something stirred deep within her soul. She paused and looked around, seeing how the sun cast a mellow glow upon the weathered, blackened stones, the cairns covered with lichen and moss. Something strong and powerful rose up within her, and she was filled with reverence and awe at the reality of walking upon the same ground where the Celts had walked.

She was about to turn back when she saw a low, stone fence around some of the standing stones and what appeared to be more recent burial slabs. The plot was terribly overgrown, and feeling the need for exercise, she began to pull weeds.

It was almost dark by the time she returned to the castle, too tired to join the others at supper in the Great Hall. As she made her way up to her room, she thought of all that had happened in the ten days since she arrived. In many ways it seemed much longer.

Later, when she went to bed, she decided that she had overdid it, for her back ached abominably and her knees, too. And her hands—she should have worn gloves. But her soul stirred with joy over the things she learned that day. She closed her eyes, and the damp breath of the Atlantic blew into her bedchamber, the past calling to her, deep, dark, and mysterious.

Chapter 22

An axe is sharp on soft wood.

—African proverb

GRIM WAS RIGHT. ALYSANDIR RETURNED ON THE THIRD day, and most of those who had been ill were over their illness, like Isobella. While the others saw to the game the hunters had killed, Alysandir went in search of Isobella. He checked her room and spoke to the servants. No one had any idea where she was, but Grim did tell him to go easy on her.

"Any special reason why I should?"

"Aye, she has been verra sick with the fever. I imagine she wanted to be away from Màrrach, where the air is fresh and clean."

"Did you know she was going and you allowed it?"

"Nae, I didna ken what she was aboot. Had she asked, I would have taken her myself."

"Ye have a lot to learn aboot the wiles of a woman, so dinna allow one to persuade ye to do that which ye shouldna."

"I dinna think Isobella has any wiles. She is gentle, kind, honest, unselfish, and principled."

"It seems she has clapped a padlock on yer mind and clouded yer judgment."

"Are ye going to look for her? Can I come with ye?"

"I can handle Isobella."

"Aye, ye ken and that is why I am worrit."

"I willna be too hard on the lass," Alysandir said, and turned away. He wondered how she had managed to disappear in a castle full of people without at least one of them seeing her.

He returned to the courtyard and mounted Gallagher, anxious to find her. He had advised her, more than once, not to wander beyond the castle walls unescorted. She did not seem to understand the danger. When he found her, he would make certain she understood.

He rode along the beach, checking the sand for footprints. He was about to turn back when he heard the musical chime of her laughter coming from the direction of the castle burial grounds. He reined Gallagher into a tight turn and rode until he saw the ancient standing stones of his ancestors jutting up from the ground not far from a burial cairn. He dismounted near an old coffin slab, marked with an ornamental cross so old that no one had any idea just who was buried there.

He stepped through the gate and saw the familiar Pictish stone with cup-and-ring engravings, but he hardly recognized it. Someone had cleared away all the lichen and wild vines growing over it, along with the weeds that had clumped around the base. He continued on and paused for a moment beside the grave of his mother, where he saw flowers had recently been planted.

HERE LYES JOANNA MACKINNON
WHO DYED IN THE YEAR OF GOD, 1507

He spotted Isobella on her knees, just as she laughed again. She was watching the clownish antics of a puffin, with its gaudy rainbow-colored beak, looking as clumsy as a whale trying to fly. He stood quietly, captivated by the slender hands pulling weeds at the base of another Pictish stone. He also saw her black satchel lying nearby.

She seemed sadly alone. It had struck him that she was alone, but the idea had never seemed as real to him as it did now. Was there something about her loneliness that drew her to the graves? Did she find some kind of solace here?

He watched her wind her hand around a clump of grass, and he thought of the way she had wound herself around him in a very short time. He continued on his way unnoticed until his boot struck a rock and she turned toward him. Her eyes widened, her expression expectant, as if she knew he would berate her for disobeying him. He wondered what she would do if he pulled her into his arms and kissed her with all the wildness of this place.

"So you are back from the hunt," she said.

"Aye. I have returned to find ye were disobedient. I told ye not to leave the castle unescorted."

She turned her head to gaze out over the water. "Everyone has been sick with the fever, so I came alone. The flowers needed watering."

"Grim told me ye were ill."

She smiled. "He was being kind. Three days ago, I was certain I was dying. He assured me that I was not. And, as you can see, he was right."

She was still holding the clump of grass she'd pulled

from beneath a stone that had been carved with a rimmed mirror and a cross-shaft. She pointed at the inscription: MAQQoᴛTALLUORRH.

"It is thought that the Ogham inscription 'MAQQ' may mean son of or descendant of. It is believed that the Picts learned Ogham from the Gaelic-speaking Scots in the eighth century."

She drew in a breath and added hastily, "That is… it is something trivial I read in a book once. I'm not sure if it is true."

She was hiding something, but he let it pass for now. He opened his mouth to question her further, but she pointed toward his mother's grave.

"Your mother's name, Joanna…"

He cut her off. "You planted the flowers?"

She nodded. "Yes."

"Why? You never met her."

"Joanna is a lovely name. I thought she deserved to have colorful flowers instead of weeds. Women are intuitive creatures, you know. We feel things. Who is to say that some of these feelings did not come from those who came before us? I know your mother must have been a remarkable woman. It matters not that we never met. I feel her presence. I think she is not opposed to my being here."

She looked at the name carved in cold, hard stone, but the name Joanna itself was soft and warm, like a baby's breath. "Joanna means 'God is gracious.' It's a beautiful name, and I know she was a beautiful woman."

The muscle in his jaw worked. He did not want to discuss his mother. "And how would ye know that?"

"By looking at her beautiful daughters."

"Aye. She was a beautiful woman," he said, keeping his tone cold and indifferent. "My father never recovered from her loss."

"I did not find a grave for your father." She glanced about. "Isn't he buried here?"

"No, he is buried at Iona, although he would have wanted to be buried here next to her."

"Then why wasn't he?"

"Our uncle intervened, and it was decided that as the clan chief, my father should be buried at the priory where our uncle is the abbot. It was the only time I have disagreed with our uncle."

"I'm sorry," she said, and he caught the sadness in her voice.

She was an easy woman to be around, gentle… He paused a moment and almost smiled as he finished the thought. Gentle, kind, honest, unselfish, and principled, just as Grim said.

She was watching him now, frowning slightly against the glare from the sun. He was distracted by the sight of her, with her skirts billowing around her with each gust of wind, and he wanted to trust her. He dropped down to sit on his haunches beside her.

When she looked up, he held her trapped with his gaze. She remained still and quiet until he picked up the hand that had held the grass only moments before. He noticed the stains and scratches, several of which bled slightly.

"These are not the hands of a lady. Ye should have worn gloves."

"I don't have any gloves. Besides the cuts will heal." She tried to jerk her hand back, but he held it fast. He brought it up to his lips to press a kiss upon it.

"I am not a lady of rank or title, and I like to work with my hands," she said, anger lacing her voice. "Why did you come here looking for me? I don't need your protection, as you can see."

"That is for me to decide. Ye disobeyed me, and if you disobey me and suffer no consequences, others will think it permissible to do so."

"So have me flogged."

"Or confined to yer room."

"Whatever you feel is necessary. I do not mind. It would be easier if you gave me permission to leave the castle. I don't like being caged. I will only do it again."

"And I will come after ye."

She shrugged and looked off, gazing out over the water. "I saw a whale earlier, and I envied its freedom to go when and wherever it pleased."

"Ye feel trapped here?"

Her laugh was soft but mocking. "I *am* trapped here."

"How did this happen? How did ye come to be here? Ye gave yer word to tell me yer story. I want to hear it now."

"You won't believe me, I assure you, and you will probably toss me in the dungeon anyway."

"I will put ye in the dungeon if ye dinna tell me yer story. The time for excuses is past."

She sighed and continued to stare at the ocean. "I am not certain exactly how it happened. My sister and I came to Scotland to visit the ancestral homes of the Douglases. We visited St. Bride's Kirk, and I cried when I put my hand on the effigy of Sir James, the Black Douglas.

"A day or so later, we visited Beloyn Castle to view the painting of Sir James. I was so captivated by the portrait of him that I reached out and touched it… just his boot…and I said something like, 'I can't believe it is really you,' and everything went black."

"What mean ye, it went black?"

She turned to look at him, wanting him to see the truth in her eyes. "It was like being in a cave where there was no light. I couldn't see anything. I don't know how long it was dark. It seemed only a second, and then a freezing wind blew over us. A green vapor that was nothing more than a mist began to take shape. The light returned. I glanced at the painting, but the image of the Black Douglas was no longer there.

"Suddenly, the mist began to swirl. It took on a human shape, and I recognized it as the Black Douglas. I remember I said, 'Oh, dear God,' and he answered me."

"Ye mean the ghost spoke to ye?"

"Yes, with a deep, baritone voice that said, 'Mistress, I am not God, but ye hae only yerself to blame for my being so hastily summoned forthwith.'"

Alysandir rose to his feet, yanked her up by her arm, and spun her around to face him, gripping her shoulders and giving her several good shakes. "Ye mock me with yer lies."

She sighed, and all the breath seemed to go out of her. She looked him directly in the eyes, and he saw the weariness there, the defeat. "And so you have the truth that you asked for. Only you do not believe it. Now you see why I wanted to postpone telling you." She shook her head.

"Do what you will with me. I don't really care. I just want it to be over. It is as I expected. I told you that you would not believe me. But it is the truth, and I am so tired of worrying about your reaction. Take me to the dungeon. Put me in irons. At least I will be able to have peace there."

He decided not to respond. He wanted the rest of her story first. "And yer sister experienced this with ye?"

"Yes. You saw her in the glen with me that day. We were talking to the Black Douglas."

"He came with ye?"

"He brought us back with him. He didn't send us alone, although for all the help he's been, we might as well have been alone." She sighed wearily, and her voice grew fainter. "He was there for a short time."

She explained how they did not know they were in sixteenth-century Scotland until the Black Douglas told them and said they could not go home.

"That was when I noticed we were in the midst of a battle. Elisabeth was furious and told Sir James, 'It was all Isobella's fault!' Then she told me, 'All I am thinking right now is how much I would love to punch you, flat out.'"

He found that humorous and said that he did not know what to think. Her story was impossible, and yet she told it with sincerity and rather wearily, as if she accepted her fate as well as the fact that he would not believe her. He had seen this type of behavior in men dying on the battlefield, resigned to their death.

"Why did he bring ye here?"

She shrugged. "I asked him that, and he spoke in riddles. One moment, he seems to be my dearest friend, and the next he seems to enjoy throwing stumbling blocks in my way. 'Ye are here because ye asked to be.' I disagreed, but all he said was, 'Ye will understand, lass, when the time is ripe.'"

She looked at Alysandir and hoped he did not see that

she was fighting back tears. "The time must not be ripe, for I do not understand why he brought us here or why he allowed us to be separated."

"Ye told me yer home was America."

"Yes, it is, but not the America you know of. I am from the America of the future."

"What mean ye, the future?"

"What year is it?" she asked.

"'Tis the year 1515."

"My sister and I are from the twenty-first century, in the year 2011."

"'Tis blasphemy."

"No, it isn't. Of course you are free to call it what you will. But believe me, it gets worse."

"Ye canna be from the future. 'Tis no' possible."

"And yet I am here. I have kept my word and told you my story. You can believe it or not. If I am ever reunited with my sister, you can ask Elisabeth before I have a chance to speak to her. She will tell you the same."

"Mayhap I willna believe her either. The two of ye could have made up this story in advance."

"You don't believe me," she said. It was a statement, not a question, because she already knew the answer.

"Nae, lass. I want to, but I canna."

"You find it too incredible?" she asked.

"Nae. I find it impossible. With no proof, there can be no belief."

Oh, great. He wants proof. Just the thing I don't have. How can I prove something that happened five hundred years from now? I can't just pull a rabbit or a bouquet of roses out of my hat. She drew in a swift breath. *But you can pull something out of your backpack!*

Elated and wondering why she had not thought of it earlier, she leaned forward to catch the strap to her backpack and pull it toward herself. She unbuckled one of the two outside pockets and removed something. She handed it to him. "You won't understand what this is, but this is my proof. It is called an iPhone."

She smiled as she watched him turn the device over with careful examination. He ran his fingers over the smooth glass.

"Now, watch," she said, and she took the iPhone, thankful she turned it off in the twenty-first century. She turned it on, held it up, and took his picture. She showed it to him. "This is you, Alysandir. The way you look right now."

"Ye have captured my spirit! How did ye this sorcery?"

She ran her fingers across the touch screen and found the trailer for *Braveheart*. *This is either going to be hilarious, or he is going to drive a stake through my heart…*

He took the iPhone from her. He did not say a word as he watched Scotland's past shown to him by an object from far in the future. He had dozens of questions, and she answered them. He also found a few historical inaccuracies, as had many reviewers in her time. He wasted no time telling her what the mistakes were.

"Wallace didna wear blue paint on his face. That was the ancient Picts."

"I know, but for the story I suppose they thought blue faces made it more dramatic."

"And the plaid? 'Twas no' worn like that."

"Actually, it was worn that way many years later, in the eighteenth century. They just moved it forward three hundred years."

"Why?"

"Maybe they thought women would like to see the men's legs."

It took a second before he realized she was teasing him. He laughed and she realized he wasn't through, for he said, "Wallace couldna make love to Queen Isabella. She was a child when Wallace died."

He gave her a look so smug that she laughed. "I know all these things. They were merely done because some-one thought it would make the story more interesting."

"It is the way of yer time to find lies more believable than the truth?"

Oh, boy, do they ever... "More often that it should be, I'm afraid."

He wanted to watch *Braveheart* again, and when it ended, he stared out over the ocean for quite some time. She wondered what he was thinking, but she didn't want to intrude on his thoughts.

Then came the flood of questions about the iPhone, and she did her best to answer them. She played a few tunes, and lastly, she showed him pictures of America and her family.

"This is my father, Robert James Douglas."

"And yer mother?"

"Victoria." She continued. "This is Elisabeth and my sister Ana, and my brothers, James and John," she said, unable to stop the seepage of tears. They talked for some time about the pictures and her family. She told him about how she had studied history.

Then she turned the phone off, explaining what a bat-tery was, how it was like a candle that provided light, but that the more it burned, the less it had left to burn.

"At some point, the battery will die and all that will be left is the iPhone."

"The magic will be gone?"

"Yes."

He was silent for quite some time before he asked, "Yer sister has this magic, too?"

She nodded. "Yes. Almost everyone in my time does."

She marveled at the oddity of observing a strong, brave knight from the early sixteenth century staring with incredulity at an iPhone.

At last, he said simply, "'Tis magic."

She smiled. "Oh, Alysandir, you have no idea just how much magic there is in my time. Only it isn't magic. We call it technology. What you are feeling now is what a caveman would experience if he suddenly found himself in your time."

He picked up her backpack and offered it to her. "Ye have more magic?"

She was thinking she had opened a can of worms, but she dumped everything out. She explained coins and dollars, and showed the dates. She did the same with her credit cards, her driver's license, her passport, and all the other things women carry. She even gave him shot of breath spray.

She handed him the romance novel. "I had no idea when I bought this book about the Black Douglas that I would end up meeting his ghost."

If he heard her, he did not let on, for he was busy looking at the items before him. After careful examination of everything, he must have been satisfied, for he grunted and handed her the backpack.

"I ken ye willna be happy aboot what I am going to

say to ye, but… ye canna tell anyone yer story. Not even my brothers and sisters. One of them might forget and mention it withoot forethought. I think it best if ye keep yer pouch hidden away. I will show ye a place ye can stash it so it willna end up in the wrong hands.

"Sorcery is punishable by death. And even I canna protect ye if ye are found oot. While my clan is loyal to me, I am no' positive they would all be so understanding and on yer side if they suspected ye were a sorcerer. There would be those who would believe ye were sent here for evil purposes."

She was quiet for a while. It would be difficult to be on her guard all the time, but she didn't want to complicate things not only for herself, but for Alysandir as well. She stared at the backpack and then handed it to him.

"Hide it where you will." She paused and said, "I am sorry for all the trouble I've been…" She caught the way he was looking at her, and added, "And will be in the future, for I know the great risk you are taking by keeping my secret."

He drew a finger along the line of her jaw and stopped at the hollow of her throat, just above her breasts. "Weel, ye will have to see to it that I am justly rewarded, no?"

"So, do you think Elisabeth is being treated well?"

The Mackinnon's laughter took flight.

He took her in his arms. "Ah, lass, ye do bring back the laughter that has been long missing in my life. The Macleans willna harm her. She will be treated like a lady of high rank, accepted by the clan and as free to come and go as ye are. They have no quarrel with her. She is a pawn. That is all."

"For what?"

"To extract what they want from me."

"What do you have that they want?"

"My sister Barbara."

The hope in her eyes faded. "Then we are doomed, and I will never see my sister again."

His expression softened. "Dinna look so sad. Ye will be with yer sister. Have I not promise ye that already?"

"Yes, you have. Do you know how you will go about it?"

He shook his head. "No, but we are working on a plan. I am no' going to try bartering with Angus Maclean any longer. He finds too much pleasure in thinking he has a noose around my neck, and it delights him to yank it."

She felt guilty. Heretofore, she had seen everything through her eyes, never once considering what this was costing him. It wasn't as if he could jump in his SUV, buzz over to a neighbor's house, and kick in his door to rescue a damsel in distress. Nor could he turn everything over to the sheriff. He was the sheriff! And the judge, caretaker, arbitrator, defender, provider, protector, and decision maker.

"You won't have to resort to bloodshed, will you? My sister is a healer… what you call a chirurgeon. She would not want anyone to lose his life to rescue her."

"Like ye, I want no bloodshed over this, but trying to avoid it takes time."

She nodded and turned away, hoping to regain her composure and to chase away her disappointment. She understood what he was saying. She could not blame him. His brothers and clan members were as important to him as Elisabeth was to her. She knew from her studies that Duart was known to be an impenetrable castle, so he spoke the truth when he said it would take planning.

She had no map and could not pinpoint exactly where Màrrach was located or how far it was from Duart, but she had a general idea. So she made an educated guess that Duart was at least two days' ride. He had said the Maclean would not harm Elisabeth, and she believed him. She knew Elisabeth well enough that she would be willing to bet that her sister wasn't half as worried over being reunited as Isobella was.

She felt his hands, warm upon her shoulders. He drew her backward, and she nestled comfortably against him. He must have understood how alone she felt and that she was moved at the depth of his compassion.

His breath was warm against her hair as he said, "Ferment not yer mind with worry nor fill yer heart with cares. Ye have my word that I will reunite ye with yer sister. I canna tell ye when that will be. But before yer sister arrives, I want to hear how it was possible for ye to make the journey back five hundred years."

"I don't know how it was done, only that it was. If that wretched ghost will ever show himself while you are around, you can ask him."

Her words surprised him. "Ye have seen him here at Màrrach?"

"Oh, yes, more than once. He knows I am upset with him, so I don't know when he will decide to show himself again. Actually, I never know. Sometimes he talks to me. Other times he just stirs up a wind, or I hear him laugh at something I said. And then there are times when there are none of these outward signs, and yet I know that he is present."

"Ye are na alone," he said.

"Yes! Exactly! I am not alone. I always feel his presence out there somewhere." She smiled. "Even when I wish he wasn't."

A breeze stirred itself into a small whirlwind and blew over them, causing the puffins to take flight. Then everything was as it had been.

"That was yer ghost?"

She nodded. "That's his usual way of letting me know he is around."

His knees were starting to ache, so he sat down next to her. Without really deciding to do so, he took her in his arms. "Dinna worrit. I'll no' chain ye in the dungeon… at least not yet."

"You do believe me now, don't you?"

"Yer story is difficult to accept, but I canna find another explanation for the things ye have shown me."

His lips brushed hers delicately. "Dinna worrit. The burden is lifted."

For the time being anyway, she thought, her expression wary.

He pulled her close and continued to hold her, neither of them saying anything.

She could be quiet… Not many women had that virtue. He found that besides desiring her and wanting to bed her, he truly liked her. To his knowledge, he had never truly liked a woman, other than his sisters, before.

He kissed the top of her head. He did not know how he would handle all of this, but he had her in his arms, and for now, that was enough.

A few days later, Isobella stood at the window looking
out at the sun as it began to shine upon the castle walls.
Soon, the lilacs in the garden would be full of whistling
blackbirds, and the pleasant scent of baking bread from
the kitchen ovens would drift by her window. But now
the bailey was quiet, almost deserted. Alysandir had left
Màrrach before daylight to sail to Iona with Gavin and
Grim. He wanted to talk with Barbara.

After two days of rain, Isobella decided to take
advantage of the beautiful weather. She was dying to
go outside to feel the sea air upon her face. How she
missed the warm Texas sun! She inhaled deeply, taking
in the scent of the sea. She knew the moisture in the air
would make her hair curl in coiling ringlets, not that she
cared. The day was far too lovely to spend indoors. She
dressed in a simple brown dress and went downstairs.
She ignored the curious stares of guards and castle-
folk who knew she was going against the Mackinnon's
wishes by leaving.

Then she was free. She turned toward the ocean and
went for a walk along the beach. Invigorated after what
seemed to be at least an hour-long walk, she was about
to turn around when she happened upon a young boy
about seven or eight. He was sitting in the sand, working
on quite an impressive sand castle and moat.

He wasn't exactly ragged, but his clothes, while obviously of good quality when new, were beyond worn and
his cast-off shoes looked too big for his feet. She noticed
his socks lying nearby, and her heart wrenched, for they
were as full of holes as a colander.

She stopped. "Hello, that is a lovely castle you have built. Is it Màrrach?"

He tilted his head back to look at her, but he did not speak. He studied her from beautiful, dark-blue eyes framed by an exquisitely handsome face. His silence did not deter her, for she had two younger brothers and a younger sister who often gave her the silent treatment. So she gathered her skirts about her and sat down beside him. He smelled of peat smoke and little boy.

"My name is Isobella Douglas. Who are you?"

He remained silent, and she knew he was contemplating whether to answer or not. She was about to ask another question when he said, "Bradan Mackinnon."

A Mackinnon? How could he be? She had seen other children about the castle dressed far, far better than this urchin. She had never felt such pity for a child in her life. That he should be a Mackinnon and dressed like a ragamuffin. It was beyond appalling. Why was this child an outcast? What had he done wrong, and for God's sake, who were his parents? She had to look away for a moment to gain her composure, and she stared at the ocean to clear her mind. She did not want to scare him. He probably had enough troubles as it were.

The tide was going out, and the water lapped the shore in little wavelets that left curving ripples in the wet sand. Further offshore, she caught a glimpse of a white sail in the distance. It was peaceful here. She understood why he was drawn to this place.

"When the tide is oot, ye can gather a peck o' shellfish." His accent was thickly Gaelic, and his speech resembled that of the poorer Highlanders who worked at Màrrach, rather than that of the more educated Clan Mackinnon. Was he an orphan? But even an orphan with the Mackinnon name should be treated as well as the other children.

"Who is your father, Bradan?"

He was patting the sand into a turret, and he did not pause to answer. He went on working as he said, quite simply, "He doesna want me to say he is my father, so I dinna call him father and I canna tell ye who he is."

Isobella was surprised at the strange answer, for why would any man not want to claim this adorable child? "May I help you with your castle, then?"

He shrugged.

She scooted closer until she was sitting with her backside plopped flat on the sand and her legs crossed, just as his were. She leaned forward and cupped her hands to scrape the sand and drag it toward her, so she could start a pile of her own to work with. Soon, she had a large mound of damp sand.

"I think I shall be your neighbor, and I will make another castle nearby… one with a loch beside it."

He did not say anything, so she went to work on her castle. All went well until she tried to make a round tower, which kept collapsing. "Blast and double blast!"

Bradan looked at the fallen tower and then at her. "Ye canna make it so tall, or it willna stand."

"Ahhh, so that is the secret," she said and tried again. This time the tower stayed together.

They worked in silence for a while, and then Bradan dusted his hands against his breeks and took a piece of cloth out of his pocket that looked like a scrap from a well-worn plaid. He unwrapped two oatcakes and extended one to her. "Will ye have an oatcake now?"

"Only if you will take one of my scones," she answered, and withdrew a kerchief from her pocket. She unwrapped a triangular-shaped scone made of honey and oats and baked on a stone. It was quite different from the scones at Starbucks in the twenty-first century, but then, scones had originated in Scotland only about ten years before.

They exchanged an oatcake for a scone, and she observed the way he turned it over and over in his little hand, observing it carefully in that curious way children have. He looked back at her, and she could tell he didn't know what it was. Her heart cracked a little.

"Have you never had a scone before?"

"Nae, I dinna ken how I will like it."

"Take a bite. I think you will like it better than an oatcake. In fact, I believe you will think you have never tasted anything so good."

She could never remember such pleasure over watching somebody eat, for he truly relished it. When it was gone, she handed him the kerchief that contained three more. "Take these with you."

He took the kerchief and looked down at it and then at her. He said nothing as he busied himself with tucking the kerchief into the doublet he wore.

"Who is your mother, Bradan?"

"I dinna remember my mother, but I know she is in France."

Isobella decided to move the conversation away from his family and to concentrate on him. "Do you come here often?"

"Aye, 'tis a nice place to be and I dinna get into trouble when I am here."

"And are you often in trouble, or does it just seem that way?"

"When I was little, I would get my ears boxed about when I displeased them. They said trouble followed me like a mangy dog, but not so much now, for I have learnt to be verra careful."

She could not help smiling at the way he stressed the pronunciation of "verra," but the overall message was heart wrenching. How could anyone be so unfeeling to a child? She was willing to bet they treated their horses and dogs better than this motherless child. She gave his black hair a tousling.

"Boys are supposed to get into a little trouble now and then," she said, and decided to change the subject yet again. "Where do you live?"

"At Màrrach," he replied

"Màrrach?" How odd, she thought, for she had never seen him about the castle. "In what part of the castle do you live? Where is your room?"

"In the tower."

She thought the tower was an odd place to put a young child. "Who stays in the tower with you?"

"No one, but I am not afraid. I can look out my window and see the ocean, and sometimes I can see there is more land floating on top of it."

"More land on top… oh, you mean the land looks like it is sitting on top of the water?" she asked, thinking that was a clever way to describe an island.

"Aye, it sits there, floating on top of the water, but I dinna always see it."

"Have you ever been to any of the other islands?"

"Islands?" He cocked his head to the side and looked at her with a frown.

Lord, did he not know what an island was, even though he lived on one?

"Do you know what Scotland is?"

"Aye, 'tis where I sleep."

"What is Mull?

"'Tis where Màrrach is."

"And what is Màrrach?"

"'Tis where I live."

"You do know Mull is an island and there are many other islands out there scattered in the water, don't you?"

He shrugged. "I dinna ken aboot that," he said.

"What do you know about England?"

"'Tis where the bad soldiers live and sup with the deil."

"Bradan, do you have a tutor... a teacher... a person who shows you how to write letters and read books?"

He went on perfecting his sand castle. "Nae, I havena learnt my letters or my numbers."

"Do you have anyone who teaches you about history and geography?"

"Nae, I dinna, but I have been taught to groom a horse and skin a hare, and I can write my name. I can make arrows and shoot a crossbow, too." He stopped long enough to write his name in the sand.

"Bradan," he said proudly. "And I can muck out the stables, and I sometimes get to help with minding the sheep." He stopped suddenly, and she was puzzled by the fearful expression that came over his face.

"What are ye doing doon here?"

Isobella gave a start. She turned and held up her hand

to shield the sun from her eyes, puzzled that Alysandir had returned so soon. Why had he ridden Gallagher down here? She wondered if he often did that, or was it because he was searching for her.

"You gave us a start," she said. "I thought you were not coming back until tomorrow."

"A change of plans," he said curtly. "I dinna want ye roaming around out here like this. It could be dangerous. I have told ye before that ye are na to leave the castle unescorted. Hie yerself back to Màrrach. Now."

"This is Bradan," she said as she came to her feet. "We are building castles. Do you want to join us?"

"I know who he is," he said, his voice as cold as ice.

Isobella noticed how Bradan seemed to shrink away then, and how he kept his head down as he crawled sideways, like a crab, until he was several feet away. Then he snatched his too-large shoes, stood up, and ran down the beach.

"Bradan!" she called, but he did not stop.

She stood and started to go after him.

"Leave him be!"

She stopped. "What's wrong? He is such a beautiful little boy. It saddens me to think…"

"Stay away from him."

She was shocked. "What?"

"I said stay away from him. I dinna want ye to have anything to do with him."

She was aghast. "For the love of God, Alysandir, why? Why are you being callous toward him? He is not old enough to have done anything. He is only a child."

"He is the spawn of the deil," he said, with intense hostility that struck her a bitter blow.

"What are—"

"Leave him be. I forbid ye to have anything to do with him."

Forbid ye… Oh, he had said the wrong thing that time. She bristled, and the hair at the back of her neck stood up. "I'm sorry you feel that way, but I like him. In fact, I intend to teach him to read and write."

"I warn ye… dinna have anything to do with him."

"Why?"

"It is time to go. It will be dark soon."

She turned away, giving him her back as she tried to still her pounding heart. She sought to gain control of her runaway emotions, for two angry, unreasonable people would solve nothing. "I will be there later."

He dismounted, and she hardly knew what was happening before he swept her into his arms and plopped her in the saddle. He mounted swiftly behind her so she barely had time to grab the pommel before he spurred Gallagher into a gallop. They did not slow down until they were almost through the gates of Màrrach.

By the time he lifted her down, Isobella was seething. If he noticed, he did not let on as he said, "I will not tell ye again, mistress. Leave the boy be. He is the black-haired spawn of Satan."

"His black hair is the same color of yours, and his eyes…" Oh, my God! It struck her then… those beautiful blue eyes, the black hair. Alysandir was Bradan's father. But what could have happened that caused him to hate and despise his own child? "He's your child, isn't he? Bradan is your son," she said, surprised at the calm control she possessed.

"He is a bastard."

"A lot like his father, but whether you admit it or not, his face speaks the truth. He favors you too much for you to deny him."

"Dinna mention him again to me."

"Refuse and reject him all you wish, but you are wrong to blame him for the spilling of your seed. From a bitter seed a beautiful flower has grown. You punish yourself by not knowing him. He is as innocent as a babe." She saw that her arrow had hit its intended mark. She would give it time to fester.

She realized this was not the time to stand here and bandy words with him, but she knew what was right. Alysandir was as hard and craggy as the granite mountains of the Morvern Peninsula, and just as easy to move. She was not stronger than he, but she was softer, and not every obstacle had to be overpowered with brute strength. It was amazing, really, what strong defenses one could bring down with persistent softness, like water that turns mountains into sand.

They had arrived back at the keep, and when they stepped through the door, he said, "I will see ye at supper."

"Not if I see you first. And to be certain I don't catch even a glimpse of you, I will take a tray in my room."

He paused, and the hardness of his face subsided. "It was not my objective to raise yer ire."

"Whether it was your objective or not, you raised it. A tyrant's plea does not excuse his offense."

"I was not angry with ye," he said.

"I know and that makes it all the worse. To be angry to that degree with a child over the misfortune of his birth, I find abhorrent. I am disappointed in you, Alysandir." He started to speak, but she held up her hand. "I have nothing more to say on the subject, for you are behaving like a brute and I don't want to be around you."

She did not join him and the others in the hall for the evening meal that night but took a tray in her room as she said. When he came later and knocked on her door, she did not answer. After he left and Mistress MacMorran came to take her tray, Isobella said, "I met Bradan when I walked along the sea today. He would not tell me who his father is, but I suspect he is Alysandir's child. Is he?"

"I canna speak of the child, mistress."

"Why?"

"Dinna ask me anything aboot it, please, for I canna discuss it. None of us can. If ye canna get yer answers from the Mackinnon, then ye willna have an answer."

Sybilla and Grim came by not long after Mistress MacMorran left. "We missed ye at supper and wanted to make certain you were not feeling poorly," Sybilla said.

"I feel fine, but I am so angry at your brother that I dared not go to supper for fear I would say something I should not. But never mind that. Come, let us sit and visit."

The three of them sat in a solar off the main part of Isobella's room. "As you can see, I am the picture of health," she said, touched at their concern.

"We are glad to hear that," Sybilla said, "for we were afraid ye might have fallen ill again."

"'Tis not such a bad thing that ye were absent. Alysandir was like a red deer in rut. Ready to fight anything that moved," Grim said. "Has he been by to see ye since he returned?"

"He has been by, yes, but I haven't seen him since before dinner. Nor do I want to."

Grim was grinning at her as he spoke, "He will come to ye if ye dinna go doon, for 'tis easy to see he is itching to have words with ye."

"It won't do him any good to come here. I intend to keep my door locked."

Grim gave her a serious look. "That willna keep Alysandir oot, not if he has a mind to speak with ye. If ye dinna gain him passage, he will kick the door doon or have a battering ram brought up, if need be."

"I am not afraid of him."

"Tonight, ye might want to be," Sybilla said. "He barely touched his food, but he did drink a week's ration of ale and that was afore he opened a bottle of brandewijn."

"He can have poison for all I care."

Sybilla reached over and took Isobella's hand and gave it a squeeze as she said, "Grim is right. If he wants to speak with ye, ye canna keep him oot. He would level the entire castle if he has to."

"Then the two of you might want to sleep elsewhere tonight," she said. The three of them laughed, but Isobella noticed it was a bit forced.

After they departed, she locked the door and readied herself for bed. Let him come, she thought. There isn't anything he can do or say that would make me open that door.

It was an eerie wind that came into the room and billowed the tapestry over the window. Then the mournful weeping of bagpipes snuffed out one of the candles.

"Blow them all out and see if I care. You men are all alike," she said, and went to change into her sleeping gown. "Nothing but hot air!"

———— ∿∿∿ ————

Alysandir could not erase the memory of his hands around her small waist as he lifted her from Gallagher's back, or the way she fled into the castle to the sanctuary of her room the moment they returned. On the one hand, he admired her courage, for she had the heart of a lion, the patience of a rock, an abundance of compassion, and more stubbornness than he had ever come against.

She infuriated him and he had nothing to measure her by, for there was not a woman in the whole of Scotland like her. It was as if God had created one of her and decided mankind would not survive and he changed his design. She talked too much; she would not listen; she would not obey. She would argue with the pope himself; she would fight him to the bitter end; she had an opinion about everything whether he asked for it or not.

She was too stubborn, too determined, too beautiful, and too desirable, and he wanted her so much he ached. But a woman like her would strip a man bare, down to the very marrow of his bones, until he was mindless as a beggar. He poured the last dram of brandewijn in his goblet and drank it faster than he should. He paced the room three times and decided what he had to say to her could not wait until the morrow.

It was the second time he took the stairs three at a time, and it was the first time he wanted to throttle her, especially when he found her door locked. No amount of knocking, pounding, or brash threats changed that. He stared at the door for a few minutes. He turned around and headed back toward the stairs. But instead of going down this time, he went up.

Not more than ten minutes passed before he had ripped the tapestry drape in the room above hers from its moorings, cutting it into strips with his dirk and then tying them together. One end he fixed to the post on the heavily carved bed. The other end he tossed out the window, and then he followed it, scaling down the wall until he reached the top of the window of the room below… Isobella's room.

He pushed himself away from the wall to swing out just far enough to let a few inches of the tapestry slip through his hands. When he swung back, he caught a glimpse of her standing by the bed wearing a white linen gown, just as he sailed forward and through the open window into her room.

Chapter 23

I am not quite sure whether
I am dreaming or remembering,
whether I have lived my life
or dreamed it.

—Eugène Ionesco (1909–1994)
  Romanian-born French playwright

ALYSANDIR PLOWED INTO ISOBELLA, WHO WAS ABOUT TO climb into bed, and the two of them went sprawling on the floor. He heard her gasp, then hiss, "Are you insane? Get off of me, you big oaf! And then get out of here."

He had her pinned beneath him. The warm feel of her softness caused him to forget the flaming reprimand he planned to give her. Suddenly, chastening her did not seem as important as it had a few minutes earlier. He couldn't seem to take his eyes off her. He could see that she had nothing beneath that gown but lush, firm breasts, long legs, and the shadow of what lay in between.

She must have felt his desire, for she sucked in a horrified breath and shoved at him. "Get off before someone comes in and catches us like this."

"I find I am quite comfortable just as I am. 'Tis the first time I have been on top of anything since I met ye. Ye have led me on a merry hunt, mistress, but the chase ends here."

"I don't know what you're talking about. What merry hunt? Are you feeling well? If you are, then you've got your facts all wrong. You've been gone most of the time since I arrived. How could I lead you on a merry anything?"

He stroked and nuzzled her with his nose, nibbling and kissing her throat and neck, then her eyes. "Ye have done nothing but give me torment and trouble since I met ye. Ye willna listen to anything I say. Ye disobey my orders. Ye provoke me at every turn. Ye tell me preposterous stories."

"That is easy enough to remedy. Let me go to the Macleans. I want to see my sister. Let me go, and rid yourself of me and my troublesome ways."

Wait a minute. This was not going according to his plan. Leaving was precisely what he did not want her to do. He looked at her beautiful face with the flashing green eyes that said she cared for him, even if she was furious with him. Alysandir was angry. By staying angry, he could hold his yearning at bay.

Although he did not want to admit it even to himself, he realized that ever since he first met her, he was afraid, deep within his very soul. He feared he might fall in love with her, and loving a woman like her would strip a man bare, until he was naked and vulnerable. Already, he feared that after making love to her, he would not want to leave her as he did with other women. He feared he would want to hold her close. That he would wrap his arms and legs around her and surrender to the perfect peace of her closeness.

He couldn't marry her and he couldn't let her go, but he didn't know how that equation equaled out. He wanted her, had wanted her for too long. He wasn't going to wait any longer. He started kissing her neck and stroking just beneath her ear, which was soft as a moth's wing, with the tips of his fingers. Then he was kissing the side of her face, her eyes, and the slender length of her nose. His lips brushed across her lips, skimming lightly over them, once... twice... thrice... until he groaned. He took her firmly in his arms and pressed himself against her, bringing his mouth down upon hers.

His hold on her was firm but gentle, his kiss long and drawn out. By the time it ended, he knew just what she liked, and how and where she liked to be kissed. He knew how to kiss a woman into submission, and he took his time, allowing her to warm up to the idea, to follow his lead, to become so full of desire that she forgot that only moments ago she had wanted to leave.

He sensed intuitively the moment the long and drawn-out heat of passion took over, burning away her anger. He felt her body relax as she melted, gasping a soft little cry when his hand slipped lower and touched her. She opened to his hand like a lilac in the sun. She was sweet... And lovely... And warm... And all his.

God, she was beautiful to touch, responsive to even the lightest caress. His hands cupped her face, and his fingers threaded through the long filaments of her hair. He found a sensitive spot at the nape of her neck and felt the first trembling of a shudder ripple across her shoulders. He lowered his head to the cove of her shoulder.

She moaned. Her head fell back to expose the full lustrous length of her warm throat. His lips moved lower, and he knew she felt the instant betrayal of her body rushing to meet him. She was intoxicated, mindless with wanting.

"Ye seduce me with your little moans," he whispered, his voice husky as his mouth glided over her skin. He knew she was floating away from herself, that she was out of touch with all reason. For this moment, nothing was important but the feel of his arms, the taste of his mouth, the rough texture of his face, the fragrance of his skin. She whimpered softly and tried to pull away, but he held her against him.

"Tell me what you want. Am I frightening you? Don't be shy… not with me… never with me."

He released her with a gentle nuzzling as his tongue followed the outline of her ear. Her arms went around him, and she spread her fingers flat against his back as her other hand slid behind his neck and into his hair, pulling him closer.

He was undone. "I want to make love to ye."

"Why?"

"Why?" He had never had a woman ask that. "Because I desire ye and canna think of anything else." As soon as he said the words, he saw the disappointment on her face. She wanted something more from him. Something he could not, would not, give.

"You are taking unfair advantage," she whispered.

"The rules of conduct do not apply in love or war."

He felt her bubbling laugh just before she said, "So, which one are we doing now? We switch so often that I have trouble keeping up."

<hr />

He kissed his way across her face. "War is the furthermost thing from my mind at the moment." He kissed her tenderly and long with a shattering intensity that left her feeling liquid and warm inside. He wanted to make love to her. She wanted him to make love to her, and she feared she was well on her way to being head over heels in love with him…

But, was he falling in love with her? No. That reality hit her flat out, and she felt devastated. How could she have been so naïve? He had said nothing, done nothing, to make her think he was even close to loving her. Where did that leave her? He would bed her for a while and move on to someone else. What if she got pregnant? She had already seen firsthand how he treated his bastards.

She couldn't think because he was kissing her throat, his lips traveling across the untouched softness of hidden places. Her body seemed to melt into his, and she wanted him to be her Mr. Darcy. She was in love with him but couldn't bear to be a temporary lusting. God, she yearned for him, torn between what she wanted and what he offered her.

A static charge hung over the room. She knew he was frustrated, but she didn't dare tell him that she was one of the weird ones who wanted to hold out for love and marriage. She looked at the bewildered face and almost gave in. Just once, she was thinking. What would it hurt to make love to him just once? *Because you wouldn't stop at just once, and you know it.*

His arms went around her. "I know what ye want, lass. Ye want it all done proper with marriage and children. I canna promise ye any of those things. Dinna fear me or worrit aboot my casting ye aside. I willna hurt ye, Isobella. Not ever. I dinna want ye to fear me any more than I want ye to distrust me.

"I canna say I love ye. I dinna think I understand what love is. I dinna care aboot going there again. Some people are na destined to fall in love and live happily together until they die. Some people destroy each other. That doesna mean we canna be happy together or even grow old together. I desire ye. I care aboot ye. I dinna want ye to fear me."

"I don't fear you, Alysandir. I am not made of stone. Maybe it would have been better for both of us if you hadn't rescued me. Or kissed me. I want to make love to you... so much that I ache. Stop looking at me like that."

Her mind was racing. She had ruined Elisabeth's life, dragging her back through the centuries to Scotland. She missed her family. Her heart ached for Alysandir and his wounded heart. *Why does it hurt so much?* She couldn't bear to look at him.

"I know I'm making a complete fool of myself. I'm surprised you haven't bolted from the room before now." She was afraid she might cry so she turned away, but he caught her by the arm and whirled her around. She accidentally stepped on the front of her gown and heard a loud rip about the same time she felt the fabric slide down over her breasts.

He made a noise that sounded like a growl, followed by the calling of some ancient saint's name. She started to speak, but her mind went blank. It was too late for words. What they thought, what they felt, whatever their differences didn't stand a chance now. Their attraction was primal. Just one man and one half-naked woman. The rest was left to nature.

He said softly, "Aye, ye can make love wi' me, lass. And I will prove it to ye." And with that, he swept her up into his arms and carried her to her bed, pressing her back into the clean sheets that had been so carefully turned down earlier.

He covered her with his weight, his hips grinding against her with an agonizing heat that would have scorched the clothing between them if he wasn't busy peeling it away. Soon their warm, naked flesh was pressed intimately together. Each time she opened her mouth to resist, he covered it with a mind-erasing kiss. She wanted him so much that the joy of it caused tears to seep from her eyes.

"I will have to say that this is the first time I have made love to a teary woman, but if ye are thinking it will cause me to change my mind, it willna. I intend to bed ye this night and bed ye well."

She would have to say that he was a man of his word, for his hands knew precisely where to touch to make her moan with painful intensity while the rhythm of his hips filled her with a maddening throb, a throb that beat against her with the acute awareness of something beautiful happening between them.

For a fleeting moment, she imagined she was dreaming again and in the arms of her dream-lover and she held onto him tightly, afraid if she released him he would disappear forever. She felt the warmth of his palms cover her breasts, forming them like potter's clay to the contours of his hands. She felt like she was floating, buoyant and weightless.

She gazed at him as if she had never seen him before, every square inch of her body acutely aware of him with such fierceness that it frightened her. Her insides felt like an overwound clock that had suddenly gone haywire with springs popping and flying everywhere, and she feared that she would never put herself back together again.

While his hand wreaked havoc at her breast, his lips began their own assault on her face, throat, and neck. She was breathing so rapidly that she barely managed to say four little words.

"You don't play fair," she whispered, then bit him on the shoulder.

He was kissing her face but paused long enough to say, "When ye are involved, I always play to win." This time when he kissed her, it was hard, forceful, and passionate. She whimpered from somewhere deep inside and could not stop her hands, which slid upward to lock around his neck, pulling him closer and closer still.

"I won't let ye go, Isobella. Ye are safe with me."

He was wrong. She wasn't safe. She was in over her head now, and she knew it. She kissed him intensely and felt a corresponding stab of longing curling deep within her. He was the embodiment of her fantasies, her dreams, and the reality of her imaginings.

She had to know what it was like to make love to him. She had to experience what it was like to have him want her to the point of insanity, even when she knew the insanity would pass, just as the wind passes, and the leaves are still once more.

Tomorrow she would regret this, she was certain, but for now, nothing mattered but him and the delicious stroke of his hands, the warm, soothing phrases that he uttered, and the lazy movement of his tongue — everything working separately, yet coming together to leave her incoherent.

"Make love to me, Alysandir. I want to make love with you. I have wanted you since I first saw you that day in the glen, and I have wondered with it would be like to lie with you like this. I don't want to wonder and imagine anymore. I want to know. I want to feel. I want to live. I want to feel you inside me, not because you want it, but because I do."

He groaned and rolled onto his back, flinging his arm over his eyes. "Don't say it if you don't mean it," he said, his breath coming in short pants, his face contorted in discomfort. Her hand shyly eased into his, and he pressed her fingers against him, his hips anxious for their merging and rising up to meet her. "*Mon Dieu!*" he said.

The overwhelming desire to share this moment overrode any hesitance, and she moaned when his hand slipped over her breast. His thumb brought her to the point of readiness. His kiss grew more urgent now, his breathing harder and more ragged. Then his body slid over hers, and he spoke softly in Gaelic. He was turgid and so vulnerable that she ached inside.

Her hands wandered with slow, easy movement to learn the contours of his back and then explore the strength of his neck before she threaded her hands into the silky texture of his hair. She luxuriated in the weight of his body pressing her down. He pressed hard against her, and her legs parted. A mounting heat began to build, spiraling around her with such intensity until she whispered against his ear, "Please…"

He eased himself inside her, feeling the heat, the aching warmth, the velvety drag as he began to move, slowly at first, until they moved as one, his strokes swift and sure. This was more than coupling and far different that it had ever been with any woman. There was rightness to it, a peace that drew him further, faster, and harder into her.

She cried out his name, and he covered her mouth with his kiss until he felt the crashing waves of pleasure that shot through him, intense and drawing him deeper into her, until he could no longer control it and the warm, liquid heat burst forth.

Her arms were around his neck. She drew him closer, and he could feel tears upon her face as she whispered, "So beautiful. I never knew it could be so beautiful."

He rolled to one side, taking her with him, and her head nestled in the cove of his neck. He kissed the top of her head, and his hand stroked the silky length of her body. He kissed her eyes and her lips and held her close, and the two of them fell asleep.

She never knew how long they slept before she awoke to the touch of his hand stroking her until she writhed beneath him. She wanted to tell him to stop, that she couldn't stand the torment any longer, yet somehow he knew. He covered her mouth with his kiss, and the objections died in her throat. She began to move, tentatively and slowly, until her movements began to match the rhythmic pace set by his hand. Then he kissed his way downward.

His mouth was warm, and she gasped at the intensity. Her breathing was ragged. She grew impatient and restless, her arms flung away from her body to grip the edge of the blankets, her sweat-dampened head turning from side to side. It felt so good, and yet it was like dying with slow agony. She moved against him in uncontrollable passion as strange rhythms washed over her, each ripple unbearably shattering and the next one stronger and more intense.

When she felt herself at the point of near insanity, he filled her and she cried out and called his name. From the ashes of the woman she was came the birth of a new being. Instinctively she knew the world would somehow be different, that she would never be the same.

She felt the solid burning warmth of his loins against her, his sweat-slicked body arched in driving need. He wrapped his arms around her and she did the same, hoping that she could hold him close enough that when the first rays of morning came through the window and she opened her eyes, she would not find him gone.

She was still asleep the next morning when he awoke. He kissed her cheek and then dressed quietly. He started to leave, but something seemed to reach out and touch him, as if she was calling him back to her side. He returned to her bedside, quiet and content to simply look at her. He thought of her amazing story, the undeniable and inexplicable proof of her truthfulness. It had been good with her, better than with those who had come before. He counted himself fortunate to have experienced it, for he doubted it could ever be that way again.

But she had surprised him before.

A beam of sunlight slipped between the drawn tapestries to bathe her in a golden frame of light. He released a long-held breath, fought the urge to undress and make love to her again, and then turned and quietly quit the room.

Later, when Isobella awoke, she lay in bed for quite some time, reliving each moment of the evening before. She no longer wanted to dream about the perfect man, for she had met him. She paused and looked around. It was a perfect time for the Black Douglas to poke his meddlesome nose into her affairs and voice his opinion.

Nothing…

She stretched lazily and curled her toes. Never had she dreamed it could be as it had been between them the night before. If she had any regrets about the Black Douglas bringing her back in time, they had evaporated in the heat of her lovemaking with Alysandir. She had never known there were so many ways to make love: her on top, him on top, face up, face down, hands and mouth. She smiled and hugged herself. Last night, Alysandir Mackinnon had flipped her like a pancake, and she had enjoyed every moment of it.

She was in love with him, and that scared her. She had no idea how long she would be here. The Black Douglas gave her no hope of returning one moment and made it seem like it could happen at any time the next. How could she be in love knowing she could declare her love one moment and vanish the next?

What if she was pregnant with Alysandir's child and suddenly found herself back in the twenty-first century? He would never know his own child. And what if she had a child? Could she be taken back and her child left behind? It was a sobering thought, for how could she plan for the future with Alysandir when there might not be one?

She didn't get to think further on the subject, for

Mistress MacMorran came into the room with a breakfast tray. "The Mackinnon said to bring ye yer breakfast. Ye are na feeling the fever again, are ye?"

Isobella smiled and pulled the sheet up. "No, I'm just being lazy this morning."

Mistress MacMorran nodded, as if giving her approval. "'Tis part of being human, to take it easy now and then," she said, as she put the tray down.

After she was gone, Isobella finished her breakfast, stretched luxuriously, and hopped out of bed. She opened the lid of her trunk and withdrew the first garment her hand came in contact with, unaware of what she selected, her mind preoccupied with dreamy remembrances of the previous night. She hugged the dress against her and closed her eyes and wondered if she had ever been this happy.

She dressed, did her hair, and was about to depart when a chill went up her spine and settled across her shoulders. The window tapestries billowed. She looked around the room.

"I know you are here," she said. "You are playing games again and moving your Alysandir and Isobella chess pieces. I recognize your manipulations. Show yourself, and admit your tampering!"

She waited to see if a ghostly chuckle would float into her consciousness, and when none was forthcoming, she said, "I would be reluctant to comment on this mess you've made of things, too, if I were you."

"Vex not a ghost," a voice behind her said.

She let out a yelp and turned quickly. Today, she didn't see merriment dancing in his eyes, but something more along the line of mischief.

"I have learned that you come only when it pleases you and not when I invite you."

"I am here, am I not?"

"Yes, after the fact."

"Aye, I heard yer grumbling aboot being a chess piece."

"Yes, and a good analogy, I thought. Strange things are going on here, and I am certain it is mostly your doing. I'm beginning to feel like I'm standing on a chessboard where all the players are human and someone is moving us around, for our feet move of their own accord and we are helpless to stop them. Does that sound familiar so far?"

He shrugged. "The absent are always to blame."

"But I do turn to you. And I trust your judgment and do as you suggest."

When he raised his brows, she added, "Well, at least most of the time. And even when I have doubts, I always think of you as my *éminence grise*. Please don't tell me that you are not."

His image glowed just a little bit brighter, and she thought even a ghost has his pride. "Mayhap I concur," he said, "for 'tis true that I am secretly powerful."

She was thinking controlling. "And you exercise great power and influence over me."

"Aye… secretly, of course."

"Of course… So, use some of your exceptional powers and tell me why all of this is happening?"

"'Tis yer fate. 'Tis a misconception ye mortals have… thinking ye are the master of yer fate, when, in truth, man is completely helpless in manipulating or changing his future. Affairs dinna always prosper. Friends are no' all true. And happiness is never assured. Ye must learn to live each day as it comes."

"That makes it frightfully difficult to plan for the future," she said. "What do you know of mine?"

"I could tell ye more aboot cabbages."

"Thank you. That was a great deal of help."

"The future? What is there to know? Everything happens. Nothing happens. The unexpected happens. And life goes on in between. Ye want me to give ye a fixed image of yer future, and 'twill no' happen. Mayhap I canna predict yer future. Mayhap I can. Mayhap I try to prevent it, or is it that I can change it? Ye canna have everything ye want, and ye doona want everything ye get. And yet there is balance of life."

"My, that really makes me feel a whole lot better. Pardon me while I get my sackcloth and ashes and take a pilgrimage."

"Ye worrit about the future when the effort is wasted. 'Tis like playing chess with the deil. The future is a deceiver, and he never tires of being a cheat. Heads I win, tails ye lose."

"But…"

His image began to fade as the evening twilight fades… gradually… and by the time it is noticed, the sky is black and filled with stars. Only in her case, her room was empty, and her heart filled with hope.

Chapter 24

A guardian angel o'er
His life presiding,
Doubling his pleasures,
and his cares dividing.

—"Human Life," 1819
Samuel Rogers (1763–1855)
English poet

ISOBELLA DECIDED TO PAY A VISIT TO THE TOWER IN SEARCH of Bradan. Once there, she was surrounded by nothing but the cold, stone walls of the hallway, and a stout wooden door with iron hinges barred her way. She knew the unsurpassed strength of this mighty castle, for inner doors were almost as strongly fortified as those facing the outside. She remembered Alysandir once having mentioned that each of the towers had two upper floors reached by spiraling stairs, so she searched until she finally found one of them.

The door opened easily enough, for which she was thankful, and soon she was climbing the narrow, circling staircase until she reached a door on the first floor. She knocked and then tried the door but found it locked. On the second level, the door opened. The room was small with a narrow bed along one wall. A pail of cold ashes stood beside the fireplace, where fresh kindling had been laid in the grate.

She picked up the tinderbox sitting nearby and smiled. She imagined Bradan giving his patient attention to the ten or fifteen minutes of painstaking work needed to light a fire and then coaxing the first, timid tongues of flames to life. The chimney was still warm, so he had not been gone long.

She noticed a square of muslin cloth and the crumbs of what she supposed was an oatcake. Breakfast. She considered the bed, and her heart turned as she imagined the small hands that smoothed the bedding and folded the change of clothes lying on the chair near the wash bowl.

A clatter of hooves in the courtyard drew her to the window, but it was difficult to see more than mounted horsemen and Grim standing near the two riders. She caught sight of Alysandir framed like a painting in the slim rectangle of an open door, and her heart pounded at the sight of him, tall and slim hipped, waiting on the groomsman to bring his horse. Mistress MacMorran had mentioned to her earlier that the Mackinnon would be away from Màrrach to meet with the chief of Clan Macquarrie. Isobella was actually glad to see him go, for it would give her time to become better acquainted with Bradan.

Just as she turned away from the window, she noticed two speckled gull eggs sitting on a small table. They were placed next to a small bird's nest that contained a pinecone. A crude knife lay near a piece of greying driftwood that he was carving, but it was too early to tell what the end result would be. She touched another of Bradan's treasures, a small clay deer, and spotted a broken chessboard and two crudely carved knights and then a small wooden whistle. Leaning next to the table was a Celtic short sword, carved from driftwood, its handle tightly wound with brown yarn.

She thought of the other children in the castle, blessed with their loving parents and siblings, playmates, tutors, clean clothing. The unfairness of Bradan's circumstances broke her heart and made her more determined than ever to put things right.

She was on her way toward the beach when she caught sight of Grim walking across the courtyard, and she called out, "Grim! Wait up!" She was a bit breathless by the time she caught up to him, still not accustomed to the weight of petticoats and long skirts—not to mention the clodhopper shoes—while dodging horse droppings.

Grim turned around.

"Ah, a lass with a bright face to rival the sun, and she seeks my companionship," he said as he gave her a sweeping and much exaggerated, bow.

She laughed. "I need your help."

"Weel, I can give ye my help, but it might cost ye a favor one day," he said, with a mischievous smile rivaled by the teasing gleam in his eye.

She smiled. "Fair enough," she said and fell in step beside him. "Where are you going?"

"I am off to the stables to see a newborn foal of great size."

"I take it that it is larger than any of your other horses."

"'Tis no' so large now, but 'twill be when grown, for it is the much awaited foal sired by an English war-horse."

Isobella was intrigued. She knew from her studies that the Scots' horses, known for their endurance and sturdiness, were of small stature of about twelve to fourteen hands tall. It was extremely rare for a Scot to own one of the war-horses ridden by medieval knights, which were no more than fifteen hands.

"Ahhh, yes… English war-horses are difficult to come by, are they not?"

"Usually impossible, ye ken, because for centuries the English have thwarted attempts to smuggle war-horses from not only England, but France and Spain, although a few were smuggled across the Borders."

"And smuggling is preferable to buying them?"

"Buying is not a choice we have. 'Tis a felony in England to sell horses to the Scots, for fear that we will improve our stock."

They stepped into the stables and made their way to a large stall where a sturdy grey mare gave suckle to a long-legged foal of a chestnut color. Isobella crossed her arms over the stall door and leaned forward as far as she could to observe.

"It would seem this leggy little creature is destined to father many foals, for he seems to be in perfect health and nurses well."

Grim turned to look at her. "Ye surprise me, mistress, for ye are a woman with a breeder's knowledge. How came ye by it?"

She shrugged. "I have been around horses all my life."

"Then we shall go riding one day soon. Mayhap ye would enjoy a gallop down by the sea."

"I would love that," she said, and left a soon after. She walked along the beach a short while later, enjoying the fresh air and sunshine, her thoughts upon the horses she had at home and how her father taught her and Elisabeth to ride.

She thought about Bradan, reminded of just how little she knew about children, and then thought of how she would like to thump Alysandir Mackinnon on his stubborn head for ignoring his son.

She caught a glimpse of Bradan just ahead, with the sun glinting off ebony hair that was badly in need of a good trimming. She saw him running at the water's edge, his shadow keeping pace with him, and when he saw her, he changed direction and ran toward her. His smile reached her before he did, as if hanging in the air like that of a Cheshire cat.

"Hello, Bradan. I was hoping I would find you here."

"Ye were looking for me, then?"

"Yes, I was. We cannot become good friends unless we spend some time together, now can we?"

A frown parked itself between his brows. "I do not know if the chief will let me have a friend."

"You let me worry about the chief," she said. "He's not here, so there is no need to worry. I am new at the castle and very much in need of a friend."

His nose crinkled adorably as he stared into the sun to look at her. "What do I have to do?"

She smiled. "Why, nothing other than be my friend, and I will be your friend."

"I have not had a friend before."

"Well, don't worry. Being a friend is the easiest thing you will ever do," she said, and then asked, "Have you seen the new foal in the stable?"

His eyes brightened. "Ye have seen it, then?"

"Aye, I have seen it standing on wobbly legs beside its mother."

"Have they named it?"

"I don't think they have. What would you name it, if the foal was yours?"

"Cahir!" he said without thinking.

"Cahir… it's a Gaelic word I don't know, but then, I know very few Gaelic words. What does it mean?"

"Warrior," he said proudly. "Mayhap I would call it Cahir Mor."

"Big Warrior, a perfect name for such a fine foal. He will breed fine foals to improve Mackinnon stock," she said, wondering if she was speaking over the boy's head.

But his face lit up, and he replied quickly, "Aye, I ken this is true, for I heard the men speak of it."

"You are a very smart young man," she replied.

"Aboot things I hear others say, but I have no book-learning."

"Would you like to study with the other children?"

He looked down at his hands. "I am not allowed. 'Tis against the rules."

"What happens if you break the rules?"

"I dinna ken, for I have never broken one."

She leaned forward and gave his black hair a gentle tousling. This darling boy had been deprived of a mother's love and devotion for so long. Isobella was determined, if not to make up for it, at least to see that he received it from now on. In spite of everything, he had done a remarkable job of raising himself.

"If I arranged for you could study with the other children, would you like to?"

"Nay, they are verra smart, and they would tease me more than they do now."

"And if I could change that, so they would not make fun of you, would you enjoy having studies with them?"

"Ye canna change it, for I am not allowed with them."

"You will be," she said with a positive air.

His dark blue eyes measured her in a way that only a child could do, with hope, trust, and just a little bit of uncertainty.

She smiled at him and said in a light-hearted tone, "But, enough of that right now. Come along with me, and we will go look at Cahir Mor."

Chapter 25

I can play at Tafl,
Nine skills I know,
Rarely forget I the runes,
I know of books and smithing,
I know how to slide on skis,
Shoot and row, well enough;
Each of two arts I know:
Harp-playing and speaking poetry.

—from an Old Norse manuscript
   Rognvald Kali Kolsson (1100?–1158)
   Norwegian skald poet and Earl of Orkney, Scotland

ALYSANDIR AND HIS MEN DID NOT RETURN UNTIL LATE the next afternoon. Isobella and Bradan were returning from another visit to the stables when Alysandir and his clansmen rode through the gates at a canter and into the keep. She and Bradan paused a moment to watch them dismount and kick the mud off their boots as they tossed their reins to waiting groomsmen.

But what caught her attention was the carcass of a large stag slung over the back of one of the horses. She rested her gaze upon the drooping head and imagined him racing for his life across the moors with a hunting party and deerhounds in pursuit, and she wondered if the Scots field-dressed it in much the same manner that her father and brothers did. She decided that probably that had not changed much over the centuries.

Alysandir had not told her they planned a hunt, so she supposed they happened upon the stag and took advantage of their good fortune. Children were gathering around the carcass, so she asked Bradan if he wanted to join them. He shook his head. She smiled, not certain if Bradan was interested more in the children or the stag, but then decided it was the latter. He seemed fascinated with the dead stag, the sightless eyes still open, the tongue lolling down like a red pennant from a castle tower. It was exactly as her brothers had done, and she decided boys also had not changed much over the centuries.

She was standing with her arm around Bradan's shoulder when she noticed Alysandir gazing at her. He acknowledged her with a slight dip of his head; the second time he had done such. She smiled, a flood of memories of their lovemaking warming her until her toes curled under with delight.

Bradan had the opposite reaction to the sight of Alysandir, however, for the moment Bradan saw him, he broke away from her and lit out like a legion of devils were after him. She knew it would do no good to call him back, so she watched him disappear faster than a rabbit darting into a hole.

***

It was almost suppertime, and Isobella assumed Bradan was already safely ensconced in his tower hideaway and would not be leaving it until the following morning. She was walking down the hallway thinking about what she was going to wear to dinner when she was caught off guard by someone grabbing her arm from behind.

With a gasp, she turned around and saw Alysandir gazing at her warmly. She smiled, not bothering to hide the delight that shone in her eyes.

"How was your meeting with the Macquarrie?"

"'Twas an attempt at peacemaking between the Macquarries and the MacDonalds over a romance between Macquarrie's daughter and the son of Robert MacDonald. It seems lovers' spats are a favorite pastime on Mull."

She tried to hide her disappointment over learning the trip had nothing to do with Elisabeth. "I was surprised to see the stag in the courtyard. Did you encounter it by chance?"

"Aye, but he was a smart one and tried to swim across the inlet. We gave chase, for we couldna let such a prime stag get away."

"I am glad you were successful."

He pulled her against him. "Not as successful by half as my tracking ye doon."

She heard someone coming up the stairs and tried to step away from him, but he held her tightly.

"You don't need to hold me in place. I am not going to bolt."

"Is that the only greeting I am to receive from ye?" He loosened his hold, but he did not release her. "Is there no warm and welcoming kiss awaiting me?"

Laughter danced in her eyes. "I thought about grabbing you by the hair and dragging you off to my lair, but I was afraid the clan would frown upon that. It has been only two days since I saw you last. What did you want me to do, rush out to greet you with a kiss in the courtyard in front of everyone?"

His look sent a ripple of desire through her. "Aye, 'twould not bother me, for everyone will know soon enough that ye are my... that ye are mine." He released her arm. "Ye will sit with me in the hall tonight."

His words had a sobering effect, and she wondered what he had been going to say at the end of that phrase: "...know soon enough that ye are my—" My what? She had a feeling he almost said "mistress," or whatever the going term was here on Mull for a woman who was a little above a prostitute and well below a wife.

"I prefer to dine with your sisters," she said, raising her chin, icicles dripping from each syllable.

He cocked his head and studied her face a moment. "Ye will sit beside me."

"That makes it difficult. I am trying to blend in here and become friends with some of your clanswomen. They are, for the most part, aloof and distant towards me. They obviously know you have come to my room and why, for you have not taken great care to hide the fact."

"Who has treated ye this in this manner? Give me their names."

She placed a hand on his arm. "Don't involve yourself in women's folly. It would only serve to make things worse. Please... let me handle the matter in my own way. Once they realize that I am not a threat to any of them and that I do not have romantic notions about you, they will come around."

She saw a flash of anger in his eyes, his face turning hard and dark. "I have my ways of finding oot. If anyone is beastly toward ye, they will answer to me. I expect ye in the hall and seated next to me, and if ye dinna come, I will have ye carried doon by the guards."

She almost laughed at his protectiveness, yet his autocratic attitude that riled her. She did not want to have it out with him now, so she tried to soften things with a spirit of willing cooperation.

"I don't plan on entering the Great Hall like Cleopatra sailing down the Nile, if that is what you had in mind, but I will come on my own two feet. I am not a cantankerous woman, Alysandir. I do not like disagreements. I am a peacemaker, and believe it or not, I do not thrive on discord. I am meek as a shadow and mild as a moonbeam."

He ignored her sarcasm. "After the meal, ye shall come to my study. I wish to see how well ye play Hnefatafl."

"We call it Tafl in my time."

"I expect to see ye at supper."

She smiled, thinking how much she genuinely liked him, even when he played the dictator. He had been her friend before he was her lover. He started to turn away, but she detained him with a hand placed on his sleeve. "Please, I have a favor to ask."

"And what is this favor?"

"I would like to name the new foal sired by the English war-horse."

His brows went up in surprise. "And what name would ye give him?"

"Cahir Mor."

"'Tis a fitting name ye have chosen, lass."

"I take that to mean you agree to name it Cahir Mor?"

"Aye, the name suits me."

"Thank you," she said, and came up on her toes to kiss his cheek.

"Ye stir my bluid." Before she could turn away, he took her hand in his and placed a kiss upon her wrist. He drew her into a small, dark alcove behind the stairwell and surrounded her with his warmth, enveloping her in a cocoon where nothing else existed but the closeness of his body, the comfort of his arms, and the security of knowing that he would protect her. His mouth found hers and she surrendered to his kiss, her hands soft against his neck.

She never wanted to leave. And yet she had no control over her life. She could find herself back in Texas a minute from now or tomorrow or next month or next year. Her happy thoughts of a future with Alysandir vanished. Caution took its place. She pulled away from him, breathing unsteadily while her pulse pounded in her ears. She brought her hands up between them and pushed him away as she took a step back.

"We need to go, or we will be late."

She had to end it now before they both were carried away. She turned and started down the hall at a fast pace, her skirts rustling about her. She was almost to the door of her bedchamber when he laughed and said, "Ye told me many things aboot ye, that ye are not cantankerous, do not thrive on discord or disagreements, that ye are a peacemaker that is mild and meek. What ye did not tell me is that ye are faint of heart."

"I run away to live and fight another day. In essence, I am merely regrouping."

The sound of Alysandir Mackinnon's laughter rocked down the hallway and whispered along the spiraling stairwell. It floated past the Great Hall and through the massive studded door of the donjon, where it was caught by a breeze, as it drifted through the barbican and over the heads of the two guards standing there. It was swept into the current of a whirlwind and rode on the back of sand eddies along the beach and swirled around a tousle-headed lad building a turret out of wet beach sand.

— ∿ —

Alysandir did not understand Isobella's tendency to blow both hot and cold, but he did not have time to linger on the subject for long. As he went down the stairs, he heard the sound of horses coming through the gate and a commotion in the bailey, so he went to investigate. Thunder rumbled in the distance. The sky darkened and a heavy, black cloud settled over Màrrach, but the air did not hold the smell of rain. An uneasy wind stirred as he stepped through the door and saw his uncle Lachlan's men from the monastery in Iona. Then he saw his sister Barbara.

Gordon McMurry rode closer and dismounted to greet Alysandir with a hearty hug and a slap on the back. "We have escorted Barbara home for ye," he said, obviously making a valiant effort to hold back laughter.

Alysandir frowned. "'Tis a favor ye are doing me, then?" he said, his voice dripping with sarcasm. "Did she ask ye to bring her here, or did ye grow weary of her steel will and bossy manner?"

"Aye, 'twas both and then some," Gordon said and laughed. "'Twould seem yer uncle, Lachlan, grew weary of her daily bombardment of requests to return to Màrrach, so he decided to save ye the trouble of fetching her yerself. 'Twas he who asked me to escort her back to

Màrrach and to place her under the care of her brother, the chief o' Clan Mackinnon."

"Are ye saying she was a wee bit o' trouble to my uncle?"

"Nae, not a wee bit o' trouble, but more a monstrous amount o' it, she was. 'Tis a woman of strong opinion and demanding ways ye have on yer hands, Alysandir. Faith, such a woman would expect ye to peel her grapes afore she would eat them."

"I don't suppose ye would be interested in taking her off my hands now, would ye, if I threw in the peeled grapes?"

Gordon did not laugh when he replied, "Nay, not for all the grapes in Italy. She is a comely lass, that is true, but I would sooner take vows of celibacy than to live with a cantankerous woman."

"She only needs a man with a gentle touch."

"Och! The deil is in her tongue, Alysandir. She would devour a gentle man. 'Tis an ogre that she needs."

Barbara, who had just dismounted, walked by and gave Gordon a swift kick in passing. "Keep yer opinion and yer hostile words to yerself. The nunnery would be preferable to being shackled for a lifetime with a brute like ye."

Gordon grinned as he watched her walk away.

"'Tis a pity ye are no up to the task of taming the lass," Alysandir said. "I thought ye had an eye for her."

"Aye, the sight o' her warms my bluid, but I canna let her know that I fancy mysel' to be exactly the kind o' man she needs to tame her. 'Twill take a great effort, ye ken, but once I have won her heart, I shall go after the rest o' her."

Alysandir laughed heartily and clapped Gordon on

the back. "Come inside, and we will have a dram or two before we sup."

———————

Isobella stood at her window trying to see what was going on in the courtyard. She saw a lone woman and a group of men dismounting… none of whom she recognized.

She turned away when she heard a knock at her door. "'Tis Sybilla and Marion, and we have brought our sister Barbara to meet ye."

Isobella hurried to open the door and found herself surprised, for no one had mentioned Barbara was such a beauty. No wonder Fergus Maclean was determined to have her. With her wealth of luxuriant red hair and fiery green eyes, she would be a standout in any crowd. Isobella was willing to bet Barbara had a fiery temper and a strong will to go along with it, for she had seen the way Barbara had kicked one of her escorts.

Isobella knew immediately that there would be no middle ground between the two of them. They would be either very dear friends or archenemies. Isobella was praying it would be the former.

Barbara looked her over and then said, "I hear ye have a sister who was taken by the Macleans. My sisters seem to think it is Alysandir's place to tell me aboot it, but I prefer to hear it from ye."

Isobella laughed outright, both delighted and relieved it was not hatred at first sight. "Shall we take a walk? We have some time before dinner. I will give you the short version as we go."

They went downstairs, walking past the Great Hall and Alysandir's library and into the garden. Barbara and

Isobella were walking arm in arm, auburn head next to red one, as they talked, Sybilla and Marion following close behind.

Gordon and Alysandir were standing at the window. Gordon said, "I thought ye said Barbara had not met yer visitor."

Alysandir had his gaze fixed upon Isobella. "Apparently, she has now. I have never known Barbara to make such fast acquaintance with anyone, especially another woman, and to see her arm in arm— 'tis hard to believe what my eyes see."

Gordon laughed. "'Tis a much gentler version of yer sister I see now than during her stay on Iona. I think she began to complain aboot it right after ye left."

Alysandir barely heard. He was watching Isobella intently. *What mischief do they plan?*

Isobella saw Alysandir, but she was too occupied with the fact that Barbara liked her. It validated her as a member of the family, for several women smiled at her as they passed by. It was a happy moment, for she caught a glimpse of her future here. But, she reminded herself her future was not hers to plan. At least for now.

Marion and Sybilla left to change their clothes. Isobella and Barbara remained seated on the stone bench, while Isobella told her how Alysandir had rescued her and her twin, and Elisabeth's fate in the hands of Angus Maclean.

When Barbara asked about her odd speech, Isobella told her that their family had been shipwrecked on an island for several years, during which time her parents taught them and gradually their accent had changed.

"We were rescued eventually."

"And ye and yer sister were separated again," Barbara said. "By another ship?"

Isobella nodded, careful to stick to the story as Alysandir had outlined it. "Yes."

"If I were ye, I wouldna put one dainty slipper on board another ship," Barbara said, and the two of them laughed, but Isobella's was more of relief than good humor.

Later, they ended up in Barbara's room so she could change for dinner. Isobella thought she was on safe ground with Barbara, safe enough to be able to discuss Alysandir, and even if she wasn't, she had to ask. "I know we've just met, and you have a right to refuse me, but I must ask. Will you tell me about Alysandir's marriage and Bradan?"

Barbara's brows went up, and she smiled. "Ye have met the lad, then?"

Isobella nodded. "Yes, and I adore him. So much that I intend to see to his education. He is a bright boy, and it is a shame he has been an outcast. I want to know why Alysandir refuses to have anything to do with him, for whatever it is, it is not Bradan's fault. And there is no way anyone could ever convince me that Bradan isn't Alysandir's son. He favors him too much."

Barbara nodded. "Aye, he does, and Alysandir knows Bradan is his son, but whenever he sees him, he is reminded of the disastrous marriage that produced him."

"I know he was married, but I do not know anything about the circumstances," Isobella said, leaning forward with her hands folded in her lap, her gaze attentive upon Barbara's face.

"Her name was Janet. It was an arranged marriage between the fathers. They were young and Alysandir loved her, but she never wanted to be married and she begged her father to let her join a convent. From an early age, she had her heart set upon becoming a nun. The idea of mating with a man was abhorrent to her.

"After almost a year of marriage, she left to visit her family and never returned. Alysandir learned later that she had fled to France. When she discovered she was expecting a child, she waited until after it was born and then sent the wee bairn to Alysandir. She sought an annulment and the protection of the church."

Isobella was shocked. "And she got it?"

Barbara nodded. "Aye, it was granted. The church decided a nun was a higher priority than was a wife. The marriage was annulled. Her rejection hit Alysandir particularly hard."

"Understandably," Isobella said. "It must have been a terrible shock to him, but the child was his and totally innocent of wrongdoings."

"Och! What ye say is true, and we all know it, but unfortunately Alysandir did not see it that way. He was away at the time trying to find Janet, and when he returned, he was furious to find another man's bastard being foisted off as his. Even when it was pointed out that the age of the child coincided with the time that Janet was in residence at Màrrach, Alysandir refused to accept it as the truth and consequently, refused to acknowledge Bradan."

Isobella was puzzled. Alysandir had shown himself to be compassionate and caring to her, a stranger. How could he be so cruel to his own flesh and blood? "But why?"

Their eyes met and Barbara shook her head. "'Twas

twofold. He had no proof that Bradan was his lad, but more important was the annulled marriage. If Bradan was his, then he was conceived when his parents were married, yet the annulment invalidated the marriage.

"We dinna know if Janet told the church about the child. So no one knows if Bradan would be considered a bastard or a legitimate heir. If Alysandir should be forced by the king's regent to marry again, and if he should have a son, recognizing Bradan could jeopardize the position of a legitimate son."

"But this could all be worked out, surely. Your uncle is the abbot."

"Aye, and Alysandir would cut with him if our uncle went around him and tried to settle this. Any recognition of Bradan will have to come from Alysandir's heart."

Isobella sat back and thought there had to be a way to soften his hard heart. Although the sort of treatment Bradan received was never justifiable, she was ashamed to think she had been guilty of misjudging Alysandir. She understood him better now.

She realized why he was at war with himself and how he could be a man who yearned for the softness and companionship of a woman, yet feared one bad marriage would only lead to another. It was sad to think how one woman could so damage both father and son. With a sigh, Isobella stared down at the hands folded in her lap before she said softly, "I had no idea he suffered so much pain from such a short marriage."

"And suffers still. I hope I have no' said too much," Barbara said. "Ye have fallen quiet and pensive."

"No… no, you haven't said too much. As for pensive, I was thinking of a saying… *Two men look out through the same bars: One sees mud and one the stars*. I am ashamed to admit that when it came to understanding Alysandir, I saw mud."

Barbara smiled. "'Tis what anyone would have thought if they did not know the entire story. Mayhap ye understand my brother a little better."

Isobella was about to say it helped a great deal, but the door opened and Sybilla poked her head inside. "We should go down to the hall now or risk Alysandir's displeasure."

Isobella soon found herself being escorted to the empty place next to Alysandir, with his sisters to her left. The men were discussing their recent hunt and how the deerhounds, Duff and Malcolm, had brought down the ten-antlered stag.

Drust said, "Duff's quick eye caught sight of him immediately. He stood still as a stone, with his ears erect and one foot lifted off the ground."

"And then he looked straight at Alysandir," Gavin said, "like he was asking whether it was time to give chase. Puir Malcolm, being young and not so well trained, sprang forward pulling Alysandir doon. Had it no' been for the rope wound around Alysandir's hand, Malcolm would have taken off after the stag."

Colin cut in, "Alysandir came close to changing his name from Malcolm to 'Muckle Fule' as he kept calling him."

"By that time, the stag was on his way to Iona," Drust added.

Everyone laughed. Isobella glanced toward Alysandir and almost overturned her goblet at the smoldering desire in his gaze.

Conversation died down by the time everyone finished. Isobella smoothed the dark green fabric of her skirt and toyed with the goblet of ale she did not touch, hoping all the while that Alysandir had forgotten her promise to play Tafl. She didn't trust herself alone in the room with him.

The thought had no more than formed in her mind, when he stood and offered her his hand, saying, "And now, Mistress Douglas, ye shall accompany me to the library where ye will demonstrate yer skill at Tafl."

"Ye play Tafl?" Barbara asked, obviously astonished. "'Tis no' a game women play."

Isobella nodded, thinking that she wasn't going to explain how she became intrigued with medieval games in college and joined an extracurricular group to learn how to play many of them. "My father taught me to play."

She put her hand to her head and was about to plead a headache when she glanced at Barbara, who gave her a look that said, *I wouldn't if I were you…*

Well, a bargain was a bargain. She might as well get it over with, so Isobella placed her hand in Alysandir's extended palm and accompanied him from the hall, relieved to see that Colin, Grim, and Gavin fell in line behind them, with Barbara tagging along.

Hnefatafl was an old Viking game dating to 400 AD. It was played in Scandinavia, Greenland, Britain, and as far eastward as the Ukraine. Its popularity began to wane with the introduction of chess in the eleventh and twelfth centuries, but there were still many, like Alysandir, who enjoyed playing it.

The beautifully carved wooden board was more than

a foot square and bore some resemblance to a modern-day chessboard, with a central square in the middle. Alysandir's pieces looked to be carved from ivory and onyx, with a larger king and smaller pawns and rooks that numbered twelve light pieces and a king facing twenty-four dark pieces.

The white king was placed in the central square, or throne, surrounded by his white men, which Alysandir gave to Isobella. He, appropriately she thought, took the black pieces, which would try to keep her king from reaching a corner square. She won two of the four games they played.

"Hout! She plays like a man," Colin said. "I doubt any of us could beat her. You were verra fortunate, brother."

"Aye," Alysandir grumbled, and everyone laughed.

"I consider myself very fortunate to win two games," Isobella said.

"Ye play verra, verra well," Colin said.

"She amazes me on a daily basis," Grim said.

At that point, everyone looked at Alysandir, who had remained quiet throughout the discussion. He gave her a frank stare and asked, "Is there anything ye canna do?"

"Be quiet," Isobella said so candidly that everyone fell into fits of laughter, Alysandir included.

Chapter 26

*A little rebellion now and then
is a good thing.*

—Letter to James Madison, 1787
   Thomas Jefferson (1743–1826)
   U.S. president, political philosopher, architect, inventor

ALYSANDIR'S BROTHERS BEGAN TO BID HER GOOD EVENING. Isobella stood and walked beside Barbara. She got as far as the door.

"Mistress Douglas, I would have a word with ye," he said.

Barbara squeezed her hand, and Isobella glanced quickly at Colin, who gave her a sympathetic look before he ducked through the door, dragging Barbara along with him.

Isobella turned, and her heart began to pound at the dark look of desire she saw gleaming in the depths of his eyes. Her own heartbeat began to escalate. She was held immobile and speechless for a moment, as if caught in the blinding reflection of headlights. Her mouth was dry. Her heart pounded. Her body grew warmer beneath the heat of his gaze.

She felt hypnotized and completely under his power. So much so that she was not aware she made a small moan of distress and suddenly found herself in his arms.

Nothing was more treacherous than her own body or so capable of betrayal, and it left her with her defenses down. The warmth of his body penetrated hers and left her weak, and she melted against him.

He pulled her so close her leg was pressed against his knee. She tried to step back, but he caught her, and the next thing she knew, she was in his lap. It was, by her estimation, a rather awkward landing, remindful of the clumsy puffins, but with the heady pull of attraction between them, that did not seem to matter. She felt her body melt into his until it was difficult to discern just where hers ended and his began.

His lips closed over hers tenderly, moving slowly over her mouth, gentle, yet demanding. Without breaking the kiss, his hand slid over her skirts until it reached the hem, where it disappeared. Instinctively, she shuddered and started to pull back, but he sealed her mouth with another hot, impassioned kiss as his hand moved higher until he was at the juncture of her thighs. He found and pulled the drawstring and peeled away her undergarments. While he increased the pressure of the kiss, his hand began to stroke her.

She wanted to cry out from the sheer pleasure of it. He was whispering words in Gaelic against her skin, and her heart began to pound in unison with the tempo of her body. Again… again… and again until she wanted to cry out in agony. Oh, God, she couldn't stop him even if she wanted to, for she wanted this as much as he. Her breathing was slow and thick, and she found her legs parting of their own accord.

"Yes," he whispered. "Yes, sweet Isobella, open yerself to me and dinna hold back."

Hold back? Was he crazy? She couldn't hold back even if she wanted to. Her body had taken control, and she shamelessly writhed in his arms, moving in rhythm with each stroke of his hand until the intensity, the liquid warmth, the words he whispered against her hot skin were more than she could bear. She began to pant and press against his hand until she cried out and her body collapsed against him.

He tied the drawstring, pulled her skirts back down and held her until her breathing was back to normal. She wasn't certain if he would let her up, but when she made the attempt to stand, he let her go, saying nothing but keeping his gaze upon her face.

"Is this what you wanted to talk to me about?" she asked weakly, as she strove to control her rapid breathing and still her runaway heart.

"Ye would have preferred to talk?"

"I wanted to know why you detained me."

"Ye did say ye had trouble sleeping."

She had an acerbic retort ready when she suddenly burst out laughing.

There was a gleam of wicked delight in his eyes. "Tell me on the morrow if it worked."

It worked. But Isobella did not tell Alysandir that it worked, nor did she tell him that, with the help of his sisters, she found a room in the main part of the castle for Bradan. The room was one floor above Isobella's room with a small corner fireplace and two windows with a view of both the sea and land. After much pillaging, the girls found a few odds and ends of furniture and a nice feather bed the perfect size for a boy. A small wooden table with two chairs would serve well enough for a desk where Isobella could begin his studies, using three books she had found in Alysandir's library.

When she brought Bradan to see the room, he was both awed and terribly frightened. "The Mackinnon doesna care if I have this room?" he asked, while turning his head this way and that to survey his new room and its contents.

"He will not bother you about it," Isobella said, not missing the way Barbara and Sybilla both closed their eyes and crossed themselves, while Marion had her head down and stared at the floor.

"We will start your lessons in the morning after we break our fast," Isobella said.

The lessons were going smoothly that first morning, but Bradan was nervous, so Isobella distracted him by showing him maps. "This is what the world looks like, Bradan. This is Scotland, and if you will look here, this tiny little brown spot is the Isle of Mull."

While he studied it, she placed a larger map of Mull that she had sketched next to the first. "This is another map of Mull."

"'Tis bigger."

"Yes, they are pictures of what Mull looks like, because it is much, much larger than this map, isn't it? Now watch, and I will put an X where Màrrach is." She marked the spot, and his eyes widened. "See, this is the Atlantic Ocean and the beach where I met you, and way over here is the island of Iona, where your great uncle, Lachlan Mackinnon is the abbot."

"'Tis where Barbara was."

"Yes, and over here where this X is placed is where the Macleans live at Duart Castle, but we dinna want to go there. They are on the ocean, too." He put his finger on the blue water. "Have you ever heard of the Sound of Mull?"

"Aye. The Duke of Argyll lives across the Sound of Mull."

"Very, very good, Bradan. How did you know that?"

"I heard the guards talking aboot it. They dinna like Argyll."

She ruffled his hair. "Observant, lad! Now, this water is the Sound of Mull. Here is Duart Castle, and over here is Argyll. And over here is where the Atlantic and the Sound of Mull come together."

They spent the rest of the day with her introducing short sessions of learning the alphabet and then letting him try his hand at copying the letters. That afternoon, they went down to the beach and drew letters in the sand and wrote a few words. He wanted to learn how to write her name so she showed him both Isobella and Alysandir.

Then they sat on a boulder and ate a scone and talked about oceans and countries, the sky and stars and constellations. And before they returned to Màrrach, they watched the tide come in and wash away all they had written there, as one would erase a chalkboard at the end of the day.

That night when she lay in bed, she kept seeing the wonderment in Bradan's eyes and thought it must have been the same expression on the face of the first cave-man who made fire. How much we take for granted in the twenty-first century, she thought, and felt blessed to be the one to open this beautiful little boy's eyes to the universe he was part of.

Several days later, Isobella encountered Alysandir on the stairs, just as she was returning to her room. Before she could greet him, he grabbed her upper arm and es-corted her to her room and closed the door behind them.

"You are angry."

"I am beyond angry, Isobella. Ye have gone too far with this and without my consent."

"What can it hurt to treat Bradan in the manner he deserves?"

"What do ye mean by that?"

"He is your son, whether you want to accept him as that or not. You only have to look at him to see he has your face, your coloring. He is tall and slender like you. For heaven's sake, Alysandir, are you blind? Everyone at Màrrach knows he's your son, but they do not speak of it out of respect or fear.

"I'm not saying you have to claim him, but he is your legitimate issue, your flesh and blood, and because of that, he should be afforded a place to sleep that is better than that of a stable hand. I am appalled that you would let him go uneducated. If you should never marry again and have a son, Bradan could be your heir. Would you have him be an illiterate lout if the mantle of chief is placed upon his shoulders?"

She watched the muscle in his jaw work, but she wasn't finished. She figured she had already gone this far, so she might as well wade into it with both feet.

"If it would make things better in the eyes of your clan, punish me for what I have done, but don't take it out on Bradan. He has been punished enough for being born."

"I canna allow ye to disobey me. You will confine yerself to this room and take all yer meals here until I decide what to do with ye."

She nodded, and before she could speak, he departed.

The next morning, she was up early, and she debated only a moment whether she would disobey him. Soon she was on her way to the beach, where she found Bradan, and they walked together, talking about the ocean and the changes in his life. He wrote their names in the sand, and they finished their morning school lessons and then stopped to share the lunch she brought.

"Have you ever been inland... away from the sea?"

"Aye, I go there when I want to look for birds and nests or to catch a fine troot in the burn."

"Did you see any big stones that stand straight up like they are pointing to the sky or a cave with drawings?"

"Aye, there is a cave near the kind of stones ye speak of not so verra far away, but ye canna go into the cave except when the tide is oot."

"Can you take me there?"

"Aye."

"Would it be better if we went on horseback?"

"I canna ride a horse."

"I want you to show me where the cave is. We will go to the stable for a horse, and you can ride behind me."

They returned to the castle, but the grooms refused to give her a horse. She found Colin who not only ordered her a horse saddled but also one for him. "I shall accompany ye so Alysandir willna lop off my heid wi' a claymore for allowing ye to go."

He ordered a sidesaddle for her, but Isobella quickly said, "Please give me a saddle like you would ride. I don't know how to ride sidesaddle, and I don't have time to learn today."

If she hadn't scandalized everyone at Màrrach by now, she soon would, for she not only ordered a horse saddled, but she asked Colin to find her a pair of trews she could wear under her skirts. Once she had climbed onto the saddle, Bradan was boosted up behind her.

The cave was almost an hour away. They were fortunate that Colin brought a torch as Bradan suggested, and he lit it before they entered the cave. Inside, they found two stone slabs covered with ancient markings which Isobella immediately identified as Celtic. Bradan found two flints and a bronze pin, while Colin found a bone-scraping tool. Two pottery vessels were unearthed near a circle of blackened stones that had probably ringed a fire. One of the pottery vessels broke when Colin lifted it.

Upon close examination, the relic showed signs of residue inside, and Isobella wished she had some twenty-first-century tools to date her finds. She would have to find a way to preserve the artifacts and to leave as much information as possible for future archeologists. She didn't want them to be stolen or damaged by anyone who did not recognize their true value to mankind. However, she knew that finding the artifacts was one thing. Finding the right place to stash them was another.

Time passed quickly, and the sun eventually began

to drop toward the horizon. She knew they did not have time to look any longer, for the torch would be out soon and the tide would be coming in. Neither Colin nor Bradan thought their finds were half as remarkable as Isobella did. She, on the other hand, could not contain her excitement as they rode back to Màrrach. She needed to find a way to document the site and preserve the major pieces... that was her first objective.

She was still lost in similar thoughts as they arrived at the castle gates. Bradan abandoned her immediately by saying he needed something from his room. Shortly after Bradan disappeared, Colin said, "Mayhap I will see ye at supper."

He seemed just as anxious to leave her as Bradan. "Where are you going?" she asked.

Colin rubbed his midsection and replied with charming affability, "I am off to the kitchen to find something to quiet my hunger afore my stomach decides to digest my doublet. Would ye like me to fetch something for ye?"

"Thank you, no," she said. "I think I can wait until supper."

They parted ways, and she continued down the hall, passing Alysandir's library.

"I would have a word with ye, Mistress Douglas," a voice called out from the room.

Oh, my, she thought, I must have really offended him. She knew she might as well get this over with, so she walked into his library and stopped before his desk. "You wish to discuss something?"

"Aye," he said, looking her up and down. "Where have ye been dressed like ye are?"

"Digging in a cave some distance from here. It is by the sea and its mouth fills with water when the tide is in."

If she had told him she was frolicking naked in the ocean, she did not think he could have looked more astonished or angry. When he spoke, his words were cold and perfectly measured. "I thought I forbid you to leave the castle. I explicitly told ye yester eve that ye were confined to yer room until I decided what to do with ye. Ye deliberately disobeyed me."

Her hands flew to her mouth. Oh, dear Lord, she thought. She had forgotten all about that. "I forgot, Alysandir. Truly, I—"

He slammed his hand down on a stack of papers which, thankfully, muffled the sound, just before they slid off the desk and onto the floor.

She made a move to gather them, but he shouted, "Leave them be!"

She took a step back. "I forbid ye to go wandering out alone, and if ye ever disobey me again, a trip to the dungeon might be in order. Ye would do well to remember that."

"For your information, I was not alone. Bradan and Colin accompanied me, and it was all terribly exciting. You won't believe what we found. I want to go back tomorrow."

"Didn't ye hear what I just said? Are ye not aware of the danger of wandering into caves, especially along the seashore? If the tide had come in, ye would have had no way to escape."

"I know, but Bradan is very knowledgeable about the timing of the tide."

"Bradan! I grow weary of hearing that name, and I rue the day I allowed you to befriend him. I warned you…"

"Yes, I know you did, and I am ready to take my punishment. Have you decided what it will be?"

That seemed to catch him off guard, and his tone was somewhat tempered when he said in softer tones, "I will think upon it, but if you go wandering off again, you may find yourself captured and in the hands of the Macleans."

"Perhaps that would be the best solution for both of us. I wouldn't be a burden to you any longer, and I would be with my sister."

"If ye disobey me again, it will be an end to yer freedom. If I have to lock ye in yer room, I will. Do not test my patience, for I am fast running out where ye are concerned."

"And it will be the end of the friendship that we have found. Shall I remind you that force is not a remedy? Even if it were, I do not respond well to it. I can be persuaded to go along with reasonable requests, yet demands from overbearing tyrants don't do anything but bring out my rebellious side."

He raised his brows in obvious surprise at her outburst, but his words were hard, harsh, and final. "If you find yourself captured, mistress, Bradan goes back to the tower, and his schoolwork will be terminated. That should control yer rebellious side."

"You wouldn't dare use a child as a pawn," she said.

"Aye, I would, and ye are welcome to try me and find oot. I will brook no more disobedience from you."

"Disobedience can be a virtuous undertaking. It has paved the way for many discoveries and motivated scientists and explorers. Would you like me to tell you about them?"

"What I would like is for ye to stop turning my life upside doon. Ye seem to have a rather curious way of distracting me and creating difficulties wherever ye go."

"I am sorry if you think I create difficulties for the pure pleasure of it. That is not the case. You seem to find fault with everything I want to do. I cannot sit twiddling my thumbs and staring out the window all day. I am horrible at knitting. I cannot thread a needle. I sing like a lovesick goose. I cannot read your poetry so that anyone can understand what I am saying. I am an educated woman. I like to be active, to learn, to expand my knowledge, and stimulate my mind."

"Yer mind is over-stimulated as it is."

"Perhaps, but it would be nice to have a kind and considerate jailer."

"God, would that someone could send me a quiet, understanding prisoner!"

She sighed and decided to remain quiet, or they would continue this "tit for tat" for the rest of the evening.

He stood, and the chair scraped the floor as he leaned forward and placed both hands on his desk. "Ye are a great deal of trouble, Isobella. Would that I could stuff a sock in yer mouth and clap a padlock on yer mind and have done with it."

"I could sooner reason with a block of wood than get anything through your thick head. It seems impossible for us to discuss anything. We can't agree. Perhaps we should try again and start over at another time when we have both had time to think about it."

"The quickest way to end a battle is to lose it, but I can see that ye never give up, even though surrender is oft more palatable than resistance."

"Well, I daresay we are well suited in that regard, although I am your prisoner and you have the advantage of me."

"Nay, not yet, but I will, and soon."

"Not if I have anything to say about it," she replied and left.

She had class with Bradan the next morning, and that afternoon she taught him and several other children how to make kites. Since she was forbidden to go to the beach, she convinced Gavin and Grim to take Bradan to the beach so he could fly his kite. She gave them basic lessons in the courtyard, and by the time they went to the beach, they were followed by half the castle. Isobella stood on the parapets and observed, occasionally cupping her hands around her mouth and yelling orders to add more to the tail or to let out more string.

For the rest of the day, she did not see nor hear anything of Alysandir—or the Black Douglas, for that matter.

Chapter 27

Ah, colonel, all's fair in
Love and war, you know.

—Nathan Bedford Forrest (1821–1877)
  U.S. cavalryman and general in the Confederate Army

HE CAME TO HER ROOM THAT NIGHT WHILE SHE SLEPT. HE
lay quietly beside her, as he had done the night she slept
beside him in the glen, gently pulling her close. When
she awoke, she was surrounded by the warm, male scent
of him. Warm. He is so warm everywhere. His lips found
hers, and his mouth was hot and tasted sweetly, faintly
of ale.

The kiss was long and hungry as his mouth moved
over hers coaxing, teaching her of his need, and urg-
ing her to express hers. His words were delicately erotic
and whispered warmly against her skin. His kisses were
gently offered, but his body, heaven help her, was hot
and hard and so right. Him and no other, she thought,
for she knew she would never feel about another man as
she felt about Alysandir.

I love him.

She did not want to think about the fact that he did
not love her, that he would never again allow himself
to love another woman. She was the right woman for
him, but they were out of sync, for she had come at the

wrong time. Little did it matter that she had traveled back through centuries to meet her soul mate. She had arrived too late. Nothing could change that.

She relaxed against him, wanting him, needing him, and willing to have him without love, if that was the only way. When he kissed her again, she responded more than she had before, showing him with her mouth what she felt in her heart. He groaned deep in his throat and crushed her against himself, burying his face in her hair. She was certain he felt something more than lust.

He started to pull away, and her hand came out to touch his arm. "What is wrong?" she asked, and he jerked as if her touch had seared him like a white-hot iron. She waited as he threw back his head and closed his eyes, beads of sweat gleaming on his skin, visible in the moonlight, and she could see the strong cords of his neck standing out. His breathing came fast and erratic. But the anguished expression on his face told her he was fighting his devils now.

Sadness crept over her and wrapped her in its smothering cloak of despair.

He wanted her, but he did not want her. He wanted to make love to her, but he did not love her. He wanted her with him as his woman, but he did not want her as his wife.

It wasn't fair. He wanted everything from her, yet he offered her nothing in return. Would she ever come to understand him completely?

She knew that tenderness lay buried somewhere deep inside him. He had loved another woman who hurt him deeply. How could she peel away the layers of pain, betrayal, disappointment, and aching sadness to find the wonderful man burdened beneath the weight of his past? And was she certain she wanted to go that deep to release the devils from their shackles? What if something fiercer, more horrible, more dangerous was imprisoned there? Well she knew that once they were out, the devils would never go back inside again.

And what about you, Isobella Catriona? she asked herself. Yes, he enjoys you now, but you are nothing more than a shiny new bauble that will soon tarnish. Then he will be drawn away by the bright shine of a newer, shinier bauble, while you will continue in a downward spiral, passed from clansman to clansman until you are too old to care anymore.

She closed her eyes, overcome with an aching sadness that gripped her from within. His hand slid down her throat, lingering a moment at the soft beginning swell of her breast. "I never grow tired of touching ye."

You will… one day you will… She could almost hear her heart cracking, but he began nuzzling her, telling her how fragrant her hair was, how soft the feel of her skin was beneath his, how her soft, panting breaths aroused him and made him want to be inside her.

"No," she whispered, afraid now. Afraid that he was asking too much and on the verge of receiving it—and she did not want to give him everything. She wanted to keep a little of herself for her own. Yet his words and the way he stroked and touched her made something primitive and urgent leap within her, something too strong, too overpowering, and too desirable to stop.

"Dinna hold back."

"It's is too much. You ask too much," she said, wondering if the husky tones of desire she heard were actually coming from her lips. The heat of his touch unlocked all her well-guarded feelings and secrets, releasing, like the evils flying out of Pandora's box, the love and passion she felt for him. When his mouth came searching, he found hers waiting and she melted against him, returning his kiss with a fervor she had never experienced before.

He was touching her in a way that wiped out all rational thought. She wanted to live, to feel, to pretend, just this one time, that they were man and woman with one driving need to be together, drawing them deeper into the swirling whirlpool that gradually began to pull them under.

She moaned when his mouth covered hers, and he began kissing her with a burning intensity that left a trail of fire everywhere he touched. She wasn't so foolish as to think anything was different, but she had this moment, this night, and it would have to be enough.

"I never grow weary of touching ye this way, and when ye open to me, ye canna imagine how it feels."

For a fleeting moment, she could not help wondering to how many others he had said those same words, kissed this same way. His experienced hands moved over her as if he had been touching her like this forever. He knew how make her body jerk in response, when to gently coax, and where to put his hand to make her cry out.

"Touch me," he said, taking her hand and drawing it down between them. She closed her hand around him, and he said something softly in Gaelic. He rolled over her and pushed her legs apart, fitting himself between them. She felt light-headed and could not stop the groans that came from deep in her throat when he moved against her.

Her mind did not seem capable of clear thought. She only knew she wanted him with such fierceness she was close to screaming. She knew she would go insane if he didn't make love to her soon and put an end to the writhing torment. She ached for him, and her legs opened further until he found the place where he belonged.

He had never made love with such intensity. What he had with Isobella was stronger than anything he had ever experienced, and the memory of it would be forever etched upon the inner chambers of his mind. *If only I could give her what she wanted.*

He looked down at her, wearing nothing but the ghostly light of moonbeams blessing her skin. Her hair entwined him like coppery links of chain, binding her to him. He could love her for her glorious hair alone… if he was a man who could love. The blood in his veins ran hot and thick, but soon duty would call and this moment would become a memory and his blood would, once again, run thin and cold.

In his thoughts… she was always in his thoughts, night and day, sometimes a welcome diversion, sometimes an unwanted visitor he tried to push away. But now, in this moment, she was oh so welcome and he felt at peace with her. He wished he could paint this moment in his mind like a portrait so he could enjoy it time and again.

Did she know how he ached for her? Did she know that he had memorized the way the firelight kissed her skin and turned her hair to fire? That he grew painfully hard watching her dress in the darkness? How badly he wanted to pull her back into bed with him and touch her until she cried out from the pleasure of it?

He did not know if he would be able to hold her forever or if he truly had a right to try. She did not even belong in his world. He knew what she wanted, but it was all the things he could not give her. He had obligations. He fought battles. He knew, or at least expected, that he would end up dead in one of them, just like his father and brother.

A woman could break a man in a way that wars or physical labor could not. A woman always fell in love and ruined it all. They wanted to attach all kinds of weights to pull down a man until he could not walk for tripping over them.

Women could not be trusted.

And it was that last thought that ruined it all.

―⁂―

The next day, Isobella was on her way down the stairs as Alysandir came in from the stables. When he saw her, he paused to watch her make her descent. As she stepped off the last step, she said, "I was looking for you."

"And so you have found me," he said, his tone cold and emotionless.

She noticed he still wore his gloves, and she assumed he had been out riding. "May I have a few words with you?"

He looked like he was going to tell her he did not have time for such feminine foolishness, but he seemed to check the thought. With a sigh of resignation, he said, "We are close to the library. We can talk in there."

Without waiting for her, he turned and strode down the hall. By the time she arrived, he had removed his gloves and tossed them on the desk he was now sitting behind, framed in a square of sunlight.

She took a seat in the chair near the window and enjoyed the warmth of the sun against her back.

"Ye wished to speak to me about…?"

"Bradan," she said.

"That is not a subject for discussion. Have ye another to talk about?"

"No. Bradan deserves the same kind of life the other children have."

He shuffled papers on his desk, a sign that he was ignoring her or that she was not ranked very high in order of importance. When he did not say anything, she made a move to get up. He stopped shuffling papers and sat back, giving her a blank look.

"What is it that ye want?"

"I want you to leave Bradan out of our quarrel. I want your word that you will let him continue living in the castle and not use moving him back to the tower as leverage to keep me in line. Bradan and I are two separate issues. It is unfair of you to combine them."

Instead of answering her right away, he sat there with his hands holding a small silver dagger that he twirled slowly. She wondered if he was thinking of using it on her. At last he said, "Verra well. I will agree to allow him to live in the room where he now resides, and ye may continue to instruct him, but keep the little bastard out of my sight."

Elated, she rose from her seat. "I know you won't regret it."

"I regret it already."

For the next two weeks, she put all of her efforts into training Bradan. "When will I study Latin?" he asked.

Happy he yearned to learn more, she said, "As soon as you are further along with your English." He was smart and he learned fast, but he kept one eye on the door. He acted nervously, always looking over his shoulder. If he happened to see his father, he would run and hide. Sometimes it took hours to find him.

During the third week of it, she was sewing—yes, she was starting to get the hang of sewing—in the solar with Alysandir's three sisters. They were discussing Bradan.

"I have finally accepted defeat, and I must accept the truth that Bradan will never be free to become the man he is capable of being if Alysandir does not accept him."

"I agree," Sybilla said. "But what can we do aboot it?"

Isobella smiled. *What can we do aboot it, instead of what can you do aboot it.*

She did not get to think further upon it for Barbara said, "The way I see it, Isobella has only one choice. She must take Bradan and leave Màrrach."

Her sisters gasped in horror. Isobella was dumbstruck.

"But where can she go?" Marion asked.

"To the Macleans to be with her sister," Barbara said.

"Alysandir will be furious," Marion said, "and if he finds oot we had anything to do with it, I shudder to think how angry he would be."

"Weel, he willna kill us," Barbara said. "I am certain of that. Anything else, we can handle."

"I dinna have yer confidence," Marion said.

"I don't want to involve you in my dilemma, but I do

think Barbara is right. Bradan needs a normal life, and the only way he will have it is if he is away from his father," Isobella said.

"Ye canna take Bradan and go to Duart alone," Sybilla said. "Ye will need help."

"She will have it," Barbara said. "Our brothers will help. They all care about Bradan and want the best for him."

"They better all go together, for it will be more difficult for Alysandir to kill all of them than only one or two," Marion said, and they all laughed.

"I have only one question," Sybilla said, "and that is, have ye considered that life at Duart could be worse for both of ye than it is here?"

Isobella nodded. "Yes, I have considered that. I have had no word from Elisabeth, so I don't really know how she is being treated. I only have what Alysandir said when I asked how she would fare. He said, 'She will be treated the same as ye. She is a pawn, nothing more. They willna harm her.'"

She looked down at her hands clenched together and forced herself to relax. "I have to believe that Alysandir knew what he was talking about and go on faith. And we will not tell the Macleans who Bradan is. We don't want them to think they have the possible heir of Clan Mackinnon under their roof."

Isobella was saddened to think she would not see Alysandir again, but she knew that sooner or later Alysandir would tire of her. Because she loved him, she would never be able to stay here day after day, watching him with another woman. And what if she were to have a child? She feared it would be treated the same as Bradan. She had been terribly foolish to risk getting pregnant for a few moments of passion.

She sighed wearily. She had no choice but to leave Màrrach. A little heartbreak now was preferable to a huge one later. With the help of Alysandir's sisters, Isobella began to plot her escape.

It was Barbara who went to her brothers with the news and to enlist their help in escorting Isobella and Bradan to Duart to live with the Macleans. But they refused.

Finally, Isobella said, "Then, Bradan and I will go alone."

"Ye willna be able to get a horse from the stable," Drust said.

"Then we shall walk."

"Ye dinna ken where Duart Castle is. How will ye find yer way?" Colin asked.

"Sooner or later we should meet someone who could help us," Isobella replied.

Drust and Colin exchanged glances, and Ronan said, "I will escort ye to Duart."

"Do ye realize what ye are saying?" Drust asked. "Alysandir might disown ye and cast ye oot of the clan."

"Aye, I ken he might, but Isobella and our sisters are right. 'Tis wrong the way Alysandir has treated his own son. Bradan is a good lad. He doesna deserve to be an outcast. We are his uncles, and I am ashamed that none of us have come forward to acknowledge that before now. Since none of ye will take the step, I will. If Alysandir casts me aside, Bradan will have at least one Mackinnon uncle residing wi' him at Duart."

"We canna let ye take the burden on yer shoulders. We are all Bradan's uncles," Drust said, "and we will all help him. Probably for the last time, for I will be an outcast when Alysandir realizes I am the one who made the decision for all of us." Then he looked at Isobella with a grin and said, "'Tis the right thing to do, aye?"

"Aye," Isobella said and hugged him. "I love you, Drust, for what ye are doing."

"What aboot us?" Colin and Ronan asked, and the twins chimed in.

"I love all of you," she said, and realized suddenly that it was true.

Later, the three sisters came up with a plan to get Alysandir out of the way so he wouldn't see them leave. Isobella and Bradan hid out of sight, while Drust and his brothers planned a hunt and rode away. When Alysandir could not find Isobella, he asked Barbara if she had seen her. "Not since she left to go down to the cave with Marion and Sybilla."

As soon as he departed, Isobella and Bradan fetched their horses from the stables and rode away for their planned rendezvous with Alysandir's brothers. Once they caught up with them, Isobella said, "I am worried that Alysandir and his men will find us and this will all be for nothing."

"I wouldna be worrit aboot that," Drust said, "for Ronan took the big lock from the dungeon and put it on the door where the saddles and bridles are kept. It will take them several hours to tear doon the door, for they canna break the lock."

"I am so sorry I agreed to your helping. I had no idea just what we were all getting into."

"Contention is the bone we brothers cut our teeth on," Drust said. "He will be angry and will see we are punished, but he will forgive us because deep in the best part o' Alysandir's heart, he will know we did the right thing."

Isobella said a prayer right then and there that God would put the perfect woman for him in his life, for he deserved nothing less.

When Alysandir arrived at the cave and saw only Sybilla and Marion, he knew he had been duped even before he asked, "And where, pray tell, is Isobella?"

"She is no' here," Marion said, sounding, she knew, like the idiot she was.

Chapter 28

"Will you walk into my parlour?"
said a spider to a fly:
"'Tis the prettiest little parlour
that ever you did spy."

—"The Spider and the Fly," 1829
  Mary Howitt (1799–1888)
  English poet, author, and translator

AS GENTLY AS A BLOWN-OUT TORCH, THE SUN SLIPPED beneath the horizon. The wind stirred in the trees, their lofty branches dark silhouettes against a darkening sky. And all around them was nothing but the clip-clop of hooves and the silence of the night.

It was almost midnight when they arrived at Duart Castle, standing proud and defiant on a crag like a sentinel guarding the Sound of Mull. Isobella looked at the steps leading to the gatehouse while Drust spoke to the guards inside. She waited, fighting the panic that rose to tighten like hands around her throat.

When he did not return, a strange sense of foreboding threatened her iron will, eroding the feeling that she had made the right decision to come here. Doubt filled her with despair. She longed for the familiar surroundings of Màrrach. She glanced at the pale face of Bradan, and although he did not show it, she knew the lad was scared. *What have I done?* She glanced around her. The brothers were quiet, but there was no hostility in their silence.

At last, Drust returned with two guards and they were escorted to the entrance of the castle. A hoof pawed at the cobblestones as Ronan helped her down. Bradan's horse tossed its head, and the metal bit clanked as Drust lifted the lad and took him by the hand. Isobella hugged Colin, Gavin, and Grim, saddened that she would never see them again.

"My heart breaks," was all she could manage, and then she pulled away and joined the others, drawing her cloak more closely about her as the four of them were escorted inside.

The evening meal was long past, and everyone was abed. The interior light was smoky and dim; the late night sounds strange, the scent unfamiliar. The loneliness that filled her quickly changed to fear as she listened to Drust and Ronan refusing to hand them over to anyone but Angus Maclean.

As they waited for the chief of Clan Maclean, her hands felt clammy and cold. Somewhere in the castle a door slammed. Footfalls echoed down passages. Imagined images of the Maclean swirled around in her head. She envisioned him as Blackbeard with lit cannon fuses in his hair, the ends of his pigtails smoking, pistols jammed in his bandoliers, and a bloody sword in his hand.

She heard voices close by, but only one that was gruff and authoritative. She swallowed a gulp of air. She glanced at the doorway and the black depths behind it. A candle appeared. Her gaze was frozen upon the frame of candlelight centered in the doorway. And then, a shadow appeared, growing larger and darker as it drew near.

Isobella watched, dry mouthed, as Angus Maclean walked into the room. He was the stuff of myths and fairy-tales, the quintessential monster. His face was expressionless, as if it had been carved from granite. His cheekbones were prominent and his brow broad, and she couldn't decide if he looked like he had just stepped from the pages of mythology or a nightmare.

She was right to compare him with Blackbeard, for he did embody the pirate. He was tall, dark, and swarthy, with shaggy black hair and heavy-lidded, piercing black eyes that missed nothing. Upon first inspection, his gaze moved rapidly from Isobella to Bradan before it rested upon Drust and finally Ronan.

"And to what do I owe the honor of a visit from the Mackinnons at this hour?" the Maclean asked.

"I have brought Isobella Douglas, the sister of Elisabeth. She wishes to be united with her sister," Drust said.

The Maclean looked Isobella over. She felt like a prisoner on the auction block. "Yer sister spoke the truth when she said she had a twin." He smiled triumphantly and hooked his thumbs proudly in his belt. "'Twould seem I now have the complete set."

That sent a cold shiver over her, and she glanced at Drust, who purposefully did not look at her.

"And the lad?"

"Bradan," Drust said, and Isobella saw the muscle work in his jaw and saw, too, Ronan's clenched fists.

The Maclean's gaze rested upon Bradan for some time. Isobella was willing to bet that he had already figured out

the lad was Alysandir's son, but if he did, he did not mention it. Instead, he turned to the two guards at the door.

"Take the lass and the lad to the quarters of Elisabeth
Douglas and see they are well cared for."

She was sure everyone in the castle could hear the
release of her long-held breath. When she glanced at
Angus Maclean, she saw amusement gleaming in the
depths of in his black eyes. She turned and hugged Drust
and Ronan, and thanked Drust for at least the tenth time
for bringing them here.

"I will never forget this. Never. I know I don't need
to tell you… all of you, how much I love you, but what
you don't know is that I will miss you every day of the
rest of my life."

And then she was hurrying up the stairs, wiping away
tears as she held tightly to Bradan's hand. They followed
behind the two guards, and then they turned down a
long, dark hallway.

Elisabeth's room was at the far end, but that did not
matter. Isobella felt like she was walking on air. The
guard rapped swiftly upon the door with the hilt of his
sword, so loudly that she was certain it echoed throughout the castle.

"Just a damn minute! Do you think I'm deaf?"

Isobella smiled. Elisabeth!

The door swung open. "You better have a good reason
for… Oh, my God! Izzy!" She grabbed her sister in a
bear hug. Isobella was not sure if she squeezed Elisabeth
tighter or if it was the other way around. She would have
said something, but Elisabeth beat her to the punch.

"I never thought this would happen. How did you get
here? How did you know where I was? Come in!"

Isobella followed Elisabeth through the door, and Bradan accompanied her.

Elisabeth looked down at him. "Well, he cannot be yours, so where did you find him?"

"He is Alysandir's son," she whispered.

Her brows rose in unison with the sly smile. "And Alysandir is obviously someone important… to you, I take it?"

Isobella gave her a miserable half-smile. "Most of the time."

Elisabeth laughed. "Oh my, I cannot wait to hear of it. Come, sit down and tell me everything that's happened since we've been apart." She looked at Bradan again and said, "Let me put down some bedding for the lad." She had barely spoken the words when someone knocked on the door.

Elisabeth opened it, and in walked a servant with the things Isobella and Bradan had brought with them from Màrrach and a stack of bedding for Bradan. There were also a tray of cold food and a container of wine. Isobella wasn't hungry, but they made a pallet for Bradan by the fire. They watched him eat while the two of them talked over a goblet of wine. Later, Isobella glanced at Bradan and saw he was asleep.

Elisabeth and Isobella sat in the bed talking.

"How have they treated you?" Isobella asked. "I was so happy to see you weren't locked in the dungeon or the tower."

"Oh, never that. Actually, they have treated me like one of the family. Angus explained his grievance was not against me, that I was…"

"A pawn."

"Exactly." Elisabeth's brows rose questioningly. "You have also been free to come and go?"

"Yes, except for this trip. Alysandir's brothers escorted us here, unbeknownst to him. They will not have an easy time of it."

"And other than this trip, you were treated fairly?"

"Of course. I wasn't allowed outside the castle gates without an escort, but I went anyway."

Elisabeth laughed. "I do the same."

Isobella smiled. "So, is there anyone special in your life?"

"No. I think Angus has ideas of a match between his son, Fergus, and myself, but that will never happen. But that is another story. Right now, I want to hear about Alysandir. Is he handsome?"

"Oh, Elisabeth, you have no idea."

"Oh, my, you're in love."

Isobella sighed, "I'm afraid so."

"Then why are you here?"

"It's too long a story to go into tonight. Have you told them how we arrived here?" Isobella asked.

"You mean the time travel?"

"Yes."

Elisabeth said, "Are you crazy? I don't want to be burned at the stake."

"No one quizzed you about our sudden appearance in the glen?"

"No, but I can tell that you were."

"Yes," Isobella said. "Alysandir is smart and very observant. He immediately began asking questions." Then, she explained how things went until she told him the truth.

"You're lucky you weren't thrown in the dungeon, and braver than I," Elisabeth said. "Although it has been difficult at times for me to keep my mouth shut. I've had some close calls when I referred to something in our time, but so far I've been able to charm my way out of it."

"Have they commented on your strange speech?"

"Yes, I explained our father was a linguist who studied many different varieties of English spoken elsewhere. I said he devoted himself to reconstructing the evolution of English to a more pure form, that our vocabulary and pronunciation was different from everyone else."

"My, you do excel at fabrication."

Elisabeth nodded. "How about you? What did you use for an excuse?"

Isobella spoke of the shipwreck that never happened, and Elisabeth laughed. "Lord, if our parents only knew what a couple of creative liars they raised."

Elisabeth shrugged. "At least our stories are similar. I didn't know how long I would be here, but I didn't want my head lopped off the moment I arrived. Necessity, as they say." She put her hand on Isobella's. "Do you think Douglas will always be evasive about our going back home?"

Isobella replied, "I feel we are caught in a battle between gods and mortals. Perhaps Douglas is a puppet on a string the same as we are."

"Or he may be the one pulling our strings," Elisabeth said. "Is he still being evasive?"

Isobella nodded. "Most of the time. Have you heard from him?"

Elisabeth smiled. "Just once. On the way here when he told me…"

"...*Fear na ye?*"

Elisabeth nodded. "How often do you talk to him?"

Isobella shrugged. "It varies. He has a way of popping up uninvited and then staying away when I summon him. He laughs one moment and jerks my chain the next. I am amazed to see such affected trickery in a ghost." She paused a moment, then said, "You only heard him speak, but you haven't seen him?"

"Not even a twinkle of one of his blue eyes. I don't think he likes me. I wasn't very nice to him that day in the glen."

"He can be a bit strange sometimes," Isobella replied.

"Everything about our coming here is strange," Elisabeth said, "but what do you mean?"

"Just that I'm not always certain just whose side he is on."

Suddenly Elisabeth hugged her. "Oh, Izzy, life has been lonely without you. I have missed you so much. You won't believe it, but I've learned to be more patient, so that now I'm no longer saying that when I see you, 'I'm going to poke both your eyes out for getting us into this bind.'"

Isobella laughed. "I must admit I wasn't certain when the door opened if you would hug me or punch me flat out as you once said you wanted to do. I was afraid you would be angry or hate me for this."

"Never," Elisabeth said.

They talked until the sky was turning a pale grey. Isobella yawned and said, "Good night, Izzy."

"Night, Lizzy," Isobella said, using the pet name from their childhood before Elisabeth announced she never wanted to be called Lizzy again. When Elisabeth didn't rebuke her, she thought her sister truly had changed. Isobella smiled and whispered, "I'm sorry I said you were the crabgrass in the lawn of my life."

"When did you say that?"

"On our sixteenth birthday."

Elisabeth burst out laughing. "Oh, Izzy, there will never be another you."

The next two weeks were almost magical, with picnics and dances and boat rides. Elisabeth commented that it had not always been like that. "It's because you're here and he wants to make certain you remain."

"He would let me leave if I wished?"

"You came of your own accord. You would leave the same way. There is a strange code of honor among these Scots."

"Yes, Alysandir told me about it. I…" Isobella suddenly felt terribly nauseated. She barely made it to the chamber pot. When she felt a little better, Elisabeth made her lie down. She put a cold cloth on Izzy's head. "How long has this been happening?"

"This is the first time. I'm just not accustomed to the food here."

"What you aren't accustomed to is being pregnant."

Isobella gasped. "I can't be pregnant."

"You've had sex with Alysandir and more than once. Did you use the withdrawal method?"

Isobella's face turned a ghastly white. "Maybe I have a bug."

"That will grow into a full-blown baby in about nine months."

"I don't need a baby right now. I don't have a husband."

"Well, the baby doesn't know that," Elisabeth said.

Isobella walked to the window and stood watching Bradan and some children playing in the courtyard below. *What would Alysandir think if he knew? Would he be furious? Would he marry me? Send me away? Ignore me, or replace me? Should I return to Màrrach? Should I remain here?*

Elisabeth answered the question for her. "You have to return to Màrrach, Izzy. If Angus finds out, he may not let you leave. A child of Alysandir's would be the ultimate pawn. It's hard enough keeping Bradan's parentage a secret. I don't think we can hide the baby's, too."

The back of Isobella's hand covered her mouth, and she fought against crying. She turned back to Elisabeth. "Oh, Lord! Not after what I've done. How can I go back?"

"How can you not? It's his child. He has a right to know."

"He may not take me back."

Elisabeth gave her a look that said how stupid she thought that last comment was. "For a smart woman with two degrees, sometimes you are just plain stupid, Izzy. He did not send you away. You left. And stop wringing your hands. We can work through this. After all, it isn't the first stupid thing you've done or the first child born out of wedlock."

Isobella took a deep breath. "You're right. So, who can we trust to ride to Màrrach and tell him?"

Elisabeth sat down to think about that. "I don't know, but I'm sure we can come up with something. As a last resort, we could speak to the priest here."

"Yes! Alysandir's uncle Lachlan Mackinnon is the abbot at Iona. Surely the priest could get word to him." She sighed. "How have I gotten myself into such a mess?"

"By being human?" Elisabeth's countenance brightened. "You're in a predicament but not an impossible one."

"It seems that way to me. His brothers and sisters turned against him in helping us come here. His feelings toward me won't ever be the same now. How can they be? How can I expect him to forgive me?"

"Don't fret. We will work through this. Eventually, the tides will turn in your favor. Your life isn't over. You're simply having a life reassessment."

Two more weeks of reassessments passed slowly for Isobella. Elisabeth said it was because she was plagued with bouts of morning sickness. "It usually goes away by the fourth month."

"Arrrggghhh…"

Although the morning sickness didn't disappear, it began to lessen enough that Isobella took a stroll outside. The garden at Duart was almost as beautiful as the one at Màrrach. She sat upon a stone bench with a furry grey kitten on her lap and watched the antics of six downy ducklings making squishy, rippling noises as they paddled in circles around a water-lilied pond.

Nearby, the song of birds quietly ushered in the evening and the gloaming settled softly about her while bees droned in innumerable trees; busy like mothers whose work was never done. She was thinking there was nothing lovelier than a sunny burst of golden daffodils growing among mossy stones.

As changeable as Mercury, her mood suddenly became deeply, sadly pensive. What was she going to do? Abandoned to her own fate, she had been in residence at Duart Castle for almost a month and she still did not know what the future held for her.

For every door that closes, lass, ten will open.

Suddenly, Sir James was standing by the fountain a few feet away.

"I'm not very happy with you or the way things are going. If this is your idea of playing matchmaker, you would be better off sticking to ghosting… or riding a broom. I feel like I am adrift in a leaky boat without oars, in case you haven't noticed."

She looked off and did not say anything for some time, and when she did look back at him, she thought he must have seen the forlorn expression on her face and the frown between her eyes.

"Ye are no' the architect of yer future, Isobella, but dinna be distraught, fer ye are allowed to paint it with yer favorite colors and redecorate it now and then. Ye are feeling as if ye have been tossed into a maelstrom and fear ye are being swept away. But nothing remains the same and fortuitous circumstances shape lives as surely as calamity."

"And are there fortuitous circumstances in my future?"

His features softened, and she wished he was mortal so she could give him a hug. "'Tis not my place to foretell yer future, only to help ye doon the right path until ye reach the crossroad."

"And then what?"

"Ye must choose."

"By myself?"

The musical chime of his laughter rang out in harmony with the gleam in his eye. "Aye, by yerself. But fear na ye, chance favors the prepared mind."

"Bah! If there is anything I don't feel it is mentally prepared."

Up went his brows, and his words were spoken in a playfully mischievous way. "Ye will, in time."

She put her hand to her head. "There is so much I don't understand."

"Ye can follow a course of action without understanding it, lass, just as ye can follow an unknown river knowing it will eventually lead to civilization. Be of good cheer. 'Tis no' so gloomy as it appears."

"I'll try to remember that while groping around in the dark with no map and no destination in mind."

"Understanding is a dark shadow that always looks darker, emptier, and further away than it really is. Ye are young, impulsive, ardent, and impatient. Those same qualities drove Adam and Eve out of Paradise." His image faded, and the sound of his laughter fell around her like a million tinkling bells.

"Thanks, I feel ever so much better," she said.

"Are you talking to yourself?"

Isobella gave a start. "No, I was giving our shimmering friend a hard time."

Elisabeth sat down. "He is here."

When she saw the expression on Elisabeth's face, she knew. "Alysandir?"

"He wants a word with you."

Isobella hated being separated and yearned to see him. She ached for his touch, but it was too soon. "I am just now at the point where I can go more than two hours without crying. I can't see him. I'm afraid to."

"You have important things to discuss, like your future, which isn't just yours any longer. Tell him the truth about what has changed and how you feel about it. Say what you want. He can't fix what he doesn't know about."

"I doubt he will fix it regardless. He has one child he does not want. The last thing he wants is another one."

"That may be, but refusing to talk to him won't settle anything. It's *your* baby. That might make a difference. He has a right to know. Now, where would you like me to tell him to go?"

"To the devil!"

Elisabeth laughed. "I mean, where shall I send him to meet you?"

"Here, where it's peaceful and private, yet in plain view, in case he decides to throttle me."

Elisabeth stood and smoothed the skirts of her brown silk gown. "Be of good cheer, Izzy. Alysandir may be a blockhead, but he is a kind-hearted blockhead and he loves you, even if he doesn't know it."

Isobella turned to watch a peacock strutting toward her. The kitten in her lap arched its back, leaped to the ground, and darted into the lilies.

"They say they are two of the most useless things in the world—lilies and peacocks. I should have known you would choose the garden as the place to meet."

And you always linger in the back of my mind, silent as a butterfly… She did not turn, but she heard his approach across the gravely ground. "I loved being in our garden when I was a child. My father always told us there were fairies living there, but I never saw them."

Suddenly, he stood before her with a frown on his face, and her heart lurched. "Ye are thinner."

"Yes." It was true she lost weight grieving and suffering through morning sickness, but she was not going to tell him that.

"Are ye no eating?"

She looked down and smoothed her skirts. "Not very much."

"And the reason for that?"

"I haven't been hungry."

"And the real reason?"

"I wrestle with demons that steal my appetite." She lifted her head and met his gaze. She saw by the pain in his eyes that he had missed her, too. "Elisabeth said you wished to speak with me."

"I have come to take ye back to Màrrach."

"Why? You know why I left, and I have no desire to return under those circumstances. So you must give me a reason to return."

"Because I want ye there."

"Why?"

"I want ye. Isn't that reason enough?"

"You want me. May I inquire as to in what capacity… your prisoner, a dalliance, your mistress, your wife?"

"I told ye that I will never marry again."

"Yes, I remember all too well. Nothing has changed. I see no reason to return to the very thing I ran away from."

"Not even if I agree to accept Bradan as my son?"

She studied his face. "You are asking me to become your paramour in exchange for Bradan's rights as your son and rightful heir?"

"'Tis no' so bad as it sounds."

Her heart cracked and she turned her head away, not wanting him to see the disappointment, the aching pain, the utter devastation that she felt. She looked in the direction of the pond, not really focusing on anything, but doing so simply because she needed to have him out of her line of vision. She could not think clearly when she looked at him.

The silvered reflection of a spiderweb caught her eye… an unsuspecting fly, the ever-present spider, a wisp of gossamer, the struggle within the cocoon of death, and it was over. She could feel the wisp of gossamer tightening around her neck. Like the spider, Alysandir was sucking the life from her. She exhaled wearily, her mind not wanting to do this; her heart saying she had no choice.

As the ancient saying went, of two evils, the lesser is always chosen. Bottom line was that Alysandir would accept Bradan, and she hoped that would include her child. He would care for her, at least for as long as she pleased him.

What did it matter, really, for as Søren Kierkegaard had said, "My honest opinion and my friendly advice is this: do it or do not do it—you will regret both." She sighed resignedly, ready to have it over and done with.

"Come with me, and I will take the lad hunting for one week; just the two of us. Would that please ye?"

She nodded. "It would please me greatly, but it will please you even more."

"I will inform the Maclean we are leaving. I will ask him to allow yer sister to accompany us, but do not get yer hopes up in that regard. Angus is a prideful and stubborn man, and he longs to have the upper hand. He gains nothing by letting her go."

He must have seen the hurt in her eyes, for he continued, "My hands are tied, lass. I am on Maclean land. Your sister is their property by right of capture. I canna make demands, but I will try to persuade Angus. 'Tis a verra awkward position I am in, and the opposing faction has me over a barrel."

As expected, Angus was steadfast in his determination to keep Elisabeth, unless Alysandir wanted to exchange her for Isobella. "I am feeling charitable, and as long as I have one of the two lassies, it matters naught which one it is."

Alysandir declined and assured the sisters their separation wouldn't be much longer.

Isobella, Bradan, and Alysandir departed and spread their plaids beneath the stars that night. The next morning, after tea and oatcakes, they mounted, and with an uneasy wind at their backs, they rode into the wilds of Mull. Isobella found it difficult to maintain her resolve. She was lonely and felt forgotten in a world that closed in around her, cold as the shoulders of Ben More.

It grew cooler, and Alysandir told Bradan to wrap himself in his plaid. He removed his own from his saddle pouch and wrapped it around himself and Isobella. The timing was perfect, for the sky loosened a torrent of rain. They threaded their way through massive boulders and sodden turf, climbing and then descending until the rain stopped and she could catch the scent of the sea. Before long, she would see the towers of Màrrach rising in the distance.

It wasn't until they rode into the courtyard that she realized how tired she was, physically and emotionally, for the journey had taken much out of her. She felt some sense of happiness at arriving back at Màrrach, and she tried not to think about what lay ahead.

Alysandir handed her down from his horse, and

Isobella found herself surrounded by his sisters, who greeted her with hugs and questions.

"We have missed ye!" Sybilla said. "'Tis no' the same with ye gone."

"Marion also chimed in, "I'm so verra happy ye are back!"

"Well, that doesna leave much for me to say," Barbara said, and hugged her. "I ken ye are tired."

"I passed tired hours ago," Isobella said, smiling as she went into the castle, arm and arm with Barbara, so very happy to see things were back to normal between Alysandir and his sisters.

Their departure being something she did not want to miss, Isobella was up early the next morning to see Alysandir and Bradan off. She paused in the doorway and observed the quiet way they checked their packs carefully. Then Alysandir said, "Mount up."

Bradan mounted, rode a few feet, drew rein, and waited for his father to take the lead. Bradan's lip trembled, and she placed her hand over his, resting against the pommel. She understood his fear and dread and assured him that he had much to learn and gain from this outing.

"Be yourself, and he will see you are a son to be proud of. He will be proud of you one day, but for now, listen well to all he says. He is a good man, and no harm will come to you."

Alysandir gave her a nod and rode toward the castle gates. Bradan fell in behind him, trailed by two deerhounds, Duff and Bran.

When the gates closed, Isobella went to the curtain wall and watched until they vanished in the mist. The week would be a long one, but if she was right, it would change their lives forever.

Chapter 29

From bad matches good
Children can be born.

—Yiddish proverb

ALYSANDIR HAD NEVER SPENT MUCH TIME AROUND YOUNG children, and now he was going to spend an entire week with one. Judging from the way the lad was looking at him, Alysandir wasn't convinced Bradan would utter one word the entire trip. Alysandir had never considered that he could come to love the lad, especially if forced to acknowledge him as his son. That he was beginning to warm to the idea of having a son surprised him. Although the words were difficult for him to say, he had to admit that he had denied Bradan's existence so he could deny the woman who bore him.

By taking the lad on this hunting trip, he was officially accepting Bradan as his son. And by accepting him, that meant Bradan would one day be chief of Clan Mackinnon. This would please Drust, who had never wanted to succeed his brother and said quite frankly, "I dinna want to be chief."

One fear Alysandir had was that the boy was too soft, too timid to be a leader and would prove to be a disappointment as chief of Clan Mackinnon. So now he was here, sitting by the campfire, watching the lad roast a grouse he had killed with a remarkable shot from a bow.

The week had passed quickly, with their first days spent hunting small game and bobbing for burn trout with a line and hook. Alysandir saw immediately that Bradan knew all about bobbing for trout and was expert at catching them. He could also clean them faster than Alysandir.

He picked up one of Bradan's arrows and twirled it around in his hand. "How did ye come by these arrows? Have ye made friends with the castle fletchers and persuaded them to give these to ye?"

Bradan shook his head. "Nae, they didna give them to me. They said they didna mind if I watched them make arrows, if I was quiet. I learnt from watching. Sometimes they would let me try while they watched me, and they told me what I was doing wrong. Now, I give them my verra best arrows for yer warriors to use."

Alysandir steadied the arrow on his extended finger. It was perfectly balanced and made of yew. The shaft was straight and smooth, the point perfectly fitted. Goose feathers had been carefully selected and attached with glue and thread to stabilize the arrow during flight. Even the most difficult part, the nock, was damnably close to being perfect and remarkably executed by one so young.

"And the crossbow and longbow ye have? Ye made them as well?"

"Aye, but the crossbow was easier to learn."

Alysandir smiled at the truth of Bradan's words, impressed with the boy's ability to teach himself and the discipline that required. "I have noticed that ye have always managed to stay out of my way. Is that because ye are afraid of me?"

"Nay, I stay out of yer way because I dinna want to know if I am afraid of ye or not."

Alysandir wanted to laugh, at not only the lad's honesty, but also his deductive reasoning. He studied the boy while his dark head was bent. He was a handsome lad, tall for his age, slender, and brave, for he knew the lad had not found it easy to accompany him. If anything surprised him, it was that Bradan seemed quite accepting, in spite of Alysandir's hostility and coldheartedness. He could only surmise that the lad was the forgiving sort and not one to harbor a grudge, both of which spoke highly in his favor.

"We should bed down for the night," he said. "We'll be up before daybreak to track roe deer."

They gathered up dry heather and made it into pallets and then covered them with their plaids. Soon, the dogs came to lie beside them and share their warmth. Alysandir looked over at the boy, watching how naturally he fit into this setting. He did not want to think that Bradan reminded him of himself. But, sleeping under the stars, building sandcastles, hunting and fishing were the same things Alysandir had loved as a lad—before duty had intervened.

The next morning, they found a grassy burn where the deer were in the habit of feeding and hid downwind from where the deer would arrive. The sky began to lighten, and they heard deer as they came down from the heights to search for grass and rushes. Alysandir signaled the dogs. They picked up the scent and took off, noses to the ground.

Before long, they returned, covered with blood. "Where is he?" Alysandir said. "Show me!" The dogs tore off again, with Alysandir and Bradan loping behind them on horseback, until at last they came to a rocky outcrop where a stag lay dead, his throat torn open by the dogs.

Bradan had never hunted a stag before, so Alysandir said, "'Tis time ye learned to dress the carcass." Once that was done, he showed Bradan how to load it on the packhorse.

"Check the cinch first. It should be not too tight but not loose." He ruffled Bradan's hair to show his approval. "Now, grab the hindquarters, and we'll throw it over the back like this." Together, they secured the rope and mounted and led the packhorse back to camp, where they feasted on oatcake and cold grouse after they skinned and dressed the deer.

Later, they sat around the fire and talked about the day's events. Alysandir wondered how he could have been so consumed by his own pain that he had never taken the time to notice the pain he had caused his son. Had it not been for Isobella... He sighed, almost breathing the sound of her name.

"Ye are verra fond of Isobella, no?" he asked Bradan.

"Aye, she is my best friend. The first time I saw her, I was afraid. I thought she was an angel."

"She has made ye verra happy, just as ye have made her happy."

"Aye, 'tis true, but she is also verra sad."

"Sad? Isobella? Why do ye think her sad?"

"Because her heart aches. She thinks no one can see it."

"Why is she sad? Do ye think she is unhappy and wants to leave?"

"Nae, I ken she is happy here, but she is sad that she will never marry."

"How do ye know she willna?"

"She told me so."

"Why is that sad?"

"Mayhap it is because she willna have a bairn and she likes them verra much." He said that quite matter-of-factly, so matter-of-factly that Alysandir smiled at his innocence. For someone who doubted he could love anyone again, Alysandir felt what could only be described as fatherly affection for Bradan. He liked being with the lad and enjoyed listening to his soft voice and the way he explained his feelings with such maturity and honesty. He also realized that he wanted Bradan to like him in return.

They hunted a few grouse the next morning and then ate and packed up their belongings in readiness to leave. As Alysandir walked down to the burn to clean his knife, the dogs started barking. He passed a thicket, so dense that rain could not penetrate it. He was thinking that something lay hidden in the dark tangle of bracken, when suddenly a huge, wild boar charged out of his lair, the coarse hairs on his back bristling and his eyes glowing like red-hot embers from the devil's hellfire.

Bradan saw the dogs and heard the noisy thrashing. He grabbed his crossbow and followed, arriving as the boar hooked one of the hounds and tossed him in the air. Bran lay where he landed, mortally wounded. Then the boar turned back to Alysandir, who had only his knife for defense.

Before the boar had time to charge, Bradan aimed and let the arrow fly. It lodged in the boar's tough hide, but the blow was not fatal. The boar squealed and turned toward Bradan and charged. He fired again. The boar kept running. Bradan jumped to one side, just as the boar drove his sharp tusk sideways and ripped up the boy's thigh.

The boar turned and charged again, but the damage from Bradan's arrow was done. The boar dropped to the ground, squealing and kicking until it stilled and fell silent.

Alysandir knew only a shot to the heart or lungs would have dropped the boar as quickly as it had, and he was amazed at Bradan's sensibility and quick thinking. He set up camp again and tended to Bradan's wound. He gave the boy several sips of brandewijn to ease the pain and poured some over the wound, which he then stitched and bound tightly with an old plaid. Alysandir did not leave camp, occupying himself with dressing the boar. That night, he managed to get enough mead down Bradan that the lad began to grow sleepy.

Alysandir watched the fire burn down as Bradan slept. His son had saved his life. He did not know many men who could think so quickly or display such a level head and unbelievably steady hand. And Bradan had never made a sound while Alysandir stitched his leg. He was brave beyond his years, and Alysandir wondered how he thought the lad too soft?

Bradan stirred and opened his eyes. "How do ye feel, lad?" Alysandir asked.

"My leg doesna hurt," he answered, albeit groggily.

It had to hurt like the devil. "Can ye stand the ride back to Màrrach if we leave early in the morning?"

"Aye, I can make it." Bradan paused a moment as if thinking long and hard upon something. "I am verra sorry that ye have to care for me."

Alysandir pushed Bradan's hair back. "I owe ye fer saving my life. 'Tis I who owes ye." Bradan closed his eyes, and a faint smile turned up the corners of his lips. The sight of it put a tiny crack in Alysandir's heart, for he knew that the lad had had little in his short life to smile about. Alysandir vowed to change that.

They left at daybreak. By the time they arrived at the castle gate, Bradan was riding in the saddle in front of Alysandir. Just before dismounting, Alysandir leaned close and whispered, "'Tis a fine way ye handled yerself. I am proud to call ye my son."

Having heard a commotion at the gate, Isobella was waiting for them in the courtyard when they arrived. She watched with an aching heart as Alysandir handed Bradan to Drust before he dismounted.

She rushed to Bradan's side. "What happened?"

"He saved my life and was gored by a boar." They followed Drust to Bradan's room.

"He is burning with fever, so the wound is infected," Isobella said. "We must take him to Elisabeth."

Alysandir shook his head. "The lad may not survive more travel."

"We cannot let him lie there and do nothing."

"I agree, but he canna travel."

"What other choices do we have?" Angus would never let Elisabeth leave.

"I will take care of it," he said, and departed before she could say anything more.

Isobella was infuriated at Alysandir's callousness, but

she put it out of her mind for the time being. She had a lad to tend, and she set to work doing what she could, while fearing it would not be enough. She slept beside his bed, awakened the next morning by the sound of Bradan talking out of his head. He was still burning with fever, so she kept bathing him with cold water.

She was wishing she had a bottle of aspirin, when she remembered the aspirin from her backpack, lying in her trunk. She dashed to her room and hurried back with the aspirin. She crushed two tablets, mixed them with water, and fed the mixture to him with a spoon. She checked his wound, still red, angry, and oozing.

When Mistress MacMorran arrived with a tray, Isobella asked about Alysandir, who had not checked on his son.

"Och! Dinna be angry wi' him. The chief left last night."

"Where did he go?"

"I didna have time to ask, fer he rode away with Colin and Drust like the deil himself was a-nippin' at his heels."

Isobella returned to Bradan's side, happy to see the aspirin had brought his fever down. But she had only one bottle, and it did nothing for infection. She needed antibiotics or the sixteenth-century medical equivalent, or better yet, Elisabeth.

The next day was a repeat of the first—Bradan burning with fever, her giving him aspirin. Mistress MacMorran helped with his cool baths. Later that evening, Isobella fed him broth again, and when he slept, she put her head down beside him on the bed.

Sometime later, she was awakened by a commotion in the hallway. She had barely raised her sleepy head when the door to Bradan's room flew open and Elisabeth walked into the room. Isobella gasped and sprang to her feet.

"Oh, thank God! I've never been so happy to see you!"

"Yes, I am here and happy to see you, too," Elisabeth said in a professional voice as she gave Isobella a quick hug, for she was already turning toward the bed. "How is he?" she asked as she made her way to Bradan's side.

"He's been burning with fever. I found a bottle of aspirin in my backpack, so I have been giving it to him since yesterday."

Elisabeth began to examine Bradan, and he opened his eyes. "Don't worry, Bradan," she said, speaking in soft tones.

"Elisabeth," he said.

"I've come to take care of ye if you will let me."

"Aye," he said, with a dry, raspy voice.

Without looking away, Elisabeth asked, "Has he been drinking plenty of water or other liquids?"

"As much as I can get him to take," Isobella replied.

She smoothed the hair from Bradan's brow. "I want to look at your leg. May I do that?"

He nodded.

Elisabeth pulled back the sheet and removed the cloths tied around his thigh. Isobella winced. The wound was worse than it had been before, now bulged apart and almost bursting with infection. The margins of the cut were a dark brownish-black color, surrounded by a ten-inch perimeter of bright red skin. Elisabeth turned to Mistress MacMorran, who was standing nearby.

"I will need you to boil water and bring it to me along with another container of boiled water to which soap has been added. Bring some clean cloths and soap to wash my hands. If you have brandy, bring that. I also want a bowl of mashed garlic, enough that I can pack the entire wound with it."

Mistress MacMorran disappeared through the door.

"You are using garlic," Isobella said. "I know people in this time period sometimes used garlic and honey. I wasn't certain which you would choose."

"Honey certainly has antibacterial and wound-healing properties because it produces hydrogen peroxide on dilution of the honey with wound exudate. However, this wound has progressed too far for honey to control. I'm sure the tusks were covered with all kinds of nasty bacteria that have spread quickly in that bound wound."

Isobella's jaw dropped, for she had never heard her sister speak like... well, like a doctor. It struck her suddenly that her sister really was a doctor, and that meant more than just being able to write "MD" after her name.

Colin entered with Gavin and Grim, joined a moment later by Drust and their three sisters. They stood quietly to one side, and Isobella glanced around the room.

"Where is Alysandir?"

"He stayed behind," Drust said.

"Behind where?"

"Angus wouldn't let me leave unless a Mackinnon stayed to take my place, so Alysandir stayed," Elisabeth said.

"But Alysandir is the chief. Why didn't one of you stay?" she asked, looking at Drust.

"Because he *is* the chief, lord, and protector," Barbara said. "He would never ask his brothers or his men to do something he would not do. If ye are worrit aboot the Macleans harming him, they willna. Angus will release Alysandir when Elisabeth returns. That was the agreement, and Angus will abide by it."

Elisabeth turned back to further examine the wound. "It is abscessed, and it is surrounded with cellulitis. I need to clean it thoroughly." She placed her hand on Bradan's arm and smiled down at him. "You needn't be afraid, Bradan. Once I have it all cleaned up, I will fill it with mashed garlic. That will kill all the bacteria."

"Will ye sew it?"

She patted his cheek. "No, laddie. It must be left open so it can drain in the fresh air and then it will close on its own." She took his hand in hers. "Do you have any questions?"

"Can I see the bac-tera after ye kill it?"

"No, you cannot see it and neither can I, because it is so very, very tiny. No one can see it unless they have a very thick piece of glass to look through that makes the bacteria very large."

"How do ye ken that the bac-tera is there if ye canna see it?"

"I can tell by the symptoms—that is, by the way the wound looks and your high fever."

"How will I know it is deid, then?"

She ruffled his hair. "Because you will get well. The garlic should kill all of the bacteria, right down to the last little devil."

They plied Bradan with brandewijn, and Elisabeth set to work. When she pulled the wound open to clean it, what she called purulent matter began to run from the wound.

Mrs. MacMorran arrived with two maids carrying basins of water, mashed garlic, and cloths. Elisabeth scrubbed her hands and set to work, cleaning the wound, first with warm water and then with warm, soapy water.

"How many people did you have helping you to peel garlic?" Isobella asked.

Mrs. MacMorran replied, "Aboot half o' the castle, I think. Màrrach and everyone in it smell o' garlic."

As soon as Elisabeth finished cleaning the wound with the soapy water, the redness began to recede markedly. "I am going to put the garlic in the wound now. You won't notice anything right away, but it will start to improve some by tomorrow. Then it will get better day by day."

Once the wound was packed full of garlic, she said, "There! We are all finished." She patted Bradan's arm. "And you, my brave laddie, were by far the best patient I have ever treated. I heard you haven't eaten anything, and it is very important that you do. Will you try a little soup?"

Bradan nodded, but by the time it arrived, he was asleep.

"Why did you leave the wound open?" Isobella asked.

"If you suture it, an air-free environment is created for anaerobic bacteria to proliferate. That is the bad stuff that causes botulism and gangrene and lots of other baddies you don't want to have."

A melancholy cloud settled over Isobella. "I wish you didn't have to go back. We seem to be like two stars in separate constellations.

Elisabeth seemed amused. "Remember the saying, Izzy... 'Distance endears friendship and absence sweetens it.'"

Isobella's brows raised and she gave Elisabeth a

questioning look, while inwardly she was wondering just whose absence was being sweetened by all of this.

"Has some handsome Maclean caught your attention?"

"No, but there's a Mackinnon who has."

"Drust?"

Elisabeth smiled a cat-like smile. Suddenly, Isobella knew who it was. *Oh my, Elisabeth has gone over to the dark side.* The image of Ronan, the Greek god of the Mackinnon family, popped into her mind's eye. Ronan the Rogue, as she called him, with the strong, arrogant face, hawkish nose, sensual mouth, killer smile, and mane of glossy black hair that hung past his shoulders. Ronan could have his pick of any woman alive.

"You're after Ronan."

Elisabeth ignored that and said, "You have a fine man in Alysandir, and I hope you work out your differences. They don't come any better, and you know that." Then she asked, "Have you told him about the baby?"

"No."

"You must tell him."

"I will when I am ready."

"It better be soon because you can't hide it indefinitely."

Chapter 30

The heart of a woman falls back with the night,
And enters some alien cage in its plight,
And tries to forget it has dreamed of the stars
While it breaks, breaks, breaks on the sheltering bars.

—"The Heart of a Woman," 1918
  Georgia Douglas Johnson (1880?–1966)
  U.S. poet, playwright, and musician

A WILD WIND MOANED OVER DUART CASTLE AS A HURRYING
shape made his way slowly down the winding passage-
ways. Silently, he kept close to the damp, stone walls
until he reached the stairs and went down them sound-
lessly to the ground floor. The night was pitch dark
and moonless, and most of those in the castle had been
asleep for hours by the time he reached the door and
stepped out into the night.

Alysandir crossed the bailey, staying close to the wall
and out of the rectangular shaft of light coming from
the guardroom. He could hear the guards talking, inter-
spersed with some good-natured cursing as he slipped
into the stable. He found and saddled Gallagher quickly.

The night sentries would be returning soon, and he
waited quietly in the dark shadows near the portcullis for
their arrival. When they rode into the bailey, he spurred
Gallagher into a full gallop and thundered past the

sentries and out of the castle before anyone was aware of what had happened.

Soon they vanished into the arms of the night, accompanied by the commotion coming from the castle — shouts and the sounds of horses being mounted. By the time the guards gave chase, Alysandir and Gallagher had already vanished into the cloak of darkness.

After a lively meal in the Great Hall with much laughter and dancing, Isobella decided to call it a night. She didn't worry about keeping Elisabeth company, for Ronan kept dragging her out to dance. In good spirits and happy for her sister, she walked from the room, smiling.

She was almost to the stairs when a hand closed around her upper arm. Alysandir pulled her down the hallway with him, stopping long enough to unlock a door before he pulled her inside. He locked the door before he turned back to her.

"I have missed ye."

"How did you talk Angus into letting you go?"

"I escaped."

"Oh dear, does that mean war?"

"Nae, but he will want to even the score. Ye dinna seem glad to see me, lass. It makes me question my long, wet ride from Duart Castle."

She smiled at him and put her arms around his neck. "Of course I missed you, and I'm happy you are back."

She rose up on her toes to give him a light kiss and found herself swept into his arms. He moved his hand to the back of her head, drawing her lips against his. The feel of his mouth, warm against her trembling mouth, was painfully tender, and she wanted him, wholly, completely, almost desperately, but she also wanted him properly—and that put them on two different planets.

She pulled back, glanced around the room, and gave a start when she realized she had never been here before. Curiosity got the best of her. The room was designed for a woman, and judging by its size, the number of windows, and the beautiful furnishings, it belonged to a woman of great importance. Surely he had not brought her to a room occupied by his long string of mistresses?

"Just who does this room belong to?" she asked, tiny shards of bitterness creeping into her voice and penetrating her bones. That he would think so little of her...

"'Tisn't the abode of a woman I have bedded, if that is yer concern," he said, almost affably. "I might have expected such a reply from ye, for ye do have more than just a hint of red in that hair of yours. However, to answer yer question, 'twas my mother's room. I wanted to show it to ye. 'Twould please me to have ye move here."

She could not hide her amazement. The bed was large and covered with handwoven coverings of fine embroidery. The tapestry on the wall represented the coronation of Robert the Bruce, with an angel placing the royal crown of Scotland upon his head. But most impressive was the oriel window, corbelled out from the wall that extended outward, much like a modern-day bay window, but in this case, a much more ornate and beautifully designed piece of architecture.

An abundance of cushions was scattered over a covered seat beneath the windows. Along one wall was a small but very fine library with a French writing desk in front of it. She ran her hand over the writing box sitting to one side. "It looks like it must have looked when she lived in it."

"It is just as she left it."

"And none of the other occupants wanted to leave their mark upon it?"

"No one has been in this room. I locked it the day our mother was buried. I opened it fer ye. I want you to have this room and everything in it."

Too much, her mind cried out. It was too much. She shook her head, and holding her hand up in supplication toward him, she began backing away. "No, I cannot. It is truly beautiful, and I am touched that you would offer it to me, but I couldn't accept it. I don't belong here."

"It is mine to do with as I please. I am giving it and everything in it to you." He went to the bookcase and pulled on one of the shelves. It sprang open. Behind it was a small casket full of jewelry. "I want you to have these."

"Oh, Alysandir, I cannot. You should give them to your sisters."

He slammed the casket down upon the desk and put his hands on her shoulders to prevent her from leaving. "Dinna be such a little fool. Dinna ye see what I am offering ye?" His eyes were dark, stormy, and blazing down at her. She made a move to turn away, but he tightened his grip on her shoulders. "Nae, no running away. Not this time," he said, looking angry enough to shake her.

He yanked her hard against him. She tried to move, but he held her head firmly against his chest. Her heart was pounding wildly, and she could not seem to catch her breath. Everything about him was over-powering. His breath was warm upon her skin, his eyes penetrating her defenses, his arms too strong, his mouth deliciously close and then coming down hard upon hers, hard.

She pushed against him with clenched fists and tried to turn away, but his hands cupped her face and held her in place. She fought against it, but as always, she ceased to struggle after a few minutes. She had no willpower strong enough to withstand her feelings for him or to resist the unrelenting demand of his lips. Nor could she ignore the hard strength of his body, the throb of the rhythmic beating of his heart piercing her defenses, and the ungovernable desire for him that swept through her like a runaway fire.

Then everything changed. Now he kissed her with surprising gentleness, and she felt herself responding in earnest. She wanted him to keep on kissing her until she melted. She relaxed against him and followed his lead. She savored the strength in his arms and the hardness of his body. Even his scent was arousing, and when his mouth closed over hers again, a long-held moan vibrated from low in her throat.

This time, his kiss was hard and seeking, almost brutally erotic, his lips moving over hers again and again. He kissed her cheeks, her throat, and her ear, tugging on the lobe. Her heart pounded painfully, and the blood pulsed into her starved lungs.

He lifted her into his arms and backed her against the bookcase. His hand searched for the hem of her skirt and then traveled warmly up her leg to the juncture of her thighs. She made one weak attempt to push him away, but his hand found the place that it sought and he pressed himself closer, touching her over and over again until she gasped. She no longer had the will to resist him. A moment later, she began to pant and her hips began to move in rhythm.

She could not control her body. Mindless with desire, she was barely cognizant that his other hand had begun to work the buttons down the front of her gown until it opened. He left her long enough to push the garment apart, slipping it over her arms and down to the floor. Her undergarments followed until she was completely bare. He held her arms immobile as he kissed his way downward, torturing her with his mouth until she cried out, digging her fingers into his hair.

She was so weak. She could not stand, and she thought surely they would move to the bed, but he turned her to lie across the desk. He entered her, moving with sure strokes until she shuddered and cried out and called his name, begging him to stop. Instead, he continued until she was mindlessly consumed by desire once more.

Alysandir began to kiss her, with kisses as soft and gentle as they had been hard and passionate before, and she writhed against him, wanting him to be more forceful. She wanted him, needed him to stop the agony, but he tortured her, bringing her close and then pulling back until she was crying for him to give her release. When he began again, she cried out.

She was intoxicated with feeling, as if her blood had turned to brandy, flowing hot, raw, and burning in her veins. It touched every part of her, searing one moment, freezing the next. She was smoldering and then shuddering over and over and over until he groaned with his own release. She did not know what happened after that, for everything went blank and she could not speak nor think, for all was feeling… exquisite, beautiful, unbelievable feeling. Nothing existed but him.

He was the only man for her. He knew how to touch her in a way that called forth her wildness, her untamed spirit that so perfectly matched his. She had opened beneath him and cried out his name, wild with wanting him as much as he wanted her and feeling no shame. She lay completely spent beneath him, as spent as he, her hands moving absently in his sweat-dampened hair. His scent floated over her, a fresh, wind-whipped smell of the outdoors, of grasses and moors, of wild things and the harshness of the sea—the very the essence of life.

She knew the magic of his hands and mouth. It did not matter that others had shown him or had lain beneath him as she had done, burning with need, opening beneath the quest of his mouth and his hands, feeling the size and strength of him when he ended the torture and gave her peace.

No matter what he said, he was hers. She belonged with him. She understood now why the Black Douglas had brought them together. That dear, beloved, unflappable ghost knew she belonged with Alysandir and had done the impossible to right a wrong that had placed them eons apart in different centuries.

Douglas knew she was destined to be in Alysandir's arms since before she was born, not by forfeit, or capture, accident, or betrothal, but because it was meant to be. She yearned to tell Alysandir of her discovery, of the newborn love that grew inside her. She would hold the secret for a little longer, tucked away in the center of her heart until he spoke, at last, the words she yearned to hear.

I love you.

When sanity returned, he silently helped her dress. Then he kissed her again, not with passion this time, but softly, gently. As he turned to lead her from the room, he picked up the casket of his mother's jewels.

"These were meant to be yours."

A gentle wind swept into the room, warm and fragrant, and she knew the ghost of the Black Douglas was nearby. She was almost giddy, believing somehow that his presence blessed this moment, this oneness she shared with Alysandir. But then the wind changed suddenly, bitter cold replacing the warmth, and she shivered. It was as if she was standing alone on a great summit covered with snow, while the world basked in warmth and sunlight below. She did not understand what was going on. But before she could react, Alysandir spoke again, distracting her.

"Take them. They are yours," he said. He thrust the casket into her hands.

Confused, she stared down at the box. Was this his way of telling her he cared enough for her to make her his wife? Just as his mother had been wife to his father? As his wife, the jewels would belong to her. Her heart swelled with delight for it was his way of saying that he loved her. She was about to pour her heart out to him, but something held her back.

His gaze traveled over her, slow and deliberate, as he said, "There is no dishonor in being my woman. All will know when ye move into this room that ye are, in my affections, far above any mistress whose bed I have shared."

Mistress... back to Square One, after all they'd just shared. Couldn't he see that they were meant for each

other? Was he truly incapable of loving her? If he had
taken his dirk and stabbed her in the heart, it would have
wounded her less. She felt her legs weaken. Her head
began to spin, and she knew she was going to faint.

Please, she whispered in her mind. I don't want him
to know how much I care. Not now. Not like this.

A crack of thunder rent the skies. A fierce wind blew
down the chimney and swirled around them. Isobella
felt the weakness, hurt, and shame flow out of her. She
was a Douglas; her baby would be a Douglas. Good
blood flowed in her veins… the blood of warriors who
didn't cower or bow, no matter what they endured. She
raised her chin and looked up at Alysandir, his proud,
dark head hovering like a bird of prey over her. He regarded her silently, searching her face, waiting for an
answer that was not forthcoming.

Her body rested, but her mind did not, and when she
awoke, the memory of the previous night was there
waiting for her. She lay abed for some time before she
dressed and went downstairs to breakfast. Thankfully,
she had slept later than usual and she was the only one
in the hall, other than the servants. She ate enough to
rid herself of hunger, but she had no real appetite. She
was worried.

She needed to think about the future and the child
she carried, so she slipped away to the stables. No one
saw her as she took one of the horses and rode down
the beach toward the cave. She always felt happy there
among the relics of the past, along and a feeling of being
connected to her family because she hoped that one day

they would learn of the work she had done here and the treasures she left behind.

She was almost there, when part of the embankment gave way and the horse reared as it tried to gain its footing. Isobella was thrown and fell over the edge. She hit the bottom with such force that she was knocked unconscious.

~~~

Alysandir missed seeing Isobella at breakfast and assumed she was sleeping late. Later, when she did not appear, he checked her room. Afterward he made a few inquiries of the guards and servants, but no one had seen her. He went to see Bradan, partly to see his son and partly because he thought Isobella might be there fawning over the lad. He was surprised to find she was not there either.

"Perhaps she is in the solar with Sybilla and Barbara," Marion said.

Alysandir shook his head. "I checked there."

"What aboot the garden? She likes to sit there," Colin said.

"I just came through the garden," Gavin said. "I did not see her."

Elisabeth asked, "Did you check her room?"

"Aye, she wasna there," he said. A muscle in his jaw worked. "I will have the castle searched, and I will find her if I have to take it apart stone by stone."

Elisabeth frowned. "It is not like Isobella to just disappear this way."

"I will find her," he said, and left. Colin and Gavin ran after him. They had barely caught up with him when they were met by one of the guards. He told the brothers that the horse Isobella had ridden earlier had returned without a rider.

Alysandir rushed downstairs and had Gallagher saddled before his brothers could catch up with him. He rode at a gallop down the beach, retracing a fresh set of hoofprints in the sand. He could never remember being scared before, and he prayed that she had not gone to the cave. The tide was almost in now. She could be trapped inside before he could reach her.

He found her lying on the other side of the embankment, unconscious and crumpled and limp. He was off Gallagher before the horse stopped. He had Isobella in his arms by the time his brothers arrived. For a moment, he stood there, whispering her name softly. He handed her to Ronan, and then he saw the blood. He mounted quickly and took her in his arms. Cradling her against him, he whispered desperate words, pleading with her to not give up as he rode back to the castle.

While Ronan was helping Alysandir with Isobella, Gavin had ridden back to the castle to alert everyone. By the time Alysandir arrived, Mistress MacMorran was waiting at the entrance. "Take her to her room. Elisabeth is waiting for her there."

Alysandir took the stairs two at a time, whispering words of encouragement as he searched her ashen face for some sign that she might have heard, but she was silent as stone. He carried her into the room, with Mistress MacMorran huffing and puffing behind him.

Elisabeth had a basin of water and several towels ready. A fire blazed in the grate, and the bed coverings were turned down. She seemed to know something he did not. Several servants came into the room carrying more supplies, followed by Alysandir's brothers and sisters.

"Put her on the bed. Then I need you to leave," Elisabeth said.

Alysandir was puzzled. "But I..."

"No. Please, Alysandir. Give us some privacy." She gave him a sympathetic look. "I need you to wait with your family while I examine her. Mistress MacMorran will stay to assist me. She will give you a report once I have finished."

Outside the room, Alysandir spoke with his family and then they all went down to the Great Hall to wait. Everyone was seated at the table, talking quietly, while Alysandir sat in a chair by the hearth, his hand absently stroking the head of one of the dogs, who watched him with mournful eyes.

It seemed like forever before Mistress MacMorran came down. She looked at Alysandir with a sympathetic expression, and fear gripped his heart.

"Elisabeth said ye may come up now." He was almost to the door when she said, "But the rest of ye will have to wait."

The walk to Isobella's room seemed longer than it ever had. When he reached her door, he hesitated for a moment, suddenly frightened at what he might find. Why had Mistress MacMorran only sent him? Did that mean something was seriously wrong with Isobella?

With dread mounting, he opened the door. Elisabeth was bathing Isobella's face in the darkened room, lit by only a few candles, but even then, he could tell that Isobella's face was terribly pale. When she saw him, Elisabeth turned and walked to the end of the bed. He stopped to gaze upon Isobella's still form, so tiny in the big bed.

"How is she?"

"She has a nasty cut on her head, which I sutured." She placed her hand on Alysandir's sleeve. "I regret having to be the one who has to tell you this." Her voice caught, and she had to pause for a deep breath. "Isobella was with child. I am sorry, but she has lost the baby."

Alysandir reeled from the shock of Elisabeth's words. He closed his eyes and threw his head back. A child? His child?

"Did she know?"

Elisabeth nodded.

Why? Why couldna ye tell me? He recalled the previous night. Dear God, now he understood why she had reacted as she did. *If you had only told me of the bairn.* Remorse ate at him. While she carried his bairn, he had offered her the role of mistress, shiny baubles and all. He had humiliated her in the worst way.

"I had no way of knowing. Why did she keep it to herself? Why could she not tell me? I wouldna have turned against her. 'Tis no' her fault but mine."

Elisabeth nodded. "Yes, it is your fault, in that you should have had a care not to get her with child, but it isn't your fault that she was foolish enough to ride a horse when she knew of her condition. However, none of that really matters now."

"Is she going to recover?"

"Yes."

"Is the blow to her head severe enough that she might not wake up?"

"No, she was awake shortly before the baby… before the bleeding stopped. She is simply exhausted now but doing fine. She is distraught and blames herself. She is strong of body and mind. Right now, she needs rest. And even if she denies it, she needs you, Alysandir. You are the only one who can truly console her, for you have lost a child as well."

Elisabeth's words cut into the heart of him. "Did ye have knowledge of the bairn before the accident?"

"Yes, I recognized her symptoms while we were at Duart."

"That is why she agreed to return to Màrrach with me," he said. "She did it for the bairn."

"That is only partly true, Alysandir. She considered the child, yes, but she loves you. I know because she told me. She did not want to tell you of her love or the child because she knew you did not want marriage or children. I'm her twin. I know her better than anyone.

"It won't be easy now. She will tell you she wants nothing to do with you, perhaps she will even ask to leave, but you must remember it is her pain speaking and not her heart. Whatever you do, don't take her rejection seriously. Hang in there and be there for her, even if she tries to drive you away. She loves you and will tell you that, but she will need time."

Alysandir felt as if something deep inside him had been ripped out. He wished he could go back, to undo the wrong that had been done. Guilt ate at him. And he was wounded to the quick that Isobella had not told him about the bairn. "I had a right to know."

"Yes, you did and I told her that, but she thought you might offer her marriage if she told you."

"Aye, 'tis true! I would have taken her to wife, had I known."

"She did not want you that way, Alysandir. She wanted you to want her because you loved her as much as she loved you. She told me of your marriage—how your wife had the marriage annulled and then sent Bradan to you after he was born."

"My fault. 'Tis all my doing. Did it… that is, will she… can she…"

"Have other children? Is that what you want to know?"

"Aye."

She nodded. "There was no damage that I can see. She is fine and should be able to have a house full of children if that is what she wants."

"What can I do?"

"Nothing. All we need is time."

"I will wait here with ye."

Elisabeth put her hand on his arm. "Let me talk to her first. I will try to get her to see you, but if she does not want to, it would be best if you stayed away, at least until she is ready. I am so sorry, Alysandir. Truly I am."

Alysandir gave her face a caress. "I ken ye speak from yer heart," he said. "I thank ye for it and yer understanding and no' blaming me."

She watched him go, hating the fact that she had had to be the one to tell him. She turned back to the bed where her sister lay, unable to forget the anguish she saw on Alysandir's face and the pain she heard in his voice.

"Oh, Izzy, why didn't you tell him? He had a right to know. He seems so broken. No one deserves to go through this sort of thing. He does love you, you know."

Isobella slept almost two hours, and after she awoke, Elisabeth told her about the baby.

"No! Oh please, no! Oh, God, what have I done? I wanted this baby with all my heart. It was our baby, a part of Alysandir no one could ever take away."

Elisabeth ran a cool cloth over her sister's face. "Now, now, don't take on so. It isn't good for you to be upset. You need to rest and let your body heal."

Tears ran down Isobella's cheeks. "I shouldn't have gone off like that. It is my fault. I killed my baby. I killed my own child."

"It was an accident. Things like this happen all the time." She smiled. "If you will remember, you were always having accidents when we were growing up."

"When will I ever learn? What was I thinking?"

"I don't think you were thinking when you left. You were obviously upset and did not consider the consequences. It is called being human, Izzy. We have all done things we regret."

"Have you told anyone… Alysandir?"

"Mistress MacMorran knows because she helped me. Otherwise, I told only Alysandir. I felt he had a right to know. I hope you are not angry."

"No, I'm not. I should have told him. I doubt he will forgive me for doing something so stupid."

"You are wrong, Izzy. He is brokenhearted that you lost the baby and that you did not tell him, but he is more broken over his own guilt in all of this. He blames no one but himself."

"He told you that?"

"Yes, he took full blame. He is so broken over this. He wanted to see you."

Isobella turned her head toward the wall. "I have ruined everything by my foolishness. I want to go home. There's nothing for me here. The Black Douglas ignores me when I seek him."

"Izzy, you know you cannot leave Alysandir. You love him, and he needs you."

"Alysandir needs no one."

Elisabeth put her hand on Isobella's arm. "You are wrong, but try to rest now. He wants to see you. Let him."

"No."

"Don't be that way, Izzy. Let him comfort you, and you can do the same for him."

Isobella turned her head to the wall and closed her eyes.

Chapter 31

Alas, regardless of their doom,
The little victims play!

—"Ode on a Distant Prospect of Eton College," 1742
  Thomas Gray (1716–1771)
  English poet

A MONTH LATER, A DARK, THUNDEROUS CLOUD HUNG heavily from the sky, bringing ominous rumblings of discontent, while the wind blew and battered the castle walls like wings of an ill-omened bird. It had been raining for days.

Alysandir had a feeling something bad was about to happen. Still recovering from Isobella's rejection, he did not need more problems. It bothered him that all of his family was not safely ensconced within the walls of Màrrach Castle. The two youngest siblings, Artair and Margaret, were visiting their maternal grandparents in Argyll. Alysandir wanted them home and asked Gavin and Grim to fetch them.

"Are they in danger?" Gavin asked.

"I have a feeling they are, but I have no proof. Have a care, lads. I sense there is mischief aboot. Twenty men will accompany ye."

When a week had passed and they had not returned, he decided to send Drust and Ronan with a full company of soldiers to find them. Before they could leave, Colin found him in the stable examining the injured leg on one of the horses.

"Ye may not need to send Drust and Ronan. There is a courier from Angus Maclean with a letter for ye."

Alysandir gave the gelding a pat and turned away. "Bring him here," he said, knowing Maclean had his brothers and sister in his cold clutches, but he read the missive anyway. It was obvious the courier feared for his life, but Alysandir put him at ease.

"No harm will come to ye on Mackinnon land."

He turned to Colin. "Tell Duncan to see that this man is given something to eat and send him on his way."

After they departed, Drust inquired after the contents of the letter.

"It was to be expected," Alysandir said. "Angus Maclean has the four of them and our soldiers, which he will exchange for Elisabeth."

"And if we do not comply?" asked Ronan.

"He will execute the male captives and return Margaret to us."

"The bastard!" Drust said.

Ronan turned to Alysandir. "What is our plan?"

"I havena a plan as yet, but I will inform ye the moment I do."

The next morning, Alysandir showed the letter to Elisabeth. "I'm sorry to cause you more complications. I will gather my things while you decide who will escort me to Duart."

"No." Alysandir looked at her, his eyes quiet and sad, for he knew what this would do to Isobella.

Elisabeth sighed. "You have no choice. You know

that. I hope Angus wouldn't harm them, but you can't risk it. Isobella is well. She no longer needs me. I will tell her I am leaving."

"I will go with ye," he said.

They found her in the garden, sitting on a stone bench beside a basket of flowers she had gathered. She must have sensed something was wrong, for her expression was both suspicious and guarded.

"I am the bearer of bad news." Alysandir handed her the letter from Angus. She read it and handed it back to him.

"So, you are sending her back."

"Izzy, you can't expect him to keep me here," Elisabeth said.

"I don't." Isobella looked at Alysandir. "But I do expect you to let me go with her. You have no right to keep me here."

"Izzy, you are not well enough to travel that far on horseback," Elisabeth said.

"Ye will remain here. You have my promise that I will bring Elisabeth back if I have to exchange myself for her."

Eyes downcast, Isobella walked away, turning over the basket of flowers on her way.

"I am sorry we have brought so much angst into your life," Elisabeth said. "I feared this would happen, but I was hoping for more time."

"Are ye fearful of what might happen when ye return?" Alysandir asked.

"Yes. Fergus was grieving over Barbara, but before long he began to transfer his amorous intentions to me. Angus intervened with a threat that I would never see Izzy again if I rejected Fergus."

Alysandir nodded. "I will put an end to this, but I need time."

"I have precious little of that. Before I came here, I was measured for a gown for my marriage."

"Try to delay things as long as ye can. I will bring ye back."

"I will be ready to go in the morning."

Alysandir found Isobella in the solar alone. "I understand why you are letting her go, but I cannot make myself like it," she said. She looked at her hands folded in her lap as she spoke. "I know you and I have made a royal mess of things. Neither of us is blameless, just as neither of us is right. I should have told you. I should not have held it against you when I lost the baby. There has been enough blame and pain. Enough to last a lifetime. We have both suffered."

"Isobella…"

She looked at him. "I don't hate you, Alysandir. I don't want to hurt you. You were honest with me. You never promised me anything more than passion. How can I fault you for that? I allowed it to happen because I was in love with you and I read more into it than was there. Like too many women, I thought it would be different for me. The romantic in me believed in stories that ended with happily ever after."

She heard his mournful cry. She saw the anguish in his eyes when he threw his head back and closed his eyes tightly against the pain. She loved him. That was her fault, her crime and her punishment. She had never felt so alone. She could not stop the tears that rushed to the surface, and she wiped them away.

She did not want his pity. She stared at his broad

shoulders, slim hips, and long, well-formed legs and wondered with what demons he wrestled now. *Strange, though it is, I know you would give your life for me, and yet you cannot give me your heart.*

He was watching her now, waiting, but she had no words for him. "I ken Elisabeth told you Fergus wants to marry her," he said, his eyes softening. "I promise ye that I will rescue her before that happens. I want to ease yer torment. I will…"

She rose to her feet. He was close enough to reach out and touch, but he had never been further away. She placed her hand against his cheek. "I know you will try to bring her back. I am not angry at you. I don't hate you. I will probably never stop loving you." She sighed deeply and realized how very tired she was. "I just want to go home."

"I would give all I own if I could make it up to you, if I could change what happened."

"I know you would, but we are at a stalemate. I don't want you without marriage, and you don't want me with it. Sometimes love just isn't enough. That is why I want to go with my sister. I don't belong here anymore."

"It will never be over." She heard the anguished break in his voice and saw the despair in his eyes. But she was not moved. She had lost him and the baby, and now she felt nothing. She was empty inside. She rose on her toes and placed a kiss upon his warm mouth. When he started to speak, she placed two fingers over his lips.

"Don't say anything. I know your heart, Alysandir. You are a good man. I couldn't love you if you were not."

Without another word, she turned and left him standing in a shaft of sunlight that suddenly broke through the clouds.

Isobella went to see how Bradan fared.

"I am fair to sick o' this room," he said, "and I long to walk in the sand along the sea barefoot."

"How about we go down to the stables to see Cahir Mor?"

"Cahir Mor!" Bradan said, "'Tis the name I gave him!"

"Yes, it is. Come along now."

Bradan still walked with a limp, but he assured her his leg was just sore and not painful. She looked at him, seeing his trusting innocence. He had no idea what his future would be or the challenges he would face as chief of his clan, if that was his future. His Scotland would be conquered, as the Picts and the Celts had been before them.

She knew his proud world of tribes and feuds would someday be remembered only through the words of bards, historians, and poets, and their way of life learned through writings and artifacts unearthed by romantic academics like herself, who were devoted to bringing to life the vestiges of the Scotland that was.

She couldn't stop the inevitable, but she could teach Bradan about preserving artifacts and even recording some historical documents. Thinking about devoting herself to her work, Isobella was more optimistic about her future. Perhaps there might be a silver lining to this time-travel business after all.

Chapter 32

Any solution to a problem
changes the problem.

—R. W. Johnson (b. 1916)
   U.S. journalist, newspaper executive

FIVE DAYS LATER, THE MACKINNONS WERE REUNITED WITH
much laughter and celebration. Isobella was there to
greet them the moment they entered the Great Hall, and
she was quick to hug Grim and Gavin before she turned
her attention to Artair and Margaret. She would have
recognized them anywhere, for they had that remarkable
Mackinnon stamp.

Artair was a miniature Ronan—tall, slender, and black
haired, with a secure future as a heartbreaker, for he was
positively saturated with charm. Margaret was a study
in rosy hues, for everything about her was rose tinted—
strawberry-blond hair tied back with bands of a rosy hue,
blushing cheeks, and rose-petal lips, all offset by the darkest of dark blue eyes.

"Grim said ye like to visit caves and look for things
left by the Picts and Celts," Artair said.

"I do love it. Did he tell you I have a room where
I store a lot of the interesting things I find? If you like,
I will show you the cave and some of my artifacts."

"I should like very much to see yer things. I ken

I would like to see yer cave, for I havena been in one before," Artair said.

As for Margaret, she was primarily focused on Isobella's braided hair. Enraptured would have been a better word, for she did not understand how one managed to French braid and interweave it with ribbons. "Will ye braid my hair with ribbons like yers?"

Isobella hugged her and assured her she would.

Across the room, Alysandir watched with interest. He could not remember seeing Isobella so animated, for she seemed to bring the room to life, from the riot of fairy-tale tints to the ribbons braided into her hair to the radiant greenish-gold hues of her velvet gown. The exquisitely clinging fabric wrapped itself around her, as soft as silk draping a body pulsing with life.

Out of the shadows of his mind, out of the mystery of secrecy, appeared reality. Isobella, alive, warm, captivating, all wrapped up with a warm, calm competence rarely seen in one so young. She seemed relaxed and confident, and he marveled at the difference he saw in her. Aye, she was graceful and beautiful; yet underlying her beauty was something delicate and sad. Was this the bloom of motherhood he saw, tinged with the sadness of having lost a child?

He would have given a fortune to have a portrait of her just as she was tonight.

He left the hall to retreat to the inner sanctum of his library, where he caressed a goblet of wine, his brow furrowed and his mind awhirl with decisions. He could not remember being weary, drunk, upset, remorseful, and enamored with a woman all at the same time. It was pure hell.

An obstinate, wrong-headed woman, intractable to the end. She was worse than a broody hen sitting on a china egg, determined to prove it would hatch. There was no convincing her. He was certain the problem that existed between them was because she did not know what she wanted. To get what he wanted, he had to give her what she wanted—and therein lay the beating heart of the beast.

What did she expect him to do? He had rescued her. He had brought her to his home, made her a part of his family, and not lain with another woman since he met her. Didn't he accept Bradan as his son because he knew she wanted him to? He had tried to console her after the loss of the babe, and he had taken Elisabeth's advice and given her plenty of time to heal her body and her mind.

What more did she want?

A dark cloud gathered in Norway and crossed over the sea to give birth to a cold wind that rode great waves to Mull. The wind wrapped itself around the towers of Màrrach Castle, penetrating cracks and crannies as it climbed higher, howling and swirling. It encircled the tall spires and then went whistling down the chimney to make the fire crackle and glow as it sent a sweeping shower of sparks flying into the room.

Alysandir stared into the leaping flames, and as if by magic, he could see his lady mother walking across the stone floors of the solar in her gold brocade kirtle, her flaxen hair braided like the Crown of Denmark upon her head. His father appeared, went to his wife, and put his arms around her, folding his hands across her belly, great with child.

Alysandir could not take his eyes from her face, not because of her beauty, but because of the expression,

serene and peaceful, he saw there. He saw himself as a
young child and his older brother, Hugh, playing at their
parents' feet.

Then he watched as the flames became the ghostly
figure of a knight. He recognized the three white stars on
the tunic as those worn by Sir James Douglas. Alysandir
opened his mouth to speak, but no words came forth.
They were not needed, for he knew what the Black
Douglas had come to tell him, and the words danced in
his head.

*She wants what all women want, a husband to love
her and babes playing at her feet.*

The moment the thought penetrated his consciousness, the vision faded. The flames in the fireplace vanished, and his mind was blank for a moment. When it
cleared, he doubted that he had seen a vision at all. He
glanced downward, and he saw his clothes were covered
with ash.

Marriage…

That dastardly word. That deadly, dreaded union of
misery, betrayal, and pain. He did not need the ghostly
Douglas floating and hovering about, directing his life
and leading him down a path he had walked before. He
would never again pledge his troth and commit himself
to the agony that came with it. His heart was beyond
hardened. He would not, could not, force himself to
marry again.

Hell and damnation. Was there anything that he could
do or give her, besides love and marriage, that would
please her? Wasn't there anything else she wanted that
he could do to prove how much he cared for her?

Only Elisabeth…

It wouldn't be easy to steal Elisabeth from under old Angus's nose and bring her back to Màrrach. That would mean putting Duart Castle under attack and he, his brothers, and his soldiers at great risk. And Duart had never fallen, even against the bombardment of kings.

If they laid siege successfully, they had to get back out, once in, and more than likely many Mackinnons would die. If only he could come up with a plan to get them inside the castle without a fight or without being seen. The thought clung to him as cold and bleak as a wintry landscape, robbing him of his peace of mind and leaving his heart heavy.

Isobella heard the ring of spurs echo against the turret walls, but she went back to sleep without much thought. It was not until morning when she went down to breakfast that she discovered to whom the spurs belonged and where they were going.

"Good morning," she said, greeting Alysandir's sisters, who were scattered about the long table. She looked around. "Where is everyone else?"

"The men broke their fast early," Sybilla replied. "Didn't you hear them?"

"Alysandir, Drust, and Ronan left before daylight with a small band of soldiers," Barbara said, when Isobella sat down beside her.

Isobella felt her heart drop and her appetite wither away. "Where were they going?"

Barbara said, "I wish I had more to tell ye, but all I know is that Ronan said Colin was in charge while they were gone." Barbara buttered a breakfast scone and drizzled it with honey. "'Tisn't the first time we've had to wait until they returned to learn what they were up to."

Sybilla stirred her tea. "If ye are thinking about asking Colin, dinna, for it willna do ye any good. We tried, and he clamped his jaw tighter than a mussel shell."

"It had to be something out of the ordinary," Marion said, as she finished the last bite of oatmeal, "for they were accompanied by Mackinnon soldiers."

———*m*———

After the evening meal, Alysandir and his brothers sat around a roughly hewn table with their uncle, Lachlan Mackinnon. They had arrived at the monastery on Iona earlier in the day.

"God's blood, Alysandir, I canna give ye the monks' robes. Ye ken old Angus Maclean would be angry enough to go to Rome to complain to the Pope. He will say that I was taking sides between two of ye and favoring my kin."

He paused and looked at Alysandir, then poured him another goblet of wine. "Faith! I would give ye anything ye ask, if it were in my power, but as abbot, I must serve all my sheep, not just the hard-headed rams that I am related to. Ye should have known that when ye decided to come here."

"It is more as if I was hoping ye might be off the island on business. Then, unbeknownst to ye, a thief would have absconded with some of yer robes."

Up went Lachlan's brows. "I am glad ye reminded me, for I suddenly remember that I need to go to the Abbey at Paisley to attend to some matters there with Robert Shaw, the Cluniac abbot."

"We will be sorry to have missed ye when we arrive to borrow yer monk's robes."

Lachlan grinned at Alysandir and pushed aside his wooden trencher, reaching for his tankard. "There is a slight problem. We havena received a shipment of new robes from Rome for some time, so there are only the robes the monks are now wearing. Be not disheartened, though, for there are ample numbers of nun's habits that ye may pilfer."

"God's teeth, uncle. Ye expect us to enter Duart as an order of nuns riding on the horses of knights?"

"Or ye could ride in on the back of an ass, as did our Lord and Savior when he entered Jerusalem."

Alysandir did not have a reply to that one, so Lachlan went on to say, "Ye could be an order of Augustinian nuns bound for Iona whose ship sank in the Sound of Mull. They wouldna expect ye to come from the sea garbed in nun's habits. Or ye could be set ashore by pirates who absconded with yer ship." The old man chuckled.

"Ye do look mighty pleased with yerself, Uncle," Alysandir said.

"Aye, I am at that. And now, if ye dinna mind my leaving ye here, I find 'tis time fer me to make my departure for Paisley. Ye do ken how to find the nunnery, do ye not?"

"Aye," Alysandir said, grinning, "'tis where Barbara stayed."

"One and the same," Lachlan said. "God's bones, Alysandir! Ye make me wish I were a younger lad and not yet given over to a life in the church, and I would join ye!" With another hearty laugh, he gathered his robes and quit the room.

Two days later, the Mackinnons waited until after dark and then sailed into the Sound of Mull. They traveled in a small boat that was well hidden under the starless sky, rendezvousing with the rest of the Mackinnon's men on the rocky shore.

Alysandir glanced at the men around him and said a short prayer for their safety, the successful rescue of Elisabeth, and a grateful Isobella to greet him with a kiss, and hopefully more, when he returned home. He was about to add wishes that his clansmen would arrive soon when Simon McLeish suddenly appeared out of nowhere to greet them.

"'Tis good to see ye, Simon," Alysandir said, "for I was close to cursing ye for leaving us stranded and at the mercy of the Maclean."

"Ye willna see Angus, for 'tis good and bad news I have to tell ye. Angus and about four hundred of his men left at dawn for Ardnamurchan. It seems there are troubles brewing between the MacDonalds and the McLains."

"What kind o' trouble?" Alexander asked.

"We intercepted a messenger leaving Duart day before yesterday. He brought word that MacDonald of Lochalsh was attempting to lay claim to the lordship of the Isles and is now laying siege to Mingary Castle."

A frown made two deep furrows between Alysandir's brows. If this wasn't handled properly, the entire Western Isles could end up fighting over control of the Sound. "Is this related to McLain murdering MacDonald's father two years ago or a new matter?"

Simon stroked his chin and said, "It seems MacDonald still festers over his father's death not being avenged."

"God's bones!" Alysandir said. "Does he not understand what he is starting? The Duke of Albany sanctions whatever McLain does."

"Aye, but McLain's loyalty has earned him the vengeance of nearly all his tenants. When ordered under the Privy Seal to support him, they refused and MacDonald attacked. So Angus and his Macleans have gone to support MacDonald and lay siege to Mingary Castle, after hearing that Argyll was on his way to Ardnamurchan with an army of men."

Alysandir's face was unreadable. "I am certain Argyll has his own plans to take advantage of the turmoil and thereby seize Ardnamurchan and Mingary for himself, and gaining control of the gateway to the Sound of Mull."

"Does this change yer plan to rescue the lass?" Simon asked, "Or do we involve ourselves with Argyll and Ardnamurchan?"

Alysandir did not have to think about his response. His plan had not changed, and the news that the Maclean and his men were away afforded an even greater possibility of success. Alysandir had the advantage of time and place, and that was half the victory. He would seize the moment to rescue Elisabeth. He would return to Màrrach and keep his nose out the troubles brewing across the Sound of Mull. Whenever Argyll was involved in something, it did not bode well for the others.

Alysandir's reply was firm and spoken with conviction. "We will trick them with our ruse and rescue the lass as planned," he replied, "and then we shall return to Màrrach and leave Maclean and Argyll to themselves to settle the dispute with McLain over Ardnamurchan. 'Tis of no concern of ours, at least not for the present."

He gathered his men close about him, and with his boot, he cleared a small patch of sand of all debris. He dropped down on his haunches with a stick in hand to sketch the layout of Duart Castle, so his men could see how they would enter once the nuns were inside and had gained control. And as he did, he did not think of the victory he could reap but of the danger that might incur.

Chapter 33

Come, pensive nun, devout and pure,
Sober, steadfast, and demure,
All in a robe of darkest grain,
Flowing with majestic train.

—"Il Penseroso," 1645
  John Milton (1608–1674)
  English poet

IT WAS ONE OF THOSE TALES THAT WOULD ONE DAY BE told by bards. Accompanied by the minstrel's lyre, they would sing of how the mighty Mackinnons came, a dark-veiled silhouette of holy nuns approaching Duart Castle and telling a tale of woe about being cast adrift in a rowboat by unscrupulous pirates. Only the coldest of hearts could turn away the poor, the chaste, and the obedient. The gates of Duart swung open to grant them entry.

But the scorpion stings him who helps it out of the fire.

Pensive, devout, pious, and pure, they walked slowly through the gates, heads bowed, in their coarse woolen robes of darkest brown, their faces hidden beneath flowing hoods, a blessing in disguise. From beneath their robes, their swords came, and they had the advantages of surprise and the absence of some of Duart's soldiers. Their weapons sang as the ring of clashing metal rang out, steel against steel, clan against clan, and the commotion of battle echoed throughout the bailey and the keep.

The Mackinnons fought with the strength of twice their number, for Alysandir had much to gain and his brothers and his men rallied behind him. Exhausted and overpowered, the guards would be spared if they threw down their weapons.

"In exchange for Elisabeth Douglas," Alysandir said. He was utterly weary to the bone but filled with iron-willed resolve to see this thing through. "I will ask ye only once," he said. "Where is she?"

"In the north tower," a voice answered.

While Drust and Alysandir went after Elisabeth, the defeated Macleans were locked in an abandoned cell. When they arrived at the north tower, Drust and Alysandir crept quietly into Elisabeth's room and found her asleep. With a puzzled expression, Drust glanced at Alysandir.

"How shall we wake her?" Drust whispered. "There isna a safe place to touch withoot getting yer face slapped."

Alysandir reached over and gave a gentle shake to Elisabeth's shoulder, and when she gasped, he clamped a hand over her mouth.

"Say naught," he said. She nodded, her eyes wide with fright. He removed his hand and realized she did not recognize him in the murky darkness, so he pushed back his hood. "'Tis Alysandir Mackinnon."

When she saw who it was, she asked, "How…"

He shook his head, put a finger to his lips, and motioned for her to get up. In the meantime, Drust had fetched her cloak from the peg and handed it to her. "Put this on," he whispered. "Ye havena time to dress."

And that is what the bards and minstrels would tell of the night that the Mackinnons rescued Elisabeth Rhiannon Douglas out from under the Maclean noses, how they rode into the enchanted world of Celtic antiquity upon Maclean horses while showers of arrows fell down around them as plentiful as drops of rain. And how one found its mark lodged deeply in the back of their beloved leader.

Alysandir swayed in the saddle and fell forward, his face alongside Gallagher's neck, his hands clutching the stallion's mane. He managed to stay in the saddle until they were safely away and the horses had slowed their pace. But the Mackinnons could not afford to stop.

After some time, Elisabeth saw Alysandir's blood-soaked horse and, reining her horse, she said, "We must stop! Go on if you wish, but I refuse to go any further. Can't you see that you're killing him?" It may be too late already."

Surrounded by frowning cliffs, they were without a place that could provide them shelter except for the nearby ruins of a castle, which Elisabeth aptly named Castle Desolation, a once proud fortress now deserted and devoid of inhabitants. It stood ghostly silent among ancient standing stones and beneath a silvered moon that sent shadows scampering about.

They made camp not far from what had been the postern gate, near a tower, its seaward side whitened with spray as it stood as it had for centuries, a sentinel looking over the wild surges of the Sound of Mull. She could almost feel the encroaching spirit of some ancient ruler reaching out from the weather-beaten walls to chastise them for the intrusion upon his castle.

Around them, the night was full of noises, but she was not afraid, for they were the sounds of the sea, while a sweet, fragrant scent of salty air wrapped around them, haunting and quiet. Was Queen Mab galloping by?

As soon as Alysandir was out of the saddle, Elisabeth felt his cold, clammy skin. "He is chilled to the bone from blood loss. We must have a fire to warm him while I see to his wound."

With nothing but the light of the fire, Elisabeth examined him, terribly afraid that the arrow had passed through his lung. Then there would be nothing she could do to save him. But upon closer observation, Alysandir did not have trouble breathing, and no air was bubbling up from the wound. A very good sign.

She inspected the entry point at his back and then his chest. It would be too dangerous to push the arrowhead on through the chest and break off the point. She glanced at Drust and said, "It must be removed from the back."

With no medical supplies and a campfire for light, she was at a loss as to how she could remove the arrowhead. She knew no traction should ever be made with the shaft unless the arrowhead has been removed. There were two problems with simply pulling on the arrow. First, pulling it with the arrowhead attached could loosen the head and leave it in the wound. Second, if the arrowhead did not pull loose, the two barbed fangs above the arrow point would tear his organs to ribbons.

"Do ye need help to pull it oot?" Ronan asked.

"We cannot pull it."

"How will ye get it oot then?" Drust asked.

Elisabeth was already thinking about something she had heard about the Indians. A couple of years earlier, she and Isobella had been traveling in Colorado with their family when they stopped at the cliff dwellings near Durango. They were discussing the hard life and short life span the Indians had, with their limited medical knowledge and even less in the way of painkillers, antibiotics, and surgical supplies.

"Back then, if someone was shot with a musket ball, he might well end up carrying it with him for the rest of his life, rather than risk death if someone tried to remove it," their father had told them.

Isobella had mentioned then that she had been on a dig in North Dakota while in college. "We unearthed a human lumbar vertebra in which a small quartz arrowhead was encased. It was completely overlaid with new osseous formation, which proved the wounded man had lived for several months, at least, and possibly years with that arrowhead lodged in his bone."

"Why didn't they remove the arrowhead?" their mother asked.

Elisabeth remembered she had explained that the Indians had had no way to surgically remove an arrowhead.

"Oh, but they did," Isobella said. "It was so ingenious that it was adopted by U.S. Army doctors in the old West, after they observed the method the Indians used."

Elisabeth closed her eyes, thinking back to that day and trying to recall precisely what Isobella had said. After a few moments, she took a deep breath. She turned to Ronan and said, "I will need a willow limb this long."

She measured about a foot between her open palms. "Rub the limb as smooth as possible with your knife. Split it lengthwise into two halves, and hollow out the pith of each half.

"When that is done, taper the ends to narrow, rounded points. Those are the ends I will insert into the wound-track. And bring a flask of anything you have. If we can get him drunk enough, he may not remember my prodding about."

Alysandir was stirring and moaning in his sleep. Drust plied him with drink, while Elisabeth and Ronan set themselves to the task of preparing to remove the arrow, shaft and all. Ronan handed her the two limbs he had prepared exactly as instructed. She smiled as she took them. "Perfect."

He grinned down at her. "I have three older brothers. I am good at following orders."

Mesmerized by his eyes, she did not realize for a moment that she was staring at him. "Well... then I shall have to remember that next time I feel like giving orders."

He raised his brows and grinned widely at her. "Is there anything else ye will be needing now?"

"Yes. I will need something to bind these two sticks to the arrow shaft once I have them in place. Perhaps if you have a thin strip of leather."

"I think I have something that will work," Drust said. He went to the pouch hanging from his saddle and removed a small leather bag, tied with a narrow length of leather. He removed the leather strip and handed it to her.

"Hold him steady, Drust," Elisabeth said, "for his life

depends upon it. If he moves while I am working, it could kill him." She then turned to Ronan. "I want you to hold the leather strap and be ready to bind the limbs tightly to the shaft when I tell you."

"I hope he doesn't thank me with a punch later," Ronan said.

"Nothing would please me more than to see him do just that," she said, "but I don't think he will remember much of what happens." She said a quick prayer that all would go well.

She glanced down at Alysandir, lying on his stomach, his head turned to one side. "Look at him. Smiling like a babe, innocent as you please, and drunk. Now, if you are ready." She took a deep breath and carefully introduced one stick into the wound-track. She pushed until she reached and covered the uppermost fang of the arrowhead.

Alysandir stirred and mumbled. Elisabeth knew what he felt was a paralyzing pain, so she waited until he settled. Then she introduced the second limb and pushed it along the same wound-track as the first. She manipulated the second stick into place to cover the lower fang of the arrowhead. Once she had both fangs covered, she held the two limbs pressed together tightly against the arrow shaft.

"Are you ready, Ronan?

He nodded.

"Bind the two limbs securely to the arrow shaft while I hold it in place. Try to get them tied as close to the entry wound as possible. We want the limbs to hold fast against the arrow fangs. If one should slip off, it could kill him."

She could hear the whispers of Alysandir's men watching from some distance away. She ignored them and concentrated on Ronan as he secured the willow limbs tightly together. When he had finished, she held the bound shaft firmly in both hands. Slowly, carefully she withdrew the arrowhead without doing any noticeable damage to the wound-track.

When the shaft was out, Elisabeth released her long-held breath and felt her body shudder. She went limp as she sat back and would have fallen if Ronan had not been there to catch her. She leaned against him and closed her eyes, taking several deep breaths. A few moments later, relief washed over her when she looked at the bloodied shaft still in her hand and saw the arrowhead held between the two limbs.

She ignored the increased whisperings around her. "I need a knife," she said as she pulled her cloak back. "I'll cut some fabric from my nightgown to bind the wound."

With Ronan's help, she hacked several inches off the hem of her gown and tied it firmly around Alysandir's chest. She wished she had some antiseptic, but she would have to wait until they reached Màrrach for that.

Drust came over and offered her some of their meager food, but she shook her head and turned away. She could not eat. She had so much adrenaline rushing through her that it would need some time to dissipate. She cleaned her hands with sand and accepted a cup of mead from Ronan.

She turned away to walk among the ruins, inhaling the fresh night air and welcoming the chill that rippled over her. She stood for a time, watching the eerie shadows cast upon ancient walls by the firelight. When she turned back to join the others, she was warmed by the sight of Ronan standing guard on a boulder not far away. She smiled. Who said chivalry was dead? It was functioning perfectly in sixteenth-century Scotland.

When she returned, the men were gathered together some distance away, eating and talking softly. She checked on Alysandir. His skin was cold, his pulse rapid. His core body temperature was lower than it should have been, and she was concerned that he could go into shock from the loss of blood. She covered him with her cloak and sat in her nightgown on a pile of stones near the fire.

As she watched him sleep, she was mesmerized by the rhythmic rise and fall of his chest and praying earnestly that the movement did not stop. The night was quite cold. He needed rest, but they faced a long, arduous journey before he could be put to bed beneath thick furs in a fire-warmed room. And they would have to wait until morning.

She was shivering when Ronan came to sit beside her. He wrapped her in a plaid, "borrowed from one of the men," he said. Suddenly, she turned her head against him as tears began to flow silently down her cheeks. She knew her tears would ease some of her stress, but she was still terribly afraid of losing Alysandir.

She felt hopeless and then thought there was only one thing she could do. Her hands shaking, she dropped to her knees and began to pray. Then Ronan went down on his knees beside her, and soon all of the Mackinnon's men joined them.

—⁓—

Hours passed, and Elisabeth lost track of time. They would leave at daybreak, but she was too weary to sleep.

She felt so helpless for she had nothing with which to treat Alysandir other than her knowledge. She was afraid the trip back to Màrrach might well be the last journey he ever made. She shivered, aware suddenly that a peculiar silence had gathered around her. A thousand fantasies fluttered in her mind, and out of the shadows he came… a glowing light bright as a celestial torch.

Transfixed, she might have cried out in fright, but the figure bore an uncanny resemblance to the Black Douglas. As he approached, she was spellbound by his twinkling blue eyes and his floating hair as he spoke to her.

Why grieve ye? He lives still.

He has lost too much blood. I have done all I can to save him, she said, not with words but with thoughts. *Even now his body temperature falls dangerously low.* She wiped away tears, which were soon replenished. *If his condition doesn't change, he will be dead before we reach Màrrach.* She began to cry softly. *I fear I have failed him… Isobella… myself.*

Have ye no faith, lass? Do ye no' believe in the impossible?

Yes, but…

Are ye consumed by fear o' the night the moment the sun goes doon? Be of good cheer, lass. This night, he shall not drink the milk of Paradise.

You don't understand. He…

Touch him! Is he not warm?

With a confused frown, she went to check. She crouched down beside Alysandir and placed her hand across his brow. It was as warm as mother's milk. With a bewildered expression, she turned toward him. *You have healed him with magic?*

Nae, lass, he heals not from false enchantments, for 'tis written that naught of man created shall harm him.

But how…

Ye stand upon holy ground, for once a priory stood here and the fervent prayers of the righteous availeth much.

A scripture-quoting ghost? I don't understand what is happening. Or why.

I have found ye a solution, lass. I am no' obliged to find ye an understanding o' it. His image became more and more transparent, growing fainter and fainter still until he was gone.

Wait! Please come back! But he was swallowed up into the night. Still not trusting what had happened, she sat nearby, watching Alysandir, her head resting upon Ronan's shoulder. Alysandir slept fitfully and as if in a delirium, and he kept repeating himself over and again.

She went to his side and knelt beside him. Her hand went to his forehead, and she found it was still warm. She leaned closer and listened. *Marcy?* No, that wasn't it. *Darcy?* No, that couldn't be right. She leaned closer. Her heart began to pound. *Darcy.* That was it. *Darcy!* The realization sent a chill rippling over her. How could he possibly know of Isobella's longing for her own Mr. Darcy?

She stayed there, pondering, until Ronan came and crouched down beside her and covered her with the plaid. "'Tis too cold for ye to be in nothing but yer gown. How fares he?"

"He is warmer now and talking in his sleep. He keeps saying 'darcy.' Is that a Gaelic word? What does it mean?"

"Nae, 'tis only a name. Our father's name was Darce Mackinnon."

Fear na ye...

A whisper of wind blew through the roofless ruins. She glanced at Ronan, but he apparently had heard nothing. Nor had the men behind them, for they were up and about, rolling up their plaids and gathering the horses. Somehow, she knew that the Black Douglas was still nearby, and she found the knowledge comforting.

Elisabeth stayed right by Alysandir when they moved him. "He cannot ride alone. Someone will need to ride with him. He will need support."

They helped Alysandir into the saddle and Drust mounted behind him. Ronan helped Elisabeth to mount, and then he gathered Gallagher's reins and handed them to one of the men. She turned her horse, and her gaze rested for a moment on the place where Douglas had appeared. *Thank you.*

A breeze stirred. A sweet fragrance settled around her, and the ears of her horse pricked forward as he snorted, the bit ringing against his teeth. As she followed the men in front of her and began her journey back to Màrrach, she listened to the soft wind breathing through the trees and over the rippling grass, and she wondered if she had, indeed, heard the sound of angels taking flight.

Chapter 34

All, everything that I understand,
I understand only because I love.

—*War and Peace*, 1869
   Leo Tolstoy (1828–1910)
   Russian writer

A MONTH AFTER HE WAS WOUNDED, ALYSANDIR DECLARED himself healed and life at Màrrach returned to normal. It was a warm, sunny day, and Elisabeth and Isobella were working in the cave while Bradan played in the sand below with Artair and Margaret. Gavin and Grim had left only moments before to return to Màrrach as they had promised to go fishing for salmon with Alysandir, Colin, Barbara, and Drust.

That left the two Douglas girls alone, organizing the collection of artifacts they found that day. Isobella was humming gaily as the sisters packed their finds in peat to preserve them. The artifacts would be hidden to rest for centuries until some fortunate archeologist stumbled upon the stash and the letter in the oiled pouch left with them.

The sisters were deep in conversation as they worked, and Elisabeth's blue eyes were alive with laughter. She was once again telling Isobella about the night Alysandir had rescued her from the clutches of the Macleans. They had more than one good laugh when she described what a beautiful nun he made and how he had frightened the wits out of her.

The laughter faded and her tone turned solemn when she said, "If it had not been for the volley of arrows that followed our departure from the castle, we would have made the perfect getaway. Alysandir was the only one who was wounded because he waited until the others were out of the castle before he followed them. He risked his life and those of his men to rescue me. I owe him a great deal."

The humming stopped. A mood of pensive reflection settled over Isobella, filling her mind with remorseful awareness. She was filled with guilt.

"I am so ashamed."

Elisabeth almost dropped the magnificent eighth-century Celtic cross she was holding. "Well, talk about a mood swing! Did you accidentally dig up some old Druid curse?"

"No, just a bad case of R-E-M-O-R-S-E."

Elisabeth was smiling. "Hmmm… wasn't that a song?"

"It isn't funny!"

"Izzy, you were always funny when you got a case of the glums. So what caused it?"

"My selfishness almost got Alysandir killed."

Isobella watched Elisabeth as she carefully put the cross down on a bed of straw. Isobella clapped her hands on her hips, as if about to start singing "I'm a Little Teapot" without realizing she was posed as a sugar bowl.

"Yes, it did almost kill him, and I'm glad you finally realized that. Here's something else you might realize:

From what you've told me about your relationship with him, it's been pretty one-sided."

"How do you mean?"

"Listening to you talk about it is like looking at a painting with no depth. It has no center. It lacks breadth and proportion like a close-up photo, when it should have been painted from much further away. Put yourself in his boots. He saved your life by bringing you with him that day in the glen. He brought you into his home and treated you like family.

"When you asked him to wait for an explanation about your past, he granted it. And when you finally did tell him, he accepted your story. He let you educate Bradan. He let you move him into the castle. And he accepted Bradan because he knew it would please you. When you told him you wished to be reunited with me, he explained why that would not be easy, yet you kept complaining about it until he almost died doing it."

"But…"

"Yes, I know he was unrelenting in wanting to bed you. And although I'm guessing here, I think he was quite persistent in overpowering your resistance. But at some point you relented, and that was your choice. I know Alysandir would never have raped you."

"No, he would never do that."

"I'm not painting him as totally innocent by any means. Obviously, he did not take into consideration that you could get pregnant. He put his own needs before yours. He wanted you and was determined to break down your defenses no matter the cost to you." She paused. "Izzy, I'm not saying these things to make you sad or to make you feel guilty or bad. I am simply hoping to help you to see there are two teams here on the playing field, and the score is not even.

"He's done an awful lot to please you, but aside from what may go on beneath those wolf-pelts in the bed, I haven't seen much along the same line from you. However, to your credit you have united him with his son. You have saved Bradan from a life of drudgery, and more importantly, I think that, in the end, you will be instrumental in showing Alysandir how to love again. And that is a good thing, because if I've ever seen a man who should pass on his genes, it's Alysandir."

Isobella sat down on a large rock. She stared at the hands folded in her lap. "I feel terrible, but I'm glad you told me. I guess I couldn't see the forest for the trees. I see now that I had a lot of preconceived ideas about how things should be."

"Well, you were working with a handicap. I mean, who has ever had a romance with an age difference of five hundred years?"

Isobella stood up and gave Elisabeth a hug. "Thank you for telling me, and thank you for saving Alysandir's life so I have the chance to change things. I don't want to lose him."

"I don't think you have to worry about that."

Isobella gave a start. "You certainly said that with a lot of confidence."

"Let me tell you about a strange thing that happened after I removed the arrowhead from Alysandir. We had plied him with drink before the surgery, and then he slept most of the night. I was not far away, in case he awakened. Sometime during the night, he woke up and

I heard him talking. When I went to see about him, he kept murmuring, 'Darcy.'"

Isobella's head jerked around, and she looked at Elisabeth.

"I asked Ronan about it, and he told me it was his father's name. And, get this… it isn't spelled D-a-r-c-y, but D-a-r-c-e." She paused, as if giving Isobella time to absorb what she was telling her.

"In case you're interested, Darce is an ancient Celtic name that means dark," Isobella said. She held a small clay lamp and dusted it carefully.

Elisabeth picked up a pair of bronze earrings and began to wipe them with a cloth. "You know, I found it odd that the name of Alysandir's father was Darce and here you have this thing about Mr. Darcy. Uncanny, is it not?"

Isobella gave her a puzzled look. "Uncanny? Why? Are you thinking there is some connection?"

Elisabeth almost dropped the earrings. "You're kidding, right?"

"No. I don't see the connection. It's just a coincidence, that's all. The names aren't even spelled the same way."

"Well, maybe you should try seeing it from my perspective. Remember when we left St. Bride's Church, driving back to Edinburgh, and your comment of 'I think I was born a few hundred years too late' almost made me run off the road?"

Isobella nodded, not certain at all where this was going.

"I asked you what you meant, and you said, and I quote, 'I long to find Mr. Darcy, and he does not exist in the world I live in.'"

Isobella was still looking puzzled when she replied,

"I still don't get the connection between that Mr. Darcy and the name of Alysandir's father."

"Okay, forget it. I'm starving. Let's call it a day and round up Bradan."

It wasn't until later that night, when she was back in her room after dinner, that Isobella gave the matter of Darcy and Darce considerable thought. She thought back to that day they had been driving to Edinburgh, and she recalled that she had asked herself, "Just what do you want?" Her answer had been, *My very own Mr. Darcy.*

And hadn't she wished for a "darkly handsome man, heroic, upstanding, and moral, with a heart filled to overflowing with love to come to her rescue and sweep her off her feet and into his arms?" She nodded to herself. *Yes, I did.*

And didn't that fit Alysandir, right down to the rescue and sweeping her off her feet and into his arms?

This was really starting to get a bit creepy, but she couldn't let it go... *a man of deep feeling, inner struggle, and fiery pride... a man of strength and quiet reserve, a man of brooding countenance, who, instead of drawing attention to himself, would play the hero in the background.*

Fear na ye...

She looked around the room, searching for the greenish glow or the wind rushing down the chimney or a fragrance filling the room, but none of these things manifested themselves. But that did not mean he wasn't here. She knew that voice.

And her own thoughts came back to haunt her. *To find Mr. Darcy, she would have to go back in time...*

"Oh, my God!" she said, her mind spinning backward to recapture a moment from the past. She closed her eyes and saw herself that day in the glen when she had asked the Black Douglas why he had brought them to the Isle of Mull.

"Ye are here because ye asked to be."

Isobella understood now that they had been taken to Mull because Alysandir Mackinnon was the one man who truly fit her dream ideal, her very own Mr. Darcy.

She glanced at the fireplace and smiled. "Well, I suppose you are feeling pretty happy with yourself about now," she said, not expecting an answer.

"Och! The time for celebrating will be when the two of ye reconcile your differences and realize ye have more to hold ye together than ye do driving ye apart."

She turned around quickly. "I thought you were in the fireplace."

Douglas laughed. "A ghost, like a woman, never likes to be predictable."

A smile born of her fondness for him settled upon her lips. "You always manage to sneak up on me and give me a fright. One would think I would have become accustomed to it by now."

"I hope ye are not begrudging me that wee bit o' enjoyment because o' it."

She laughed, feeling warm at the sight of his merry eyes. "No, you can sneak up on me whenever you like. I suppose that means you know how things have been going for us of late."

"'Tis a troublesome world ye are in, that is for certain. Full of misgiving on one side and bullheaded determination on the other. Necessity will make ye seek a common ground. Courage grows best when watered with occasion."

"I don't see how we can ever come together. We cannot agree on anything."

His face seemed to light up. "'Tis good for a man and a woman to disagree now and then."

"What is good about it?"

"The making up."

She had to smile.

Chapter 35

*For God's sake hold your
tongue and let me love.*

— "The Canonization"
  John Donne (1572?–1631)
  English metaphysical poet and clergyman

ALYSANDIR WAS SUCKED INTO THE VIOLENT CIRCULATION
of a waterspout that drenched the castle, sent a flood
of water gushing down the gargoyles, and nearly
drowned him in a puddle with the cocks in the courtyard below.

He awoke with a start and sat up in bed. His heart
pounded. He looked around the room, breathing with
rapid pants, but at least he was breathing. A dream, he
thought, and he fell back in bed. And what a dream. He
hadn't been this shaken by a nightmare since boyhood.

For some time, he lay there thinking…

His life had been a lot like a waterspout since the day
he met Isobella, for it had become a tumultuous rush of
confusion toward an unknown ending. Things were not
going well. He wanted to change that. He did not know
how. How could he end this stalemate between them and
come out with both of them getting what they wanted?

His passion for her was now raging at its highest
peak, and during his convalescence, his pent-up anger

with himself had time to gather like rain in a Highland tarn. He realized that he was a man with a heart as hard as a grape stone and that he had, as she had once told him, the brains of a bowl of oatmeal. He smiled.

He knew now that he would do whatever it took. To win her favor, he would face a volley of arrows, a shower of stones, and a hailstorm of cudgel blows, but inwardly, he knew it would not be as simple as that.

With a curse, he left the bed, dressed, and went to find Drust. He wanted to saddle Gallagher and ride away from the castle for a while. A deer hunt would get him out in the open, and he could leave the Mackinnon chief behind and be Alysandir for a while.

The problem was that even out in the open, he could not stop thinking about her. He knew what Isobella wanted. All he had to do was to get over his fear of giving it to her. He had confessed that he wanted her in his life, but he stopped short there. He could barely force himself to think of the word, and he certainly could not say it. Not to her. Not to anyone. And therein lay the problem, for if he did not say it, and soon, he feared he would wake up one morning and find her gone.

"Are ye trying to find answers to a question you keep avoiding?" Drust asked as he rode up beside Alysandir. "She loves ye. Ye love her. 'Tis simple, no?"

"Aye. And for all yer nosey prying, ye can see to the deer carcass," he said, handing Drust the reins to the packhorse.

With a laugh, Alysandir tuned to watch Bradan's horse ambling along behind him. "What say ye that we race back to Màrrach and leave Drust and Colin to see who wins?"

Bradan's eyes lit up. "Aye," he said, and kicked his horse into a gallop. Alysandir watched him go, feeling pride in his heart at the fearlessness his son possessed. He remembered having thought the boy was soft, but now he knew that one day Bradan would be a man of dauntless courage. And he would have never known that had it not been for Isobella.

Finding her wasn't as easy as he had thought, for after searching and asking about the castle, he decided she must be in that place he was growing rather jealous of. The cave. He invited Bradan to go with him, and the two of them rode down the beach.

He knew they had found her when he saw Artair and Margaret playing in the sand near the cave. They called out to him, and Bradan dismounted and led his horse over to where they sat. Alysandir rode on, listening to Bradan telling his young aunt and uncle about the hunt.

After bumping his head on the entrance, Alysandir followed the glow of light until he found her. Along the way, he noted that the rock-paved floor was strewn with bits of charred firewood, limpet shells, animal bones, and the skeletons of three infants near a crude altar at the back of the cave.

He stood for a moment without announcing his arrival, content to look around at the cave walls marked with signs of fire, ashes still adhering to one side. Her back was turned toward him as he walked close enough to see she had a plaid stretched out on the floor, on which she had arranged tools of stone, flint, and bone. There also were a few seashell ornaments and a bronze torc.

He shook his head. Any other woman would want silks and jewels, but not Isobella. Just give her a little dirt to dig in, and she was happy. He would never find another woman like her.

"I thought I would find ye here."

She gasped and turned around quickly. He noticed a knife in her hand and saw the belt and the scabbard around her waist. "Ye were not thinking of stabbing me with that, were ye?"

"No, of course not. Why are you here? I was about to finish up and return to Màrrach."

"I came to see ye."

"Why?"

"Mayhap I enjoy seeing ye standing amongst ancient burial urns, digging in the graves of those who spoke deceased languages. Your face is dirty."

She smiled hesitantly and wiped at the smudges. He stepped closer. "Ye only made it worse," he said, and wiped the dirt away with his thumb. "It will be dark soon. I will ride back with ye."

Elisabeth walked out of the shadows. "Hello, Alysandir. Here to drag us out, are you?"

Isobella glanced toward the entrance to the cave, where long shadows stretched like returning spirits across the stone floor. She caught a stray wisp of hair and tucked it behind her ear as she glanced around the cave. "I suppose I should stop now, but there is so much to do here."

"Aye, there is much history in this place." He picked up the bronze torc. The metal had been twisted to fashion a woman's necklace that fit like a collar. He placed it around her neck. "This dates back to the times of the Norse. The Celts were exceptional metal craftsmen. It has been waiting a long time for ye to find it, but it is safe to return home now, for it will still be here on the morrow."

As they left the cave, Alysandir called out to Bradan, Artair, and Margaret that it was time to go. He felt a surge of pride followed by a bubble of humor, as he watched Bradan mount his horse and jovially hoist the other two upon the bare back. "They line up like peas in a pod."

"You are proud of him," she said.

"Aye, he is a good lad." He laughed. "And Margaret as well, for she rides like a lad, and I am sure my mother must be frowning."

Elisabeth mounted her horse. "I'll ride with the bairns," she said with a laugh as she rode off.

Alysandir mounted Gallagher and grinned down at Isobella. "'Twill require me putting my arms around ye, if ye can bear the insult."

"I have managed so far, and your touch is preferred over blisters."

"'Tis good to know where I stand in the order of pestiferous things." He leaned from the saddle and gathered her into his arms, lifting her with such ease that she could have been as weightless as a feather. He placed her on the saddle before him as he guided Gallagher into a wide turn toward Màrrach.

They rode a while before he broke the silence. "Since ye carry on yer work with great attention and care, if it interests ye, I will show ye some artifacts of another kind. There are musty and sometimes nearly illegible charters in my library—manuscripts, rolls, maps, records, letters, two very old scrolls, and other written documents that have gathered there over the centuries."

"Well, by chance, I have nothing to do when we return," she said so quickly that Alysandir laughed heartily.

It was turning cooler, and a fine mist was falling by the time they reached Màrrach. He dismounted and lifted her to the stones of the courtyard. "If ye still have an interest in seeing the things I spoke of, wash off the sand and dry the mist from yer hair, and join me in the library."

Her face seemed to light up from the inside. "Oh, I shall look forward to it," she said, and hurried off, as if she was late for an appointment with a ewer of water and a comb.

I look forward to it as well.

When Isobella arrived an hour later, he took note of the fact that she looked fresh in a low-cut gown of deep burgundy, a fierce and passionate color of desire and warm pulses of the heart.

He was sitting by a blazing fire, a goblet of wine dangling from his hand. Her gaze went to the small table between two chairs, where a round of cheese, a small plate of fruit, and a few slices of crusty bread waited near a bottle of wine and an empty goblet. Her brows rose in question as she looked from the gourmet display to Alysandir for an explanation.

"Doubt is perfectly companionable with supper. 'Tis simple enough fare, and it will allow ye ample time to riffle through my collection at yer leisure, but be careful that ye dinna riffle them."

She smiled at his use of the two meanings of the word 'riffle.' "I promise to look and withstand any temptation to steal."

"Fair enough," he said, and poured her a goblet of wine. "Join me," he said, and she sat down warily.

They spent the next several hours pulling out relics. Then he sat back in his chair with his wine and his dog, watching the myriad of expressions upon her face as she reverently handled each thing she touched. Around her, the thick scrolls and books of papyrus and parchment looked terribly fragile on the library table surrounded by other relics—quill pens, silver ink pots, a letter opener carved from horn, and a silver crucible that burned oil.

He poured her another goblet of wine and continued to watch her, wondering if it would be possible to bewitch her or cast a spell upon her that would make her do his bidding. But he did not want that. He wanted her passion and her fire, yes, but only if she wanted him.

For some time, he watched her practically worshipping an illuminated medieval manuscript that was richly decorated with vivid colors and gilded with gold. Without speaking, he finished off the last of his wine and went to stand behind her. He put his hands on her shoulders and began to knead the muscles of her neck.

"Mmmmm… that feels so good." She relaxed back against him, and he could see the soft, white mounds of her breasts rising and falling with each breath. Something deep and instinctive stirred within him: primeval, arousing desire. His hands moved over her shoulders, and he made love to her neck while his hands slipped further down to dip into the bodice of her gown. There he cupped her breasts in his hands, his thumbs teasing her until her breathing increased and little moans escaped from her lips.

Once, she made a move to turn toward him, but he held her in place. "Not yet," he whispered, as he began to undo the buttons down the front of her gown, kissing her neck and shoulders. After he had the buttons undone, he peeled the gown away from her. When she tried to turn to him a second time, he said again, "Not yet."

Her undergarments came next, until she was wearing only a chemise. His hands moved downward over the curve of her hip and the softness of her belly, calm and coaxing. He knew the stir of her body awakening beneath his hands, and he whispered warm, provocative words in her ear.

She was like butter melting against him, and each time she moaned, it made him want her all the more. She was ensnared in the web of passion as tightly as he. There was no escape for either of them, save satisfying the very urge that drove them. He dropped down and began to make love to her with his mouth. She protested. "No, I can't do this anymore."

"Aye, ye can," he said, and he proved it with his mouth, which gently persuaded her until her body convulsed. She was too weak to stand, so he gathered her in his arms and carried her to his chair. He pulled a plaid over her and held her close. He never took his gaze off her lovely face until she fell asleep. Then he followed her into the arms of Hypnos, the god of sleep, and his brother Morpheus, the god of dreams...

And Alysandir dreamt of children.

It was still dark when he awakened, but Isobella remained sleeping in his arms. He wondered if that was because of the lovemaking or the wine, or both.

He thought of the children in the dream and found

that something strange had occurred during his sleep, for he suddenly felt he truly wanted children, lots of them, scampering about.

And he wanted them with Isobella.

It was that simple. He vowed then to give her what she wanted. He would persuade her with charm, kindness, flowery praise, and good deeds. He had seduced her before and torn down her defenses, but this time it would be different. He had been a fool to think he could win her by force or skill. It would take gentleness to turn the current of her strong will. He would caress her with words, for a woman wooed was a woman won.

Chapter 36

*Today I begin to understand what love must be, if it exists…
When we are parted, we each feel the lack of the other
half of ourselves.
We are incomplete like a book in two volumes of which
the first has been lost.
That is what I imagine love to be: incompleteness in
absence.*

—Edmond de Goncourt (1822–96)
 and Jules de Goncourt (1830–70)
 French writers

A WEEK PASSED. ISOBELLA WAS READY TO TEAR OUT HER
hair. She was frustrated. She did not understand what
was going on between herself and Alysandir. How had
it come to a complete standstill?

Everything had been absolutely perfect between them
that night in his library. Truly, she was positive there had
been a change in him that night; something beautiful had
happened. She was certain. But what glittered like gold
that night had turned to dross.

Now they seemed to be falling into a polite pattern
of high regard. It was almost as if each of them was trying to outdo the other. She was upbeat and positive and
pleasant. She laughed a lot and showed him her charming side. She was amiable, interacted with the family in

the most positive way, and involved them in her digs, giving history lessons as they worked and explaining the value of what they were doing.

As for Alysandir, he spent more time around her. He was attentive, romantic, and devoted. They played games, danced, went riding, sat by the fire in the evenings, and talked. She taught him much about the future and modern civilization.

It was like the early days of courtship, but she wanted more than hand-holding and pecks on the cheek. Didn't he understand he did not have to impress her? Didn't he realize that she had been destined to love him from the moment he uttered his first words to her?

Her mind spun back to that day in the glen when he had flown down the side of the crag like a mythological being and into her life. She recalled how she had forgotten all about her throbbing ankle when he crossed his arms over the pommel of his saddle and leaned forward, his cold gaze going over her with slow ease as he spoke those magical words... "'Twould seem ye have yerself in a bit of a predicament, lass."

Dammit! There had been so much promise in that face, those eyes, those words that flowed over her like molten lava. She wanted fire. She wanted passion. She wanted action. She wanted a declaration of love. She wanted marriage. She wanted children. She wanted a future... She wanted Alysandir.

But he seemed to be stuck on third base. And she needed a home run. She needed... She paused in thought, and then she smiled. She needed the Black Douglas.

Aye, anything is possible... if ye believe...

She plopped down on her bed. She closed her eyes. *"I believe…I believe…I believe…"*

Nothing happened. She opened one eye, then two. No ghost. No green vapor. Not so much as a puff of wind coming down the chimney. She stood up.

"I know you are there, and I know you can hear me." She walked around the room. Finally she gave up. She had no idea how to summon him when he did not want to be summoned.

"All right! Throw away all you worked on! Don't offer to help. We have a damozel in need of some major counseling here, in case you don't know. What kind of family ghost are you?"

The tapestry over the window billowed out, and a great wind blew into the room. A candlestick fell over and rolled across the floor. Then everything died down.

"All right. I'm sorry. I'm just at my wit's end. I don't know what to do about Alysandir. He is being too nice, and it's driving me crazy. At this rate, we'll both be moldering ghosts before we come together on anything. You were my dearest friend and confidant, and now you have abandoned me."

Another gust of wind came into the room, stronger than the first, swirling around her with great promise. Then poof! It was gone. Everything was still and quiet. The tapestry dropped back into place.

Where is he? Humph! Maybe that legend about him and the Countess of Sussex was true. Maybe he is gallivanting around the universe with her.

From somewhere behind her, a deep baritone voice seemed to rumble out of nowhere. *I have passed o'er mountains old, through dungeons deep and caverns cold. I was not gallivanting with the Countess of Sussex.*

She turned around, just as he folded his arms across his chest. "I thought we had the matter of ye and Alysandir settled."

"Alysandir has changed. He seems stuck in neutral. We are going nowhere. I don't know how to progress from here."

"There is a time to retreat and a time to charge."

She frowned. "I don't understand."

"Ye will when the time is ripe."

"Can't you give me a hint?"

"When the right hand is wounded, the left hand takes over."

"Gee, thanks." She thought about that for a moment. Her eyes widened. "You mean me? I should take over?"

"Aye, ye are as wavering as a weathercock. Ye have fought him every step o' the way, struggling to get the bit between yer teeth and run with it. Weel, ye have it now, lass. He has given ye free rein. What ye do wi' it is up to ye. Ye are free to make a decision or to take action withoot Alysandir's approval or asking me what I think aboot it. Every why has a wherefore, every action a result. But be careful what ye ask for."

She was getting a headache from trying to follow his logic, and she decided he was either the wisest man ever created or the dumbest. "I never knew falling in love would be so difficult."

"'Tis no' so difficult once ye realize that when ye feel a great love for someone, the logical expectation is that it will bear fruit. But ye will never gather the fruit by standing still and doing naught."

"Does this mean you are going to help me?"

"Nae, lass, it doesna. I willna do yer work fer ye. I am a ghost. I am not God. Ye were created with a free will. He who dares wins. Ye are either the hammer or the anvil. Ye canna be both. Yer destiny is what ye make of it. Ye canna choose what is in yer picture, but ye can paint it wi' yer own colors."

His hand reached out, and she felt the touch of warm flesh upon her cheek. "Ye are a lass this fond heart will never forget and when slumber has bound me in the dark o' night, yer memory will be my light. Fear na ye. Yer destiny is a riddle for ye to solve. Stay the course, and ye will embrace stars."

A sudden thought penetrated her mind and drew the mirth away, for something about the way he spoke touched her. "That isn't the reason why you came here, is it? You came to tell me I won't be seeing you again, didn't you? This is good-bye."

"Aye. Everything has its end. Now it is time to bid ye farewell, for ye have made yer journey and seen it to its completion."

"But it isn't finished yet. You've always had such a propensity for poking your head into my affairs that I've come to expect it."

"Mayhap 'tis time ye learned to handle yer affairs yersel'."

"This is not like you. You are always meddlesome. You love pulling my puppet strings one moment and tangling me up in them up the next. You tease and you taunt. You come when you aren't invited and do not appear when you are."

She paused and eyed him suspiciously. "Please say

this isn't good-bye. Maybe you could simply disappear for a while."

"'Twould not be so good fer ye to become too attached to me, fer I canna remain in yer life forever, ye ken."

"You can't leave me now! This is the turning point in my life! You can't abandon a sinking ship."

Amusement danced in his eyes. "'Tis no sinking ship I ha' been visiting these past months, but a man-o'-war, sailing full speed ahead with all cannons loaded."

An aching sadness settled over her. She was not prepared for this moment. She had become so emotionally involved with him, accustomed to having him in her life. What could fill the gaping hole once he was gone?

"So, you are leaving for good this time."

"Aye, the painting misses me, and it is time to give my puir ghostly bones a rest. Go and reconcile yer differences with the Mackinnon. Ye have found yersel' a guid man. Yer future is now in yer hands to make of it what ye will. 'Tis no so verra hard to do, lass. But, before I go, I have one last thing to say to ye. If ye still wish to return to yer time, it is possible."

"But you said…" Suddenly it did not matter what he said or how many times he confused her. She could not leave Alysandir. Not now.

"So, what is it to be lass?" He extended his hand toward her forehead. "Shall I touch ye, and ye'll find yersel' back in yer time for guid?"

She stepped hastily away. "No. My place is here, and you knew it before I did."

"Aye, I had a suspicion, but there were times…"

"Yes, I know, and I am sorry."

His form began to shimmer brightly. It grew darker and filled in more deeply until he was no longer a ghostly image but a man in human form. And what a magnificent sight he was.

He smiled, his eyes bright as the stars on his tunic. "Come and give an old knight a farewell greeting and send me away with a fond memory o' ye."

He opened his arms and she ran into them, crying and talking at the same time. "I don't want to let you go. How can I, for I have become so fond of you." She realized she was dampening the fabric of his tunic, and she began to wipe at it, crying and talking at the same time. "I cannot bear this. Please don't leave for forever. Is there nothing I can say or do?"

"Nae, lass. 'Tis time ye made yer own way."

"I shall miss you forever." She pulled back and looked at his dear face. She wiped away her tears. "You don't suppose you could pay me a surprise visit a time or two, do you? Would it be possible?"

His eyes were shining with mirth as he said, "With ghosting, anything is possible if ye believe. Now, go find yer lad, for he has suffered with yer indecision long enough."

"It won't be easy. We are miles apart on issues of grave importance, and there is the matter of the baby…"

"There will be other babes."

"I've been the nice one in all of this. He's the unreasonable one. Shouldn't you be telling him that?"

"I dinna think I will have to, lass, for ye are certain to tell him yersel'."

She sighed. "Well then, I suppose I will know when the time is ripe, like you said."

"Oh, aye, ye will ken the moment it arrives," he said, with amusement in his voice. "But, I ken ye willna want to discuss it at that particular moment."

"Why not?"

His smile was X-rated, promising a vivid picture of just what she would be doing and who she would be doing it with.

"Oh." She felt her face grow warm, and she tried to be nonchalant as she said, "I suppose one has to do what one has to do for the sake of history, doesn't one?"

It was the first time she had ever seen him throw back his head and laugh heartily in his human form. Oh, how she wished she had known him as a mortal.

"Aye, all for the sake of history," he said.

As his form began to fade for the last time, she said with conviction. "I will see you again."

"Will ye now?"

She smiled. "Aye, I will, for in ghosting, like love, anything is possible if ye believe."

His laughter rang out as his body faded away.

And then he was gone, and she knew no amount of calling would bring him back.

At least not today…

⚬⚬⚬

She sat in her room in the dark for some time, thinking. Moonlight spilled into the room. She wondered how long she had slept. She went to the window. The moon hung round and low in the sky. The night was young. She heard riders come into the courtyard, and she saw Alysandir with Gavin and Grim as they rode beneath the torches.

You win by surrender…

She lit the wall sconce and opened her trunk, pulling out the scarlet velvet dress that was new and yet unworn. She dressed quickly and went to Alysandir's room. She did not light a candle but remained in the dark as she made her way to the far side of the room, away from the window and out of the moonlight.

She heard footfalls coming down the hall. The door opened, and Alysandir stepped inside. The door closed with a click. She watched his shadowy form as he crossed the room. He was pulling his hauberk over his head as he went. The metal links gleamed in the moonlight.

He paused long enough to light a candle beside his bed and then one of the sconces on the wall. He pulled off his tunic, washed his face, and ran his hands through his hair. Wearing only his trews, he turned and saw her. Astonishment plain on his face, he said, "Isobella. Why are ye here?"

She did not say anything. She did not need to. He saw the red dress wearing her. Indeed, it did look as if it had been stitched together on her body, so well it fit her form. It clung to all the right places and teased his imagination about the places he could not see. He looked her over at his leisure and felt his body respond. He liked the way the velvet clung to her slender shape, the way it outlined the fullness of her breasts. The velvet was like her, soft and smooth. Red, the color of passion.

"I did not expect to see ye here and certainly not dressed as ye are. I have never seen ye in that dress before."

"I was saving it for a special occasion."

"And is this a special occasion?"

"Aye, a very special occasion."

"There was a time when I hoped you would come and a time when I knew you would not. I am surprised to see ye now, for I had given up on finding ye willing to reconcile."

Oh, you have no idea just how reconciled we are going to be…

He picked up a decanter and poured wine into two goblets. He crossed the room, never taking his gaze away from her. He handed her a goblet.

She took it, her gaze savoring his face. "Some things come when you least expect them."

He saluted her with his goblet. "To an unexpected spark that has kindled a blaze from smoldering ash. To see ye thus." His voice broke. "'Tis difficult to keep my distance and my hands off ye. It takes a frightful amount o' restraint, and I am no' certain I am in possession of it at the moment." He drank deeply and placed his goblet on the long table that ran along the wall behind them.

She did the same. "And if I did not wish you to exercise this frightful restraint?" She asked.

He did not know for certain why she was here, dressed as she was, but he would not make the first move. He had done that too many times in the past. Wherever they went from here, it was all up to her.

"Why are ye here, Isobella?"

"I bring you a peace offering."

"And what is this peace offering ye speak of?"

She stepped closer. "Me."

She was close enough that he could see the pale, white flesh of her breasts caressed by candlelight. He did not, could not stop looking at her as he waited to hear what she would say.

"I have had a revelation tonight."

He said nothing. She went on. "I have learned that one does not always win by being the victor in battle. That sometimes you win by surrender. Being separate from you these past weeks, I died a little with each day that passed."

He heard the small, whimpering moan that she tried to hold back and saw the tracks of tears on her face. He had never wanted to reach out and pull her against him more than he did now, but he would not make it easy for her. Not this time.

"I love you, Alysandir Mackinnon. So much that I have come here to accept your offer to become your mistress. If that option is still mine to accept. I surrender to you."

He closed his eyes, pacing himself and praying for the right words. One wrong move and he would lose her forever. "I dinna want ye as a prize I have won in battle. Come to me as my equal. Canna ye no' see 'tis yer fire and yer spirit that I love the most?"

His arms went around her, and he drew her against him, his chin resting upon her head. He held her for some time, feeling the warmth of her and knowing this was not a dream. She was here. And here she would stay. Neither at his head nor at his feet, but by his side.

"It has been agony for me to lie in my bed at night and to remember what it was like with you and to have felt your passion. I felt yer absence draining the life from me as would a hole in my heart. I kept seeing yer gown lying on the floor and you in my bed. Lying in my bed after ye are gone… 'tis agony. Yer scent remains, for a bit of fragrance always clings to the hand that has held the rose. I could waste my heart upon one last kiss."

He tilted her face up to his, and his gaze wandered over her lovely features, to her slightly parted lips, then lower past the wild fluttering in her throat to the swell of her breasts.

"Aye, I have missed ye beyond compare," he whispered hoarsely, as his mouth covered hers with a wide slanting kiss that left little doubt as to what he felt. Then suddenly, his mouth left hers with trembling reluctance and he rested his forehead against hers.

"I want to love ye for all time, Isobella. As my wife."

She turned to him. "I have traveled back through time five hundred years to find you, and from this moment on, I hope never to be separate from you again. I love you, Alysandir." And in case he did not understand it, she said it again. "I love you. And once more, just to be certain. I love you."

She thought of all the men she dated in Texas and how they had all seemed to slip through her fingers. And as she listened to the beautiful sound of Alysandir's beating heart, an ancient song of courage and determination, she thanked God for the one that did not get away.

And she owed it all to a beloved ghost…

Epilogue

How you'd exult if I could put you back
Six hundred years, blot out cosmogony,
Geology, ethnology, what not...
And set you square with Genesis again.

—"Bishop Blougram's Apology," 1855
  Robert Browning (1812–1889)
  British poet

Beloyn Castle
Scottish Lowlands
Present Time

ROBERT AND VICTORIA DOUGLAS WERE A LONG WAY FROM
their Texas ranch when they arrived at Beloyn Castle. As
they walked inside, Victoria was filled with apprehension. Would they find the answers to their questions?
Would they learn anything about the disappearance of
their daughters almost a year ago?

Since the day the twins vanished, an agonizing sense of
loss had penetrated her memory. How does one get over
the loss of a child, especially when the loss is doubled?
There had to be answers here. She wanted to see the place
where the girls were last seen. She and her husband had to
realize a sense of finality, a way to come to terms with the
sudden disappearance of the twins. They needed closure.

She knew the story of the ghost of the Black Douglas. She read about Douglas having disappeared more than once from the portrait. The last time it had happened was the day her daughters had vanished.

The painting was far larger than she had expected. The Douglases paused before it, each with their own thoughts as they studied the portrait intently. The Black Douglas was rather splendid looking, standing with his legs planted far apart and his arms crossed in front of him, his great black cape swirling, a glimmer in his deep blue eyes, and a smile upon his lips.

I believe you know what happened to my daughters, just as I feel you had something to do with it, Victoria thought, as tears slid down her cheeks. Robert put his arm around her.

"I wish he would leave that painting," she said. She looked at Robert. "I know you don't believe the legend of the painting, but I do."

Having heard this many times before, Robert hugged her, but he remained quiet, allowing her to ease her pain in whatever way she could.

Victoria was still studying the face of the Black Douglas. *I know they were in this castle. They probably stood right here, as I am doing now, looking at this magnificent painting of you. I know you know their story and what happened to them that day. Can you give us some knowledge of what happened to them?*

A cloud passed over the sun. Thunder rumbled in the distance. Then all was quiet, save for the faint drone of a bagpipe. She glanced at Robert, but he seemed not to notice. Then she saw the sun was shining through the window, and there was not a cloud in sight. She noticed, too, that most of the tourists had already left.

Robert took her by the arm. "Come on, we should go now. We've seen about all there is to see here."

They turned away and walked back the way they had come. They passed a quaint alcove with a stone bench, where a small painting hung. Robert passed on by, but something about it snagged Victoria's attention. She stopped to give it a closer inspection. After a few more steps, Robert turned around.

In the painting, a group of people stood in front of a castle, but it wasn't Beloyn. It appeared to be a family, for there were two adults and several children around them, along with a couple of dogs. Victoria leaned closer and gasped.

"Robert, come here!"

He joined her. "What?"

"That is Isobella in this picture."

"Victoria, I know you…"

"I know it's Isobella. Put on your damn glasses!"

Robert put them on and leaned closer. "It does look like Izzy, but it's just a resemblance. It cannot be her. Look at the clothes. That painting must be several hundred years old," he said, but he realized she had already walked away. "Wait."

"I'm going to find someone who knows about this painting."

Siobhán McGill was the castle's administrative director and the woman with all the answers. The moment they introduced themselves as parents of the missing twins, Siobhán said, "And you are here to see the place where they disappeared."

Victoria nodded. "Yes, and we are here to find answers."

"You were here before, I believe, right after they disappeared."

"Yes, we were," Robert said, "but the investigation had just begun and it was too soon to get answers."

Siobhán smiled sympathetically, her eyes warm and kind. "And now you are back for those answers."

"Yes," Victoria said. "But first, I want to know one thing. Do you believe in ghosts?"

Siobhán's eyes brightened, and she smiled. "I am afraid not to."

"Do you think it possible that the Black Douglas had something to do with their disappearance?"

Siobhán did not take long to reply, "Scots, especially Highlanders, which I am, have always been superstitious. A study showed that a third of Britons considered themselves to be superstitious, but Scots topped the list with forty-four percent. I was reared on the legend of the Black Douglas. Intellectually, I did not believe such a legend was possible, but after what happened here, my intellect was severely challenged.

"It is hard to argue with cold, hard facts. And the facts are: The figure of the Black Douglas was in the painting the day your daughters visited here. The housekeeper saw your daughters standing before it. She stepped away for not more than two minutes to take a call. When she returned your daughters had simply vanished, along with the image of the Black Douglas.

"Your daughters' belongings were at the hotel, and their rental car was in the car park. The video cameras located around the castle showed them entering, but none showed them leaving. Hard to argue with that, my mind tells me, so, yes, I suppose I do believe it."

"Do you happen to recall when the Black Douglas returned to the painting?" Robert asked.

"I was not working here at that time, but I remember hearing it was about four months later, on Christmas Day," Siobhán replied.

Victoria had been listening carefully, but she turned and pointed to the painting in the alcove. "What do you know about this particular painting?"

"The one you see here is only a small copy. I believe the wife of the chief was a Douglas, and that is why a copy of it hangs here."

"Do you know where the original is?" Victoria asked.

Siobhán nodded. "I will check on it for you. I'll be right back."

She returned a short while later with a folder. As she sorted through it, she said, "These documents are quite old, so they may no longer be accurate, but it is noted here that the original painting hangs in Màrrach Castle on the Isle of Mull. That is the ancient seat of the Mackinnon clan."

"Does it identify any of the others in the painting by name?" Robert asked.

Siobhán nodded. "Yes, they are listed here: Alysandir Mackinnon, Chief of Clan Mackinnon, his wife Isobella Catriona Douglas Mackinnon, and…"

Robert jerked his head around. He and Victoria exchanged looks. Victoria started crying. Robert, although stunned, managed to say, "One of our daughters was named Isobella Catriona. As you can see, this is quite a profound discovery for us. We have been praying for a break."

"Oh, my!" Siobhán exclaimed before she composed herself. "I will copy everything for you."

A short while later, she returned with a folder and handed it to Robert. "I've made photocopies of several documents. There is a small map included. I also took the liberty of calling ahead for you. Màrrach is a popular setting for weddings, so they have an events coordinator. Her name is Morvern Fairbairn.

"She is expecting you and has scheduled for you to visit there tomorrow. She did mention that you might also be interested to know that Isobella Mackinnon had a sister who was married to the Earl of Kinloss and there is a portrait of her also."

⌒⌒⌒

Morvern Fairbairn met them upon their arrival. She greeted them warmly and said, "Please let me begin by saying I'm very sorry about your daughters. Siobhán McGill told me your daughters were the ones who disappeared at Beloyn. I do apologize for the noise. We are setting up for a wedding."

They were anticipating a miracle that day when they walked into the Great Hall, and they were not disappointed. Two huge, full-length family portraits hung side by side. Beautifully displayed in ornate gilt frames, each one bore an inscription.

ALYSANDIR MACKINNON, CHIEF OF CLAN MACKINNON,
ISLE OF MULL, SCOTLAND AND HIS BELOVED WIFE,
ISOBELLA CATRIONA DOUGLAS MACKINNON.

DAVID MURRAY, EARL OF KINLOSS,
MORAY, SCOTLAND AND HIS BELOVED WIFE,
ELISABETH RHIANNON DOUGLAS MURRAY,
COUNTESS OF KINLOSS.

Gathered around Isobella and Alysandir were ten children, seven sons and three daughters, while David and Elisabeth had five sons and three daughters, including one set of twins.

Morvern said, "I've requested the paintings be taken down. There is something on the back you should see."

They talked for a while until the workmen had the paintings down. On the back of each was a more complete listing, which included the names of the children. Robert was the first to notice that Isobella and Elisabeth both had children named Victoria and Robert.

Beneath the names were the words of a poem:

I shall be telling this with a sigh
Somewhere ages and ages hence:
Two roads diverged in a wood, and I—
I took the one less travelled by,
And that has made all the difference.

"Robert Frost," Victoria said. "That is from his poem, 'The Road Not Taken.' Robert Frost died in the early '60s. This painting was done centuries before he was born. Don't you see? This was their way of telling us to believe what our eyes see and not what our logic tells us."

She turned to her husband and put her hand on his arm. "They loved us, Robert, and they left this where we would find it because they did not want us to grieve. Look at our beautiful grandchildren. It is strange to think that we must trace the Mackinnons and the Murrays to find our descendants among our ancestors."

Morvern handed them a few papers. "The originals of these are in Edinburgh. This is a copy of the names and birth dates of their children. It also has the date of the marriage of Isobella and Alysandir."

Victoria leaned closer to read the document, and gasped. "Oh, my God!" She turned to Robert. "Look at the date of their marriage, Robert. It was December 25, 1515. Christmas Day."

"The day the Black Douglas returned to the painting," he said.

"We have quite an extensive collection of rare and extremely well preserved artifacts and historical documents that were discovered and catalogued by Isobella Mackinnon. She was quite an impressive archaeologist for her time. So many antiquities of this nature never made it to modern times. Scotland owes her a great debt for her devotion to preserving history. Many of her findings are in Edinburgh and a few in London.

"I wish I knew as much about Elisabeth Murray as I do Isobella. However, I can tell you that she was quite skilled and made many advances in medical science in a time when women did not excel in such.

"And now, I have a big surprise for you," Morvern said. She guided them down a long hall to a large room. "Many of these items were discovered by Isobella in the cave you will visit later," she said, as she put her key in the door and turned on the light. "These are kept under low-light conditions, "she said, "to keep out UV light and to minimize visible light. Many of the documents are hermetically sealed and put it in an atmosphere of nitrogen or helium to prevent oxidation. But what I really wanted to show you is over here."

She led the way, talking as she went. "The castle underwent some renovations recently, and a secret compartment was discovered behind a wall that had been added centuries later. Inside that compartment was something you may recognize."

She removed a covering from the glass case, and Victoria burst into tears. "It's Izzy's Prada backpack."

"There were also some items in the stone box that belonged to Elisabeth, but they are under the care of the current Earl of Kinloss in Moray. You mentioned you were going to visit there, so be sure you ask to see them."

"Oh, we will," Robert said.

"We normally don't allow anyone to touch the items, but I think we can make an exception in your case." She unlocked the glass case.

It was a moving experience to touch the familiar items belonging to her daughter, and Victoria took her time looking at each item. "Just think, Izzy was wearing this backpack a couple of years ago and yet it has been buried for five hundred years. Mind boggling, isn't it?"

Victoria went through Izzy's wallet. She looked at the photo on her license and passport and tested the breath spray, which did not work. And then she picked up the romance novel and laughed.

"Now, this is really spooky," she said, leaning over to hold the book up in front of Robert.

"*The Bride of Black Douglas,*" he read.

"Izzy read romance novels for years. It's almost as if she had a premonition, or maybe it was a sign of some sort. Whatever it was, I do not believe it was an accident that she picked this book to bring with her."

Later, as they left the castle, she glanced at Robert. "I know they were happy. I just wish there was some way I could know that in the end they had a choice of whether they remained or came back to their time. If only I could have some sign," she said, and turned away.

From somewhere deep within the castle came the haunting skirl of pipes.

Acknowledgments

A special thank you to John Everett, MD, for his patient explanation of wound infections and why garlic was a better choice than honey for my wounded character and time period.

I just love it when I learn something.

About the Author

Since her first publication in 1988, *New York Times* bestselling author Elaine Coffman's books have been on the *New York Times, USA Today* Top 50, and Ingram's Romance bestsellers lists. They also have won four nominations for Best Historical Romance of the Year, Reviewer's Choice, Best Western Historical, and The Maggie. She lives in Austin, Texas.

Look for the next Scottish time travel romance
from Elaine Coffman

Lord of the Black Isle

When Elisabeth Douglas is pulled back in time
by an ancestral ghost, she encounters a stubborn Highland laird who accuses her of witch-
craft, then becomes totally bewitched by her...

Coming in Spring 2012
from Sourcebooks Casablanca

HUNDREDS OF YEARS TO REFORM A RAKE

BY LAURIE BROWN

HIS TOUCH PULLED HER IRRESISTIBLY ACROSS THE MISTS OF TIME

Deverell Thornton, the ninth Earl of Waite, needs Josie Drummond to come back to his time and foil the plot that would destroy him. Josie is a modern career woman, thrust back in time to the sparkling Regency period, where she must contend with the complex manners and mores of the day, unmask a dangerous charlatan, and in the end, choose between the ghost who captivated her or the man himself. But can she give her heart to a notorious rake?

"A smart, amusing, and fun time travel/Regency tale." — *All About Romance*

"Extremely well written…A great read from start to finish." —*Revisiting the Moon's Library*

"Blends Regency, contemporary and paranormal romance to a charming and very entertaining effect." —*Book Loons*

978-1-4022-1013-6 • $6.99 U.S./$8.99 CAN

WHAT WOULD
JANE AUSTEN
DO?
BY LAURIE BROWN

Eleanor goes back in time to save a man's life, but could it be she's got the wrong villain?

Lord Shermont, renowned rake, feels an inexplicable bond to the mysterious woman with radical ideas who seems to know so much…but could she be a Napoleonic spy?

Thankfully, Jane Austen's sage advice prevents a fatal mistake…

At a country house party, Eleanor makes the acquaintance of Jane Austen, whose sharp wit can untangle the most complicated problem. With an international intrigue going on before her eyes, Eleanor must figure out which of two dueling gentlemen is the spy, and which is the man of her dreams.

978-1-4022-1831-6 • $6.99 U.S. / $7.99 CAN

Uncertain Magic

BY LAURA KINSALE
New York Times bestselling author

"Laura Kinsale creates magic."
—Lisa Kleypas, *New York Times* bestselling
author of *Seduce me at Sunrise*

A MAN DAMNED BY SUSPICION AND INNUENDO

Dreadful rumors swirl around the impoverished Irish lord
known as "The Devil Earl." But Faelan Savigar hides a
dark secret, for even he doesn't know what dark deeds he
may be capable of. Roderica Delamore, cursed by the gift
of "sight," fears no man will ever want a wife who can
read his every thought and emotion, until she encounters
Faelan. Roddy becomes determined to save Faelan from his
terrifying and mysterious ailment, but will their love end up
saving him… or destroying her?

"Laura Kinsale has managed to break
all the rules…and come away shining."
—*San Diego Union-Tribune*

"Magic and beauty flow from Laura
Kinsale's pen." —*Romantic Times*

978-1-4022-3702-7 • $9.99 U.S./$11.99 CAN

THE
FIRE LORD'S
LOVER

BY KATHRYNE KENNEDY

IF HIS POWERS ARE DISCOVERED, HIS FATHER
WILL DESTROY HIM...

In a magical land ruled by ruthless Elven lords, the Fire
Lord's son Dominic Raikes plays a deadly game to conceal
his growing might from his malevolent father—until his
arranged bride awakens in him passions he thought he had
buried forever...

UNLESS HIS FIANCÉE KILLS HIM FIRST...

Lady Cassandra has been raised in outward purity and
innocence, while secretly being trained as an assassin. Her
mission is to bring down the Elven Lord and his champion
son. But when she gets to court she discovers that nothing is
what it seems, least of all the man she married...

---

*"As darkly imaginative as Tolkien, as richly romantic as Heyer,
Kennedy carves a new genre in romantic fiction."*
—Erin Quinn, author of *Haunting Warrior*

"Deliciously dark and enticing." —Angie Fox, *New York
Times* bestselling author of *A Tale of Two Demon Slayers*

978-1-4022-3652-5 • $7.99 U.S./$9.99 CAN/£4.99 UK

HIGHLAND HELLCAT

BY MARY WINE

"**DEEPLY ROMANTIC, SCINTILLATING, AND ABSOLUTELY DELICIOUS.**" —Sylvia Day, national bestselling author of *The Stranger I Married*

HE WANTS A WIFE HE CAN CONTROL...

Connor Lindsey is a Highland laird, but his clan's loyalty is hard won and he takes nothing for granted. He'll do whatever it takes to find a virtuous wife, even if he has to kidnap her...

SHE HAS A SPIRIT THAT CAN'T BE TAMED...

Brina Chattan has always defied convention. She sees no reason to be docile now that she's been captured by a powerful laird and taken to his storm-tossed castle in the Highlands, far from her home.

When a rival laird's interference nearly tears them apart, Connor discovers that a woman with a wild streak suits him much better than he'd ever imagined...

Praise for *To Conquer a Highlander:*

"Hot enough to warm even the coldest Scottish Nights..."
  —*Publishers Weekly* starred review

"I have read numerous Scottish-themed romances, but none compare to this amazing book." —*The Royal Reviews*

978-1-4022-3738-6 • $6.99 U.S. / $8.99 CAN

A *Duke* TO
Die For

BY AMELIA GREY

THE RAKISH FIFTH DUKE OF BLAKEWELL'S UNEXPECTED AND
shockingly lovely new ward has just arrived, claiming to
carry a curse that has brought each of her previous guardians
to an untimely end...

Praise for Amelia Grey's Regency romances:

*"This beguiling romance steals your heart, lifts
your spirits and lights up the pages with humor and
passion."* —Romantic Times

*"Each new Amelia Grey tale is a diamond. Ms.
Grey...is a master storyteller."* —Affaire de Coeur

*"Readers will be quickly drawn in by the lively pace,
the appealing protagonists, and the sexual chemistry
that almost visibly shimmers between."*
—Library Journal

978-1-4022-1767-8 • $6.99 U.S./$7.99 CAN

A Marquis to Marry

by Amelia Grey

"A captivating mix of discreet intrigue
and potent passion." —*Booklist*

"A gripping plot, great love scenes, and well-drawn
characters make this book impossible to put down."
—*The Romance Studio*

The Marquis of Raceworth is shocked to find a young
and beautiful Duchess on his doorstep—especially when
she accuses him of stealing her family's priceless pearls!
Susannah, Duchess of Brookfield, refuses to be intimidated by
the Marquis's commanding presence and chiseled good looks.
And when the pearls disappear, Race and Susannah will have
to work together—and discover they can't live apart...

Praise for *A Duke to Die For:*

"A lusciously spicy romp." —*Library Journal*

"Deliciously sensual... storyteller extraordinaire Amelia Grey
grabs you by the heart, draws you in, and does not let go."
—*Romance Junkies*

"Intriguing danger, sharp humor, and plenty of simmering
sexual chemistry." —*Booklist*

978-1-4022-1760-9 • $6.99 U.S./$8.99 CAN

AN Earl TO Enchant

BY AMELIA GREY

HE'S DETERMINED NOT TO BE A HERO...

Lord Morgandale is as notorious as he is dashing, and he's determined no woman will tie him down. But from the moment Arianna Sweet appears on his doorstep, he cannot resist the lure of her fascinating personality, exotic wardrobe, and tempting green eyes...

Arianna never imagined the significance of her father's research until after his untimely death. Now she is in possession of his groundbreaking discovery, one that someone would kill for. She can't tell Lord Morgandale her secret, but she knows she needs his help, desperately...

Praise for Amelia Grey

"Bewitching, beguiling, and unbelievably funny."
—Fresh Fiction

"Witty dialogue and clever schemes...Grey's characters will charm readers." —Booklist

"A gripping plot, great love scenes, and well-drawn characters...impossible to put down."
—The Romance Studio

978-1-4022-1761-6 • $7.99 U.S/$9.99 CAN/£4.99 UK

Lessons in French

by Laura Kinsale
New York Times bestselling author

> "An exquisite romance and an instant classic."
> —*Elizabeth Hoyt*

HE'S EXACTLY THE KIND OF TROUBLE SHE CAN'T RESIST...

Trevelyan and Callie were childhood sweethearts with a taste for adventure. Until the fateful day her father drove Trevelyan away in disgrace. Nine long, lonely years later, Trevelyan returns, determined to sweep Callie into one last, fateful adventure, just for the two of them...

"Kinsale's delightful characters and delicious wit enliven this poignant tale...It will charm your heart!" —*Sabrina Jeffries*

"Laura Kinsale creates magic. Her characters live, breathe, charm, and seduce, and her writing is as delicious and perfectly served as wine in a crystal glass. When you're reading Kinsale, as with all great indulgences, it feels too good to stop." —*Lisa Kleypas*

978-1-4022-3701-0 • $7.99 U.S./$8.99 CAN

SEIZE THE FIRE

BY LAURA KINSALE
New York Times bestselling author

"Magic and beauty flow from
Laura Kinsale's pen." —*Romantic Times*

AN UNLIKELY PRINCESS SHIPWRECKED
WITH A WAR HERO WHO'S GOT HELL TO PAY

Her Serene Highness Olympia of Oriens—plump, demure,
and idealistic—longs to return to her tiny, embattled land
and lead her people to justice and freedom. Famous hero
Captain Sheridan Drake, destitute and tormented by nightmares of the carnage he's seen, means only to rob and abandon her. What is Olympia to do with the tortured man
behind the hero's façade? And how will they cope when
their very survival depends on each other?

"One of the best writers in the history of the
romance genre." —*All About Romance*

978-1-4022-4683-8 • $9.99 U.S./$11.99 CAN

THE
PRINCE
OF
MIDNIGHT

BY LAURA KINSALE
New York Times bestselling author

INTENT ON REVENGE, ALL SHE WANTS FROM HIM IS TO LEARN HOW TO KILL

Lady Leigh Strachan has crossed all of France in search of S.T. Maitland, nobleman, highwayman, and legendary swordsman, once known as the Prince of Midnight. Now he's hiding out in a crumbing castle with a tame wolf as his only companion, trying to conceal his deafness and desperation. Leigh is terribly disappointed to find the man behind the legend doesn't meet her expectations. But when they're forced on a quest together, she discovers the dangerous and vital man behind the mask, and he finds a way to touch her ice cold heart.

978-1-4022-4686-9 • $9.99 U.S./$11.99 CAN

MIDSUMMER MOON

BY LAURA KINSALE

New York Times bestselling author

IF HE REALLY LOVED HER, WOULDN'T HE HELP HER REALIZE HER DREAM?

When inventor Merlin Lambourne is endangered by Napoleon's advancing forces, Lord Ransom Falconer, in service of his government, comes to her rescue and falls under the spell of her beauty and absent-minded brilliance. But he is horrified by her dream of building a flying machine—and not only because he is determined to keep her safe.

978-1-4022-4689-0 • $9.99 U.S./$11.99 CAN

My
UNFAIR
Lady

BY KATHRYNE KENNEDY

A WILD WEST BEAUTY TAKES
VICTORIAN LONDON BY STORM

The impoverished Duke of Monchester despises the rich
Americans who flock to London, seeking to buy their way
into the ranks of the British peerage. Frontier-bred Summer
Wine Lee has no interest in winning over London society—
it's the New York bluebloods and her future mother-in-law
she's determined to impress. She knows the cost of smooth-
ing her rough-and-tumble frontier edges will be high. But
she never imagined it might cost her heart…

978-1-4022-2990-9 • $7.99 U.S./$9.99 CAN